DRIFTING THRO[UGH...]

"Steve?"

It was a voice he somehow knew. A voice that somehow should have made him feel— something.

"Kris?" He said it, or did he just think it?

"I'm here, Steve. What do you remember?"

"The water. We spun into the water. I sank—"

"Steven, listen. We found you. You should know that you've been aboard the Ark for six weeks now. You've been unconscious. We've been working on you."

"Kris, I can't move. What's wrong with me? Where are we?"

"I'm in the processing center. You are, too. In a way."

He knew. "I'm in the computer." After a pause, Li said, "I'm dead." Virtually immortal. He thought fleetingly of eternity, and a flood of symbols filled his mind, the formulae generations of mathematicians had designed to deal with infinity. "Too much," Li said. No human being should have such power, such knowledge, such control. No human being.

"That's why I chose you, friend . . ."

THE FUTURE IS UPON US . . .

ARK LIBERTY

Will Bradley

A ROC BOOK

ROC
Published by the Penguin Group
Penguin Books USA Inc., 375 Hudson Street,
New York, New York 10014, U.S.A.
Penguin Books Ltd, 27 Wrights Lane,
London W8 5TZ, England
Penguin Books Australia Ltd, Ringwood,
Victoria, Australia
Penguin Books Canada Ltd, 10 Alcorn Avenue,
Toronto, Ontario, Canada M4V 3B2
Penguin Books (N.Z.) Ltd, 182–190 Wairau Road,
Auckland 10, New Zealand

Penguin Books Ltd, Registered Offices:
Harmondsworth, Middlesex, England

First published by Roc,
an imprint of New American Library,
a division of Penguin Books USA Inc.

First Printing, April, 1992
10 9 8 7 6 5 4 3 2 1

This is for Mark Stevens and Bill Amis, partners in crime—and science fiction.

BOOK ONE

TERRACIDE

Chapter 1

1: Kingstown, Maine

The government had migrated north early that year. Hurricane Alita had pounded into Washington on May 5, threatening the sea walls and hurling a wind-lashed tidal bore kilometers up the Potomac. By the end of that week, the Senate and House adjourned to Kingstown (back in 2051 when Congress had approved the construction of a summer capital, the new city was to have been Lincoln, but a Maine delegation loyal to the state's first governor carried the day when the formal christening took place eight years later).

The President and cabinet followed within a few days. The Supreme Court had been permanently housed in Columbus, Ohio, since the Washington tornadoes of 2076, and so the nine justices did not have to move—they had only to endure the swelter.

Now it was August, and Hurricane Thomas had just breached the dikes protecting Old Jacksonville, had veered north, and Stefan Li found himself mightily put out—at the weather, at the government, at the Rising Nations and their petty wars, at everything. The latest hurricane had not affected the weather this far to the north—another ten kilometers and Kingstown would have been in Canada—and beneath a clear blue sky and a pitiless summer sun the Executive Building (North) shimmered in 38-degree heat.

Standing at the double-glazed window gazing out over the east lawn (kept reasonably green by a combination of subsoil irrigation and bioengineered grasses), Li relished the air-conditioning and gritted his teeth as he waited for the secretary of the interior to see him. Though the window was constructed of high-filter glass, Li kept his shades on, the better to hide his eyes and his true thoughts from the secretary, assuming he would eventually get to see McMurphy.

Out on the lawn two figures moved with the apparent indolence necessary in steamy tropical heat, clipping the hedges with efficient human-powered shears. Li could not tell if the two people were male or female, for both wore the white reflective anti-solar coveralls and hoods that were mandatory for any prolonged exposure to the sun. He knew that both were miserably hot, even inside the garments. He had worn them himself often enough to discover that the fabric's highly touted cooling capacities were vastly overrated.

Beyond the laboring pair the St. John River sparkled, visible in the gaps between the low buildings comprising the nation's alternate capital. Beyond it was the hilly countryside rolling away toward Canada and, presumably, coolness. Here everything looked peaceful, calm, and torrid. Li sighed and turned back to McMurphy's secretary. "The appointment was for eleven," he said.

The secretary was a middle-aged woman with the prim mouth of an elementary school teacher, and she gave him a cold look. Her anti-UV contacts gave her doll's eyes, solid black pupils with no hint of iris. "Mr. McMurphy is busy with the Florida emergency," she said.

Li took a deep breath of cool air, artificially scented with pine. "I know. I'm part of the emergency. *Liberty* is part of it. He's got to see me."

"I'm sorry, Mr. Li. He will be with you as soon as he can." The secretary pointedly turned away from him and touched a pad, activating her data monitor. The seal of the presidency showed momentarily in blue, red, and silver before fading to a blank screen. She touched the pad again, pulling up a document which she officiously studied, to the exclusion of Li and all his problems. On the wall above her head a painting showed Old Washington as it had looked back in the twentieth century, everything glittering and blinding white, and the streets crowded with green, white, red, black, blue—with a rainbow and more of private automobiles. Incredible.

Li grunted and checked his watch again: 1:21. Fleetingly he thought of the construction, of the great undersea Ark, and of the damage the storm could do to it. Might do to it. It was supposed to be secure, damn it. If the engineers' figures were correct. If the materials met the specs. If, if, if.

It was foolish to be so personally concerned about a mere structure, but Li couldn't help it. Designing and building the Ark had occupied the last decade of his life. Now that it was complete (ninety-eight percent complete, he reminded himself), now that he lacked only the President's order to power it and staff it, *Liberty* was more than domes and tubeways, power plant and air cyclers, greenhouses and waste processing facilities. It was in some way his baby, and he'd be damned if he'd let McMurphy or any of the other politicos take it away from him.

Li sank into a soft upholstered chair to wait McMurphy out. He opened the portfolio that rested on the floor beside the chair and pulled out a personal databoard. The secretary glanced up briefly as he powered it. The versatile board, flat and the size of a large notebook, could be many things: an audio-visual recorder, a communications terminal, a reference library, an entertainment console, or a computer. Li tapped a labeled spot on its surface and it became the latter. A virtual keyboard, a holographic replication of a standard board, appeared on the pad itself, and a holographic virtual flat screen shimmered into existence over the board.

Li's fingers tapped the nonexistent keys, and the board's electronics gave back audible clicks and provided his fingertips with the tactile sensation of pads being depressed. Data began to flow across the illusionary flat screen, data relating to other Arks and their states of readiness. Either the faint clicking of the keys or the soft illumination of the screen seemed to irritate the woman at the desk. With a flicker of annoyance, she said, "We might already be at war, you know."

Li ignored her. He was checking the status of the other Arks, searching for leverage to use against McMurphy should the need arise. After all, he told himself, *Liberty* is the ninth Ark (though the first undersea one). If the others have been approved, if they're up and running, there's no justifiable reason to delay startup—

He took them alphabetically. *Ark Appalachia* first, in the West Virginia highlands: five thousand hectares housing eleven hundred species of plant and three thousand-odd species of animal life, including insects. Staff was 1722, they had been operational for nearly two years, and according to the figures the installation's performance was right on the predicted curve. *Columbia* next, down in Virginia. Twice the size of the prototype *Appalachia* and already operational. And so down the line. Six of the nine were staffed and working. Only *Ark Pacifica* (California), *Ark Paradise* (Hawaii) and *Ark Liberty* were still waiting to begin operations, and of the three *Liberty* was by far the most nearly complete.

Li grunted, settled back in the chair, and began to review his figures. His ammunition.

Somehow he sensed that this was going to be one hell of a fight.

2: Old Savannah

The ocean had come to town.

Mountainous gray seas, whipped to fury by Hurricane Thomas, surged over shallows to the north and east of the city, broke over the reef that once had been Yamacraw Bluff, roiled into a dirty brown foam, and swept the deserted historic section. The city had been founded in 1733, and it had celebrated its three hundredth birthday intact. It would never see four hundred.

The brick-and-ironwork houses of the old city stood abandoned, windowless, weather-broken. Most lacked all or at least part of their roofs; some had collapsed entirely. The wind, gray with salty spray, made visible shock waves as it blasted the walls that still stood. Streets that once had been shaded with gnarled and ancient oaks now churned with a meter or more of brown-foamed seawater. Waves broke over the jumbled wreckage that had been the River Street water frontage, spilled into Broad Street and Pennsylvania Avenue, into Abercorn and Bull Streets, and assaulted the remaining structures. A church steeple gave way, bowing away from the wind, breaking to fragments as it fell, the din of its collapse lost in the howl of wind and surf.

From her post a kilometer and a half away Keli Sumter watched the steeple go. She spoke into her transceiver: "The northeast seawalls are down. I'm pulling out now." She didn't wait for a response.

No part of Savannah is very high, but the section that Keli was in, several klicks south and west of the mouth of the swollen Savannah River, offered some protection. Still, Keli wondered how long the steel-reinforced window that she had sheltered behind would hold out against the blows of Hurricane Thomas, the third that year to buffet the city. Gritting her teeth, she left the observation post, clambered down four flights of stairs, and stepped out into a torrent that tore at her legs.

The winds of Thomas had weakened as the storm tore northward along the Florida-Georgia coast, and now they roared out of the northeast at velocities under 190 kph. Still they ripped into Keli, threatening to tumble her head over heels into the foaming street. Turning her face away from the blast and the blinding, pelting rain, she gasped at the sight of the historic old cemetery wholly awash, with tombstones leaning crazily this way and that, the few braced trees that remained leaning away from the gale, their branches broken and flopping.

Keli had no time to shed a tear or spare a thought for the unlucky dead. With the wind at her back she fled toward higher ground and safety. She had to lean back into the wind, resisting its pressure, and before she had gone ten steps she was soaked through. But she made good time, everything considered; within thirty minutes she had covered more than a kilometer, and there was the bunker dead ahead, on relatively safe ground.

Dave met her at the entrance and helped her in. It took their combined strength to close the reinforced door against the wind. The howl, suddenly reduced, became the faraway yammer of a madman. Keli leaned against the door, taking deep breaths. The bunker smelled of kerosene, and the light inside gleamed the sodium-yellow of a pressure lantern.

Dave, his crooked smile rueful, said, "We've lost it, huh?"

Too winded to speak, Keli nodded. Her red hair, trimmed to nothing more than a tight-fitting skullcap, dripped salty water into her eyes, and she swept a palm back over it. After a few gasping moments, she said, "Everything below Wheaton and Skidaway is gone or going. How about the others?"

Dave shook his head. "Eastern sea wall's breached in half a dozen places. The fringes are all gone."

"Damn."

"Coffee?"

"Yeah. Let me get into dryer clothes."

The bunker had three rooms, counting the bathroom. Keli unpacked underwear and a red jump suit from her duffel, snatched a towel from a stack, and went into the bathroom ruthlessly toweling her hair. She returned, barefoot but otherwise dressed, to accept a steaming mug from Dave. She took a long drink.

Dave, whose blond hair was cut just as short as Keli's, offered a philosophic shrug. "What the hell. All the old coast cities are going. Miami, Jax, even Boston. You can't keep the ocean out forever."

The coffee scalded its way down, bringing something like life back into Keli's numb limbs. "Yeah. And it's worse in Europe, I know, blah, blah, blah. Venice is completely gone, and Marseilles is a wreck. But, damn it, they weren't *home.*"

The radio receiver squawked, and Dave turned to respond. "Come on in," he said over the mike. "We're packing to get out as soon as we can." He thumbed off the mike, leaned against the wall, and folded his arms over his chest. "The hell with it," he muttered, the fingers of his left hand absently stroking the round patch on the right sleeve of his jump suit: U.S. HISTORICAL SERVICE.

"New York," Keli said.

Dave looked up. "Huh?"

"New York. Manhattan will be next."

With a gruff bark of a laugh, Dave shook his head. "Not a chance. Too much investment there. They've brought in Dutch experts and have the best ocean-management system in the country."

Keli took another gulp of coffee. "And they've been lucky. No force 5 hurricanes that far north in twenty years. But wait. It'll come." She finished the coffee. "I hear the old subway tunnels are flooded now."

"Groundwater seepage. They have pumps."

Something battered the bunker, something the size of a large tree branch, making both of them jump. Dave grinned and Keli gave a bitter laugh. "Pumps. What good are pumps against that? You wait. The ocean currents will change, a hurricane will come slamming straight into the city, and then see what good the pumps will do."

Dave shook his head. "They wouldn't let Manhattan go. Too symbolic." He stretched. "Well, I checked with the NWS while you were making your way back. Thomas is holding to a north-northwest path. We should be able to head out by this evening. Better pack."

"Yeah."

"Anyway," Dave said, "why worry about Old Savannah? If it's gone, it's gone. You've got a place to escape to, haven't you?"

Keli shook her head. "Doesn't look like it."

"I thought your application was approved."

"In theory," she said. "But until somebody in the administration gives the word, the Ark sits empty." Again something caromed into the bunker, something that boomed like a nearby cannon shot and sent vibrations through the entire structure. Keli grunted and added, "And God knows if there'll be any Ark left after this."

Dave ran his hand over the reinforced door. It had

buckled inward near the outer top corner, and a spray of rain whistled through.

"God knows," he agreed.

3: *Ark Ouachita*

"Gimme," Johnny Wolf ordered, reaching for the binoculars.

Hack Bloodworth jerked away from him. "God damn," he said. "Would you look at them sonsa-bitches. And us dying out here."

"Let me see," Wolf said. "Damn it, you talk and talk but you won't let me see."

With a grunt the bearded Bloodworth passed the binoculars over. Both men wore reflective white coveralls and hats, both wore shades, and both had smeared their exposed skin with sunblock. But on the sandy hillside they felt like a couple of pieces of bacon sizzling in a skillet. Small wonder. The high on this fine sunny day in south Kansas would hit 135, the forecaster said. That was a quirk of the American Midwest: while almost everyone else had switched to degrees Celsius, the weathermen there continued to give Fahrenheit equivalents. Somehow 135 Fahrenheit *seemed* hotter than 57 Celsius.

The rubber eyecaps of the binoculars flattened against Wolf's shades. He took off the dark glasses. "Burn your eyes out," Bloodworth warned.

"Shut up." Wolf twiddled the focus knob until he, too, saw what Bloodworth had seen: a man and two women inside the nearer of the hundred or so geo-desic domes that made up the Ark. He sucked a sharp breath. The women wore shorts and halter tops, and they were laughing.

"Yeah," Bloodworth whispered. "Bet they got a damn swimmin' pool in there. While we die out here."

Wolf did not reply as he peered through the binoculars at the group just inside the dome. Of the three people in the field of vision, Wolf ignored the man, a stooped old geezer of seventy or more. One of the two women in focus was a skinny strawberry blonde, an older woman—hell, from her figure and face, he guessed she had to be forty at least—and the other was fifteen years younger, black-haired, dark-skinned, and buxom.

A gritty blast-furnace wind kicked up, pelting Johnny's face with stinging sand particles. Next to him Bloodworth spat. "Hell, le's go. They catch us here we're in for it."

"There's plants in there," Wolf said. "Wheat."

Bloodworth snorted. "Wheat, my ass. You wouldn't know wheat if you saw it."

"I seen pictures, Hack."

"Come on, this wind's blistering."

After a last look through the eyepieces, Johnny gave the binoculars back to Bloodworth, slipped his shades back into place, and pushed off backward. The two of them wormed down the slope for a few meters, then stood and slapped dirt off their chests and bellies. Neither had spare flesh, though the older Bloodworth, with his beard and shock of hair sun–bleached to dry brown, was somewhat heavier. They retreated downhill, through a dry wash that fifty or a hundred years ago had been a creek bed, and came to the point where they had slipped through the fence around the Ark's property.

"Watch them sensors," Bloodworth said.

"Yeah, yeah." They had blinded the electric eyes with mud made from their own urine, and so far no one had come to check the malfunction. Johnny had predicted that: as long as only one small sector was out, he had said, the bastards would wait until the cool of evening before snooping. He and Bloodworth eased under the fence, walked a kilometer farther along a concrete road that was half-obscured by drifts of sand, and came to the truck.

The truck alone marked them as outlaws. Private transportation had not existed for longer than the creek had been dry—not even converted methane burners like the junker that squatted behind a fallen barn. But there were ways around bans, ways to get fuel and tires from government sources if one were clever enough or brutal enough.

"What you think?" Bloodworth said as he slid into the driver's seat. He produced a pair of gloves from the pocket of his coveralls and slipped them on. The bare metal steering wheel could blister his hands. He started the engine and warped the truck into a tight U-turn. It farted a couple of times and began to pick up speed, rattling and jolting along the ruined surface of the road. Speed made the temperature somewhat better, because the truck had long since lost all its windows and its windshield. "Johnny? What you think?" Bloodworth repeated, shouting over the clatter of the truck.

"We take 'em," Wolf responded. "We got the manpower, got the weapons."

"Yeah, but it's a federal offense."

The younger man snorted with laughter. "Federal offense. When have the feds been here, man? They're busy enough with the risers. Hell, they say California, Oregon, and Washington's all cut loose already, declared independence. That's where the army's gone, try to get 'em back in the fold. Kansas an' Oklahoma both are deserted. No fed forces *left* here. You tellin' me the feds gonna do something about this little pissant resort?"

"It ain't supposed to be a resort," Bloodworth said. "Supposed to be a Ark."

"Uh-huh." Wolf tilted his head back and let the hot

wind dry the sweat under his chin. "That's bullshit,
too. You're too new here to know about these things.
Retirement parks for the hot shots, that's what they
are. Gonna get in there and ride out the heat in their
damn air-conditioning, then when the rest of us're
dead and gone, they come out, these white bastards
and their big-tittied girlfriends. Gonna rule the goddam world, man."

Outside the truck, mile after mile of Kansas rolled
by, bare rock and scoured fields, farm compounds fallen
into ruin, all of it sun-baked and dead. A generation
ago the government had tried to establish swaths of
plants adapted to more arid conditions, but heat had
surged northward too fast, and the experiment had
failed. Kansas had dried out even more rapidly than
the old twentieth-century worst-case scenarios had predicted, and even the tougher grasses had withered and
died. But all on their own, the cacti had found Kansas,
and here and there green lobes sprouted. Aside from
them the whole vast flat landscape might have been the
Sahara.

"Got swimming pools in there," Johnny crooned.
"Got wheat fields and corn. Could be room for fifty
thousand people in there, man. We gotta take it for
the people. For us."

Bloodworth nodded and kept the truck moving.
Whereas Bloodworth was a newcomer, a refugee from
the salty lower Mississippi, Johnny Wolf was old-time
Kansas, or so he claimed. He resented the scalding,
killing heat that had ruined the state, that had sent its
people north as emigrants to the fertile fields of Canada, to work as hired hands, as bonded labor, as virtual slaves on the big labor-intensive farms there. And
he didn't buy the government's story about the Arks,
no sir.

People like Johnny and Bloodworth, the ones who
stayed behind and scratched out some kind of living

in the few irrigated areas of the state, they were the ones who deserved to be inside the Arks, not a bunch of pale-assed government types and their women. Johnny thought of the dwindled Arkansas River, a brown trickle barely five meters across the last time he'd seen it. A dead stream, just as dead as they'd like him and his kind to be.

"The weather," Johnny intoned suddenly in a voice quite unlike his normal one, "is a weapon of the ruling classes. Once the need for cheap muscle labor had passed, the workers became superfluous to the economy. The rulers and their techies then decided the time had come to end the superfluity. That was when they changed the weather. The end goal is the genocide of the under-classes, and when that objective is accomplished, the ruling classes will alter the earth into a paradise."

"I read Krantz, too," Bloodworth reminded him.

Johnny tapped his forehead. "But I got it here, man, inside my skull. When we take the installation, I'm gonna be the ruler one day. You know why? 'Cause I use my brain." He slouched deeper in the seat. The hot wind from the shattered road poured over him. "Gonna raise wheat," he murmured. "And cattle and corn, just like my forefathers." He laughed. "Gonna get that dark-colored bitch just for myself. Live like a king, man. Live like a goddam king."

Bloodworth, perhaps lost in plans of his own, did not answer. They sped down the road, two sun-dark men, one of them twenty-six, the other just seventeen.

4: Southeastern Marine Mammal Station

The dolphins screamed.

Luce Norden, stripped to the skin, stepped off the edge of the huge tank and plunged into warm salt water. Immediately the two dolphins, Seela and her mate Chang, were on either side of her. "It's all right," she crooned. "It's all right. I'm here now." The tank, twice the size of a football field, was only partly domed. Through the opening Luce could see the forbidding Atlantic, scudding low clouds lashing its surface to white-capped fury.

"Bad," Seela squealed. "Bad come. Bad, bad, bad."

"We'll be all right," Luce said. In her heart she cursed the government; just when the program had succeeded in the effort to boost the intelligence of dolphins to the point where they could communicate on the level of a three-year-old child, the funds had vanished, the staff had murdered the experimental animals, and the unit had closed.

Well, not entirely. Luce had saved two young ones, Chang and Seela, and for the last two years she had lived here with them—and without electricity or any other conveniences. But her portable radio told her of the storm's approach, and she had always trusted Seela's uncanny gift for seeing into the future.

"Is the storm the bad thing you see?" she asked.

"Bad," squealed Seela. "Bad, bad. Baby?"

"What?" Luce rested an arm on Seela's broad back. "Your baby? What about your baby?"

"Dead," wailed Seela. "All gone. Dead, dead."

Chang, who did not fully share Seela's ability, took up the cry. His was less understandable, more drawn-out, more hopeless: "De-e-ad! De-e-ad!"

The wind howled outside as if in grim acknowledgement.

5: Beneath the Atlantic

Sixty meters above the continental shelf the back-wash of the storm surge bucked and heaved across the face of the Atlantic. The surface writhed, a madness of gray water, whipping white lines of foam, and lash-ings of rain that struck the surface with the impact of bullets. The ocean was a howling wilderness here, deadlier than a desert, louder than five Niagaras put together. During every hour of its existence, Hurri-cane Thomas expended more energy than twenty-five thousand Nagasaki bombs.

The story was different below.

Ark Liberty felt something of the strain, but only as a person might be aware of the buffeting changes of March winds. Her instruments registered changes of pressure that hinted of mountains of water rolling overhead, and her remote sensors monitored the di-rection and velocity of the winds. But neither winds nor pressure mattered that much here, where an in-sulating layer of water offered protection from the uncertainties of surface life. Which was as it should have been; which was, in fact, exactly what Kris Harris had planned years ago.

Harris had many favorite spots in the *Liberty* envi-ronment. For the freshness of the air and the sheer abundance of life, he loved the greendomes, where piped-in sunlight, toned down and reduced in UV, shone down on tilled hectares of growth. There he could lie at full length on a strip of real honest-to-God grass, with its blades prickling his legs and back and the sweet smell of clover in his nostrils.

For a promise of better things to come, he liked the cold-storage tunnels of Level 25, lodged in the bed-rock of the ocean floor itself. Here in the form of cryonically preserved genetic material rested hun-dreds of thousands of species, some already extinct on the surface (elephant and rhino, whooping crane and mountain goat), others heading that way. Here, where the cryonics kept the air so cold that Harris's nose ached to breathe it, they waited for a second chance.

But most of all, Harris loved the place where he now sat: the data center of the installation. The brain of *Liberty*.

It was a small windowless room, three meters by two and a half by five, smelling vaguely of salt and sweat and plastic. But here, on two hundred different screens, Harris could reach out into the ganglia of the beast and discover what she was feeling, what she needed, what she—almost—was thinking. The computer complex that he had designed was by far the closest thing to human intelligence yet produced, with room in it for a dozen human minds. If *Liberty* was not truly self-aware, she was close to it; a sleeping, dreaming behemoth, knowing her moods if not truly knowing thoughts.

Harris grunted in satisfaction, for right now *Liberty* was feeling secure. He tapped in a relay setup request, and the main computer instantly slaved a secondary unit, accessed the data, and produced a readout showing in schematics the path of the hurricane overhead.

"We made it," Harris said, though he had not activated the vocoder and the computer was deaf to him. "By God, we made it." His voice sounded flat in the room, dying without an echo, its vibrations soaked up by plastics and insulation. He pushed back in his chair and took a deep breath.

The screen in front of him showed a closeup of the Florida-Georgia border, as seen from a weather satellite. The image was a virtual one, reconstructed from other measuring criteria than visual, but it glowed in startling realism. Ghost images of Thomas in pale blue showed its course over the past ten hours: straight over

Liberty, then west, then curving to the north, hitting Old Jacksonville and running right up the coast, eroding the sandbars that were the remnants of the Golden Isles of yesteryear, slamming into Old Savannah.

Harris tapped a second request, and the screens flanking the image immediately glowed amber with facts, figures, and statistics: wind velocities and pressures, cloud heights, temperatures, energies. Thomas was turning more northward—bad news for the Carolinas, but good for *Liberty.* The central screen reduced magnification until the entire eastern seaboard was visible, with Thomas a sprawling schematic whirlpool centered just north of Savannah. In translucent red, its projected path took it in a shallow sweep up to Virginia, then just north of Washington and out over the Atlantic again.

Harris tapped again, calling up a scene of the Atlantic and the Caribbean, with other storms plotted on them. Ursula bore down on the eastern tip of Cuba already, and waiting in the wings in mid-ocean was Victor. Depressions off Cape Verde had the potential of spawning Wilma and Xerxes. Harris shook his head. Hurricane season had never swallowed such a chunk of the alphabet before. The record season five years back had ended with Walter.

Well, Ursula wasn't a danger, and as for the others—they were too far away to tell. Harris wiped the screen and then switched to communications mode. He saw an image of people at work: fifty men and women, perhaps, laboring at a complex structure of girders and panels, the middle reinforcing area for the last of the three "bays" that would preserve ocean environments. Most of the heavy work was being done by robotics slaved to human operators clamped in remote-simulation pods, but some final touches required the hands of men and women. Several looked up at the camera as the communicator pinged.

"Yes, sir," one of them, a blond young man, said into his transceiver. The remote camera immediately froze on him and enlarged until Harris could see his face.

"Just checking," Harris said. "No weather problems there?"

The blond man grinned. "Lots of creaks and boings and groans, but no leaks so far. The main hull seems sound enough, even on this wing. If you're looking for trouble, better contact the outside team. We're ahead of schedule. Think the old man's gonna bring us back some more women?"

Harris laughed. "Already run through the three hundred we've got? I wouldn't worry about it, Landsberg. Not if I had your sort of luck."

Harl Landsberg chuckled at that. True, he had been through six contract marriages by the age of thirty, but he was the first to admit that the novelty of a new experience soon wore off with him, and he'd never blamed any of his wives for ending the contract at the one-year option. "Always hoping my luck might change," he said.

"Hope that the weather pattern changes."

"I don't know. Anything that makes northern geography less attractive to the Rising Nations is all right with me."

"You may have a point. Check back with me when you're ready to begin installing the bay floor liner."

"Right."

Harris keyed off. Then he leaned back in his seat again, exhaled, and listened in contentment as *Ark Liberty,* a great empty beast, breathed all around him.

6: Kingstown

McMurphy deigned to see Li at last, late that afternoon. They sat in the secretary's office, a fashionably windowless room with one wall entirely given over to information readouts. "Look at that," McMurphy said. "Then give me your argument again."

That was a compilation of public opinion judgments regarding the Arks. Currently, the display said, 50.01% of the population was against further construction of Arks. "They're wrong," Li said. "You know that as well as I do."

"It's the will of the people," McMurphy returned. "See it from their point of view. What does it mean if we establish fifty Arks, spend God knows how much money?"

Li regarded the secretary for a long moment. The politician was stocky, silver-haired, red-cheeked. His bland features displayed no sign of discomfort under Li's hard scrutiny. "I give up," Li said at last. "You tell me."

McMurphy shrugged. "Means we've given up," he said. "Means we can't help anyone. Means the ones in the Arks will live and everyone else will die."

"Bullshit!"

McMurphy raised an eyebrow. "You differ?"

Li took a deep breath. "We can turn it around," he said. "It will take a long time, but we can turn it around. The problem is that we won't have much left afterward. Maybe fifty percent of the plant species will make it through the heat, maybe only twenty percent of the animals. It's a big death no matter how you look at it, but the Arks will at least give us a chance to reestablish some of the extinct species—hell, you know all this—"

"You want to tell the whole country that story?"

Li snorted and rose from the armchair McMurphy

had pulled up for him. He paced the deep carpet. "Secrecy wasn't my idea. Don't you think they should understand that without the Arks we'll lose eighty percent of all animal species, maybe half of all plants? Don't you think they should know what that means for human survival? Even if the engineers do get a handle on the weather—"

"Defeatest talk. Look, Li, we're doing all that we can. Even with the military crisis, the President has authorized another study—"

"The time for studying is long past, and you know it," Li retorted.

"Anyway," the secretary continued, "implementation of the Arks might stand in the way of the unification talks with Canada."

Li paused in his pacing. "Is that what this is about? Is abandoning the Ark project the price Canada wants for taking us over?"

McMurphy shook his head. "Canada's got its own preservation projects. They wouldn't object—"

"Then what the hell is the problem? You say the voters have soured on the idea. So what? Mount a campaign to swing public opinion back around. Change their minds. You've done it before, for lesser causes."

"It isn't that easy." McMurphy leaned back in his chair and tented his fingers. "You think the Arks are everything? You think the administration can risk public relations capital on them? Have you been following the news?"

"I've been under the ocean," Li said.

"Time to surface, friend." McMurphy stabbed a finger at Li. "The country's falling apart. We've got three western states in open revolt against federal authority. The Gulf States are already talking about a new confederacy. Face it, Li: the country has too many problems and not enough money. Here, look at this." He touched a pad on his desk, changing the wall display. A multicolored map of the continental United States and Canada appeared on the wall. "Here's the population a hundred years ago."

The country became a cool pale green, with orange concentrations along the east and west coasts, with the Sunbelt shading into yellow. New York, Washington, Los Angeles were all hot red. Canada was almost a uniform blue, with a few greenish-yellow highlights marking the larger cities. "Now let me show you what's happened." McMurphy touched the pad again, and the colors began to flow northward.

Canada became green as the southernmost United States faded to blue, with Florida especially paling as its shorelines visibly shrank inward. New York cooled to orange as the vast midwestern section of the nation went turquoise. McMurphy swiveled in his chair and pointed. "Look at the guts of the nation. Empty. We've had flight northward, and they didn't stop at our borders. Now Canada's complaining about illegals, and they're offering aid if we consider their consolidation program. What choice do we have? What good is all that real estate with no people on it, with the weather making it unlivable?"

"What if it doesn't stop?" Li asked.

"What, the flight north?"

"The weather."

McMurphy thumbed the pad, and the wall went dark. "Impossible. The planet's big enough to adjust."

Li shook his head. "That was true two hundred years ago. It might have been true even a hundred years ago. But not anymore. Not with the Rising Nations using fossil fuels at the rate they are. Not with deforestation so far advanced that we can't stop it. Not with a nuclear brushfire breaking out every two years as the population centers struggle for resources. Our projections—"

"I'm sorry," McMurphy said. "Look, at least we

aren't ordering the dismantling of the Arks. Not yet. If we can convince the people that things will get better, then we can go ahead and staff. But it would be breaking faith with the electorate to go against their expressed wishes."

"I want to see the President."

McMurphy's face twisted into a wry expression of amusement. "You think she'll help?"

"I think someone has to."

But no one, it appeared, had to do anything. Not when the Latin Alliance was threatening war if the United States failed to surrender territory and resources. Not when a hundred thousand people were homeless and clamoring for aid after a major hurricane. Not when the hottest August on record fried people's brains and hatched plots in their skulls.

Only three days after his arrival in Kingstown, Stefan Li boarded a military aircraft and it flew him to a compound in North Florida. Stepping out into the dazzling sun, Li saw the destruction the hurricane had wrought even this far inland: gullies opened by torrential rains, palms toppled, flat puddles everywhere ruffling in the breezes, windblown trash lodged in trees and in chain-link fences. But at least the storm, sweeping up through Virginia and then out to sea, had pumped cooler Canadian air south. The temperature stood at a bearable 33 degrees.

A red-faced, solidly-built young man greeted him with a grin. "What did you work out, chief?"

Li shook his head.

At twenty-four, Daley Burnford was the youngest engineer ever entrusted with so complex a task as designing an electrical generator capable of powering an Ark for five hundred years. "Oh, damn," he said with a sigh. His shades hid his eyes, but a frown pulled down the corners of his mouth. "Delay?"

"Shut down."

"My ass!"

Li took out his handkerchief and mopped his forehead. "Let's get inside."

In Burnford's cluttered office Li explained Kingstown's position. "That's it," he finished. "We're to halt operations."

"We're four days from completing work. Four damn days!" Burnford's red hair was plastered to his skull, and his blue eyes glared a challenge. "I say we go."

"Daley, I can't tell you to—"

Burnford's grin was sardonic. "Of course not. But I can't cease operations until I see written orders. And I'm going to be out of touch for the next week or so. Have a good trip to the Ark, chief. Your chopper should be ready."

Two helicopters took off within minutes of each other. Daley Burnford was traveling to the Gulf Power Array; Li's took him to the Ark construction tower, the largest man-made island ever to rear above the waves. He arrived there at 1400 hours, E.D.T. The tower, rooted to the ocean floor by four massive legs, was a lot like an offshore drilling rig of decades past. But the drilling rigs didn't have elevators, and the construction tower did. Li slowly rode fifty meters down, the gradual pressure change making his ears feel stuffed even at the slow pace of the compression lift.

He got out at the top level of *Liberty*'s north wing. The outer lights were on, for sunlight was feeble this deep, and refracted blue ocean light poured through the row of observation ports, making the corridor seem cool and welcoming as Li hefted his bag down to the circular hub of the "immigration center," where new arrivals would one day process in. If the administration ever let them come. The burly Harris was there to meet him, with his sardonic grin in place. "No luck, boss?"

Li shook his head. "Damn right. Well, give me your report. How did you get through the storm?"

"Storm was no problem." Harris took one of Li's bags and they stepped into a lift. As the doors hissed closed and the lift began to descend, Harris said, "Rode it out all right. We pulled the tower crew inside, but the platform was never stressed to more than seventy-eight percent of tolerances. Bay Three's about finished. Waiting for your inspection. I'd say *Liberty*'s ready to go."

Li took a deep breath. It seemed to him that the air in *Liberty* was salt-scented. It certainly was cool, making his jacket and shirt feel clammy against his ribs. "Ready to go," he said. "Ready to go and no one to fill it up."

But that was about to change.

7: North American Air Quality Monitoring Station #1

From the August 1 Report

The so-called "greenhouse gases" have not significantly increased since the July report. Carbon dioxide remains at 559,125 ppb, up only 5 ppb. Methane has held steady at 2675 ppb. Chlorine atoms in the upper layers of the atmosphere are approximately 7 ppb. The ozone layer stands at .56% of standard.

The hoped-for reduction in carbon dioxide has not materialized principally because of deforestation in Latin America and the continued unrestricted use of fossil fuels in Asia, Africa, and Latin America. Current plankton fertilization programs in Antarctic waters are proceeding in the hope of encouraging a bloom that will absorb a significant portion of free atmospheric carbon dioxide. The consensus of the monitoring team is that global temperatures will increase by no more than .5 degree C. in the coming year. This translates to no more than a 10 cm. rise in sea level.

Weather patterns continue to change unpredictably. . . .

Chapter 2

1: The North Atlantic

The *Reina* had weathered heavy seas on the way north. Now, at the latitude of Nova Scotia, it had rolled into choppy water. Captain Ernesto Gasset y Santo Marco was satisfied that they had come this far undetected, the trawler's true mission still a secret.

As far as anyone in these parts knew, the *Reina* was a floating cannery, a factory ship that harvested and processed the shrinking tuna population of the far northern waters. The worst that she could expect would be a shelling if she ventured too near Icelandic Territory. But the plan did not call for such a venture.

Gasset woke early on a mid-August Wednesday, thirsty for coffee. Being a somewhat ascetic man, he did not ring for the steward immediately but instead set about making himself presentable. He sponged himself clean, thinking that if more of the earth's people had been sailors, then they would have proved more conscious of the need to conserve water. Then perhaps the great Chinese and Indian famines could have been averted. Perhaps a billion people would not have died.

Too late to worry about that now, though. Facts were facts. As of that year, Gasset knew, experts estimated the world population at 9.7 billion people, down from a high of 10.4 billion thirty years ago. Great dyings in Africa, India, and China had accounted for most of the decline. Not that his homeland had escaped. Gasset smiled a bitter, private smile at how easily he could forgive the deaths of Chinese, of Indians, of Africans, and at how difficult it was to forgive what had happened to him personally.

He was thinking about famine, about hunger, as he left his cabin. He could have stopped in the wardroom for his coffee, but the thought of death by starvation had somehow made the notion shameful, and so for the first time on the voyage north he came to the bridge without a cup in his hand. His second in command waited for him. "Any communication?" Gasset asked him quietly.

Jorge Esteban shook his head. "Nothing, Captain."

Gasset sighed. "If only they had listened to reason."

Esteban shrugged. His dark eyes were unfathomable.

The captain took a few moments to scan the empty horizon. Once these waters had been rich in sea life, but a hostile sun had depleted them. The ultra-violet rays streaming through the damaged ozone layer had killed perhaps half of the species of phytoplankton in all the seas. The remnant, more resistant, sank lower in the water and sometimes even flourished under the bombardment. But they were the wrong type of plants to sustain the zooplankton. The little animals died, too, and they fled to deeper water, seeking shelter from the sun. There they bred less effectively.

And so the slightly bigger animals had less to feed on. And animals slightly bigger than they found less in turn, and so on and so on. Human greed had reached far and deep. The whales were mostly gone now, except for a few dwindling species in high latitudes. The giant billfish were no more. A diver here would wonder at the profusion of life, for in the lower latitudes the warming sea held less oxygen, and the fish had become radically scarce.

But Gasset knew that the apparent abundance was illusion. Compared to fifty years ago, a hundred years ago, the Atlantic, even this far north, was almost barren. Gasset cleared his throat. "You realize that we have almost no chance," he said.

Esteban nodded. "We all know that, Captain."

"Very well." Esteban glanced at his chronometer. "We have eleven minutes. Let us go."

They left the bridge in the hands of the second mate and clambered down a long ladder that led to the bowels of the ship. If she had been what she appeared, an ordinary fishing craft, the hold would have been crammed with processing equipment. Instead it held banks of electronics and two widely separated command stations.

Gasset occupied one of these, Esteban the other. For some minutes they busied themselves switching various computer systems on, correlating and crosschecking, verifying. Then there was nothing to do but sit and wait. There would have been time for a little cup after all, Gasset thought. Aloud he said, "Perhaps one of us should check to make sure there has been no message."

Esteban looked at him with what seemed to be mild surprise. "For what purpose? If a message had been sent to the forces, we would surely know here, of all places."

Gasset nodded. "You are right."

A screen before him gave him a count-down from sixty seconds. During the first half minute he found himself wishing with insane regret that he had taken a cup of coffee. There might be no time later.

He fitted his key in the lock at thirty seconds. To his left Esteban mimicked his movements with his own key.

"Fifteen seconds," Gasset and Esteban said in unison.

Then ten.

Five.

The computer beeped.

With a twist of his wrist Gasset turned the key. Esteban did the same with his key, in exact coordination.

For a second nothing happened.

Malfunction, Gasset thought.

But then from behind him the roar began. He clapped his hands to his ears. He felt the deck shudder, saw the numerals on the computer screen blur from vibration. The echoes seemed to roll through the ship long after the actual sound had ceased.

Gasset pushed back from the console, rose from the swivel chair bolted to the deck. He straightened his uniform.

"All three missiles away," Esteban reported. "Tracking looks good."

Gasset nodded and sighed. In something less than ten minutes the three missiles, flying quite low, should explode over Kingstown. Each carried a 10-megaton warhead, primitive by all modern standards but effective enough. Of course, satellite tracking would very quickly identify the *Reina* as the source, and within a very few moments they could expect retaliation, even if the missiles should be intercepted. Of course, even if the three missiles the *Reina* had launched somehow failed, the Alliance had other ships, other captains. He wondered how many targets there might be in all. Washington, certainly. New York. Perhaps a few in Canada.

Esteban said something to him. Gasset started and said, "Pardon me? What?"

"I said we have time for coffee now, sir."

Gasset made a face. "I would not care for any," he said.

2: *Ark Ouachita*

Gene Handelsman fumed about security. "Damn it," he finished at a fine high pitch of indignation, "no one even checked. God knows how many hogs broke through the perimeter, and no one even went to check for three hours."

Adriel Volker reached across the table to pat his hand. It was a big hand, for Gene was an immense man, nearly two meters tall, with dark hair and brooding brown eyes—black now, with the UV contacts in. "Maybe it was nothing," Adriel said. "Maybe animals—"

Handelsman snorted. "Animals, all right. Animals smart enough to piss in the dirt to make mud to smear over the contacts. They're out there watching us, 'Driel."

"You sound a little paranoid."

Handelsman toyed with the last of his food. Soybeans were practically extinct out in the open, for they were one of the species most sensitive to increased UV radiation, but the Ark produced bumper crops of them, more than enough to support the population. "We ought to have sweeps," he muttered. "I've seen them out there, beyond the perimeter, looking at us."

"They're probably wondering what we're up to in here."

"They're probably wondering if we're armed." Handelsman pushed back from the table. "Trouble is, we're not."

Adriel shrugged. They sat at a table that was, almost, in the open air. At least the only thing separating them from the real sky was a high layer of structural transparent plastic, honeycombed into the configuration of a geodesic dome, formulated to filter out UV-B and a great deal of infra-red while transmitting enough UV-A and visible light to allow their precious crops to grow. The little terrace café in the corn section was not strictly necessary to the functioning of the Ark, but it made life a little more pleasant. They had waited a quarter of an hour for a table, and now they were one of fifty or sixty couples and groups on the terrace above the field.

A dry wind rustled the leaves of the corn, bringing its sweet, dusty aroma to them. It was a good crop, nurtured by subsurface irrigation, nearly ripe, with the stalks green, healthy, and tall. A hundred workers made their slow way through the rows, inspecting for disease or for insect infestation. Though disease was a real possibility, bugs were only a theoretical concern, since any corn-loving insects had long since perished in this part of the world. As the workers moved through their bounty, their banter and chatter came faintly to the terrace of the café, sounding pleased and cheerful.

Adriel could appreciate their accomplishment, even though her own specialty was a more humble one, concerning itself with algaes and planktons. She picked up her drink (cool water) and sipped it. Handelsman muttered, almost to himself, "Have to ask Kingstown for another troop detachment. Even a small one."

"Come on. Army gikes swarming over the place, slapping me on the butt? I haven't missed the soldiers."

"You will if the outsiders ever come over the hills in force. And I'm pretty sure it's gonna happen."

"You're serious, aren't you?" Adriel asked.

"Damn right I'm serious." Handelsman swept his right arm out in a curve indicating the corn field, the dome, and by implication the hundred square kilometers of the Ark. "We've got eleven thousand people here, most of 'em techies or scientists. The security force is only three hundred altogether. And we're not really armed. We have some shotguns and rifles, a raft of stun guns, that's about all. If they decide to take us—"

"Why would they want to do that?"

"Have you been outside lately?"

Adriel sighed. "I know, I know. But they have to understand that our mission is to protect life, to carry the species through—"

"All they see is a bunch of us growing crops where they can't grow any. All they see is a place where they'd like to live."

Adriel shook her head. "But they couldn't live here. They wouldn't be able to operate the Ark."

"They don't know that."

Adriel tried another tack. "Anyway, haven't most people moved? I mean, are there enough out there to be a threat to us?"

"You'd be damn surprised to know how many hogs still scratch out a living around here. There are enough. If—"

A sudden squeal from the transceiver on his belt interrupted Handelsman's words. With a roll of his eyes heavenward, he snapped the unit out of its holder and held it to his mouth. "Yes, Handelsman here."

A scratchy voice rasped from the small speaker: "Report to Central at once."

Adriel caught her breath as she saw shock register in Handelsman's face. He lowered his voice and said, "Are we under attack?"

"Don't know."

"What is it?"

There was a momentary pause before the voice added reluctantly, "It's not local, anyway. But we've lost contact with Kingstown. Looks like EMP."

"On my way," Handelsman said, rising. He left without bidding Adriel farewell.

She rose, her legs shaky, and concentrated with all

her mind on the everyday task of cleaning the table, of moving the silverware, plates, and glasses to the cleaning station. EMP: electro-magnetic pulse. It was an old term, one that she had heard frequently enough whenever people discussed the nuclear flamewars in Latin America, Africa, elsewhere. It was a disruptive effect of a nuclear explosion, destroying electronic components in everything from transport vehicles to computers to communications devices.

She found her way down to the research level somehow. Patsy Grice, her cricket-like partner, swung away from the data terminal. " 'Driel, hi. I can't get a damn thing on screen. Everything's preempted for Security. What's going on?"

Adriel shook her head. "Some flap about Kingstown."

Patsy's face, elfin and boyish—Peter Pan, someone had said to Adriel once, and she'd had to look up the reference—showed annoyance, not concern. "I need to enter the data on the last generation. When will the lines be free?"

"I don't know."

"Hey, you look like it's serious."

"I think it is."

But despite Patsy's questions, Adriel would not speculate on just how serious. She had concerns of her own. That afternoon she filled a number of 10-ml test tubes with brownish-green powder. She sealed the tubes.

From that hour on, she planned to keep them with her at all times.

3: Atlanta

The southeastern headquarters of the U.S. Historical Service once had housed a major electronics company's North American branch. But the Japanese owners had followed the exodus of business and industry northward, and now the great compound stood mostly empty, with only a few tenants left to disturb the silence of its glass-walled offices and corridors. Because of the high cost of air-conditioning, these had settled down to the second and third floors, which remained a relatively bearable 32 degrees, while the upper, empty floors steamed.

The Historical Service occupied six offices. At the moment some thirty employees were there, sixteen of them members of observation teams newly returned from the devastation of Hurricane Thomas. They were all subdued, exhausted.

In one of the small corner offices, Keli Sumter spun away from her data terminal with a muttered, "Damn!"

"What's wrong?" Clay Elmore asked, swabbing his bald dome with a bright orange-red handkerchief. He wore a matching pullover shirt and olive-drab shorts, his chubby, hairy legs startlingly pale and bare.

"Kingstown's off-line."

Elmore, the paunchy elder statesman and guru of the outfit, shrugged and massaged his considerable stomach. "They'll straighten it out. Probably power problems in the Central Seaboard grid. You know what it's been like."

Keli drummed her fingernails on the desk. The laminate felt slick under the heel of her palm, lubricated with sweat. "Yeah. Well, I might as well add the rest of the damage reports to my file while I'm at it. Can you send me Charleston and the Triangle?"

Elmore settled his bulk behind his own terminal and tapped his entry pad a few times. "Damn shame about Savannah," he said for the fourth or fifth time.

Keli nodded, tight-lipped, as the information from the other teams began to stream across her terminal. Charleston had survived this time, though the city's Battery had long since been claimed by the sea. The

Triangle (Raleigh, Durham, and Chapel Hill) had suffered spot flooding but no lasting damage. Both localities had applied for nonexistent federal relief.

Keli packaged the reports with her own, consolidated the files, and then tried again to transmit. "No good," she said. "They're still unreachable."

"Let me try."

Keli moved aside and Elmore settled into her chair. He frowned as he tried to route the information four different ways, failing to connect each time. Finally he sighed. "Hell, I'll store it in temp memory with a 'transmit' tag attached. It'll go immediately as soon as they're up again. Want to call and see what's blocking the lines?"

"Okay." She picked up the telephone, but replaced the receiver almost immediately. "Dead."

Elmore gave her a curiously quizzical look, then picked up the phone and listened himself. He hung up and slowly rose from her chair. "I think we might as well call it a day."

Keli laughed. "But it's only—"

Elmore seemed not to hear her. "I was in Brazil," he said, "when the Andes War broke out."

For a moment his reference to the first of the Western Hemisphere's localized nuclear conflicts seemed a non sequitur. Then an icy hand squeezed Keli's heart. Numbly she followed Elmore into the main office, where the others tapped at keyboards or entry pads or scribbled notes. "Folks," Elmore said, hardly raising his voice, "I've just declared a legal holiday."

Puzzled looks, a growing murmur of inquiry.

Elmore held up his hand. "Now, it may be nothing, but we're out of touch with Kingstown. Washington, too, and New York. Y'all go on home now and report in tomorrow. I'll let you know then if there's any news."

The office crowd broke up very slowly. Without re-

ally registering their remarks or thinking about what
she herself was saying, Keli spoke to two or three of
them before she plodded down the stair to the street-
level foyer, now an impromptu sort of farmer's mar-
ket. The thick hot air was heavy with the sweet smells
of corn and beans, swollen peaches, big mushy apples.
From behind their baskets and boxes the leathery city-
edgers urged their produce on her. Dark men, wrin-
kled, their faces splotched with carcinomas or the pale
white scars of cancer excisions, they wheedled, ca-
joled, and exhorted. She ignored them all and walked
out into the sunlight.

Only then did she realize she had left her suncoat
in the office. But she had her contacts in, the sky was
mostly overcast, and it was only a nine-block walk to
her apartment. The hell with it, she decided. She'd
walk on the shady side of the street.

Almost immediately a hooded figure thrust a flyer
into her hand. She accepted it, walked away, and
glanced down. It was a religious tract headed, in blazing red letters, THE WORLD WILL END IN FIRE! Keli crumpled it and let it drop. Every street corner had its
fanatics, and sometimes at night she could hear them
out under the stars, singing their lugubrious hymns,
or shouting and screeching as they prayed. Some
preached fear of the End Times, and some welcomed
them. All fervently believed the End was not far.

This time, she thought, they might be right.

Pedestrian traffic was as heavy as ever, with bicycles
weaving in and out in reckless haste. The red trolleys,
humming along on solar power, had to hesitate and
pause, give way and creep. A trolley was slower than
walking.

The quirks of warming and rain redistribution had
produced a desert in the Midwest. In the Southeast
they had brought forth a jungle. In sidewalk cracks a
crop of luxuriant milkweeds grew, waist-high against

storefronts. Palmetto scrub had claimed vacant lots. The heavy air was dense with the chirr and hum and rattle of insects, billions of them, more than the few birds could manage.

Forty percent of the birds were extinct in the wild, blinded by the harsher sun. The dusk- and night-flying species remained, and there were even a straggling remnant of jays, crows, and starlings. The insects far outnumbered them.

Keli panted as she moved with the river of pedestrians. Atlanta experienced, on the average, sixty-five days a year of temperatures above 38 Celsius, and the humidity seldom dropped below eighty percent. The abandoned kudzu wilderness a few kilometers out of town dripped and steamed with moisture and crawled with snakes. The reptiles, shaded and shielded by the vegetation, had not lost their eyesight as drastically as had the birds, and they were rapidly multiplying to fill the niches available to those species that could live on insect life.

At the corner of Peachtree and Tannover, Keli came to a halt, stopped by an unfamiliar rumbling. Heads craned as pedestrians scurried out of the street and onto the sidewalk. The sound grew louder until it was a thunder vibrating in Keli's bones, and down the street she saw a rising cloud of dust.

Engines, she realized with a start. What she heard were the roars of dozens of internal-combustion engines.

The lead vehicle came into view: a bulky, clanking, rattling truck painted a dull green.

An army vehicle.

More followed, a staggering line of them, each one loaded with grim-faced young men who did not respond to the questions shouted at them by the spectators. Keli coughed in the rising dust and the reek of gasoline fumes. Hurriedly she turned and made her way to the next block, less crowded now that the noise of the passing parade had drawn people over to Peachtree.

Keli walked on under an increasingly gray sky, her heart sinking. Why on earth would the army be mobilizing, unless—

She left the thought unfinished.

A warm drizzle started to fall, as it did close to two hundred days out of the year. Settle the dust, Keli thought. While the Midwest parched, the Southeast nearly drowned under more than twice the normal rainfall of a century ago. Keli found a back alleyway choking with trash, scurried through it, and turned onto a less crowded side street. Her red hair felt soaked. Her eyes brimmed with tears.

She had seen video records of the way it had been. Before the air changed. Before the big heat.

Damn them, she thought. Damn them!

Her stride grew longer, more determined. She was no longer headed for her apartment, at least not to stay there. Not to return to work. Not to fight the forces that were too great for her, too great for all of them.

Her destination had changed for good.

Come hell or high water, now she was going to *Ark Liberty*.

4: Off the Coast of North Carolina

"More babies?" Seela squeaked from the water.

At the wheel of the absurdly small cruiser—ex-property of the United States Government—Luce Norden wiped her eyes with the back of her hand. "Yes," she called.

Yes, more babies. More to replace the stillborn pup.

She felt in the pocket of her windbreaker for the

hundredth time that day. The letter, damp and stained, was there. Her invitation to *Liberty*.

It would be a hell of a run in the small boat. She planned to coast along down to Old Savannah, where she would be desperately short of fuel. There she would somehow, legally or illegally, find a supply of synthetic gasoline or even the real stuff. Then down to the Florida land station for bearings. Then across open water to the Ark. And if they took her—

"More babies," Seela cried plaintively.

Sobs shook Luce Norden. An hour earlier she had opened the locks to the Atlantic by main force, pulling muscles in her back and shoulder. The dolphins had ventured out shyly, slowly. She had packed the little burden aboard the cruiser and had met them in the bay.

They took the death with more acceptance than she could muster. Seela's pup, born too soon after the hurricane, had not lived, had not even taken a breath. Luce had sewn it into a weighted canvas bag. Crazy. Burial at sea for a sea creature.

With the cruiser bobbing at anchor, Luce had climbed down into the water. Chang and Seela came to nuzzle, to be stroked. "This is your baby," Luce had told them. "We are giving him back to the sea."

And she had let go. The two dolphins disappeared. She caught a glimpse of them circling the sinking canvas package, pale through the water. She began to weep.

After a few seconds both dolphins surfaced again. "Baby gone," Seela moaned.

Luce climbed back aboard the cruiser. Leaning over the transom, she explained what they would do. "You guys have to catch your own food," she said. "What does that mean?"

"Fish!" exulted Seela, and Chang imperfectly echoed "Fiss!"

"That's right, fish. And then we'll go to a place where there won't be any storms. You'll be safe. Do you understand?"

"More babies?" Seela asked.

"Yes," Luce had answered, and then the tears began again.

Dolphins do not weep. They stared at her in silence until she raised anchor and started the engine. Then they began to pace the boat, as their kind had done for thousands of years.

5: Ottawa

The missiles had come too close for comfort.

The sun shone on streets nearly empty of traffic, for the radiation spike (though within medically defined tolerance) had frightened most people indoors. The newer buildings, reflective aluminum and aluminized glass, stood just as solidly as ever. People moved in them, talked in them, worried in them.

The acting President of the United States sweated profusely as he met with the Canadian cabinet and prime minister. No help for that: the conference room wasn't on the emergency electrical circuits that allowed for limited air-conditioning. The tall windows, not designed to be opened, had been removed, and a sluggish breeze oozed in.

"Deaf, mute, and blind," the President finished. "The whole eastern half of the country, everything this side of the Mississippi, lacks any central communication facilities. We need your assistance in coordinating military operations—"

"Our power has been disrupted too," the prime minister said coldly. "What do you want us to do?"

"Canadian power has been only marginally affected," the President said. "You could route through

Toronto or through the Republique. From the spotty reports that we've received, we're anticipating an invasion at any moment."

The minister of defense looked troubled. "I assume you mean along the southern border and the Gulf coastline."

The President nodded. "That's the logical target." He fanned himself with a notepad. "Understand: the Latin Alliance isn't out to conquer territory. They want leverage, that's all. They want us to guarantee to stay out of what they perceive to be their own affairs. And they want—" he made a face— "reparations."

The prime minister gave him a long, level look. "I would say it is a problem for the United States."

The President shook his head. "No, Ed, it is not. It is a hemisphere problem, not a national one. Surely you can understand that."

"Couldn't you make peace with the Latin Alliance? If all they want is reparations, some arrangement could be made."

From behind the President, the secretary of the interior laughed bitterly. "What arrangement could be acceptable to them? The only thing we can tell them is the truth: 'Sorry, friend, you're just a little too late. We've raped the earth already. Now Canada has all the resources and half our people. We can't afford to pay you a dime.' They want the same things for their people that we have. That we had. But there's not enough to go around, not anymore."

The President held up his hand. "Ed, please. It's not a question of telling them anything, but of protecting our sovereignty."

"Protecting your sovereignty." The prime minister snorted. "With what, your bare hands? Until the computer nets died, your administration's governance-efficiency quota was riding at fifty point oh one percent. Care to guess what it might be now? The minute the net's restored, there'll be a vote of no confidence and—"

"The net won't be restored," the President said. "Not soon. Not for years, for decades, maybe. We're going to have to get used to governing again, not just appeasing popular opinion. We have to show the fighting will to—"

The minister of defense slapped the conference table, producing a moist *thap!* "Mr. President, unless you draw the states closer into the Union, you won't have that will. You need to move against the Pacific group—"

"That isn't the threat," objected the President. "There's no question of what we *ought* to do. Sure, we ought to meet the Latino threat, and we ought to knock down the rebels on the West Coast. There's a hell of a lot that we ought to do, if we had the resources. But the country is bankrupt. Where are you going to get the money to—"

The prime minister held up a calming hand. "It isn't a question of our getting the money. It's your problem. Unless we can work out some arrangement of our own."

The secretary of state, seated to the left of the President, squeezed his arm unobtrusively. The President licked his lips. "And what sort of arrangement might that be?"

"The English-speaking peoples of the North American Continent have a great deal in common," the prime minister said carefully. "With so much of the world arrayed against us, it's time that we considered a union of our people. If we could—"

"A confederation?" the secretary of state asked.

The prime minister pursed his lips. "Well, no. Not exactly."

The conference dragged on for another two days,

but the issue really was decided at that moment. Not exactly a confederation, no: rather, the prime minister proposed the absorption of the mid-northern part of the United States into Canada. The United States government—what remained of it—sought certain face-saving concessions and won a few of them. It would hold power along the eastern seaboard, at least in theory. The thirteen original states were intact. Theoretically. And if they could save anything westward, but south of the Ohio river, then Canada would not object. The secretary of state, who only days earlier had been a representative, wept bitterly when the President signed the treaty. Afterward, when they were alone, he took her in his arms. "I'm sorry, Catherine," he said. "There was nothing else to do."

Like Catherine Dearing, McMurphy was from Texas. He wondered if Texas still existed.

6: *Ark Liberty*

At the same hour, another council of war was taking place on the continental shelf off the Florida coast. Seven people, four men and three women, sat at the pale gray conference table in Ark Central, Level 1. Unlike their surface counterparts, they felt comfortable, for the air temperature here was conditioned by the water temperature outside. They paid close attention as they heard the news.

Stefan Li waited until Kris Harris had finished speaking, surveyed the stricken looks on the faces of the others, and cleared his throat. "Can you assign a probability to this, Mr. Harris?" he asked formally.

Harris shrugged. "Ninety, I'd say. We'll know more as more military channel intercepts come in. It's still spotty, but communications are firing up through Canadian reroutes."

Barbara Kluczyk, the slender blond woman who had

overseen the installation of the atmospheric control system, balled her fists on the plastic table top. "Who did it?" she asked.

Harris shook his head. "Who knows? We had the Latin Americans angry at us, but there's also the Chinese, the Arab Union, take your pick. Everybody's got nukes now, even if they haven't got food for their people."

Charlie Andrews, outwardly calm except for the dew of perspiration on the chocolate-brown skin of his forehead, asked. "Are you sure it was a nuclear attack?"

"Dead sure," Harris said. "The military intercepted some of the missiles, but the perimeter guard around Kingstown took at least one hit. Looks like a hit on the communications grid in Virginia, too, and maybe one outside Minneapolis. Satellite photos should confirm, when we raise the satellites again."

Andrews leaned back, a pained smile on his face. "All these years and it never happened," he murmured. "Then some goddam third-rate little nation—"

Li coughed. "I called you together so that all sections would be informed," he said. "Now, no matter what happened, no matter who fired the shot, it means war. I assume that the United States will win—despite our troubles, we're not too weak to defend ourselves. If anyone currently on the work crews wishes to return topside, they will be permitted to do so."

He turned to Harris. "Just bring us up to date on our state of readiness here, Kris."

Harris keyed the datapad before him, and a wall display unit came to life with a schematic of *Liberty*. "Our living quarters and life support are one hundred percent functional," Harris said, highlighting these areas. "Environments for crop production and oxygen generation already operational. Research centers ninety-eight percent. Cryo-storage ninety-five percent. Daley Burnford has the Gulf Power Array at fifty percent capacity now, and even at that it will supply more power than we can possibly use." He went through the whole list, stopping after a few minutes with, "We're ready to go. We've got everything but people."

"Maintenance capability?"

Harris shrugged. "Theoretically the structures should endure for seven hundred to a thousand years, given minimal maintenance and no unforeseen natural disasters. We've stored nearly enough materials to fabricate half the Ark over again from scratch, and we could extend even that if we cannibalized the materials on the mainland intended for *Ark Caribbean*. We could do that; Burnford has sequestered the storage unit for us, and his men have reported no attempt to reclaim the materials. Even at fifty percent output, the Gulf Stream power generators are operating at nominal efficiency, and our ground station is prepared for long-term maintenance there. Backup systems are all in place. We're set for a siege."

Li nodded and turned to the woman at his side. "Sandy?"

Sandy Dumont, fifty, gray-haired, a little overweight, smiled weakly. "We've processed nineteen thousand applicants. We've short-listed five thousand, pending further screening."

Li surveyed the faces turned toward him. They were all stricken, in different ways. Sandy Dumont looked as frightened of speaking in a group as at the prospect of nuclear war. Barbara Kluczyk was wide-eyed, strained, holding her emotions in. Charlie Andrews, outwardly calm, betrayed his emotions by his darting eyes. Donald Willis and Jean Tumlin seemed to be in shock. Only Kris Harris was taking everything in stride, as he always did. Li nodded and then said, "I propose to staff *Liberty* immediately."

Li raised his hand to ward off the babble of objections. "One at a time, please. You, Donald."

Willis, an expert in metallurgy and design, said, "I thought you'd been denied permission."

Li began to pace. The conference room was pale blue, indirectly lighted, with a tough plastic pad serving as a kind of carpet. It squeaked faintly under his shoes. "It's true that the administration failed to approve my request," Li said. "But perhaps the administration no longer exists. Certainly it has ceased to function as a government. The country has invested a staggering amount of money in our project, and we've invested a considerable portion of our lives to it. In my view, it would be senseless to lose that investment."

"Go," Andrews said. "I'm with Stefan. We go."

Jean Tumlin stirred herself. "Wait a minute," she said in her deep contralto. "What about my construction crew? They haven't applied for membership in this little club, but—"

"They stay," Li said. "If they want to, they stay aboard."

Harris gave him an annoyed look. "The point of screening the applicants is to insure a genetic pool—"

But Li shook his head. "Forget it, Kris. Look at the facts. We have a short list of five thousand. Some of them may not have lived through the attack, and some of them we'll never be able to find. Ideal start-up crew is thirty-three hundred, but we can handle nearly twice that many. A few hundred extra people won't be a problem."

Jean Tumlin nodded, her squarish chin set. "Then I'm with you," she said.

"I think we should vote," Li replied.

Donald Willis laughed. "Vote? Are you joking? Hell, Stefan, there's no choice. I'll tell you this: if we're to have a chance of making this thing work at all, if we're to fire up the Ark and try to run it with whatever rag-ass crew we can haul in, you're not going to run it with votes. It will have to be a dictatorship if you have a prayer of holding everything together."

"It isn't one yet," Li said. "In favor of populating *Ark Liberty* and bringing all systems on line?"

Six hands raised at once. After a moment Donald Willis raised his hand as well. "What the hell," he murmured.

"Good," Li said. He turned to Harris. "Kris, I'll want you to stay. We'll draft a notification document, then get it out to our short list one way or another. Charlie, Donald, Barbara, I'll want you to form a committee to work out processing of the arriving staff. Charlie, you oversee Medical personally. Sandy, you'll set up central records and information systems. We'll need a working orientation program—that's yours." Li paused. "I know it's a hell of a shock," he said. "But let's get started. We've got a world to rebuild."

Chapter 3

1: *Ark Ouachita*

Adriel Volker bent over a microscope and grunted with irritation. She saw spherical green cells, their color not uniform but darker in some areas and lighter in others. "You're almost there," she said. "Damn you, how could I have worked that much on you and still have you only almost there?" She straightened, putting both hands against the small of her back and arching until her spine cracked. She tapped her datapad and glared at the read-out.

She had begun with some fairly common varieties of phytoplankton and had worked her way down to some UV-resistant varieties. Then, using a dozen different techniques, she had tweaked and twiddled the organisms until they had begun to behave in ways slightly different from their genetic ancestors. Then a little more different. Finally a lot different.

The cells were still chlorophyll-bearing plants, and they still did the humble jobs their ancestors had always done: they soaked up hydrocarbons, water, and carbon dioxide, and they exhaled oxygen. Of course, the newer models were a hell of a lot more efficient than nature's originals had been. Adriel hoped that they were hardy and vigorous enough to grow and multiply, to spread through the world and replenish its diminishing oxygen supplies, to become a replacement for the vanished rain forests.

But she wasn't satisfied yet. Oh, this generation was

an improvement, but it wouldn't quite do what she wanted it to do. Even so, she would release these into the waterways, and they would find their way to the ocean soon enough. These cells wouldn't quite do what she wanted, but maybe the next generation would, or the one after that. The vats waited. Adriel Volker hooked a chair with her foot, rolled it over, and sank into it, frowning at the display screen.

Adriel spent a couple of hours at the datapad, rearranging configurations of molecules, sketching a different approach. Others in the lab occasionally paused to look over her shoulder and make a comment, but she merely grunted and ignored them. Finally, at least partly satisfied, she pushed back and sighed. "There. We'll try that on lot 1505-C series," she said to no one in particular. She became aware that her stomach was empty and that her left leg had gone to sleep. She massaged the muscle, yawned, and got up, stretching again.

Patsy Grice, looking tiny beside a stand of experimental corn, glanced her way. "Overtime again," she chided.

Adriel shrugged. "Nothing else to do. Any word from outside yet?"

"I heard we have troops heading our way."

"Ours or theirs?"

"Ours, silly. What would the Latin Alliance want with an Ark?"

"Maybe they'd want to wreck it. The way they're doing the world."

"It isn't just them," Patsy said.

"I know. It's all of us. Excuse me, but I'm more hungry than guilty right now. I'll be back this afternoon to see how the new strain is developing."

"It's afternoon already."

"Be back tonight, then."

"Have fun."

Adriel went to the surface level. The air inside the greendomes, cascade-cooled, was moist and muggy, but not as hot as the desert outside. She had to stand blinking for a moment to accustom her eyes to the glare filtering through the translucent dome panels. She wondered for a moment where Gene Handelsman might be, but she knew that already. He was on guard duty.

The Ark had been buttoned down tight as soon as the extent of the nuclear attack had become known. Things were more nearly normal now, a month later— if anything could be termed "normal" anymore—but the security force had been thoroughly shaken up. Adriel felt a fleeting moment of pity for Gene and his fellow security officers, for they would be outside, patrolling the perimeter in the merciless blaze of the sun.

Still, do it to Julia, she thought. Adriel had a mid-afternoon lunch, then made the rounds of the eastern greendome, checking on the progress of the various crops, chatting with the agronomists she knew. They had little news, for the Ark was a world unto itself, and not much had filtered in from outside. The usual rumors swarmed, of course. The Latin Alliance had crossed the Rio Grande and was sweeping north. No, the Alliance had fragmented into civil war, and the United States was just mopping up. No, others claimed, it wasn't the Alliance that had attacked at all, but the Arabs. . . .

Close to sunset Handelsman caught up with her. He was in a sunsuit, the hood thrown back and his hair plastered to his skull with sweat. He gave her a hug, and she suggested a shower might be in order.

They did not share living quarters, but used each other's indiscriminately, according to whichever was closest. In this case, her cubicle was. They took a regulation three-minute shower together—which meant that they could take another one later. Conservation had its advantages.

Some time later, when both were dressed again, Adriel lay on the bunk and Handelsman sat at the foot of it on the cramped room's single chair. "Hell of a day," he said.

"What happened?"

"Had to turn away this guy. Said he'd come all the way from California, most of it on foot. Ever hear of a Dr. Kito?"

She frowned. "Taniguchi Kito? The marine biologist?"

Handelsman shrugged. "Don't know. Didn't give me his specialty. Short little guy, about a hundred years old. Wanted in the Ark."

"And you turned him away?"

"Orders," Handelsman said with a stretch and a yawn. "Standing orders from the President: no admission of newcomers for the duration. Anyway, he had the wrong address."

"What?"

"Said he was heading for *Ark Liberty*. Said they'd invited him to come."

Adriel raised herself up on her elbows. "But *Liberty* was never activated."

Handelsman shrugged. "That wasn't the little guy's story. Said they'd sent for him. But he's having a hell of a time trying to get there. Flights have been canceled, travel restrictions are tight for everywhere south of the Kansas border. There's some goddam story about Canada invading Washington and Oregon, too, and the little guy was babbling about that."

"Was he alone?"

"Far as I could see."

"What did he do? When you turned him away, I mean?"

"Oh, he was very polite. Said he understood why we

couldn't take his word for who he was. Asked to buy
some food. I gave him some rations. Then he took off,
on foot, heading east. I guess if he makes it to the
Mississippi he just might have a chance. Get a boat
there, go down to the Gulf, around the tip of Florida,
and he might actually make it, if the Latino navy isn't
operating down in that area. Funny little guy."

Adriel sat on the edge of the bed, close to the foot,
close to Gene. "If it was Dr. Kito, I wish you'd let him
in. He's done some amazing work with—"

"Don't talk work. Come here." For a few minutes
they cuddled and kissed. Then through her blouse
Handelsman pinched the test tube that she wore on a
thong around her neck, like a pendant. "What is this?"

"Never mind," she said, and moved his hand to a
more comfortable place.

2: New Savannah

Keli Sumter walked the last twenty klicks into town,
her knapsack slung over her shoulder, her eyes con-
tinually straying toward the east. Earliest morning, the
pre-dawn hours—travel on foot was bearable then,
before the scorching sunrise. She made good speed
and timed her walk well, for she reached the outskirts
of town just as the sun rose off to her left. She kept
to the shadows and made her way to the city center,
where she rested with her back against the cool metal
siding until nine, when the city workers began to show
up for work. Many of them knew her, and they welcomed her into their air-conditioned sanctuary.

Keli had to wait another half-hour before Walt
Franklin showed up. Muscular and square of face,
Franklin was in charge of noncommercial boating and
dock permits. His lean brown face was more somber
than Keli could recall. "What can I do for you?"
Franklin asked without preamble.

"Hey," Keli said. "This is me, remember?"

Franklin's smile was a grimace. "Sorry. Things've gone to hell this last week. I don't know who we're answerable to or for what. Between New York and Ottawa—"

"What are you talking about?"

He gave her a look of surprise. "You haven't heard? Where you been, woman?"

Keli grinned at him. "On the road. Five days by bicycle from Atlanta to here, at least until I warped a wheel. What's up?"

"Jesus, where do I start?" Franklin tilted back in his chair and locked his hands behind his head. "Canada claims they own us now. Signed some sort of bogus treaty with some drag-ass remnant of the Kingstown government—you did know about the attack, didn't you?"

"Something about it," Keli said.

"Yeah, well. Anyhow, what's left of the Senate and House of Representatives has convened in New York and has elected an acting President—McMurphy, so you know what that means. Meanwhile, Canada claims that it has the rights to everything down to the Virginia border, then west to the Pacific."

"What about the rest of us?"

"I guess we're supposed to be under the control of the Latinos. Except they haven't showed up yet. It's a mess, girl. Why'd you want to leave nice safe Atlanta for here?"

"Not for here," Keli said. "For the Atlantic."

"I don't understand."

"I don't have time to explain. I need a boat, Walt, for a one-way trip down to the Florida border. What looks possible?"

Franklin got up and closed his office door. He stood looking down on her. "There's supposed to be a ban on boat travel," he said. "We're at war. You can't leave

port without a permit, and there ain't no permits being issued. So tell me, Keli, what's so important that
you have to get down to Florida?"

Keli opened her knapsack and rummaged through
it, finally producing a rumpled and stained envelope.
"This," she said. She passed it to Franklin.

He opened the envelope and pulled out the single
sheet of stationery. After frowning over it for a minute or so, he said, "This came surface mail?"

"I guess you could call it that. A messenger. An
Army kid on a motorcycle." She shrugged. "Didn't
matter. I was ready to leave, anyway. If he hadn't got-
ten it to me, I would have been gone the next day or
the day after."

"So you're accepted for duty aboard *Ark Liberty?*"

"If I can get there. I need you to help me get there."

"That is a problem." Franklin held the envelope out,
and Keli took it and replaced it in her knapsack.

"What keeps anyone from taking a boat out?"

Franklin settled back behind his desk. "Coast Guard,
theoretically, but they've gone north."

"So you can find me a boat?"

Franklin shook his head.

"Come on," Keli said. "When I think of all the goddam favors I've done for this city—"

"Hold on," Franklin said. "I can't find *you* a boat. I
got one for *us.* If you'll let me tag along."

For a moment Keli was startled into silence. Then
she said, "Well, sure, but why?"

Franklin's grin was rueful. "I don't want to see the
ocean come any farther into town than it has. I don't
want to ride my bike past all these damn empty buildings. I don't want to see this place die any more than
it already has. Good enough?"

"I guess."

"Reckon they'll take me?"

Keli laughed. "They're operating the ark wildcat,

without any conceivable authorization. You know computers, you know boats, you're healthy and under forty. Sure, they'll take you."

"When you want to start?"

"Now would be good. Follow the yellow brick road, huh?"

Franklin frowned. "Huh?"

Keli laughed and shouldered her pack. "Come on," she said. "I'll explain on the boat."

3: The Gulf of Mexico

The invasion fleet would have been laughable a century earlier. It consisted of slightly fewer than a hundred ships, most of them rustbuckets, some of them diesel-powered dinosaurs. The Latin Alliance had exactly one aircraft carrier to its name, and it housed only fifty planes.

The invasion had been delayed in hopes of arriving at some sort of negotiated settlement, but the first strike had done its work too well. The Alliance could find no one with whom to negotiate, no one who wielded the kind of power that would allow a government to function. But once launched, the mission was proceeding inexorably, with some success already: Puerto Rico, never comfortable as one of the United States, had fallen easily into Alliance hands. Not that Puerto Rico represented much of a victory, for it had dwindled markedly as the ocean level rose, and the stunning heat and numbing hurricanes had taken their toll on the island, making it a rutted wasteland with a population measured in the low thousands.

The victory was symbolic, but not hollow. More important had been the clashes with the U.S. Navy; two sharp exchanges in the Caribbean that had resulted in the loss of four Alliance craft and of three naval ships, one of them a submarine. Other U.S. ships had trailed the invasion fleet and had turned away, their officers confused by the lack of any ordinary chain of command, too timid to strike on their own initiative.

Captain Luis Ortez felt odd about the invasion. For one thing, his father and grandfather had been born in the old United States, in Los Angeles, and he himself had been raised there until his eighth year, when the family relocated to Argentina, drawn by the promise of land. Despite all the intervening years of propaganda, Ortez remembered his childhood fondly, recalling especially the times when his papa had taken him to the sports—to soccer, football, and baseball. He had been a follower of the New York Yankees, his father, and so Luis had become one, too. It seemed somehow wrong now to be moving north toward the land of the Yankees with hostile intent, like some grievous but unavoidable mistake.

Ortez sighed and drew his attention back to the radar screen. He flew a reconnaissance craft, a *Serpiente*, lightly armed but heavily fueled for maximum range; he was the eyes of the invading forces, and he had a great responsibility, or so his commanders repeatedly told him.

He had ventured to within sight of the Mississippi Delta this time without encountering any sign of resistance. The few surface craft he spotted were too small to be anything more dangerous than Coast Guard cutters, and he had encountered no air traffic at all. Ortez radioed the carrier with the news that he had no news, and the carrier ordered him to return in a wide circling path that would let him sweep more of the Gulf. He made sure his recorders were on—the *Serpientes* possessed complex monitoring equipment that allowed them to follow both civilian and military radio traffic—and made his long turn.

Canada, he thought. He would not mind fighting Canadians. He had never met one of them, had never attended any Canadian sports events except for the rare baseball game against Toronto or Calgary, and then he rooted for the American side. Despite himself, Ortez grinned inside his oxygen mask. He had caught the disease early, the malady of thinking the term "American" was limited to citizens of the U.S.A. His grandfather had railed at him a time or two: there were *norteamericanos* and *sudamericanos*, and both were American. But even his grandfather made no distinction between Canadians and the former designation.

Well, they were different, and from what Ortez heard, the Canadians now claimed to own the U.S.A., to have taken it under their protection. They said the Canadians were well-equipped and well-armed. He wondered if he would meet any. Ortez had never fired his weapons (two Venom missiles, four cannon), and he was half-anxious for the chance to try them out.

But he would not get a chance on this day. No hostile craft sailed the blue Gulf, none cruised the sky. Captain Ortez sighed and wondered how much longer he would have to wait for something, for anything to happen. He had waited almost all his life, he thought.

And he soon would be twenty-one years old.

4: New York City

President McMurphy was a chief executive with his hands tied, a commander in chief with little to command. The situation report on October 1 was not encouraging: Arabs had struck at Northern Italy and were reportedly on their way to Germany, satellite recon reported a sharp nuclear exchange in central

China, a naval force was closing on the Gulf Coast of the United States, Canada was becoming intransigent in its insistence on his capitulation, and *Ark Liberty* was using government channels for non-government business.

"What do we have?" McMurphy asked General Samuel Metzger, the commander of what was left of the Air Force.

"We've reestablished command links with the Eastern Bomber Wing," Metzger replied. "General Labord commanding. I finally got the son of a bitch to acknowledge the chain of command. They're on standby."

McMurphy bit his lip and considered a map, an honest-to-God paper antique. "Where are the invasion forces heading?"

Metzger put a thick forefinger down on the paper. "Our best guess is here, to Old New Orleans. If they can hold the mouth of the Mississippi, they have some leverage."

"Recommendation?"

Metzger shrugged. "The ground forces are occupied on the Western front. It'll have to be an air and amphibious assault. Of course the simplest thing—"

"Say it."

With another shrug, Metzger continued. "The simplest thing would be to nuke them. Lose the city, but we'd break this idiotic little force at the same time."

McMurphy pushed away from the desk and rubbed his eyes with forefinger and thumb. "God damn it," he said. "Is the Net anywhere near repaired?"

"That's negative, sir. We have some lines up—local New York, and part of the Virginia grid, but nothing west of the Mississippi. We're relying on military communication from the western states."

McMurphy rose and paced to the window. A touch of a button cleared the opaque glass. Manhattan lay below them, its towers shadowed by an overcast sky, the rivers on either side of it slate gray and lifeless. Off the tip of the island, the Statue of Liberty raised her torch atop the reconstructed Liberty Island. Had the work not been done in the last century, she would have stood knee-deep in water now. As it was—

McMurphy sighed. "Have you seen the weather estimates?"

"Yes, sir."

"Not cheerful reading," McMurphy muttered. No, not cheerful at all: an ionosphere depleted by nuclear explosions, an atmosphere more highly charged than formerly with greenhouse gases. Wholesale melting of the Greenland ice cap, unprecedented thawing of Antarctica. A temperature jumping not half a degree but a degree and a half Celsius. Without turning from the window, McMurphy asked, "What's Ottawa doing?"

Metzger said, "Occupying forces in the Dakotas and Iowa, putting pressure on our army's northeastern flank. No hostilities yet."

McMurphy laughed without mirth. "Iowa and the Dakotas. They want the last fertile states, do they?" With a sigh he turned from the window. "All right. I want a strike at the sea forces, not on New Orleans. Conventional weapons only. Reserve the nukes—" he twisted his mouth— "in case we need them later on. For Canada."

"Yes, sir." Metzger rose but did not leave. "Sir?"

"Yes, General?"

"The other matter. The unauthorized use of military channels by *Ark Liberty*—"

"Fuck *Ark Liberty*," McMurphy said. In a way, that would prove to be the most important decision of his short-lived presidency.

5: Kansas

Johnny Wolf had raised an army of his own. It num-
bered not in the millions, but in the thousands: grim
dark men and women with sun-bleached hair and eyes
gone filmy from the sun, people with no hope for the
future and no use for the past. Hack Bloodworth, who
was in charge of arming the multitude, found himself
impressed despite his close ties to Johnny, for until
the army actually massed he had no notion of exactly
how large it was. Because food was precious and
scarce, the isolated settlements and farms—a dozen
people here, a hundred there—had been separate to
this point.

But harvest time had come, and after harvest the
time of reckoning, or so Johnny said. They came by
night, brought by messages sent God knew how, bear-
ing with them enough food to last for a few weeks.
They took up the arms that Hack and his men had so
painstakingly gathered: stun guns, trank guns, old-
fashioned rifles and shotguns, even a few handguns.
They did not practice, for practicing would use ammunition.

The camps, scattered in the hills around the Ark
that was their goal, swelled gradually. Johnny himself
appointed the leaders, usually younger men, sun-hard
and cruel of face. In late September the decisive element fell into place: a group of disgruntled U.S. soldiers, deserters from the Northwest front, showed up,
let themselves be talked into joining the forces that
Johnny was putting together, nearly fifty men, each
one fully armed, some carrying explosives. Their
leader was a lean, sunburned man they called "Cap,"
though Hack thought he probably had been no more
than a sergeant in the regular army. And Hack saw,
as Johnny seemed not to see, that Cap was willing to
let the civilians join in, was willing to let Johnny play

leader, until he, Cap, could claim that position as his own.

Hack didn't trust the man, but he had no opportunity to convince Johnny of Cap's probable treachery. With chameleonlike eagerness, Johnny changed colors, became an ardent student of military tactics under Cap's tutelage, became too busy to listen to Hack or to his doubts. And on a dry October evening the thirty-odd leaders met with Johnny and Hack for their briefing.

They gathered around an arena made of swept sand, with lines incised in it to represent the Ark and the surrounding territory. Johnny strode about the swept circle, a pointer stick in his hand, the only one whose footprints could be impressed in the sacred area, though Cap sat hunkering on the perimeter, nodding his approval at each word from Johnny Wolf. "These are open," Johnny said, his pointer indicating the westernmost domes. "Just canopies, no walls. We'll go in there in force, with me and Cap leading, but first, here" —the pointer tapped the northern dome— "we distract them. Here's where the dynamite goes. Hack's in charge of that detail. That will draw their security men, and while they're busy there the main force will come in—"

Hack shook his head, but he kept the movement minimal. Dynamite. And the northern dome was where Johnny had seen his "wheat." God knew what would happen to that if the dome was shattered. God knew how deep the installation went—Hack's recollections of newscasts from the old days told him that the Ark delved far down in the earth, that level upon level waited there, each one defended no doubt against attack. Bloodworth glanced around at the hard men whose eyes were on the pointing stick: they headed an "army" of three, four thousand. Who knew how many were inside the Ark?

Johnny straightened up, the pointing stick switching against the leg of his antisolar jeans. "Questions?"

"What do we bust up?" one leader, a tough-looking hispanic with a scarred face, asked.

Johnny looked at Cap, and in his flat Southern twang, Cap said, "Just the north dome's all. Take out anybody who looks like he has a weapon. Don't damage the other domes if you can help it, and don't hurt any crops or animals."

"Women?" someone else asked.

"Grab 'em." Johnny grinned, and the men laughed.

Hack cleared his throat. "Johnny—"

The dark eyes whipped toward him, intense and challenging. "What?"

"What if there's other defenses? Electric fields or—"

"Leave that to Cap and me," Johnny said. "We'll take enough security forces alive to tell us what to do about them. We get into the domes, find out what we have to deal with, and then we do it, man." The grin was white and ferocious.

Hack looked away. "Yeah," he said.

"Hey, hey," Johnny said softly. "You with us, man? 'Cause if you ain't with us—"

"I'm not against you, Johnny," Hack said. But he wondered. He saw that dark, dangerous stare and he truly wondered.

6: *Ark Ouachita*

Adriel Volker awoke to explosions.

She rolled out of bed, dressed hurriedly, and ran to the lifts, only to discover that they had been shut down. She pounded up three flights of stairs instead, emerging in the central experiment station just as more explosions rattled the dome overhead, made the supporting pillars thrum with a deep submusical note.

She grabbed the arm of a technician. "What is it?"

He jerked his sleeve away. "Mines, on the north side. We got trouble there."

The dome was full of people, pressing inward, toward the center of the installation. Adriel fought her way against the flow, finding openings, diving through, making her way to the north. The soy dome lay fallow, the next crop not yet begun, and she ran across the rows heedless of any damage she might be doing to the crop. The wheat dome, so immense that it generated its own weather, lay in light fog. She saw figures here, darting toward the exits. "Gene!" she shouted, realizing how ridiculous it was to shout.

A giant hand slapped her off her feet, tumbled her head-over-heels, left her on hands and knees with her ears ringing and her open mouth full of dust. A shower of debris rained over and about her, and she bowed her head against it, rounding her back, pulling in like a desert tortoise. After a few moments she moved, feeling hand-sized pieces of plastic fall away, and she stood dazed and shaking, a hot wind in her face.

A third of the dome had been blown away. She stared through billows of dust out at a harsh red landscape, at a flat stretch of ground alive with dashing, falling figures. A faraway clatter came through the roaring in her ears and she knew it for gunfire. She felt instinctively for the familiar weight suspended from its thong around her neck; the sealed tube was intact.

Adriel stumbled back toward the central domes, disoriented and staggering. She fell sprawling across a body, recognized its blue clothing as the uniform of a security guard, and rolled it over, her heart thudding against her teeth. It was a man she knew slightly, Freddy-something, and he had been shot high in the chest. His eyes, wide in death, bore a filmy coating

of dust. Adriel took the stun gun from his grasp, un-
buckled the battery belt, and somehow got it fastened
around her own waist. Her hearing was coming back:
shouts and gunshots, screams and explosions, all of
them distant, ranging away from the gaping hole in
the dome's wall.

She found the passage to the central domes deserted, saw no one in the soy dome or in the experiment station. She tried the stairway door, found it
electronically locked, and pounded on it in ineffec-
tual despair. She thought of the airshafts and the
maintenance ladders, turned to her left, and made her
way to the service corridor that snaked in semicircles
between the domes, connecting them and tying them
into a unit.

The second service door she tried was unlocked,
but the corridor was in darkness; the surface lighting
was off, cut by friend or foe. Adriel plunged into the
darkness, extending her left hand, feeling her way,
trying to remember the exact layout of the service corridor, the location of the ladders.

She found the hatch that should give access to the
ladders, but it, too, was locked. Cursing her luck,
sweating in the rising heat—for the air-conditioning
was gone along with the lights—Adriel felt her way to
another door, pushed it open, and blinked in the light
of the rain-forest preservation dome. She gasped
moist air, heard the drumming, chirping, and screeching of thousands of insects and birds. A ten-meter high
waterfall splashed to her left, and from it a mock river
twisted and wound through the lush foliage.

The pump, then, was still working. They had power
below, she thought. They had—

Someone shouted ahead of her, and a half-dozen
green and red parrots broke from cover, flew with
their awkward fluttering strokes against the pearly
light shining through the dome—

A gunshot, and one bird tumbled in a ragged cloud of feathers. The dome shattered somewhere past it, and someone laughed in a harsh, phlegm-filled rasp. Shouting voices masked by the alarmed screeches and cries of birds, an altercation, words not clear but tone definitely angry.

Adriel crouched behind a thick bayonet bush, champing her teeth together hard. Her hand stole to the communicator on the belt battery, but she dared not switch it on.

The brush rustled along the winding path. Adriel brought the stun gun up, touched the test button, saw the capacitor light glow green. She tried not to breathe.

Five men came into view on the path, two in Army uniforms, three in white reflective shirts and jeans. One of the Army gikes was half-turned, scolding the man behind him, a dark-skinned Anglo with startling pale eyes. "No more of that shit," the gike said.

The man shrugged and scowled at his feet.

"Come on," the lead gike said. "Got to find some way to get them damn rats out of their holes."

Adriel remained absolutely silent until well after she heard them open the service corridor door, until it had closed behind them again. She gazed upward, feeling her eyes fill with tears. The dome showed a hole, not a large one, perhaps the size of a palm. A shaft of bright sun poured through, harsh and incredibly bright against the milky haze of the dome.

It was a small hole. It could be repaired.

If anyone remained in the Ark who could repair it after these—these vandals had finished.

She rose, her knees creaking, and wound her way down the path, paralleling the artificial river, hearing the new hysterical note in the cries of the birds, as if they knew their chance at life hung in the balance.

Next was the marsh dome, droning with dragonflies, thrumming with frogs. Next the tidal pool, with its ceaseless artificial waves still at last. Next a food dome, where potato and tomato plants grew, where salad greens and sturdy root crops flourished. And next—

Adriel edged through the last door and almost sobbed aloud. This dome was open to the environment, one of the western semi-enclosures where they developed and tested grasses, cacti, other arid plants, for their chance at survival in the wild sun of Kansas.

And there, not far away from her, a Security man stood with his back to her, his weapon ready in his right arm. In front of him a dozen or so of the improbable guerrillas squatted, obviously his prisoners.

Gasping with relief, Adriel ran toward him. He heard the noise, his head came up, and he looked over his shoulder—

It was one of them, in a Security coverall.

Adriel shouted something, jerked the stun gun up, and tried to pull the trigger.

The other reacted more quickly. She saw a red burst of light from the muzzle of his weapon, and all the world turned to blood and then to darkness.

6: *Ark Liberty*

"That's it?" Keli Sumter asked, squinting through the glare.

"That's it," Walt Franklin roared back, his hands on the wheel of the launch, his eyes hidden beneath the shadow of a long-billed cap and behind reflective shades. "Don't look like a whole hell of a lot, does it?"

"Looks like heaven to me," Keli shouted back. She broke out the binoculars and climbed back on the ladder to get a better look. The launch wasn't going very fast—fifteen knots, Walt had estimated—but the jarring made it difficult for her to focus the instrument. Finally she had it, and the surface of *Ark Liberty* came into sharp focus: an enormous rectangular metal island, all girderwork and radomes, with one flat VSTOL landing area and a complex of structures like the bridge of a couple of aircraft carriers put together.

"Any life?" Walt bellowed.

"Too far to see," she shouted back. She tried to steady the binoculars. "There's a sort of harbor on this end, though, and a few boats in it."

"Okay. Climb on down before you break your fool neck."

She did, grateful for their motion and for the reflective outfit Franklin had found for her. She let the "veil" cover her face—she had been exposed to sunlight before, but never in such concentrated form, with it reflecting off the ocean all around—and she chided Walt for not following suit.

He shrugged. "Covered my face and arms with that AS-40 shit. I've only had one carcinoma so far."

"Wish I trusted my skin enough to raise this thing," she said. "At least it's cool."

"Getting along in the fall," Walt replied. He fiddled with the throttle. "Come on, baby."

"God, don't let it run out of gas now," Keli said. "Not after it took us so long to find it."

"She'll do," Walt said.

Their departure from New Savannah had been delayed far longer than she'd wanted. Walt insisted on tidying loose ends, and then there were air-raid alerts, and then there was the problem of locating a craft with enough fuel and power—they had wasted days.

But at last Franklin had come up with this launch, an antique surprisingly in running condition, and they had left town in the dead of night. "Probably no Coast Guard around anymore," Franklin had grunted. "But if there are, we'll stop and let 'em board. You got your marching orders, DOD, and I got my bona fides. We'll be all right."

The trip had been less than memorable. They hugged the coast as much as possible, with Keli wincing at the crumbling ramparts of the Old Savannah seawall, at the nearly-submerged dunes that were the remnants of offshore islands, Ossabaw, Sea Island, St. Simon's, Jekyll. Another hurricane had brushed past since Thomas, and in its wake the surface lay littered with incredible things, parts of roofs, fragments of signs, once a soggy teddy bear.

They swung away from shore as they neared Jax—"Feds might have a force there by now," Franklin said. "No sense making them curious about us."

After one night at sea, they turned southeasterly and began to track back and forth, with Keli working an inadequate radio-finder and Franklin becoming increasingly worried at the coughs and splutters of the engine. Finally, past noon, Keli had picked up a strong signal, encoded and unreadable, but almost certainly coming from *Liberty*. They followed that until, like a conjuring trick, the ocean produced the tower on the horizon.

It took another half hour of maneuvering before the launch was close enough for Keli to distinguish people moving on the surface of the tower. By then she was calling, fruitlessly, on the radio. "Can't raise them," she said to Franklin.

Franklin's dark skin glistened with sweat. "Not surprised. That piece of shit set probably ain't even functional. Break out a flare and show 'em we ain't sneaking up, anyway."

The flare arched high, trailing orange smoke. After another minute or so, Keli said, "They're sending a boat."

The launch engine coughed consumptively. "Good

thing," Franklin said. "Ours is about to die on us, I think."

It took ten minutes more for the little inboard to come close. Three people were in it, a woman at the wheel and two men with rifles flanking her. Franklin killed the engine and they floated as the smaller craft came alongside. "Hi," one of the armed men shouted. "What's your business, please?"

"We're heading for the Ark," Keli shouted back.

"Authorization?"

"I've got a letter."

The wind was kicking up, and the man asked Keli to repeat. She shouted again.

"Stand by." The man spoke into a transceiver and then listened to an inaudible reply. To Keli he shouted, "Give me the authorization number, just under the heading."

Keli fished the crumpled, sweaty letter out of her pocket and opened it. "Three niner three oh," she shouted across the water.

The man spoke into his radio again, then replaced the unit on his belt. "Follow us in," he yelled.

"Easy for him to say," grumbled Franklin, struggling to start the engine.

It coughed to life at last, and the launch trundled along in the wake of the little craft. Keli kept revising her estimate of the size of the Ark tower: at first it was the size of a city block, then two, then five. The "harbor" proved to be more of a canyon cut into the side of the structure, with primer-red metal towering on either side like skyscrapers. Their pilot craft took them to a floating dock, shadowed by the sheer height of the harbor's walls.

They tied up there and clambered out of the boat. The two armed men waited on the dock for them. "Papers?" one of them said. Keli extended the letter.

The man was really quite young, probably no more

than twenty. He nodded and returned the letter. "Welcome aboard, K.M. Sumter. You, sir?"

Franklin, who towered over the youth by a head, cleared his throat. "I guess I'm sort of along for the ride," he said.

The young man looked at his counterpart, a blond, red-faced fellow who seemed hardly out of his teens. The other shrugged and grinned. "Oh, well, what the hell."

With an answering shrug and grin, the first young man let the muzzle of his rifle droop. "Okay. Name?"

"Franklin, Walter Scott. Late of U.S. Customs and Border Control."

"Okay, Franklin, Walter Scott. Don't know if they'll let you stay or not, but what the hell. I'm Ben Milvers, and this is Janko Sundersen. Let me give you the drill. We'll send you down to processing. . . ."

And processing, it seemed, would determine their fate. To Keli's surprise, they were not the only refugees: ten others joined them in a room that could have accommodated a hundred; a room that proved to be a staged elevator. After a few perfunctory greetings, they retreated to small groups of two or three, with Franklin and Keli one group. A slim woman, her head razored to stubble, wandered over, looking forlorn. "I'm Luce," she said.

Keli and Franklin introduced themselves. Luce stared at them for a moment. "Will my dolphins be able to stay?" she blurted.

Keli exchanged a glance with Franklin. "I'm sure they will," she said.

The thin girl hugged herself. "They raped me ashore," she whispered. She touched herself in an awkwardly innocent way, like a toddler gingerly probing a fresh bruise. "Men and women both." She wandered away again.

"What's wrong with her?" Franklin whispered.

"I think it's what's wrong with the whole world. We'll find out when we get aboard. It's bound to be a clummy sort of place."

"Don't know if they'll let me stay," Franklin muttered.

"Of course they will," Keli returned. "If they don't—hell, if they don't, I won't stay, either."

"Crazy talk, girl."

"Crazy girl, I guess."

Gears hummed, air hissed, and little by little the lift sank down into the sea, down into the vast body of the Ark itself, down into whatever new life awaited them there.

Chapter 4

1: Rumors of War

The *Serpiente* was not designed to be a fighter plane, but Luis Ortez fooled it into behaving like one.

The North Americans had sent a fleet against the Latin Alliance's ships, but a fleet nearly as laughable, as inadequate, as the invasion force. One ship, though, was a carrier, and it housed F-333A attack craft—sleek, fast, virtually invisible to radar, and armed with six ship-killer missiles each. Ortez could not hope to match the speed of the North American planes, but he did cobble together an eye-lock, a visual reference system that gave him a chance at vanquishing the foe by using a sight-directed laser to guide his two Venom missiles.

The key was that the F-333A's were not interested in aircraft, only in ships. Ortez took vectors from the spotters in the smaller craft, lined himself up, and hoped he was on the right trajectory. This time he was: an F-333A doing better than Mach 1.2 came out of the high overcast, arcing downward to deliver its missiles. For a moment the two planes were parallel and less than five kilometers apart, and then the North American began to pull away.

Ortez flew without reference to the controls, turning his head, activating the aiming laser. His goggles flared two vivid orange crosshairs, and he thumbed the Venom release.

The *Serpiente* juddered as the missile launched,

causing the enemy craft to blur in Ortez's sights. But he kept the visual lock, and the Venom missile followed the laser point to impact just behind the F-333A's cockpit. Plane and missile exploded in an orange fireball, and Ortez broke away, swiveling his head to try and spot any other craft in the area.

Either he missed one or the North American had fired a missile of his own just before dying.

The surface of the Gulf lit up as a tactical nuclear warhead exploded amidships of one of the Alliance ships. Ortez twisted away, his earphones rasping static. He clamped his teeth together, waiting for the shock that never came. He had been too far away from the explosion to feel any direct effects—yet. Whether he had received enough radiation to kill him was quite another question.

The *Serpiente* wheeled in a greet swooping bank that ended with the nose of the aircraft pointed north-northwest. Ortez checked his fuel: he had just under a half-hour's supply remaining. That should be enough, he thought.

He hoped.

He strained his eyes forward, looking through patchy clouds at the surface of the Gulf, willing himself to see land, the coast of Louisiana. Ejecting there was his only hope.

For the ship that had gone up in the nuclear fireball had been the carrier that the *Serpiente* had called home all through this sorry, misbegotten excuse of an invasion.

"I'm sorry," the victorious commander said.

The vanquished general shrugged. "My people can't hold together without communications, without a chain of command. I honestly don't know who I should surrender to—you or the Canucks."

The weather in southeastern Oregon had taken one

of its unpredictable turns: snow had come in mid-October, a three-inch dusting, and the temperature had plummeted to minus two. The command post overlooked the gray water of Upper Klamath Lake, cold and uninviting under a slaty sky. The victor, a squarely-built man in his mid-forties, grinned mirthlessly. "We're better than the Canadians, I think. Your men might want to join us. We've still got a long way to go."

The beaten general, older, graying, shrugged again. "I'd say that would be up to the troops. I don't know. I think I'm tired of fighting." He squinted at the patch on the other man's arm. "Union of Pacific States. That's what you're calling yourselves now? What happened to Pacifica?"

"That's still the name of the territory. Like America and the United States."

"Yeah. God, I'm tired."

"Alaska's joined us."

The older man nodded. "They'd been neutral so long I'm not surprised. You fighting the Canadians yet?"

"Not yet. Maybe it won't come to that."

The gray-haired man's smile was wry and knowing. "It will come to that."

A cold wind rattled the panes of the big window. The Pacifica officer glanced over his shoulder. "Your people will be freezing. I'd say the first order of business is to get them south, to the Eureka headquarters. They'll be fed and housed there until they make up their minds about joining us."

"You have transport?"

The Pacifica man shook his head. "We have legs," he said. "There's a general ban on fossil-fuel transport in the Pacifica area, and you people pretty well eliminated our solar and electric capability."

"It's a hell of a long way, and my people aren't equipped for this cold."

The other nodded. "I know," he said in a surprisingly soft voice. And then once again, he said, "I'm sorry, General."

In contrast to Oregon, Ottawa was a balmy 27 degrees. War had not come close to the city; the stores were already decorated for the Canadian Thanksgiving, and the electric transports hummed shoppers around with quiet efficiency. Parliament met on the question of mounting a military offensive against Washington and Oregon, the two states theoretically now belonging to it; Alaska so far was not discussed, a remote western outpost remarkable only for its remaining supplies of oil.

The debate continued through most of a bleak northern day, with proponents and opponents going for the jugular in the ancient, civilized manner of Anglo-American representative democracy. The decision, reached at five P.M., was finally against war; after all, Minnesota, the Dakotas, Montana, and especially Idaho had come into the fold already. They had the most natural resources, the most exploitable farmland. As for the eastern states, Michigan had lost the northern peninsula, Wisconsin was wavering, and only the Eastern Seaboard seemed firmly in the hands of the provisional U.S. government. God knew what was happening in the Gulf States and the arid Lower West.

Under the provisions of the Act of Union, the former citizens of the United States owed their new government a decade of bond-service before earning their citizenship. That was unpleasant, but farms had to be manned, and labor was almost as precious as dwindling supplies of oil.

All in all, the Canadian government would have

much to be thankful for this season. Oh, the British Columbia question was vexing, with unrest among the populace and at least the chance of a break-away there, of the Western renegades joining Alaska to Washington so that Pacifica would indeed be united. However, B.C. had dwindled in importance to the Canadian Union since the weather had changed: soaking rains, climate veering from broiling to freezing, altogether unsuited to intensive agriculture.

But that question could be settled later.

In the meantime, with so much new territory added to the country—yes, the government would have much to be thankful for.

The War Room of the United States government was located in a windowless inner area of a sky-scraper, one of the obsolete legacies of the twentieth century. President McMurphy brooded there over a map that covered a tabletop. A transparent overlay had been marked in vivid colors: a blue border surrounded the faithful states; a red one set off the Western rebels; a green one marked the beach heads of the Latino invasion; and yellow cross-hatching marked problematic areas, places where the government's control was questionable.

The yellow stripes crossed three-quarters of the United States: everything south of the North Carolina-Tennessee line, everything west of the Mississippi. "What about the invasion fleet?" McMurphy asked the man at his left shoulder.

"Just remnants to mop up," General Anhausen replied promptly. He touched the map. "They have scattered forces here, in the Florida panhandle, but nothing we can't handle once we reestablish command over the southern forces. They hold the Biloxi area pretty strongly. Word is that a lot of the

Hispanics in Texas and New Mexico went over to their side—they don't actually have that many troops on the ground there, but I'd say that our biggest headache is going to come in all the states with a heavy Hispanic population. Lot of sympathizers there."

"Thank God for air superiority."

Anhausen, a trim fifty-year-old, nodded his appreciation. "We don't think they've got anything floating in the Gulf now. Frankly our big worry should be farther south. The missile strikes pretty much knocked out the Alliance's main command centers, but the nukes have played holy hell with satellite communication, with strategic—"

A young woman seated at a table in the far corner suddenly looked up. "President McMurphy," she said. "A priority call."

McMurphy growled, but he strode to the table. "Who is it?"

"Coast Guard," she said.

With a curt nod, the President lifted the receiver. "McMurphy here." He listened for a few moments, then said, "Sink it."

"What is it?" Anhausen asked.

McMurphy capped the receiver with his hand. "A ship under Australian flag in the harbor. Crew seems to be Arabic."

"Sink it," Anhausen said.

The ship, which actually was neither Australian nor Arabic, removed the necessity of sinking it very simply. The crew, a dedicated group who believed strongly in martyrdom, detonated a dirty, hefty nuclear device before they could be boarded. The resulting explosion obliterated everything within six kilometers of the southern tip of Manhattan.

2: *Ark Ouachita*

As she recovered from the stun gun blast, Adriel Volker cursed the waste.

The wild-eyed man, the one who called himself Wolf, had ruled the surface levels of the Ark for more than a week, and Adriel and the other women (she had seen maybe forty in all, separately, at a distance) who had been caught on the surface served the men under Wolf's command. The men of the Ark had been killed, either in battle or afterward. One of the few things that Adriel was grateful for was that Gene Handelsman's body had not been among those that she and the other women had been forced to drag to the dry creek bed on the northern edge of the Ark.

She had the horrors during those days, fits of uncontrollable trembling, dry sobs, seeing the ravine fill with tumbled bodies, wearing a wet handkerchief tied around her face to diminish the stench. But the real horror went beyond that, beyond even the despair and outrage of violation, twice, three times a day as men of the occupying army took turns with her.

No, the real horror was that the Ark itself was dying.

She hoped fiercely that those below, the ones who had barricaded themselves beneath the surface, could hold out and prevail, that they could wipe these— these barbarians from the face of the earth. If she could be assured of that, Adriel thought, she could face even death without qualms.

But the hope was a forlorn one.

Meanwhile—

Meanwhile the men who had taken the surface domes systematically raped *Ark Ouachita*. All the domes were holed now, and badly: the rainforest dome so thoroughly that the plants were desiccating, the bird life dying in the dome or escaping to die even more pitiably in the dust-desert outside. Those below

had kept the climate controls going, but Wolf's forces
had destroyed a great many of the surface controls, had
skewed others, so that the waters were no longer aer-
ated, so that the supplies of nutrients were interrupted, so that irrigation ceased.

As long as they had food and sex, Adriel thought,
they would never think to provide for the future.

Never.

She was appalled at the creatures who crowded under the domes: the men sun-dried, faces splotched
with cancers, eyes as often as not milky with solar cataracts; the women rail-thin, muffled, veiled; the children ridge-ribbed and pot-bellied, doomed no matter
what food they found, no matter what shade they
rested under.

And all were ignorant, willfully so.

Adriel pled with the men for the freedom to make
a few adjustments, to keep the domes living and green.
They cursed her, hit her, and raped her. The first time
it had happened she fought back, only to be rewarded
with a dazing blow to her chin that chipped her two
upper front teeth and sent her into a whimpering fog.
She learned with each later time that she could not
fight three of them at once, that a pretended submis-
sion won her time, that the thing to do was to wait
and plan.

The trouble was that the others never let up. She
spent a day with a squad of soldiers, six men, and with
her were two other women from the Ark; but they had
no chance to speak to each other, kept from com-
municating by blows and threats of worse to come.
They passed her to a family group of one old man, a
couple, and five children, where she worked as a kind
of domestic for a week before being sent to yet another compound. And always she was watched.

And always she watched the wreck of the Ark. They
stripped the communications center for no reason,

ripping out microboards, toppling the satellite dishes, blasting the computer nodes with racketing gunfire. Laughing at the destruction.

They pissed in the clean water and ran the electric carts in wild impromptu races through the tilled fields, destroying the crops that could have fed them.

They acted like—well, Adriel had to admit it—like humans.

She had no idea how many people had come in from the desert, but the number was surely in the thousands. And Johnny Wolf constantly sent out patrols to bring more in. They trickled in, a dozen, twenty a day, but constantly. For the time being the food stores were paradise, the unlimited water a gift of heaven, but how long could that hold up? Not long, she thought.

And finally her chance came, in the form of a man who looked middle-aged until he spoke, and then his voice came out breaking, like an adolescent's. His name was Bloodworth, and from the way he glared at Johnny Wolf, Adriel knew there was trouble between them. She attached herself to Bloodworth, cooked for him, even washed his clothes in one of the few fountains that still worked and that was as yet unspoiled. He took her sexually, but with an awkward shyness, a hesitancy.

"How old are you?" he asked her after the first time.

"Forty this year," she told him truthfully, her cracked teeth making the "s" whistle strangely.

"Jesus God," he sighed.

He kept her. A week went by, two. Bloodworth kept her, refused to pass her along, and Adriel became aware that there was indeed some kind of rotation plan, that the captured women were to be kept on the move. She began whispering endearments to Bloodworth in the night, began to stroke his face, his neck.

Waiting for the right night, for the right time, for the opportunity.

Waiting.

3: *Ark Liberty*

"Nothing," Keli Sumter said.

Harris leaned over her and tapped the virtual keyboard. The screen remained blank. "Try reorientation to Europe-1," he said.

"Already have. They're dead, too."

Harris checked the time. "Without satellite relay it'll be another four hours before we can raise L-5, another eight before we can try Luna."

Keli ran a hand through her short red hair and yawned, her jaws aching. "Another war?" she asked.

Harris's face showed bleak humor. "I guess so. What's that, the third this month? Damn, I hate to lose the weather feeds." He slid into a chair next to Keli's station. "Anything on short-wave?"

"Short-wave transmission list, Matrix," Keli said.

The computer blanked a two-meter square section of wall and displayed a list of several thousand entries. "Clarify: government bands," Harris said.

"Sorry," Keli told him.

Harris shook his head. "No sense in cluttering up the screen with a lot of amateur stuff."

The list resolved itself into a notation perhaps two hundred items long. Harris scanned it. "Canada's still healthy, looks like. Great Britain. The German Enclave. Wonder what the hell's happened in Central and South America?"

But no one, not Matrix and certainly not Keli, could tell Harris that. November had brought, at last, the end of the hurricane season, but as the days went by, the Ark's lines of communication to the outside world began to vanish. Early on, *Ark Appalachia* had tersely advised that it was "sealing up," bracing itself against some real or fancied invasion; since then there had been no word from that quarter. In mid-month a brief communique from *Ouachita* had claimed that the surface levels had been taken by invaders and had begged for help. *Liberty* had none to give.

And other reliable lines of exchange had vanished, one by one. Harris and the others worried incessantly about weather patterns: fires in Asia and South America had apparently sent volumes of smoke into the upper atmosphere, darkening the sun over large patches of the earth. "Not bad," Harris had remarked to Keli while he was training her how to use the equipment, "if you just want to cool down for a bit. But the surface is in for some rough UV afterward, and God knows what the gases will do to the greenhouse balance."

Now at Harris's request Keli had Matrix monitor the government broadcast bands, searching for information about weather patterns and the effects of the nuclear exchanges of autumn. She could tell that the results were meager, but she dutifully stored them all and asked Matrix for a constant situation estimate, updated hourly.

Then, because Matrix did most of the work and she wasn't really busy, Keli asked for a readout of Ark occupancy. "Two thousand nine hundred and four," she said.

"Hmm?" Harris had been scanning through a European weather broadcast. "Oh, Ark population?"

"Yes, as of this morning. How many more do you think will make it?"

Harris shook his head. "Can't say. None day before yesterday, then nearly forty yesterday. And only about half of them with tickets."

"You don't turn anyone away, though."

Harris's laughter was silent. "Can't afford to. But

we're probably putting together one hell of a genetic stew." To Matrix he said, "Male/female ratio, please."

Rounded, it was 51 to 49. "Not as bad as you thought it would be," Keli teased.

"Yeah. Bad enough, though. Should be fifty-fifty. We were established under a conservative government with a strong commitment to monogamy."

"It will work out," Keli said.

"It'll have to."

Keli busied herself with the communications terminal and half wished that there were some other way of keeping busy, or at least busier. She had adjusted to life on the Ark surprisingly fast, but then she was a woman who could do that. Now and again she found herself with a fierce wish to know what had happened back home, back in Old Savannah, back in Atlanta; a maddening wish to know simply whether her friends were alive or dead (for she had no immediate family), even to know if the Historical Service was still operating or trying to.

Futile, all of it. So Keli threw herself into her training, kept up a strict round of calisthenics, toured the Ark, learned about its functions and its quirks. Her friend Walt Franklin had joined a maintenance team and seemed to fit right in there; she envied him his casual grace at forming friendships, his ability to greet her now not as a special friend but just as another Arkmate. Some part of Keli, some secret place of the heart, held her aloof from such ease.

"What?" she asked in sudden confusion, for Harris had spoken.

He shook his head. "I called up a projection of oxygen levels outside. Damn, look at the figures," he said. "God damn."

"Bad," she said, though she still didn't grasp his meaning.

"It couldn't be worse," Harris said, and the way he said it made Keli shiver.

4: Pointe Coupee Parish, Louisiana

Something moved in the jungle.

Art Trammel crouched in a tangle of palmetto scrub and held his breath. Something was coming toward him, moving north along the overgrown path that once had been Highway 190, back before the cars had died, before the river had overflowed the low spots, before the swamp had encroached. Art remembered none of this, for he was far too young, but he had learned something of the past in school, during the six years of schooling he had taken.

Now he held his breath, hunkered even lower, contracted himself, pulling his elbows close in, his knees, holding his chin close to his chest. He could tell by the sudden silences of the insects, by the change in the sodden air, that it was a person coming along the trail, slowly, probably alert for danger. Overhead a leaden sky drizzled thin cool rain, fine enough to drift almost as fog, sheening everything with a slick shiny coating of water.

Almost in sight now. . . .

Trammel tightened his grip on his only weapon, a wicked long combat knife. A U.S. Army Albrecht combat rifle hung from his shoulder, but he had used up his ammo in the fighting around New Orleans. Since Trammel wasn't U.S. Army, or anything else, he found replacement ammo hard to come by. But with surprise the knife could be enough.

There he was.

A young guy, swarthy, black-haired, eyes hidden behind mirror shades. He wore stained and tattered sand-tans, boots, and a bandolier, and he carried a short, efficient-looking carbine. He seemed to be alone.

Trammel tensed.

But the stranger himself tensed at almost the same instant, and the blank lenses of the sunglasses seemed to sweep the area. Trammel wondered if they were somehow special, infrared selective maybe. He huddled behind the palmettos even tighter, the knife grip slippery in his sweaty palm.

"Okay," the stranger said in unaccented English, "I got you there. Show yourself, slowly." The muzzle of the carbine tracked back and forth slowly, then froze. Trammel almost felt a small cold circle on his chest, where the weapon was pointing.

"Easy," he said, and he eased up, flexing his knees slightly, bouncing on the balls of his feet. He held his hands out from his sides, the knife visible in his right fist, the left hand open, palm toward the newcomer.

"You want to drop that," the other man said.

"Hey, you got the gun, man."

For a long, uneasy count of five there was silence, except for the steady background chatter of the bugs. Then the stranger took a deep breath. "Army?"

Trammel laughed. "I look like Army?"

"What are you?"

"I ain't nothing."

Another long pause. Then the man with the carbine said, "Holster it, then."

Trammel twirled the blade expertly, and it snicked home in the scabbard at his belt. "You Army?"

The other shook his head. "I used to fly a plane."

"Where you heading?"

"Up country. People there?"

Trammel shrugged. "Most of them are in and around Alexandria. Still some farming up there. You want to get to a base, you got a hell of a long walk. The government's cut us loose."

"Who's in charge, then?"

Trammel grinned. "Guys with guns, I reckon." He wiped his mouth. "Hey, you got akwas?"

"You have food?"

"Yeah. Want to join up?"

"Well—let's eat, anyway."

"This way." Trammel turned and pushed his way through the undergrowth. The other man followed, though at a cautious distance. "Name's Art," Trammel said over his shoulder.

"Call me Louis," the other said.

"Cajun?"

The other grunted.

When they reached the lean-to and Louis saw the food that Trammel had stashed, he seemed to consider pulling out of the partnership, but Trammel reassured him: "Hell, 'gator's good."

They boiled a gallon of water and Louis dropped an Akwa-Pur tablet in, designed to handle the pesky microbes that had become tolerant of short-term exposure to boiling water. "Usually I have to boil it all night," Trammel said. "Wind up with a quarter of what I started with. But around here, the untreated stuff'll eat your insides out."

Trammel roasted chunks of 'gator, muscle meat from the tail, over a hot fire of embers protected by a slantwise overhang. "What's that?" Louis asked, nodding at the slab of metal that kept the rain from the fire.

"Piece of a plane," Trammel said. "One of theirs."

The 'gator fat sizzled as it dropped into the embers. Louis took a cup of the water and waited for it to cool. Trammel, watching the cooking meat, said, "You fight down around New Orleans?"

"Over the Gulf," Louis replied.

"How was it?"

Louis shook his head. "Got rough," he said.

"Yeah, I reckon. Shoot, them bastards landed

around Old New Orleans and some of our people went over to them, you know? But others of us, the militia, and some of the regular troops down from Benning, we held them all right."

Louis looked at the Albrecht and said nothing.

"Beauty, ain't she?" Trammel turned the spit, and more fat sizzled into the fire. "My buddy's firearm. Only he got hit bad, and he told me to take it. So I did."

"But you're out of shells."

Trammel shrugged. "Hard fighting, man. We fell back. I fell a hell of a long way back when the shells were gone. I don't expect you've got any 7.75 ammo?"

Louis shook his head. "I've got forty-one 2.25's for the carbine."

"Them the explosive slugs?"

"Not much good for hunting small game."

"Reckon not." Trammel prodded one chunk of 'gator meat with a sharp stick. Clear juice ran out. "Here, put this in your belly. See what you think of lizard tail."

Trammel watched Louis as they ate. The man bit into the 'gator meat gingerly at first, then ravenously. Trammel, used to the diet, ate more slowly, chewing the stringy flesh and washing it down with gulps of hot water. "Look," he said, "night's coming on. You really set on heading up country, you might as well stay here the night. Shoot, I might as well go 'long with you, come to that. Sure ain't nothing to keep me around here."

"All right."

"I guess you, you're probably pretty anxious to join back up with the troops, huh?"

"Not particularly."

"Yeah, I know what you mean, all right. Man, this country has gone to hell in a basket. You hear all sorts of stories—nukes up North and out West, and they say tidal waves have hit Hawaii and Japan, and—"

"You want that last chunk on the fire?"

"Huh? Naw, help yourself. Sometimes I think if I eat one more piece of 'gator I'll grow scales." Trammel rose, got some damp wood, and put it on the fire, where it steamed and hissed as it began slowly to catch. "I reckon you won't have much news."

Louis shook his head. "You know as much as I do."

Dark was coming on. "Well, we can both sleep in the lean-to," Trammel said. "Plenty space. Unless you think we ought to keep a lookout."

"You probably sleep light."

Trammel laughed. "I sure as hell do."

He was crafty as they prepared for bed. He placed his Albrecht and the knife scabbard on the far side of Louis's place, without comment. The knife itself he slipped out expertly, sliding it inside the waistband of his trousers. He lay with his back to Louis for a long time, hearing the booming of the 'gators off in the swamp, the shrieks of the night birds, the eternal rasping of the insects, and—especially—the breathing of the other man.

When it became slow and regular, Trammel pulled the combat knife out slowly, stealthily. He clutched it against his chest, visualizing what he would do: a quick rollover, a thrust in and a yank up, and so much for Mr. Louis. It was tough, but he needed the carbine, the Akwa-Pur tablets, whatever else was in the rucksack. Sometimes a man had to take what he needed, that was all.

He slowed his own breathing, waited until he was sure the other was asleep. Then he rolled over.

The night outside was dark, and the fire had waned to weak red embers. Louis was only a silhouette in the gloom, but Trammel could tell from the breathing sounds that the other man lay on his right side, facing him. He shifted the knife into position and made his move.

The carbine made little noise, just a flat *crack!* of sound, but the explosive shell punched into Trammel with a wet slap, slamming his body back, so that he wound up with his torso out of the lean-to, a gaping hole in his chest, his eyes wide and startled.

Captain Luis Ortez, late of the Latin Alliance Air Force, had become a light sleeper, too.

5: Atlantic Power Generation Station 1

Stefan Li found the Gulf Steam waters soothing, relaxing. He cruised easily in the one-man submersible, inspecting the elegant and strangely beautiful array of generators, spidery "windmills" with huge sweeping arms; except of course these were water mills, driven by the incessant and dependable flow of the Gulf Stream northward.

The November light far above was subdued, though the sky was clear: atmospheric smoke and dust at high levels filtered the sunlight, reducing visibility. Normally a cool, nearly luminescent blue, the water had faded to a dismal gray-blue. Li wondered what it had looked like years ago, when the corals grew, when the fish schooled in the thousands instead of in the scores. He knew objectively, for he had seen video records; but he wondered how it would have looked to him, in the flesh.

He puttered along, a lone figure in a craft no larger than a small runabout, following the long line of generators. They swept their arms obedient to the current, as they always did, and nothing seemed wrong. Li had helped design the array years ago, not long after earning his degree. It had been intended to augment the tidal generation stations of south Georgia and north Florida, to send power to the mainland as well as a tithe of electricity to *Ark Liberty*. No one seemed to mind that he had diverted the flow, sending all of it to the Ark.

At least not yet.

Li reached the southernmost generator, and he tried the sonam. Daley Burnford, the other inspector, was not yet in range. That was fine with Li; he relished the time alone. He manipulated the craft's grapplers, latched them onto the generator's superstructure, and then cut power. The submersible swayed gently to and fro. Off to the right the great vanes spun, stately and constant.

Don Quixote would have been transported, Li thought. If his windmills might have been giants, think what these would have been to him. Titans. Gods.

He settled back in the seat, the wet suit embracing him comfortably. And what windmills have you tilted at lately, Mr. Li? Too many.

Harris was after him to seal *Liberty*. They were much too visible, he argued, much too vulnerable. So far they had been lucky, so far the navies of the world had concentrated on killing each other. But sooner or later. . . .

Sooner or later there had to be a reckoning. Harris had a plan to help, but if they put it into operation too late, it would do no good whatever. Best to seal the Ark now, to take their chances with the crew that had by guts and by God made their way to the installation.

Still—damn it, still—Li felt in his heart that the time was not ripe, that more orphans struggled toward *Liberty*. Oh, the throngs of September and October had thinned to a trickle of three, four a day, but still they came. If only he—

"Submersible one, you there?"

Li jerked from his reverie and thumbed the transmit button. "Here, Daley. How are things on your side?"

"Nominal. Yours?"

"Same here."

"Good." Burnford's voice was cheery, conjuring in Li's mind a picture of the man's broad red face and ready grin. "You scared us. It's not often that the big guy himself comes out to the boonies."

"They're not boonies to me," Li told him. "Probably easier for you to link with me. I'm moored to the port stanchion of installation 1-F."

"Be there in fifteen minutes."

"I'll keep a light on for you." Li signed off and, true to his word, switched on the visual beacon. Its white strobe lit the sea around him, freezing the tips of the sweeping vanes in a series of snapshots. A few curious fish came to investigate, but wary of this strange thing, they circled at a respectful distance.

Five minutes went by before the sonam buzzed again. "Boss," said Burnford, "we have company."

Li checked his readout. "I'm not showing it."

"It's at the far end of my range, but it's coming on fast."

"What do you make it?"

There was a long pause. Then Burnford spoke again, keeping his voice detached, professional. "A warship."

6: *Ark Ouachita*

He came strolling out of the dust desert in the dim days of late November, a figure fantastic even in the distance and close up absolutely incredible.

Adriel Volker was trying to explain to Bloodworth how they might yet salvage something of the food-production domes when they first saw him. They were in the broken north dome, and he came from the north, a striding figure taking the slope with no visible evidence of effort. One of the perimeter guards shouted a warning, and the figure stopped a hundred meters away. "What in God's name?" Adriel asked.

Bloodworth shook his head. He moved to the edge of the shattered dome, with Adriel trailing in his wake. "Do we kill him?" the guardsman who had shouted asked.

"Not yet. Get Johnny."

The figure stood with legs apart, patient as a monument. "Is it a robot?" Adriel asked.

Bloodworth took a pair of binoculars from one of the guards and stared through the instrument. "Damned if I know." He passed the binoculars to Adriel.

She focused on the figure, boosted the magnification to 12X, and realized that she did not know, either. Six feet tall and barrel-chested, the stranger wore only trousers and boots, and he carried a case in his left hand. Nobody walked about like that, bare-headed and bare-chested, not under the changed and hostile sun.

Nobody except this apparition. His skin was a peculiar color, literally bronzed, glistening and almost metallic. His eyes—well, she couldn't be sure at this distance, but he seemed to be wearing some kind of bizarre contacts, for his eyes were a uniform cloudy marbled blue, no pupils visible, no conjunctiva; it was as if his eyeballs had been replaced by blue marble orbs.

But the musculature beneath the skin looked human—misshapen, with the chest far too big, the waist impossibly small by comparison, but certainly human and not machine.

Unless some mad disney somewhere had actually made a humanoid robot for some reason. For no reason. Reasons didn't seem to matter in this latter age of Earth.

"Get him," Bloodworth grunted, and one of the guards set off at a run.

The figure outside remained motionless, expressionless, face blank as a sphinx's in the unshadowed light from the gray sky. Adriel shivered despite herself. "Hack, I don't like him," she whispered.

Bloodworth took the binoculars from her and took a long look. "I don't, either," he said. "See what Wolf says, though."

Wolf came a few minutes later, wearing a bloused white shirt and reflective jeans. At each hip a handgun rode, and he carried a snubbed, wickedly efficient carbine. "What the hell is it?" he asked. Adriel had noticed before that any real question, any question that truly bothered Wolf, went to Hack instead of anyone else.

Bloodworth shook his head. "Been standing there half an hour, just like that. You want me to check him out?"

"Both of us," Wolf said. "You guys cover us."

Adriel watched the two close the distance, carefully angling so that the guards would have a clear field of fire should the newcomer make a threatening move. He didn't. They stopped a few paces away from him, and he spoke to the two. Adriel saw him point to the case with his right hand, saw Wolf nod, and then the newcomer set the case on the ground, snapped the catches, and opened it. Bloodworth and Wolf stepped back, but nothing untoward happened. The man took something from the case and held it out on his palm. There was another brief exchange of words, and Wolf nodded again. The man replaced whatever he had taken from the case, sealed everything up, and then the three walked together back to the Ark.

Adriel shivered again as they came closer. The new

man was completely bald, and his nose was curiously flat—not broken, but low to the cheeks. In profile, the line of the nose was continuous with that of the brow, giving a simian impression. And the eyes, the cloudy blue marbled eyes: they weren't lenses, Adriel knew somehow. The eyeballs themselves had changed.

Bloodworth hardly gave her a glance. Adriel fell in behind the three, followed them through the service corridors to what had once been a storage pantry for one of the dining halls. Wolf had taken it as his office. Bloodworth, following the other two inside, turned to close the door and gave Adriel a surprised glance: you still here?

Yes, of course. Because if I'm not with you the others will take me—

Bloodworth closed the door on her.

With a sigh, Adriel sank to the floor, her back against the cool wall of the corridor. As long as she was here, within yelling distance of Hack, she felt relatively safe.

As safe as she could feel so close to that odd, inhuman form.

Chapter 5

1: *Ark Liberty*

"We lured them off-course," Stefan Li said. "But they're close to the power array. If they look hard enough, they'll find it."

"Hold still," Dr. Traubner said, adjusting the bandage on Li's chest.

"Hell of a note," Harris grumbled. "Probably they weren't even looking for us."

"Probably not," Li agreed, then grimaced. "Take it easy, Doc."

Traubner, a brisk young man with frosty blond hair, snorted. "Listen, anybody who lets one of those toy submersibles get depth-charged deserves some lacerations. You're lucky you weren't killed."

"Not depth-charged. They probably tossed a few grenades over to see if we were porpoises. The explosions didn't come close."

"Not to anyone else, maybe," Harris said. "You, you had to be in the thick of it. God damn, Steve, nobody knows *Liberty* like you. What if you'd been killed?"

"You must be angry to call me Steve. Don't worry, though. We've got plenty of engineers aboard now."

"I repeat: nobody knows *Liberty* half as well as you do. You're going to have to rein in your instincts for the good of the cause, if not for the sake of your own hide." Harris watched Li slip gingerly into a shirt and then asked, "What navy?"

Li grimaced as he began to slip-fasten the shirt.

"Who knows? Two small craft. Maybe patrol boats, could have been Coast Guard, I guess. Or maybe some stragglers from the Latin Alliance fleet. We didn't ask them for I.D."

"Have you been scanning the digests?"

Li shrugged. "I know. Civil disturbances throughout the Southeast and into the Southwest. Skirmishing on the Oregon line. Rumors of invasion along the Gulf coast. But it's all pretty chaotic."

"Getting more so. Here, let me." Harris held Li's jacket while the other man slipped his arm into the sleeve. Traubner had left them alone. Dropping his voice to little more than a whisper, Harris said, "Nobody knows this, but the L-5 station declared independence yesterday."

Li gave his friend a long, hard look. "That's ridiculous. They've got fewer than a thousand people, they're dependent on shuttle supplies for water, for air—"

"They've worked something out, I guess," Harris said. "Hell, come to that, are they any crazier than we are?"

"We've got water and air."

Harris's grin was sardonic. "And power, for the time being."

Li experimentally clenched and unclenched his right hand. It hurt, but not too badly. It would mend. "Yeah," he said.

2: The Independent State of L-5

They watched the earth burn.

The space colonists, the descendants of Poles and Chinese, of Africans and Iroquois, of Saxons and Aborigines, could not keep their eyes off the old world. They had to use magnification, of course, but they watched and gasped at the ravages they saw.

Rising Nation landscapes sparked and glared with nuclear-generated fires, trailed streamers of black or shining white smoke on the prevailing winds. Now and again a short, sharp war would break out, signalled by the pinprick suns of nukes. The pall of smoke thickened, and downwind from the fight the sky became translucent, not transparent.

The green sprawl of Canada was relatively free from such devastation, but—

But something was happening in the West. Fires burned there, too, although these had not been ignited by tactical or strategic nuclear arms. "Terrorists," some guessed. "Conventional war," others opined.

And meanwhile, according to the measurements that the L-5 observers still took, but which they no longer relayed to Washington, the melt rate of the Greenland cap, of the Antarctic shield, had increased by .2%.

In less than a month.

Nuclear winter, some of them murmured, hoping almost that the scenario would play itself out, that the ice caps would freeze up again. Because if they didn't—

Well, Manhattan would be inundated within ten years. Nothing, no sea walls, no dikes, no emergency measures, could save it. And Washington. And Rio, Hong Kong, Sydney. . . .

They had other worries.

Food? They were all right for food: the greentubes produced bumper crops, with oxygen an added benefit. As for water, they recycled every drop. Even so, there was a small loss, a gradual attrition.

Still, plenty of water was on the earth.

All they had to do was wait.

And watch.

3: *Ark Ouachita*

"Freedom," the apparition thundered. "Freedom!"

Adriel Volker huddled small in the back of the crowd. Hack Bloodworth was an arm's length away, intent on their weird visitor's pitch. Beside the bizarre man on the platform Wolf stood, his face wearing an odd, uncomfortable mixture of excitement and anger.

Their guest strode up and down the platform like an old-time evangelist working a crowd. "Look at me," he said. "Look!"

Yes. Look at the barrel-chested monstrosity, the sphinx-eyed mutant.

"*They* say the earth is ready to destroy us all." The voice was rough, gravelly, barked out rather than shouted. "*They* say that science has done nothing but pave the way for our death, for the death of the human race. But look at me!" He spread his muscled arms wide, threw back his head, and laughed.

The crowd murmured and shuffled. Some individual more bold than the rest said, "What'd you do to yourself, man?"

Adriel had the feeling that the man who spoke was a plant, for their guest smiled broadly and said, "I changed myself, friend. I adapted." More loudly, with the fervor of an Endtimer, he shouted, "Is that not the one great law of life, my friends? To adapt—or to die?"

"What about your eyes?"

"What about 'em? I can travel outside without shades, I can stare the old sun right in his face for an hour and do myself no harm. Can you?"

"Yeah, your chest and—"

"The better to breathe with," laughed the apparition. "Listen! The sun is killing plant life. That's no lie, no exaggeration. You know what's happening to the air, friends? The oxygen content is dropping. Oh, it's gradual, it's slow, but it's going right down. Used to be twenty-one percent. Not anymore! Twenty point oh five. Maybe twenty by now. What next year? Nineteen? *Seven*teen? Going down!" He slapped his chest with a flat palm, making a drum-boom. "But I'm ready. When it levels off—and it will level off—then I'm ready. Now why am I here?"

Johnny Wolf, impatience showing in his scowl, muttered something that Adriel didn't catch, but the speaker nodded. "I'll tell you—because I don't want this old world all to myself, friends. I want you to be like me."

"Shit!" someone snorted.

This time it wasn't a plant. Snake-quick, Johnny Wolf's head swiveled, and his dark gaze pinned the objector. "Hey," Wolf said, "You listen to this. Dr. Landrau come here to give this gift to the gophers. We're grabbing it instead."

Adriel pressed a fist to her mouth. *Dr. Landrau.* She had read his papers, had seen him speak once, years ago, at a conference in Denver—but then he had been an average-looking man in his thirties, brown-haired and brown-eyed, not—not the thing that stood before her on the platform.

Landrau spread his arms. "Makes no difference to me," he said. "It will work on everybody."

"Tell 'em the rest," Wolf said.

"Sleep," Landrau said. "You don't need sleep. Or you need at most two hours in twenty-four. Think of it! I'm giving you six hours of conscious life out of every day that you'd otherwise miss. A day in every four days! Three months in every year! And you're never tired—"

Adriel felt sick. She looked behind her. They stood in the ruined open space of one of the soy domes, a couple of hundred of the invaders and captives. No one was behind her. She could slip away—

Only she couldn't. Because if she were out of Hack's

sight for long, some of them would see her and grab her and start to take turns with her.

"It's a virus," Landrau was explaining. "A virus with genes tweaked and changed this way and that, with programs rewritten, with minor changes and improvements worked in. I inject it into you, and it replicates itself. In your cells it starts to rewrite your own codes, your own genetic makeup. It makes you better, stronger, more fit—"

Adriel touched Hack's arm. He looked at her, surprised. She whispered, "Ask him how long he'll live."

Hack's gaze lingered on her for a moment, became suspicious, and whipped back toward the man on the platform.

"You," Wolf said, pointing to the man who had expressed a doubt. "Up here."

The crowd laughed, jostled, and pushed until the unhappy objector stood on the platform with Wolf and Landrau. He was tall, broadly built, with dark skin and features that could be either African-American or Anglo, depending on the observer's prejudices. "You think you can take him, Felipe?" Wolf asked.

Felipe's muttered response was too low for Adriel to hear.

Landrau laughed. "You take any weapon," he said. "Any one at all. I'll face you bare-handed. Let me show you what I can do for you."

Moments later Adriel regretted that she had not tried to steal away. The crowd surged her along, through the ruined outer lock, beneath one of the broken domes, out onto the sand. The sky was copper, the sun a shrunken, glaring parody of itself, but her eyes began to tear immediately. Everyone else broke out shades and put them on—everyone but Landrau.

They made a rough circle around the two. Felipe hefted a carbine, checked to make sure it was loaded, and said something to Wolf. Wolf nodded, his eyes invisible behind his own mirror shades, and Landrau laughed.

"Okay," Wolf said. "Here's the deal. Dr. Landrau says he's faster, deadlier, than any ordinary man. Felipe, he don't believe it. So he's gonna kill Landrau. Or Landrau's gonna kill him. If Landrau wins, then we take his stuff. All of us." The wolfish grin, like his namesake. "And then, by God, we dig down into this gopher hill and kill us some gophers."

Adriel could see only in gaps, as people ahead of her leaned left or right. She saw Wolf raise his hand, drop it, caught a glimpse of Felipe whipping the carbine up—

The *crack!* of a shot, flat on the hot air, a shriek from the other side of the crowd—

Cries of alarm. Or admiration.

Felipe came into view, horizontal, on his back, as if he were levitating.

No.

Landrau's right hand held the scruff of Felipe's neck. His left clenched Felipe's buttock. As for Felipe—well, the loll of his head, the slackness of leg and arm told the story. Felipe was dead.

The crowd screamed.

"We take it," Johnny Wolf screamed. "We take the goddam stuff!"

Adriel drew disposal duty.

Hack was pissed at her: because she pled with him to find out more about Landrau, because she spilled to him the secrets she knew, he grew angry and slapped her. And then volunteered her to dispose of Felipe, while the others returned to the domes to take their shots.

All but Hack, who would supervise Adriel's work.

"It'll kill you," Adriel said in a hopeless voice. "That's the only catch."

"He looks okay to me."

Adriel bent over the body and lifted the shades. She slipped them on herself, grateful for the relief. "Bullshit. He's crazy and he's a freak and he's dying. The problem with Landrau's beasties is they don't stop. You take the shit he's shooting into people, and in two years you'll look like him. In five you won't be human anymore. And in ten you'll be dead."

"Johnny thinks he's—"

"Johnny," she mocked. "Johnny, Johnny, Johnny. Think for yourself, Hack." She grabbed Felipe's right wrist and left ankle and leaned. The body scraped across the dry ground. Adriel looked over her shoulder. The dead ditch was a quarter of a mile away, too close, close enough to smell. She bunched her muscles, took a better grip, and felt her heart flip.

Hack shook his head. "Look, those army guys are already after Johnny's ass. We gotta protect him. And you saw yourself that Landrau can walk around here in the open, that he can—"

"Help me get him on my shoulders."

Felipe's dead weight was crushing, but she staggered along under it silently, with Hack a few steps behind. The dead ditch, the dry bed of a creek, sickened her with its stench long before she reached it. The flies zinged and complained in a whirling cloud there. Adriel gagged and staggered.

Close to the edge of the ravine she dropped Felipe, hunched him off. When he hit, the air compressed in his lungs and the corpse said, "Aah!" in a mildly surprised way.

Bile flooded Adriel's throat. She dropped to her knees and turned her head away, trying to find some breath of air. Hack, thirty feet away, watched her. She pushed Felipe closer to the edge. Her hand slipped into his pants leg, found what she had felt through the material, pulled it out. She rolled the body twice, and then it flopped over the edge. The flies roared as it hit the rotting pile on the ravine floor.

Adriel backed away.

"Let's go," Hack said.

She turned then, quickly, and fired.

Felipe's little automatic pistol made an insignificant sound.

Hack's left eye broke, he staggered, sat, and crumpled sideways.

With only a glance at the domes, Adriel fell on him. First his carbine, then his side pocket. She found the keys to the ridiculous, rusted-out clunker of a truck that formed half the invaders' motor pool.

She set off at a run, already counting off mentally the ones she would have to kill: the guard at the broken dome that served as a garage, the lookouts at the intersection, anybody else she would spot within twenty klicks of *Ouachita*.

Through the thin material of her shirt, she clasped the test tube hanging from its thong around her neck.

Death. And life.

3: Calgary Grain Company

The riots began over shoes.

In the worker barracks for the great southern wheat fields the displaced Usans rested, grumbled, and finally revolted; the shoes they received, they said, were not the quality promised. For these cardboard imitations, these shapeless lumps that failed to keep out water, they gave up their citizenship, their freedom?

All two million of them?

The Usans had given up their weapons on entering Canada, of course, along with their right to bear arms. Bondservants had no such right.

Still, some had weapons, and others fabricated weapons of a sort, and still others were ready to fight with bare hands. The uprisings began on a Friday, and by the following Wednesday were widespread throughout the Calgary (south) district. The Canadian Army arrived that morning, assessed the situation, and asked for the authority to use extreme force. Authority was granted by sundown.

The next morning began the Great Murder, and the inevitable fragmentation of Canada as a nation.

4: Atlanta

The city had been without power for days.

Clay Elmore, sweating profusely, periodically wiping his bald dome with a handkerchief, roamed the offices of the Historical Service like a forlorn mother bear whose cubs had been snatched away. He paused at the deserted desks, remembering Richard, Keli, all the others. Through the ill-designed building echoed the distant sounds of gunfire in the streets. Scavengers, looters, an indigenous army more merciless than even Sherman's had been.

Well, they had fought the fight, he thought to himself. They had tried.

In the weeks since the Historical Service had disbanded, Elmore had moved into the offices, had slaved there with a dwindling staff and then, when fears of invasion grew, when worries about what was happening at home had grown too strong, he had dismissed the last of them and had finished the work himself.

Load after load of computer records, disked, bubbled, chipped, he had carted down nine flights of stairs. Sheaf after sheaf of paper had followed, neatly tagged, neatly stacked.

The basement of the building housed a vault, one with walls a meter thick, with a ponderous door as wide as his forearm was long. Who knew what it once had held? It now held History.

History stacked waist-high in ream upon ream of paper. History in the form of ten complete computer sets, together with schematics and diagrams. History in compact form, in magnetic memory. All the history that Elmore and his team had assembled, all that had been recorded up to the moment when—Elmore grimaced at the thought—when History had ended.

With the last sheet of paper in place, Clay Elmore leaned against the vault door and swung it shut. He twirled the vault's old-fashioned non-electronic combination lock, then wrote the combination on the door with paint. Someone might need it someday.

In the following weeks Elmore brought load after load of brick into the building with a wheelbarrow, moved them downstairs by elevator when the electricity was working, manhandled them when it was not. He became expert at the art and craft of bricklaying, sealing up History like a chained and senseless Fortunato.

At last the work was done. The basement room had two and a half new walls of brick, with nothing to indicate the presence of the vault. But one day, one day, someone would find it. Elmore sometimes mused that the finder might be an intelligent rat, or something equally bizarre and not human at all.

But maybe it would be a man.

Rifle shots came from close by. A window shattered somewhere in the building. Elmore shook his head and looked down at himself. The fat had melted away, and his belly was lean and hard. He felt in many ways ten years younger than his actual age. "Should've got off your ass years ago," he told himself.

Oh, well. Too late now.

Clatter of feet on the stairway.

From its hiding place in his desk drawer Elmore eased the pistol that he had liberated from the body of a dead policeman weeks earlier. This was the third time he had drawn it. So far the danger had passed him by.

The door banged open. Elmore squinted through the darkness.

Three of them, young, two blacks, one white. All carrying rifles.

"Somebody there," one of them said, pointing Elmore's way.

The rifles came to bear. "Old man," another one said.

"What you got, old man? What you got to give us?"

Elmore smiled. "Not a damn thing," he said. He rested the muzzle of the pistol under his chin, barrel angling upward, and pulled the trigger.

5: *Ark Liberty*

Keli finally asked Harris the question: "Who will it be?"

They were in the central control bay, the nerve center of *Liberty*, and they had just finished running diagnostics through Matrix, the main computer. Harris lifted his eyebrow. "I sort of thought about myself."

"Jesus."

He shrugged. "It's a kind of immortality. Oh, after the computer is loaded, after it's assumed whatever intellectual capacity I feed into it, I'll still be me, and I'll grow old and die. Or die, anyway. But the matrix, the thought patterns, the personality, will be duplicated in the core memory. *Liberty* will become a living organism, and in a way I'll live in there."

"Has it been done before?"

Harris laughed. "Sure. L-5 has a computer with SI, and the Luna colony was to have one. But they're prototypes—about seventy-five percent of the human personality survives in them. There are gaps. Our setup has more than twice their memory storage capacity, potentially, and some modifications as well. I've built in some emotion emulators, some capacity for dreaming even. L-5 has reported anomalies, you know. Their computer isn't completely sane."

"A thinking colony," Keli said.

Harris shrugged. "In a manner of speaking. But I don't know. Maybe I'm not the best candidate. The council will have to talk it over, maybe take candidates, screen them—"

Keli closed a panel. "Why, aren't you the best?"

With a grin, Harris said, "I'm a pessimist. Hell, I don't think we'll survive down here for one generation, let alone five hundred years. And if we do, what then? All my projections show the deterioration of surface conditions continuing. Five hundred years and the earth could be halfway to Venus. A thousand and it could be there. When the surface temperature gets high enough to boil away the oceans, what will be left of *Liberty?*"

"If you feel that way, why bother?"

Harris laughed aloud. "I could be wrong, you know."

6: The Mississippi

Adriel Volker had killed more than one.

When a group tried to block the truck, she had hit them, scattering bodies like bowling pins, ducking down, away from the whine of slugs. When the truck died and she took to her legs, she had fought off scavengers and rapists and—

Well, she had fought them off. Twice she had found hospitable groups, nomadic gatherings of a hundred or two hundred people, drifting east, alive with worry and fears of invasion. She traded her meager medical skills for food and shelter, set broken limbs, advised what to do about fevers, sat beside the dying and closed their eyes. And when the groups moved too slowly for her, she went ahead on her own.

Step by step. Kilometer by kilometer.

When she ran out of food, she killed animals: rats, snakes. She foraged among the burgeoning weeds for stuff she could eat: the taproot of kudzu, the seeds of grasses, wild grapes, dandelion leaves. And she kept going.

State by state. To the big river, the great muddy stream that flowed now between constricted banks cracked and crazed with the wild sun, its barrens stinking of decay but its banks lined with life, with humanity. From community to community Adriel passed, swapping news for food and companionship for a place to sleep.

Somewhere along the way she found the boy, or he found her.

It happened at dawn, a cool foggy morning pearl-gray with moisture, hooting with insects, whirring with the wings of the night birds. She slogged along the dried-mud banks, heading southward, and heard a sound like a cough.

It came from the river.

She stood still and looked out at the brown face of the water to the point where it dissolved into the gray mist. Something there, something a little more solid. . . .

A boat.

She waded, taking exaggerated steps. It was a small boat, hardly more than a rowboat, close in to shore, drifting. The cough came from inside it.

She was waist-deep. The boat was an arm's length away. She grasped the side—

With a screech the child reared up, plunged forward, sank his teeth into her knuckles.

Adriel swung without thinking, hit him square in the face, heard him thump down into the bottom of the boat. Scrambling, leaping, she fell across the gunwale, felt him pummeling her, pressed him back and down. "Stop it!"

She shook him, almost ready to kill again.

The eyes were wide and dark, staring from a hunger-hollowed face. The boy was naked, withered, belly bulging in imminent starvation. He couldn't have been more than six, she thought.

"Mama?" he whimpered, and reached for her.

She pulled away. She had glimpsed his private parts, and they were not those of a six-year-old. The boy, small as he was, had to be twelve at least. Tears stung Adriel's eyes, and, ashamed of herself, she took the child in her arms and comforted him. They clung to each other and floated down the Mississippi.

The boy's name, it developed, was Hawk, last name unknown. His father had put him and his mother into the boat away up north, and they had been together until his mother had disappeared one night, having gone ashore to scavenge for food. For some days and nights, Hawk didn't know how many, he had drifted alone. From his coloring and bone structure, Adriel guessed him to be Native American, though Hawk himself could tell her nothing about his parentage.

"Huckleberry Finn," Adriel murmured. The boy did not know what she meant.

She fed him, clothed him—that meant a night ashore with a lonely man—and the two of them traveled together a week, ten days, on the slow river. When the people ashore began to warn her of fighting farther south, of airplanes and tanks, she used a broken plank to row them across the river to the eastern shore. They left the boat there and found an old highway that headed east.

East, to the Atlantic, she thought. To *Ark Liberty*.

Hundreds of kilometers.

They walked. There was no other way. Some of the communities they passed had horses, but nobody had a horse to sell. Some automobiles and military vehicles cluttered the roads, but without fuel they were

useless. Somewhere that she hoped was in Alabama
they camped one night, finding shelter in a tumble-
down shack that might once have been a farmhouse.
Now it was a crazy leaning ruin of gray timbers and a
gaping roof, smelling of mold and of ancient shit.

They crept into the shelter well past midnight, for
the best traveling time was from early evening to the
early hours of morning, and the worst was in the heat
of the day. They lay apart but close, and Adriel listened to Hawk's breathing until it steadied and slowed.

The boy's famished state had improved, but he was
thin, thin to the point of emaciation. She nourished
him as well as she could, but the strain, the moving,
was telling on him.

The moon, half full, shone through the broken roof,
and she closed her eyes to its light.

And the instant she did she felt the point of a knife
at her throat. Her eyes opened.

The man was a shaggy-haired silhouette above her.
"This is my place," he said evenly, in a low voice.

"I'm sorry," she whispered, wondering if she could
work the gun out of her belt.

"Your son?"

"Yes," she lied.

The knife eased away. "Passing through?"

"Yes."

"Know any medicine?"

"Some."

The man grunted and shifted his weight. "Don't
move," he said. She heard a scratch, and then a match
flared to life. He was swarthy, black-haired, with eyes
that gleamed like dark coffee. The match touched a
stub of candle.

With his left hand the man lifted the candle and
held it over his leg.

Adriel winced. The wound was raw, ugly, blacken-
ing at the edges. "I know it's bad," the man said.

"Infected. If you're not careful—"

The man laughed. "Shit, I know it. What luck I have. I finally find a way to get out of this place and a gringo gets a lucky shot at me."

"You're a Latino," she said.

"My name is Luis."

"I'm going to get up."

"Slowly. And don't even think about the gun."

"I am, though."

It was brutal treatment, and it had little chance of working; but from the look of the wound, Luis had less chance of surviving. Powder sprinkled into the wound, a touch of flame, a scream of pain—they had moved well away from the boy, but he jerked awake— and the flesh had been cauterized, after a fashion. Adriel went to calm the boy. He slipped into sleep again.

When she got back to the man, he was sweating and shaking. "Damn."

"I know," Adriel said, lying down near him.

"Are you Latino?" he asked.

She laughed. "Mostly German, but a Mexican grandmother. What did you mean, you had a way out of here?"

"I was a pilot once," Luis said. "I think I could be again. There is a plane not far from here, practically an antique, but it will fly. There's enough fuel for five, six thousand kilometers."

"Will it carry us all?"

"Easy. It was a U.S. survey plane. Some gringo pilot took it with him when he left the service, I guess. It's in a barn, and the field is a long flat pasture."

"And the owner?"

Luis grimaced. "Won't be needing it again. No, I didn't kill him. I found him dead, hanging, and very rotten. I was only trying to track down the rumors of a plane—"

"Are you sure it's safe?"

"Yeah. More trouble's coming from the south. Most

people have pulled out. The plane's there, and I could fly it. Only where do I go?"

She drew him down beside her. "I have a place to go," she said. "Shall we trade?"

His fingers, caressing her neck, found the cylinder dangling on its cord. "What's this?"

"Never mind," she said, and moved his hand to cup her breast.

7: The Midwest

That spring the People's North American Expeditionary Force reached what had been *Ark Ouachita*. By then the lower sections had been penetrated and thoroughly looted. Nothing remained but the broken domes, a few odds and ends of equipment, and many desiccated bodies.

But the half-disciplined soldiers did not care to remain in the vicinity for long. Quasi-desert surrounded the cracked dome, arid flat landscape where nothing living moved ... by day.

By night someone or something picked off the soldiers one by one, even the sentinels equipped with NV goggles and sound amplifiers. The invading army left the site within a few days, heading north and east, hoping to find something worth holding on to.

As the harsh summer rose, the few people who had scraped out an existence in the dusty ruin gave up and moved away or simply vanished.

Stories began to be told of nomads who could stare into the sun, who had the strength of many men, who were part ghost.

Men called the nomads "wolves."

Chapter 6: *Ark Liberty*

1: Visitors

One year passed, then most of another. The complex hummed with life, sorted itself, rearranged itself, settled into some kind of routine. At the insistence of Li, everyone aboard *Liberty* worked at something: those who had no other skills cultivated food or worked maintenance, or else they studied to acquire the skills they needed to do other work. A child was born aboard the Ark, a girl. Couples married, either in the old-fashioned way (sometimes complete with religious ceremony) or in short-term agreements.

And the damned thing worked, as Kris Harris observed. The miracle was that the damned thing worked.

"We're still short-handed," Harris told Li one March day as the two of them stood in an observation pod watching divers reinforce the outer dome of a new agricultural wing.

Li nodded. The months had eaten away at him, had taken flesh from his already spare frame. "Not necessarily a bad thing," he told Harris. "After all, if everyone's busy, no one's making trouble."

"I suppose. We've got to bring the main computer up soon, though. Any more thought about that?"

Li's smile was tired. "Your job," he said. "Mine's just to facilitate the operation of this tinkertoy."

"This what?"

"Never mind." Li nodded toward the port. Outside,

in the dim illumination filtering down from an overcast day, the divers fitted and welded a set of struts.
"One of those guys Luis?"

"Yeah. The one on this end, I think."

"The others seem to be a little more accepting of
him lately."

Harris shrugged. "Not much point in holding a
grudge against an enemy of the nation when the nation doesn't exist anymore."

"Maybe so. Wonder if his wife—"

"Dr. Volker isn't his wife. And he isn't the father of
her child."

Li gave Harris a look of mild surprise. "Sorry. Wonder if Adriel Volker has released her bouquet this
week?"

"I'd take it more seriously if I were you."

Li laughed and clapped Harris on the shoulder. "By
God, you're in love. I had no idea."

With a rueful grin, Harris said, "Adriel went
through hell to keep that damned algae colony intact.
And she's done some surprising things with it."

"Don't change the subject."

"All right! Adriel says as long as she's stuck in this
loony bin, she intends to contribute to the gene pool.
But marriage is out of the question. She's too damn
busy."

"Sorry."

"Don't be. Worry about her algae, not about my
love life."

Li tapped the breast pocket of his coveralls, where
his datapad rested. "I haven't read the reports yet.
Haven't had time."

"Briefly, she's engineered an organism that produces hydrogen gas as a byproduct of metabolism. It
stores the gas in a membrane that gradually inflates
until the whole cell is buoyant." Harris jerked his chin
upward in a gesture that, by implication, took in the

upper levels of the ocean. "Think of the stuff as atmospheric plankton. It eats hydrocarbons and methane and produces oxygen and hydrogen as byproducts. If it's viable and reproduces, then in a few dozen decades the globe will have a floating haze of algae in the upper atmosphere to help filter out UV and build up the oxygen content—"

"A green sky."

"Maybe. It'd be preferable to that smutch that's—"

Li's wristwatch purred a signal: one long burr, one short one. "What now?" Li muttered. He tapped the watch and spoke into it. "Yes, Li here."

Keli Sumter's voice, low in volume but clear, said, "Excuse me, Mr. Li, but we have something from the shore station. You need to hear this."

"Okay. We'll be there in a minute."

Li and Harris took the lift to the comm center level, then walked the length of a thick connecting plexi tube to the center itself. "I always feel like a gerbil in this damn thing," Harris observed. Li, who had heard the remark before, didn't reply.

The comm center was a room seven meters square, with arrays of humming display terminals and recording devices, most of them idle. Keli Sumter was alone there, anxiety in her eyes. "Here he is," she said, and then keyed a console to standby.

"It's Franklin at the main installation," she said quickly to Li. "He's had a contact from the United States Government."

Li frowned and pulled a chair over. Keli moved aside, giving him access to the panel. With a touch of his index finger Li activated the transmission. "Li here, Walt. What's happening?"

Franklin's voice, audibly tense, came back immediately. "I was just telling Keli. We have people here who claim to represent the United States Government. They're demanding access to *Liberty*—"

"Give me that," another voice interrupted. "Li? Stefan Li?"

Li straightened in his chair. "Yes. I'm here."

"Do you recognize the voice of your President?"

After a moment, Li said slowly, "I recognize *your* voice, Mr. McMurphy."

2: Parley

The sky lay horrid over them.

Swagging, ragged clouds, yellow-gray, roiled over the choppy surface of a troubled ocean. A muggy western wind blew at a steady twelve knots. It was no weather for flying.

"You sure about this?" Kris Harris asked Li.

"Have to see him," Li returned.

And so he climbed into the 'copter and nodded to the young pilot, who soon became very busy. They took off, circled, and then fought the wind. Li looked behind him as the huge platform dwindled against the slaty gray ocean. They had fended off invaders three times already, and he wasn't eager for a fourth encounter. Not even if it was with the government of the United States.

The weather did not ease materially as they flew in. Li settled back, closed his eyes, and wondered how the hell things had come to this point. As far as they could tell from the scanty intelligence *Liberty* could still tap, the United States no longer existed as a going concern. Canada had fragmented into civil war, the west coast had fallen completely silent, and the other states had seemingly gone their separate ways. Fortunately for *Liberty,* no one to speak of had migrated toward the storm-lashed coast of eastern Florida.

At least until now.

The 'copter set down nervously at about 1400. Most of the shore installation was below ground, and Li headed for the lifts. Daley Burnford, wearing no insignia on his coveralls, met him. "Looks bad," he whispered, his broad red face solemn.

"Why? McMurphy has no authority."

"He brought guns."

Burnford led Li to the tech library, and the instant Li opened the door he gasped.

President McMurphy, if he was indeed president of anything, was far gone. He looked twenty years older than he had the last time Li had seen him—when? Two years ago, practically. Weight had fallen from the man, and only a little hair clung to the dome of his skull-like head. The eyes burned in deep sockets, and lesions scored the flesh of the cheeks. "About time," McMurphy said, his voice a shadow of itself.

Behind McMurphy six men stood, their weapons not exactly trained on Li but ready. They wore, incongruously, the uniform of the Coast Guard, together with Marine Corps helmets and impact vests. Their faces were grim.

"Well," McMurphy said. "I understand that you violated a direct order of the United States Government, Mr. Li."

"Am I to be shot for that?" Li asked, but no one smiled.

McMurphy leaned forward in the chair, his head bobbing loosely on a pencil-like neck. "Perhaps it was just as well. Now we have a base to fly to. A center of operations."

Li pulled a chair away from a table and sat facing McMurphy. "I don't understand. A center of operations for what?"

"The war, man!" McMurphy's chin shook as if with palsy. "They think they've whipped us. But we'll regain control from the Ark, bringing in our air power, activate the missiles—"

"Wait, wait." Li held up a silencing hand. "The war is over, McMurphy. You're president of nothing."

The man's pale face drained of remaining color. "Treason," he growled. "I knew it."

"Now, we can take you in, care for you, see that you get medical—"

McMurphy's smile was frosty. "No. You don't take us in. We take over *Ark Liberty*. It's still a government installation, and as such, it's subject to my authority."

Li tried again. "The government doesn't exist anymore. The country's in chaos, lines of communication are gone—"

"We'll fix all that." McMurphy bent forward and coughed rackingly. He gasped, "We'll show them yet. We still have weapons, and *Ark Liberty* will allow us to use them."

"No." Li pushed away from the desk. "No, that's impossible. The Arks are a way of preserving life, not of destroying it. I'm sorry. I'll offer you all the help I can personally, but—"

"Stewart." One of McMurphy's men stepped forward and set a valise on the table beside his chief. "Open it."

The valise opened to reveal a transmitter, compact but powerful. "Li, we have an aircraft currently orbiting *Liberty*. If you do not agree to my terms, I will order that aircraft to attack the tower and detonate its payload. It is a one-hundred megaton device. What will happen to *Liberty* then?"

Li swallowed. "We have nearly four thousand people aboard," he said.

"Traitors? Expendables? Or people I can work with? Let's talk, Mr. Li."

In the end talk was fruitless, and Li knew it. In the end McMurphy, a sizable contingent of his bodyguard, and Li boarded a transport chopper for *Liberty*.

The weather had not worsened, but neither had it improved.

Li sat next to the pilot, with McMurphy just behind him, as they vectored in to the tower. The colossus had come into sight on the horizon when Li spotted the second aircraft: a dirigible, making heavy going of it in the wind. McMurphy brusquely ordered the pilot to establish radio contact, and when that was done, the President ordered the crew of the dirigible to continue their pattern until he personally gave the all clear. The dirigible captain acknowledged.

"Wind's too heavy," the chopper pilot yelled as the radio conversation ended. "I'll have to come in from the southern quarter."

"All right."

Li brooded on the fate of *Ark Liberty*. As far as he knew, as far as anyone did, the other Arks were dead losses by now—broken, empty shells. And he had seen the projections, the curves plotted by their best computers, predicting the rise of temperatures and ocean levels, the diminishing of oxygen and of life forms.

Gusts of wind caught the dirigible, ahead and to their left, and it turned three-quarters away from them. They would pass it within a thousand yards, a chancy distance—

Li made his decision and grabbed the controls. The chopper pitched forward and someone yelled. Li felt hands clawing at his shoulders, heard McMurphy's shouted, strangled, "Shoot him!"

Then the dirigible filled the canopy, the blades bit into the fabric, and the whole world spun. The pilot fought the craft, partially righted it, though it cartwheeled around the rotor crazily. The gray sea came up terribly fast, the world exploded, and Li sank into cold darkness.

3: *Ark Liberty*

After endless ages of drifting through the dark there
was light, of a kind. At least there was the perception
of light, though it illuminated nothing but space itself.

"Steve?"

It was a voice he knew. A voice that somehow should
have made him feel—something.

"Steve?"

"Kris?" He said it—or did he just think it? Li felt
cold, paralyzed, unable to move. He strove to open
his eyes and the light brightened a little, but that was
all.

"I'm here. Steve—what do you remember? The last
thing?"

Such an effort to think. So far back, so dark, dark—

"The water. We spun into the water. I sank—"

"Steve, listen. We found you. You know the dol-
phin, Chang? He kept you afloat until we could reach
you."

"McMurphy? His men?"

"No, don't worry. They're dead, all of them, and
Burnford took into custody the detachment they left
behind. The airship crashed and sank. We recovered
and disarmed the nuke. It wasn't a hundred-meg
device, by the way—just a tactical. *Liberty* is safe."
A long pause. "You should know that you've been
aboard the Ark for six weeks now."

"What!"

"You've been unconscious. We've been working on
you."

"Why can't I see?"

"Just a minute."

Something happened. For a moment Li had the impression of a flow of energy, of sparks of thousands
of colors dancing before him, and then the picture

resolved into the face of Kris Harris. Had he opened his eyes? He didn't remember opening his eyes.

"How's that?"

"Better. Kris, I can't move. What's wrong with me? Where are we?"

Harris looked away. "I'm in the processing center. You are, too. In a way."

He knew.

Harris looked back. "It was the only way, Steve. They couldn't save you."

"I'm in the computer."

"You *are* the computer," Harris said. "I've absorbed your consciousness into Matrix. Tell me something. Remember something for me."

After a moment Li said, "Brazil, twenty years ago. We inspected the reforestation efforts and then got drunk together. You and that woman swam naked in the fountain." After a pause, Li added, "I'm dead."

"Do you feel dead?"

"I feel—sedated. Fuzzy, unfocused, but I feel like myself. God damn it, Kris, why me?"

"Why not you, friend?" Harris's smile was as sardonic as ever. "This whole damn circus is your show. If you're right, it's going to be here for an awfully long time. Why the hell not stick around to see what becomes of it?"

Virtually immortal. Kris Harris had once said that the personality they dumped into the computer would be virtually immortal. Li thought fleetingly of eternity, and a flood of numbers and symbols filled his mind, things he did not really know: the formulae generations of mathematicians had designed to deal with infinity.

"I see what you're doing," Kris said. "You can't do it yet because the interfaces aren't set, but eventually you'll be able to access all levels of computer storage. Read every book ever written. Feel every change in

Liberty, from the pressure of the water to the mental state of the population. It will come."

"Too much," Li said. "No human being should have that much power, that much knowledge, that much control. No human being."

"Yeah. That's why I chose you instead."

"Why can't I get angry with you?"

Harris's reply was matter of fact. "I haven't turned on all your emotions yet. Look, I'm going to phase you out for awhile. The dump is complete, but there are still things to do. I'll see you later, friend."

Friend. The word echoed in Stefan Li's mind. Friend.

His vision faded and he sank down again into unconsciousness.

Friend.

The Generations Between

One of the first actions taken by Stefan Li following his assimilation into the computer was to seek out and destroy all references to *Ark Liberty* in world databanks, a plan first devised by Kris Harris. This in itself was no small task, for the global communications net was in the early stages of what became total collapse. However, after more than a year of effort the work was done as thoroughly as was by then possible. For all intents and purposes, the Ark had ceased to exist in every outside databank. Certainly it would be most difficult for anyone to locate the exact site of the Ark using any standard references.

However, before the job had been completed, *Liberty* faced two separate threats of armed invasion, once from a few hundred refugees fleeing the increasingly uninhabitable Washington area of North America and once from a limping, battered flotilla of ships from many nations that struggled under the delusion that practically the entire United States had relocated to a safe haven beneath the waves.

In both cases, their numbers were far too great for *Liberty* to absorb.

The first threat died naturally: the two ships from Washington capsized and sunk in the raging winds of a force 5 hurricane—a nameless hurricane now, as were all storms. The second possible invasion ended only when a squad led by Luis Ortez destroyed the lead vessels with a low-yield nuke—the same device, ironically, that they had recovered from the wreckage of the dirigible. It was an absolutely last-ditch tactic, and it met the threat of a nuclear strike from the invading force that proved to be only bluff at the end. Li felt a dull sense of guilt, but not enough to distract him from the very real demands of settling the Ark and of making it livable.

After these incidents, detectable human presence on the waves above *Liberty* became sporadic, then exceedingly rare, and finally nonexistent. As far as anyone aboard the Ark could tell, the world above had forgotten that they were there. Surface communications, carefully monitored, flared, sputtered, and died, telling the dreadful story of wars, of uprisings, and famine everywhere. But even these frantic dying screams became more and more infrequent as the worldwide electronic communications net frayed, broke, fell apart.

Within ten years the global collapse seemed to be complete. Monitors aboard *Liberty* continued to pick up some intermittent traffic between L-5 Colony and Luna, but terrestrial electronic communications were dead and remained so. The greenhouse effect rapidly intensified, despite Adriel Volker's "bouquets." *Liberty's* environmental teams speculated on the role of the nuclear conflicts in causing the heating. Had they been coordinated, had the wars been fought all at once instead of being strung out over half a century, the planet should have cooled in a drastic nuclear winter. But occurring as they did, the wars merely added to the atmosphere's burden of carbon dioxide and other byproducts of burning. The air trapped more heat. The rise in sea level accelerated measurably.

Within thirty years the rotating ground crews reported a serious die-off of terrestrial species. For a time the Florida peninsula, all but deserted by humans, rioted with domestic cats and dogs gone feral, but they somehow failed to survive, their numbers perhaps diminished by sheer lack of food and by rad-

ical competition among excessive numbers of preda-
tors. On land the number of bird species continued
to dwindle. The insects flourished for a time, and it
seemed as though the common roach was poised to
inherit the earth, as had been often predicted over
the years since the twentieth century.

But another fifty years served to reduce even their
numbers. The adaptable creatures could not keep pace
with the change in global temperatures and weather,
and they began to perish in ever-increasing numbers.
Whole species of insects died out. Similar extinctions
of animal life were occurring in the sea: sensitive corals seemed dead within hundreds of kilometers of *Liberty*, and marine mammals became so surpassingly rare
that when a small whale was sighted seventy-six years
after the closing of the Ark it was an occasion for
wonder, celebration, capture, and cherishing.

By then Kris Harris, Adriel Volker, and Keli Sumter
were dead. So was Luce Norden, and so were her
charges, although genetic material from the intelligence-
enhanced porpoises now rested on Level 25, frozen,
awaiting some future rebirth. More babies, as Seela had
foreseen so long before.

By then Stefan Li, incarnate in the computer system
of the Ark, had more or less grown used to his state
and had become the benign advisor of a democratic
form of government—though his advice had become
a matter of such moment that it controlled such things
as population growth more absolutely than the command of a dictator might do. At odd times he recalled
his debates with Harris and worried. At other times
he lost his temper with his charges and did not mind
being paternalistic toward them. The last thing he
wanted to do was rule with a whim of iron.

The years passed. When one century had elapsed,
probes reported that humanity, to all outward appearances, was all but extinct south of Latitude 45. By then the

hurricanes had become five-fold more intense than even
the "ultimate" storms of the twenty-first century, and virtually no man-made structures remained intact along the
eastern seaboard. Most evidence indicated that no harbor
cities existed: they had either washed away in hurricane
rains or had been covered by the rising sea.

The number of mammal species had declined by 77%
in what had been the southeastern United States. Birds,
blinded by the UV bombardment of a nearly-vanished
ozone layer, were down to eleven species in all, three of
them owls. Reptiles had declined by one-half. No amphib-
ian species had been found in ten years. Though much
greater in overall numbers than before, owing chiefly to
a population explosion among carrion-eaters and scavengers, insect species had declined by 24%. Projections
called for the extinctions to continue onshore and off.

Another century saw the projections verified. By the
year 2400, only rats and bats remained to represent mammals in the southeastern United States. No birds flew the
skies. A few snakes and lizards remained, and about half
the number of species of insects that had formerly flown,
crept, or hopped were still there. Worse, many species of
land plants were dying, too, in unprecedented numbers,
though plankton proved more resilient than projected,
sinking lower to shield themselves from UV. By then the
average global temperature of earth had risen by 8.11 degrees Celsius and was still climbing.

The Ark colonists worked against the trend—not frantically, but with slow and undeviating determination. Each
year they released more genetically-engineered organisms
into sea and air, hoping that some strains would catch,
hold, and reverse the flow toward extinction.

And then, two hundred and fifty-four years after
the Ark had sealed itself off from a dying world, something extraordinary happened. . . .

BOOK TWO:

THE EXPEDITION

Chapter 7: The Alert

Like a slumbering leviathan *Ark Liberty* rested on the continental shelf, safe from the turmoil and destruction of the surface. In the two hundred and fifty-seventh year of its occupation, the Ark boasted a population of nearly 15,000 individuals, all of whom had been born aboard and few of whom had ever ventured shoreward. The shore station, now largely automated and manned by robots, warranted only an occasional supervisory visit, undertaken by the "Tower Crew." The tower itself, its lower landing surfaces now awash with the rising sea, was only lightly manned. Those who operated it had become something of a caste, living apart from the deep-dwellers, rarely venturing down even as far as Level 1 of *Liberty*.

The people who lived in those lower depths lived a circumscribed, cramped, crowded life. Corridors teemed with traffic. Recreation areas were loud and packed twenty-four hours a day. And yet they did not miss the surface, for they had never known it; and they kept themselves fully occupied.

For one thing, the Ark needed constant attention: each day brought a dozen or more maintenance problems, expansion problems, or environmental problems. Having chosen to use human power rather than mechanization on these—largely to give themselves something to do—the Ark population found itself fully employed. Everyone had a job to do, and there were jobs for everyone. Li, resident in the central computer, noted a developing hereditary social system. If one's parents worked in the agricenters, then one tended to become a farmer. If one's parents were marine biologists, then one tended in that direction.

The trend was vaguely bothersome to Li, but not so much that he worried about it. Indeed, although he knew all there officially was to know about each and every colonist, down to genetic profile and psychosexual adjustment, Li seldom intruded in their everyday life. True, when he wished to speak with them in an intimate way, he had a means of doing so now: a generation after Kris Harris's death, another gifted computer specialist had designed a program that allowed Li to "manifest" as a holographic projection—an illusion—of himself as he had been in the year of his death.

Unfortunately—or as Li thought in his more misanthropic moments, fortunately—the effect was quite local. Li's "ghost" could walk only in the committee room adjacent to the computer control center. But there he was available for consultation, for advisement, for the simple human acts of conversation. At times Li regretted his "presence," though he found it a relief to speak face-to-face with people once more.

The problem was that the others came to regard him with an almost superstitious awe. Many times over the years he had said mildly, "This is a matter for community decision. Let's put it to a vote." And then he could see amused exasperation in their faces; they didn't *want* to vote, they wanted to be told what to do. As Harris had warned, some of the Ark inhabitants seemed to want a dictatorship, not a democracy.

But whatever they wanted of him, still they came. Li voluntarily restricted the holographic projection to a few hours every week, partly out of concern that he was indeed growing to be a sort of benevolent dictator. Gradually over the years the means of voting on important decisions had been refined. Every citizen of *Liberty* wore a communicator, a bracelet device that allowed immediate access to the central computer and to any other citizen. By means of these, the Ark community could hold immediate plebiscites on questions of moment.

Voting was almost too easy. Li took pains to make sure that everyone understood that the vote was not a trivial matter, that every citizen held the obligation of learning the most he or she could about the question before actually casting a ballot. Li wanted them not only to vote, but to treasure the privilege.

He carelessly did not record the exact moment, but at some point a hundred and thirty years into the colony, the granting of the communication bracelet had become a matter of some small ceremony, a rite of passage marking the emergence of a boy or girl into adulthood. This occurred on the day following one's eighteenth birthday. Generally the immediate family would be there, and the investment followed a little ritual: "You are of age and may make decisions affecting us all. This is the means of your voice."

"This is the means of my voice."

"Speak for the good of all."

"I will speak for the good of all."

"Be worthy of the trust. . . ."

And so on. Harmless enough, Li thought, but in some small way the rite niggled at him, made him uneasy, a bit wary. In the past thirty or forty years he had noticed a tendency among those who consulted him to treat him with marked deference, a sense almost of worship: "O Li," one of them had actually begun before Li cut him off angrily.

The trouble, Li thought to himself in the darkness of the computer, was that he was disembodied. If he walked among them, really walked among them as flesh and blood and not as holographic ghost, they would quickly learn just how human, how limited, how

utterly ordinary a man he was. But the friendly act of
Harris had made that impossible.

And so Li dreamed without sleeping, learned about the
dying earth above, worried about the future, and became
in an unintended way a sort of demigod. At least he did
until the rogue signal came in one April morning. . . .

Carin Hawk surveyed the monitoring records for
the past week, did a double-take, and sat down at a
data center. She keyed her wrist communicator and
the impersonal voice of the computer asked, "Yes?"

"Verify this spike," she said. "It occurred at oh nine
fifteen point three one hours two days ago."

For a moment there was silence. Then the computer spoke again, this time in an exact simulation of
Stefan Li's voice. "Carin, Li here. You're right: radio
activity lasting approximately two point seven nine
minutes at the indicated date and time. Point of origin seems to be within a five-hundred kilo radius of
fifty-three degrees, eleven minutes north, seventy-four
degrees, twenty-two minutes west."

Carin furrowed her dark brows, and thought shone
in her dark brown eyes. "Canada? Can we examine
the contents?"

"Negative. The signal was too weak to carry information." Li paused, considered, and then added, "The
duration and wavelength argue against its being a
lightning-induced burst of radio emissions. There are
one or two other possible natural explanations. However, the chance of its being of human origin is approximately ninety-eight percent."

"There haven't been people there in—how many
years?"

"Last verified contact was one hundred two years,
fifteen weeks, three days ago. That was a remote flyby
sighting a thousand and fifty-eight kilos south-
southwest of the point of radio transmission."

"People," Carin murmured. "Incredible. Could they live?"

"I lack sufficient information," Li responded. "All measurements we have been able to make by remote probes indicate a hostile climate: spring rainfall averages for the entire southeastern portion of the North American landmass are very low, though the summer and autumn storms dump twice the old annual rainfall along the seaboard. The climate does improve gradually farther to the north. The percentage of oxygen in the atmosphere has declined to sixteen point zero nine percent, indicating a continued loss of plant life. The average temperature in that region, summer maximum, is forty point zero one degrees Celsius. Winter minimum is undetermined but should be in the range of minus five degrees."

An average summer maximum temperature of more than blood heat, at a latitude that once had dictated short, cool summers and long winters filled with blizzard and storm. Carin puffed out her cheeks. "Maybe we'd better review that wavelength," she said. "See if there's any other activity."

After a moment, Li reported, "None within the past thirty years."

"Well . . . let's file the information, then. And I'd like a careful watch kept on that area, especially for activity in that wavelength."

"I agree. I will arrange the data monitoring system so that it will make me immediately aware of a recurrence."

"Call me if it happens again."

"Affirmative."

Carin Hawk couldn't leave it at that. Three days later she asked for an audience with the holographic Li, which he readily granted. Carin showed up in the company of Ven Savatini, a robotics expert. For a moment before he made his "entrance" Li regarded them: a dark-skinned, dark-eyed young woman and a tall, swarthy young man. Li idly wondered who their parents were, and the computer obediently gave him an immediate family tree. With a faint sense of pleasure Li realized that one of Carin's ancestors was Keli Sumter, whose arrival aboard *Liberty* he vividly remembered, and another was Hawk, the undernourished boy that Adriel Volker had brought along with the fiery-tempered Luis Ortez and a limping, outmoded aircraft. Li had hardly known young Hawk, and he felt little nostalgia on that account. But Keli . . . he had been half in love with Keli.

Carin showed little of Keli's red-haired, blue-eyed contribution to the gene pool; physically, she was closer to Hawk's type. Still, it was nice to know that this Amerind–looking young woman was in some sense the daughter (at how many removes?) of an old, old friend.

Li's holographic simulacrum manifested. "I'm glad to see you," he said.

Savatini, twenty-five years old, 1.803 meters tall, went rigid and gave a half-bow. He had never spoken to Li personally before. Carin inclined her head.

"None of that," Li said impatiently. "Please have a seat."

They all sat at the conference table. As it almost always did at such moments, a portion of *A Christmas Carol*—one of millions of books in his memory banks—replayed itself in Li's head: "Can you sit down?" "I can."

"Marley's ghost," Li murmured.

"Sir?"

Li smiled and waved the thought away. "Nothing, nothing. I find that my mind is cluttered with all sorts of things these days. Just a random thought. Well, now, what can I do for you?"

Savatini looked at Carin. She bit her lip and blurted, "We've talked it over. We've got to go topside, sir. To check out the transmission."

Li waited.

"I can rig transportation," Savatini said. "I know we have no fossil fuels left, but with methanol and solar technology I can throw together a landbus that will—"

"I want to go," Carin said.

"Wait, wait," Li said with a smile. "Take it a little more slowly. Are you two proposing an overland expedition to what used to be Canada?"

Carin took a deep breath. "There are people there."

"I'm not sure of that," Li said. "The single radio spike may be an anomaly."

"Caused by what?"

Li shrugged his illusionary shoulders. "It's not entirely impossible that a severe lightning storm might have caused it. Or a large ionizing meteorite. It might even be an automatic beacon left over from the old days."

"You said the chances were in favor of its being of human origin. You don't really think that it's natural."

"I do until more evidence is available."

Savatini stirred. "Sir—"

"You don't need my permission to speak, Ven, and you don't need to call me 'sir.' What is it?"

"I think Carin's right. I mean—I'm sorry, sir—you've almost forgotten what it's like to be human. We haven't. If there's a chance that some group has survived, we have to go and investigate. I really don't think we have a choice in the matter."

Li regarded him for a long time. Savatini wore his black hair moderately long, in curling ringlets. Beneath heavy, level brows his eyes were dark brown, direct, and challenging. After some moments, Li said slowly, "I am more human than you think, Mr. Savatini. However, I am also reasonable. I don't think the signal warrants a ground investigation yet, but I will say this: you two have the authorization to design a land expedition. To *design* it, mind; not to implement it."

"And what happens when it's designed?" Carin

asked. "Do we build it, do we get ready to launch it, do we train?"

"We'll see. I am continuously monitoring the wavelength for additional activity. If we pick it up, if there is an indication, however small, of human activity, then we'll build, train, and launch the expedition. If not, at least you two will have been kept busy."

Savatini struggled with himself, but he laughed. Carin glared at him. "I don't think it's a joke," she said.

"He doesn't either," Savatini informed her. "Do you, sir?"

"Do you get some obscure pleasure from calling me that?"

This time Carin smiled. "It's a habit with him. Humor him."

"I suppose I can live with it," Li said. "Do I think the situation is a joke? Certainly not. Now, as to the makeup of the expedition: I'd say no more than ten at the most. They should be adequately armed and trained in personal weapons. We've had no reports of hostile animals or activity, but we're far from knowing everything about the surface. Design your landbus, Mr. Savatini. In fact, you'd better design two, in case of emergency. And I suppose you would be able to modify an MPU robot to any specifications I would draw up?"

"That's my job," Savatini said. "Why would you want to send a multi-purpose robot to the surface, though?"

"Because that would be *my* bus," Li said. "If we can rig it, I'll project my awareness into the MPU and tag along on the expedition. Oh, don't look so surprised, Carin. I've been a captive on *Liberty* far longer than you have. If anyone's due for a bit of shore leave, it's me."

The Orchards were the Ark's closest terrain to surface landscapes. By now there were some forty of these, greendomes enclosing row upon orderly row of trees, from sharp-scented pines to oaks and fruit trees.

Orchards were popular spots for outings, picnics, trysts, and exercise; the air in the domes was fresh and well-circulated (breezes helped pollination and stimulated growth), the trees themselves provided a visual treat that even holosimulation failed to duplicate, and the sheer size of the domes, with the double ceiling tens of meters overhead, was something different, something more awe-inspiring, than the endless hallways, enclosures, labs, and work areas of the Ark.

But the Orchards differed from the surface in one important respect: they were never lonely. During her free time in the days following the first signal, Carin Hawk often visited the Orchards, wandering through them, smiling at acquaintances, seeking isolation that she found only momentarily, in snatches. Never was she far out of earshot of human conversation, seldom out of sight of a group of other colonists playing, working, strolling.

When she could snatch a few moments of solitude, she tried in her mind to recreate the surface, as she had seen it in holosims reconstructed from databits sent back by remote probes.

Forests there, too, up on the ravaged land. Only they were bare and leafless, dead wood, propped upright by sheer simple stubborn habit: the habit, in some cases, of trees far older than any growing in *Liberty*. Carin recalled representations of petrified forests, of stone trunks still standing as in life the trees had stood. The forests of earth were like that now, or at least all the ones within range of the Ark's probes were. The remnants of the Amazon rainforest were leafless trunks fallen or leaning crazily on rutted, ravaged hillsides. The hardwood forests of mainland North America were fallen, dust or ashes years ago. Grasses endured, and struggling knots of conifers here and there, perhaps more farther north than in the accessible southeastern part of the continent. But it seemed safe to say that nowhere did a true woods endure, an expansive growth of trees buzzing with insects and alive with birds.

Nowhere on the surface, at least.

In the subsurface Orchards life was rich and varied. Even now, when Carin thought to pay attention, insects hummed, a few species of birds twittered, butterflies fluttered. The "rains" were regular, gentle sprinklers from the overhead network of piping, and the "sun" was the even, kindly illumination from solar-duplicators built into the greendome ceiling ten meters above the Orchard floor. On the surface there would be no sound save wind and thunder, harsh rains and hail. Carin closed her eyes and tried to imagine it.

She could not.

It was impossible to visualize, to grasp, a place where the bulkheads never interposed. She could not bring into her mind's eye the grassy plains that existed now or the fabulous older landscapes, where you could walk through a forest and on and on, never coming to the barrier a hundred or two hundred meters away. The horizon was a sight unknown to her, as to most of the colonists.

The problem was not that Carin had never been outside the Ark, for she had ventured out many times, wet-suited, breathing canned air, exploring the shallows, observing the effects of biological experiments, tasting the salt of the ocean. But she had never surfaced—indeed, given her life-long acclimation to the pressures and composition of *Liberty*'s atmosphere, to have done so from a free dive would have meant death.

What she knew of topside came entirely through holosimulations made possible by robot probes, or from ancient movies and tri-d's. These illusions were not capable of reproducing reality in all its impact, of simulating the sheer assault on the senses that a walk on solid ground must be. So she sought some inkling, some hint, of what to expect by walking here among the trees.

She knew that three centuries ago, when *Liberty* was

only a dream, people from the surface would have
wondered about life below the ocean in the same awe-
struck way she now contemplated leaving it. Her reading in history had been selective but attentive. At one
time the practicality of sea-floor installations like the
Ark was seriously in question: how would people
function, how would they live, how would they keep
their sanity, confined within a hostile element?

God, she wondered, how did those topside ever endure their exposure?

Objectively she knew of the reality outside: crushing
megatons of water waiting only the slightest breach in
the Ark's construction to slice in, to obliterate any
trace of human habitation, as it had in the collapse of
North Wing G, a portion of the Ark that had been lost
because of structural weakness a generation before. It
was a famous disaster, one in which nearly a hundred
construction workers had died. But Carin thought of
the collapse as an anomaly, for she had a strong, abid-
ing trust in the works of hands: after all, the Ark had
been designed to last, to endure, had been maintained
regularly and reinforced constantly. Endure it would.

But out there, with nothing between one and the
harsh sun—

She shivered.

Why, then, did she want so badly to go?

It was a puzzle she could not solve. She walked beneath the spearblade-shaped leaves of pecan trees and
listened to the chirruping voices of children playing
some intricate game of hide and find.

She thought of the dead surface above.

She could hardly wait to see it.

The second radio trace came three weeks and some
days after the first. This time there was no doubt: a
series of radio bursts, back-and-forth traffic, exchange
of information. But with the ionosphere devastated,

ragged, the transmissions were too faint to decipher completely. The computer did reconstruct and digitize some vocal information.

Two human speakers took part in the exchange, probably using the kind of short-range radios once known as "walkie talkies." One speaker was female, with a higher voice and a marginally more powerful transmitter; the other was male, his voice fainter, harder to capture.

Li recorded only a partial exchange, but it was enough to intrigue him.

SHE: . . . south of [unintelligible] . . . dead . . . [unintelligible; rising inflection, as if a question]
HE: Negative [?] . . . hours [?]
SHE: [Unintelligible] . . . another ten kilometers. How is [food ?] holding out?
HE: [Unintelligible]
SHE: But don't take any [chances ?]
HE: [Unintelligble].

It sounded like a live exchange, not like anything recorded. It sounded as if someone up where Canada used to be still lived. As if someone were searching for something.

On Li's recommendation Hiero Suarez and his communication staff attempted to make contact with the broadcasters on the same wavelength, using the Ark's most powerful broadcast capability. They elicited no response. Suarez prepared a repeating message, and Li saw to it that the Ark broadcast the message regularly, on an hourly basis.

By then the situation had become open news, and the colonists decided it was necessary to vote on the wisdom of exploring the possibility of human life remaining on the ravaged surface. Li organized and presented the problem, the evidence, and the proposed solution, not without some subtle biases. The population considered, discussed, and then voted 71% to 26% to launch a ground investigation to discover the source of the radio transmissions. Three percent remained either undecided or indifferent.

With the vote behind him, Li began to review all the population data. He wanted to take a group no larger than ten or twelve, plus himself, in the form of Savatini's modified MPU robot. He would need colonists of a certain stamina, a certain mind-set. Early on he decided that Ven Savatini would have to go—they needed his mechanical expertise, and he was an impressive physical specimen into the bargain.

Carin Hawk, though, was a problem.

Li wondered if he were growing old, or if it were possible for a reconstituted human personality housed in a computer to grow old. He was not used to indecisiveness, and the problem of Carin gave him a severe case.

She was in excellent health, had a high, adaptive intelligence, and in many ways would be an asset to any expedition. But on the other hand she had some tendencies toward claustrophilia, toward the cave-dweller's preference for enclosed spaces. Her psychological profile did not make clear what her reaction to open spaces might be, how she might behave when faced with wide skies and broad horizons. The element of doubt alone should have been enough to disqualify her.

Still, Li hesitated and postponed the decision in a way that—he thought privately—no efficient machine should do. What's wrong with me? he wondered. He had "lived" so long that he thought he had no more surprises within him, no unexplored regions, no room for merely human quandaries.

And yet, damn it. . . .

There was the problem of Carin Hawk.

The spring storms were bad that year.

As the expedition began to take shape, at least in

the mind of Li, winds roared across the Atlantic and slammed into the coast of Central America. By mid-May the hurricanes swung on a more northerly track, one that they generally did not take until June or July. Blinding rain clawed at the arid landscape that had been Florida, Georgia, Alabama, and Tennessee. Flood waters rose, gorged, stained, with the soil they carried away into the sea. Stripped of significant vegetation, the continent could not resist the assaults.

In the raging storms, flying remote robot probes were impractical.

So the gradually increasing group of explorers studied holographic reconstructions of the landscape and the route. At first there were only two certain of going: Savatini and Bol Killee, an experienced de-signer and operator of undersea rolling equipment. Together with Li (not in projected form, but rather speaking through the computer) these two brooded over various holograms representing the seacoasts, the interior, the pathways to the north.

"City remnants aren't much," said Killee, a heavyset, blond young man with a curly fair beard. "I thought they built better than this back in the old days."

"They built well, but they built for a human land-scape and for gentle weathers," Li responded. "As far as we can tell from records, Manhattan Island was completely abandoned a hundred and seven years ago. Within seventy years the rising sea had eroded enough of the substructures for all the great skyscrapers to fall. Now it looks like this."

The three-dimensional map, a huge one at a scale of ten centimeters to the kilometer, revealed a mounded island nearly awash with the sea, a jumble of stone and craters. Except, of course, the stone was really concrete, and the rectangular craters were weathered foundations.

"Reconstruct the island in its fullest state of human development," Savatini requested.

Li obliged. The picture shimmered, changed to a representation of New York in the twenty-first century: an imposing bristle of impossibly high buildings, their feet well clear of the ocean.

"Show the decline, say in ten-year intervals."

Again Li did as requested. The others watched in silence as the buildings began to disappear: first the southernmost ones fell all at once, victims of a nuclear device; then the others, the victims of slow time, bowed, cracked, and crumbled, and all the time the hungry Atlantic rose.

"Are all the cities this bad?" Killee asked.

"No," Li responded. "Coastal cities suffered the worst. Remotes show that inland cities—St. Louis, for example, and Birmingham—are more or less intact structurally. Transitory elements are gone, of course."

"Such as?"

"Windows, wooden structures, anything breakable."

"Human life," Killee observed ironically.

"Yes."

Savatini grunted. "Loss of perishable materials is only to be expected. What about the infrastructure we used to study? Highway systems, that?"

"We won't be speeding to Canada." Li showed them a stretch of interstate highway, hardly more than a rubbled path. Before the climate had become so bad, before so many had begun to die, the vegetation had ravaged the highways. Since then, after even the trees had surrendered the fight, the elements had taken their toll. Of the highways very little remained apart from simple direction: lanes paved with tall tough prairie grasses, leading to this or that ruin.

"We'll need to keep well inland, in case of storms," Li said. "Then there are hot spots—sites of nuclear explosions from the wars—that we'll have to avoid.

However, since we are undertaking the journey, I would like to propose some investigations along the way. Remotes can't show us everything that happened to the cities, for instance. I'd like to go by way of Washington and Philadelphia, then move northward to a point where crossing the rivers will be practicable. We won't need to remain in the vicinity of the cities for long, but we should check them out."

"Historical interest," Savatini said.

"Sure, why not?" Killee added.

"Looks to me as if we need buses that can negotiate rough terrain. I'd say treads for normal progress, grav-effect generators for short-term use: fording rivers, that kind of thing. Research has improved the sol-cell efficiency to the point where we can probably survive without auxiliary power, but that will make us slow. I'd guess maybe forty, fifty kph top speed, unimpeded terrain. Grav-effect will give us a quarter of that, at three times the power drain. Meth engines for night runs, though they'd have to be limited. We couldn't haul much fuel."

"How about a small chopper?" Killee asked. "A one- or two-person job, for aerial scouting?"

Savatini shrugged. "Sure, we could carry one atop the second vehicle. Folding rotors, methanol engine. If we find anyone, though, we may have to abandon it—assuming we plan to give whomever a lift back to the Ark."

"If we find anyone, then the job will be done," Killee said. "We won't need a chopper anymore."

"Design the helicopter," Li said.

Both of the men chuckled. "Yes, sir, Mr. Computer, sir," Savatini said. Li had noticed that when he was only a disembodied digitized voice, Savatini's deferential "sir" either disappeared or became mildly sarcastic. "Hey, are we a democratic collective or not?"

Li's computer-replicated voice carried a hint of ruefulness: "Design it, vote permitting."

Killee, who had been leaning back in one of the

chairs around the holotable, sat forward. "When should we go?"

"As soon as possible," Li said.

Savatini tugged at his lower lip. "Design and fabrication. Crew recruitment, training. This is May. We could be ready to go by the first of August."

"Historically a bad time," Li responded. "The five worst storms of the past century have hit the eastern seaboard in August. And there has never been an August without at least one force-five storm in one hundred and eleven years."

Killee tapped the holotable, summoned up a virtual command center, and called up a transcript of the radio communication. He read it over silently. "They sound as if they're in trouble already. If people are alive in Canada now, they might not be by the time good weather comes."

"True."

Savatini stood and stretched. "I propose we go in August," he said. "Run as far inland as we can and batten down through any bad storms. Put it to a vote?"

"All right," Li said, storing the proposal for transmission to all the Ark inhabitants through the wrist communicators. "We'll vote on it."

"One last thing. I've selected an MPU. You want to tell me what modifications you want to make, and how you're going to manage to control the damn thing as far away as Canada?"

"I have a secret or two," Li responded.

"Okay," Savatini said with a grin. "Magic."

"I can do magic," Carin Hawk said. "But there's a price."

Li's holographic simulation went through the motions of sighing. "You want a ticket north."

"You know it." Carin, trim and elegant in silver singlet and trousers, sat across the table from him. Her dark brown eyes were direct, challenging, and hinted at mischief. "It was my discovery, and I want to be in on the payoff."

"If I added your name to the proposed list, what could you give me in exchange?" Li tented his fingers and looked over them at the young woman. "What's the *quid pro quo?*"

Carin jerked her chin up, toward the ceiling, the fathoms of ocean, and by implication toward outer space. "There's a geosynchronous satellite up there, a communications hub. It hasn't been operational for a hundred and seventy, a hundred and eighty years. No point in it. If there's anyone left on L-5 and Luna, they probably think the damn thing's dead."

"But you think it's not?"

"Only sleeping." Carin grinned at him. "You should know this, Stef. It's all in memory."

Li's simulacrum smiled. "If I consciously knew everything I'm capable of knowing, I'd go crazy. Let me review." He closed his eyes and faded a bit. In a few seconds he came back, stronger, more solid-seeming. "I see. It was an automatic shutdown because the feeds from earth ceased."

"Right. The equipment should still be operational, barring collisions with space junk, that sort of thing. It's a matter of finding the key code and transmitting. We can then tight-beam signals directly to the satellite and have it redirect them to a receiver anywhere in this hemisphere. There'll be a slight time drag, maybe a couple of milliseconds at the most, but except for having damn poor reflexes the MPU should work all right as your ears and eyes."

"Are you sure the standby relay aboard the satellite is still functional?"

Carin shrugged. "No, of course not. But they built them to last back then. If that doesn't work, I may have another trick or two up my sleeve. Is that right?

Is that what they used to say? 'Another trick up my sleeve'?"

"That's exactly right," Li told her.

"So do I get my name on the list?"

"Quid pro quo," Li told her.

Carin stood up and hesitated. "One thing, Stef. I know why I want to go—"

"Why?" Li asked.

She blinked at his simulacrum. "Because we're supposed to go back one day," she said. "Because I've seen simulations of a goddam beautiful world and I can't believe that people did to it what all the histories say they did. Because I have to see for myself, to make it real."

"All right."

"What I was saying, though, is that I know why *I* want to go. But what about you? I mean, the Ark is your whole life, your body, your mind, I guess even your soul. Why go back?"

"To see if I can," Li answered simply.

Carin shrugged. "Good enough, I suppose. I'll get to work on that right away, Stef. And thanks."

She touched the doorpad, gave him an over-the-shoulder smile, and left. The door hissed to behind her. For a few seconds Li maintained the simulacrum. Then he withdrew his attention back within the computer net, and like a candle flame the Stefan Li sitting at the conference table vanished.

Chapter 8: Scouting Expedition

Levels 22-24 of *Ark Liberty* were the levels of fabrication and manufacturing. There efficient computer and robot-automated mini-factories produced everything from clothing to new Ark modules. All units of the fabrication system worked hard through the early days of summer to produce the things demanded by the human masters of the Ark.

Clothing was one necessity. In the climate-controlled Ark, most wore similar outfits: lightweight singlet and trousers and soft-soled shoes. "Duty" uniforms had become standard several generations earlier, with the colors of the clothing coded to one's vocation aboard the Ark: tan for engineering, brown for power production and control, gray for security and legal, blue for medical, and so on. These were cut a little more plainly than leisure clothing, and simplicity was their hallmark.

Off-duty apparel, on the other hand, tended toward the individualistic and the colorful. Patterns changed according to fashion or taste, and one could program the production computers to produce any outfit one dared to wear. Fads came and went: one season women bared one breast, the right if they were single, the left if they were married or seriously engaged. Another season saw a riot of holographic clothing, with

tunics projecting an aura of stars and comets or a
school of circling barracuda. Li noted such crazes with
detached amusement. As for himself, his holographic
simulation wore the same outdated clothing of two
hundred and fifty years before.

But now the computers had another task: to design
clothing that would be appropriate to the harsh surface conditions. It had to reflect UV radiation, provide both cooling and warmth, and be lightweight for
continued wear. The first models were one-piece jump
suits, with hoods, faceplates, and gloves. A solar-
powered waist pack provided power for cooling or (if
necessary) warming. Li had one room on Level 23 set
aside for testing purposes and simulated heat and radiation levels there comparable to what he expected
to find on the surface.

Six volunteers wore the surface suits for forty-eight
hours of working and sleeping in the test room. They
discovered small discomforts, irritating awkward-
nesses, that Li programmed the computer to elimi-
nate. The faceplates shrank to rebreather masks, the
hoods became optional, as did the gloves, and the
waist pack gained an input jack for recharging from
the landbus solar arrays. By the first of July, Surface
Suit Mark 4 was ready for production.

Meanwhile Bol Killee and Ven Savatini were busy
with the buses. Each bus could seat twenty-five (or, if
packed beyond reason, forty) and had a range of approximately three hundred kilos on an average bad
day of ten hours' sunlight. Northstar 1, the prototype,
was complete by July 4, a day when the weather was
unseasonably calm. Killee and Savatini took it to the
surface, using the construction lift, and ferried it to
the Florida shore on a transport barge. They would
run it across the Florida peninsula and back as a test,
and following that they would make any necessary adjustments before the creation of Northstar 2.

In the interval Carin Hawk had continued to monitor the radio for any additional Canadian traffic. She found three suspicious spikes, but nothing definite, not even when she managed to resurrect the dormant comsat and focus its receivers on the general area of the first transmissions.

On the day that Killee and Savatini left for Florida, Stefan Li did something he had postponed for weeks: he tried on his own "surface suit."

Multi-Purpose Unit Robot 1552 (M) was a squatty construct about chest-high to a grown man. From a broad base plated with solar cells and underpinned with a complex of miniature tank treads and wheels, a slender column of black carbon-fiber structural plastic rose to a disk the size of a small tire. The disk bore two arms, redesigned to mimic human arms and hands, and an array of sensory devices. The gleaming, silvery, round "head" crowning the column actually was a communications center, containing miniaturized inboard computers and a selective antenna designed to link the MPU to *Liberty* through satellite relay.

It was ugly enough.

Li found himself irrationally repulsed by the prospect of entering the robot. Trying to analyze his feelings, he concluded that after two hundred and fifty-four years—two hundred and nineteen more than he had inhabited a human body—he had grown used to the freedom, the omnipotence almost, of being a disembodied computer intelligence. As Harris had said so long ago, the Ark was not only a living space, a combined city, zoo, museum, and plantation, but it was Li's body. At any moment, he was literally everywhere, carrying on a hundred or two hundred different conversations simultaneously, solving problems, thinking for fourteen thousand human beings.

However, once he activated the MPU his personality would be there, not in the Ark. The computers would still function: he was not abandoning the Ark to deafness and blindness. But his self-awareness would be centered in, circumscribed by, the robot. As far as he would be able to tell, he would be the robot.

The prospect daunted him.

But he intended to accompany the expedition, and so at last the trial had to be made. Li had the robot moved to a nexus room, one of the nerve junctions of the Ark, and left there for him. He chose to activate the MPU at three in the morning, when the majority of the Ark residents were asleep and activity was at a minimum.

For the initial trial, Li used a short-range radio link. From outside the robot he activated its power (supplied for the test by a tether, not by the solar array) and its inboards (the equivalent of the involuntary nervous system), and then he took a figurative deep breath, set certain safeguards, and dived in.

Light and thunder immediately blinded and deafened him. He frantically adjusted the sensory feeds downward until both became tolerable; the unbearable glare of a star at a hundred kilos muted to the dim illumination of the computer control room, the yammering, clattering, howling of a galaxy-ripping hurricane became the soft background hum of electronics, the barely-noticeable whoosh of hydraulic systems and small motors.

Li looked around. The perspective was weird, unfamiliar; even when he projected himself as a holosimulation, Li maintained his usual godlike awarenesses, using the Ark's systems for vision and hearing. Now he seemed too short, too limited. It was like trying to walk through a maze while holding binoculars to one's eyes, wrong end to: everything seemed impossibly remote and tiny.

Li did a few more adjustments to sensory receptors,

overlapping the double field of vision until he had true three-dimensional perception. Then he moved his "arms," bringing the hands up before his visual receptors for inspection.

They closely imitated human hands, though the arms they were attached to were thin, almost skeletal. Li experimentally touched thumb to forefinger, middle finger, ring finger, and little finger, and then reversed, faster and faster. He had a sensory analog of "feeling," electronic impressions that activated tactile receptors, but touch seemed incredibly crude.

Li stretched his hands out, moved and rotated his arms, and then with a cautious move away from the tethering power line he rolled across the floor. It was a curious sensation, quite unlike his memory of walking. He reached the wall, extended his arms to feel it, and then turned around and retraced his path.

He badly wanted to breathe.

He had almost forgotten breathing.

When he had first awakened in the computer all those decades ago, Li's one panic reaction was the unpredictable sensation of suffocating, of being deprived of air. Ancient neural impulses tried vainly to activate lungs that no longer existed, told him he would die if he did not breathe. Harris had worked hard for most of a year to subdue the impulse, to edit it out of Li's consciousness. In the end Li had become accustomed to it, and now it never bothered him.

Except that, in the robot, it did.

Li concentrated on the olfactory receptors. If he could smell, then maybe his mind would believe he was also breathing. He detected and sorted aromas: the metallic tang of the bulkheads, the residue of human sweat, the ozone-sharp fragrance of electricity.

It wasn't really like the sense of smell. It was a more dispassionate, distanced sensation, a faint awareness of odors expressed as columns of figures, not as immediate impressions. But it would do.

Li experimented with his dexterity and control. At one point he accidentally toppled a chair while trying a fast reversal, and it bounced off the bulkhead, fell across the base of the robot, and entangled the tether. Rather than vacating the MPU, Li treated the accident as a challenge. He lowered the manipulative center on his stalk, gave the situation a quick survey with his photoreceptors, and then used his hands to free the tether from the chair and to set the chair upright again.

It was a minor occurrence, but Li was amused at how important it seemed to him at the time. Unwrapping the chair absorbed his full attention, his whole-hearted efforts, for all of three minutes. *It's going to work,* he decided, *I can tolerate it.*

Except there were a few refinements missing. The chair had fallen on his transport platform hard, and the impact had registered as a tactile impression, but still there was something very important missing.

Li withdrew from the MPU—it was like a man leaving a dark closet for a bright, wide-horizoned prairie—and immediately set about creating a set of intricate equations, algorithms, and simulations.

Patiently, with great attention to detail, Li set about reinventing pain.

Sam Ikoto was a trim little man, black-haired, sallow-complexioned, precise in his movements and his diction. "You should not go," he told Carin Hawk.

"I'm going anyway." The two of them had just returned from a swim. Ikoto sat on the edge of an exit aperture, like a circular swimming pool five meters across, his legs dangling in ocean water. Carin had removed her swim fins and mask and had just unsealed her personal locker.

"Stubbornness will prove nothing." Ikoto made the pronouncement sound inscrutable, Confucian.

With a wry smile Carin shrugged out of her oxygen harness and hung the unit in the locker. She tasted salt, and more salt stung her eyes. "I'm going," she said.

Ikoto shook his head. "Your psych profile shows you will have great difficulty in dealing with noncontrolled environments. You—"

"I swam beside you all the way outside. I had no problem with that." Carin touched the shower control and needles of fresh water hit her in the face. She rinsed her hair, wishing that she was indifferent enough to male reactions to strip off the wetsuit and take a real head-to-toe shower. Ikoto wouldn't mind. Most of the Ark population, used to long hours in very close quarters, had but few timid shreds of the nudity taboo left. But Carin minded. Being naked meant being vulnerable, so she left the wetsuit on, stood beneath the shower, and then after the regulation 1.5-minute flow reached for an absorbent towel.

Ikoto waited patiently while she dried her face and hair. He was always patient. When Carin had finished and had discarded the used towel in the recycle chute, he resumed: "This is different. When you leave the Ark to swim, you remain within sight of the structure, within safety distance."

"Still, it's a frightening world out there. How many fish did you see? I counted exactly none. And only a handful of shellfish and crustaceans. Except for the bioengineered plankton we release, hardly anything's alive out there anymore. One desert's pretty much the same as another, don't you think?"

Ikoto swung his legs, muscular for all his fifty years, and sloshed the salt water. "That's the point. The two deserts, as you call them, are not alike. The ocean is familiar, contained, near safety. On the surface you will be utterly exposed. I don't believe you can handle that."

"I think I have to."

Ikoto sighed. "I am a psychologist/conditioning expert. If we find survivors, they will most likely be severely traumatized by life-long exposure to hostile conditions. It will be necessary for me to evaluate their condition, perhaps to work with them to ease the jolt of contact. Whereas you—"

"I will have a function, thank you," Carin said. "Stefan Li will need my assistance the whole time. Communications between the expedition crew and the Ark will be vital, not least because Li's very presence demands an uninterrupted contact through the comsat. If you check my crew records, you will see that I am uniquely qualified to maintain communications."

Ikoto sighed. "I would like to shower now."

"Who's stopping you?"

He gave her an unsmiling look. "No one." He unfastened his wet suit, stripped out of his trunks, and walked in his curiously delicate way into the shower cubicle. Carin collected her things, gave him a last amused glance, and headed up to her living cubicle on domicile Level 9.

The passageways were crowded, as always. Now and again an acquaintance greeted her—"How was the swim?" "Great, thanks." However, she made most of the journey alone, though she pressed through crowds of people busily on their way here or there, to this level or that one.

Carin's living cubicle was standard: a space 2.5 meters deep by 3 meters wide as the main apartment, with an adjoining meter-square storage closet and next to that the luxurious 1 × 3 meter bathroom that she shared with her next-door neighbor, a woman named Althen. Everything was compact and convertible: the sofa became a bed at night, the desk could serve as a table or a vanity or a holostage or a wet bar.

Carin removed her wetsuit and swimsuit and took another minute and a half shower, her last allowed one for the day. She changed into a leisure outfit, made herself a weak drink, and keyed on the screen. A menu materialized in the space above the desk. She could summon up a new or old movie, could tune to instructional or informational channels, could learn the news, could participate in court if she cared to make up part of a jury. She settled for a music program instead.

As she sipped her drink, Carin opened the top drawer beneath the desk and took out her datapad. It was the size and shape of an old-fashioned paper book—not that she had ever actually seen such an antique. She put the drink in the holder inset into the sofa arm, leaned back, put her feet up, and activated the pad.

The "pages" glowed to soft, eye-soothing life. Carin asked for a menu of informational texts, went through five sub-menus, and came up with one called *The Eastern United States* by Schumaker, Timmons, and Cathbridge and dating from 2101. Li had once mentioned that each datapad was capable of accessing some seven billion books in more than three hundred languages. Still, there were times when Carin could find nothing to read, or at least nothing that she cared to read.

This text was geographical/ecological. Carin lingered over the photographs, old-fashioned flat ones and tri-d's alike. A major thrust of the book was the deteriorating condition of climate and landscape, but even when she regarded the "modern" views, forests waning and brown and half bare of leaves, Carin saw only lushness. And the cities—

She tried to imagine living in a land city. Some of them had been domed over when the UV became really bad: Dallas had a complex of nineteen domes, and Los Angeles more than fifty. But most of them had struggled on without the domes, finding other means of protecting themselves against the killing, blinding sun.

To live in the open, beneath a pale blue sky and a sun glaring like the ones in the time-loop tri-d's in the book—what would it be like? Carin closed her eyes and tried to imagine herself in the pictures. She could not do it.

She could barely picture a city, with buildings soaring on every side. She could barely imagine an open sky, with nothing between the street and it but air. She tried to put herself there, on the street, below the sun—

And her heart fluttered with fear.

She flicked the datapad offline. Had it been a real book, she might have flung it across the room.

Scowling, half listening to the music (a sonata by Mozart at the moment), Carin drained her glass and wondered if—if just possibly—Ikoto might be right about her.

Northstar 1 lurched to a halt at the edge of a precipice. "Get me a reading on distance," Killee said.

With a glance through the forward windscreen, Savatini snorted his derision. "What's the sense of that? You can see it's too wide to cross."

"Come on. We have to test this buggy, okay?"

Cursing, Savatini used a laser to measure the breadth of the canyon. "Looks like nineteen point oh four six meters," he said, and before Killee could ask, he added, "Eleven point nine oh six meters deep here."

"Damn," Killee said with a sigh. "Whatever happened to the things people made?" He reversed the treads and the bus moved backward, away from the crumbling lip of the ravine.

Northstar 1 edged gingerly east, then nosed forward again, heading north by northwest, skirting the course of the gully. A hazy blue sky, scored by a few wisps of cirrus, stretched overhead, and in the high east a mid-morning sun blazed down at them. The landscape they negotiated was flat and sandy, the gray-white monotony broken only by a few green splotches of lichens and some tough, stringy grasses. They had seen no trees so far, and they were already a quarter of the way to the Gulf of Mexico.

Numberless gullies and washes etched the land, testimony to the torrents that the heat-born hurricanes of the past two hundred years had produced. Old maps were unreliable; rivers had deepened and shifted, town sites had vanished beneath water-carried or windblown sand. The ravines sometimes followed courses that, according to the old charts, once had been highways. If so, no trace remained now: just an eroded valley, sharp-sided, deep, with a few embedded stones in the walls.

So far the Northstar vehicle had performed well, hopping over smaller obstructions, mounds and swamps, flat brown streams and jumbled remains of towns. When they reached a barrier too difficult to traverse, they had to skirt it, as they were doing now.

"Cooling system's got to be redone," Killee said with a grunt. His face was red and shiny with sweat, and Savatini's black curls lay plastered against his skull. "This'll be intolerable on a long trip."

"If you wouldn't use the damn grav-effect generator to jump over every little puddle we'd have extra power for cooling," Savatini replied. "Watch the washout."

"I see it." Killee maneuvered the bus around the edge of a secondary ravine, like half a bowl.

Savatini looked down into the gully and whistled. "Man, that's deep. Must be twenty meters down here."

"We'll find some way around it." They headed north, then turned northwest again. "Ought to be able to use the grav-effect on a crossing as narrow as this one."

"We could, if we had a surface beneath us. Water would do, even. But you have to quadruple the power for every ten meters of altitude. Something this deep is harder to cross than a lake five klicks wide."

"Still, I thought the damn efficiency would be better than this."

"The efficiency is fine. You're pushing it too hard."

"We're gonna have to push it if we're to get all the way to Canada and back. Help me scan for a way across."

They could see now and again a thread of water far at the bottom of the ravine, a river that should not have been there. They followed the great crack in the earth for more than an hour before the opposite bank suddenly narrowed toward them. "There," Savatini said. "Let's get close enough to read."

The ravine was only four and a half meters wide at that point. Indeed, from the looks of the far bank, a natural bridge had existed there until recently. "We can make it," Killee decided.

"It's still pretty damn deep."

"We'll put the grav-effect at full."

Savatini consulted a computer, though by now he had the various configurations of height and distance almost by heart. "We'll need one hundred percent power to traverse the ravine. We've drained the reserves with full running. The computer gives us only half a minute on full repulsion."

"Plenty of time." Killee edged the machine forward, centimeter by centimeter, until its sensors detected critical stress lines in the earth below. Then he threw switches, redirecting the power from the tractor motors to the gravity–effect generator. "Hold on."

Savatini did. The bus rose half a meter, riding on a gravity-repulsion field, and then Killee engaged the forward thrust. The bus moved over the projecting edge of the broken natural arch, and a billow of sand showed that the force of the gravity field had crumbled a considerable portion of it off. The bus wobbled alarmingly as the grav field adjusted to the sudden depth of the canyon. In frictionless suspension, the forward movement slowed to an agonizing crawl.

"Fifteen seconds," Savatini said. "Increase your thrust."

"No, no need for the additional drain. We're almost across."

The nose of the bus reached the opposite bank, but beneath the pressure of the grav field it, too, began to dissolve. "Damn it, fire up the thrusters. Five seconds," Savatini said.

"Hold on," Killee said again, and he switched off the gravity field and threw full power to the treads.

For a sickening moment they hung on the lip of the canyon, gravity hauling them backward, the madly spinning treads trying to pull them forward to safety. Savatini swallowed hard and tried to think of a prayer. By the time one popped into his head, the bus was rolling down a gentle incline away from the ravine and Killee was hooting his triumph. The engines whined, faded, fell silent.

"Might as well stop," Savatini told him. "Power reserve is critical. We won't be able to make more than three kph without full drain, and we won't be able to use the cooling system at all."

"How long to recharge?"

"Three hours, maybe a little more, and we can switch on the cooling. It'll be noon tomorrow before we have full reserve for the engines again."

"We could switch to the meth engine."

"Except we might need the fuel later on. We'd better just sit here and sweat."

Bol Killee pulled a sour face. "Damn, buddy, next time you design a bus, do a good job, will you?"

"Yeah," Savatini said with a grunt. "And next time I pick a driver, I'll try to do even better."

Nik Zimmer. Marise Lindholm. Claude Wing. And Killee, Savatini, and Hawk. And Stefan Li, in the person of the MPU.

Li worked on the crew manifest. He had more volunteers than he could possibly take, but knowing as much as he, as Matrix, did about the applicants, narrowing them down was not such a hard choice, after all.

Zimmer, for instance, was a weapons buff and a security expert. He had helped implement the Ark's current police force, a smoothly operating unit that relied less on force than on simply knowing the potential for trouble and preventing it from happening. And at thirty, he was an impressive specimen, rugged, strong, with many handy skills. Nik Zimmer would go, for he would be a good friend to have in a tight spot.

Marise Lindholm, as old-fashioned as her name: an historian, a treasurer of the old. Marise wanted to get a firsthand look at the ancient things on the surface, to glimpse the actual body of history, or at least its bones. Forty-seven but in excellent health and stronger than many women half her age, Marise brought not only knowledge but a steady kind of reliability to the group.

Claude Wing, twenty-eight, a geologist/geographer who yearned to see the changed face of the earth he studied in holoform. Wing, less active than the others, probably would have less endurance, but he was a desultory student of martial arts and did have a working knowledge of five languages, four of them dead—at least in *Ark Liberty*—but potentially living on the surface.

Brea Van Clease, thirty-seven, her son and daughter in their late teens and already on their own. Brea was an anthropologist, a linguistics expert, and a certified emergency medic. She could be useful—or she could succumb to problematic insecurities and self-doubts; old fracture lines never completely healed. Still, expertise in anthropology/linguistics/medicine made her a potential backstop for any of three other crew members.

And of course Carin Hawk's profile was wrong. There were the open spaces to consider, the sheer differentness of leaving the undersea womb for the terribly exposed outer world. Li had called in expert advice about Carin, and the weight of opinion was that she represented a risk.

But she wanted to go.

Long ago Stefan Li had been half in love with Keli Sumter.

Carin Hawk was descended from Keli.

Li heaved the electronic equivalent of a sigh.

Carin Hawk would go.

And the other applicants.... Li began to work through the second tier. He would find them, sooner or later.

And he would hope that no one would prove a bad choice for the expedition or for *Liberty*.

Chapter 9: Underway

August was not possible, nor stormy September, though in the Ark everything was ready by the end of summer. Finally, midway through October, the expedition group, eight men and women and one robot remote, assembled aboard a transport, a surface ship built over the past six months and driven by nuclear power. The transport had already been checked out with a couple of runs to the Florida coast and back, and its crew of five seemed cheerful and competent.

Still, the expedition members were subdued, almost awed. The sky above them was a clear, bright pea-green. They looked around the barren seascape and shivered despite the 39-degree heat. The leaden, greenish ocean heaved restlessly, its surface speckled with green raftlets, genetically-engineered plankton that had replaced much of the older, natural sea life. More resourceful at using UV than its natural counterpart, the plankton worked hard, oxygenating with great efficiency, but still the humans in the contingent wore rebreathers. The oxygen content at the surface was down to something more than sixteen percent, though the carbon-dioxide level was not as high as computers had once predicted. Nitrogen, water vapor, and trace elements took up the place of the diminished oxygen.

Each member of the crew tried breathing the outside air without oxygenating equipment. They could survive on it, but it left them with a suffocating feeling, as if they were in a room full of people and twice-breathed air. All preferred the comfort of the environmental suits and the oxygen-enhancing rebreathers.

"At least you won't need eye protection," Li told them. "Adriel Volker's atmospheric algae has reduced UV penetration to mid-twentieth century levels."

"Ready to cast off," Brea Van Clease said.

Finally, after long deliberation, Li had determined to man the landbuses with a total of eight: the drivers plus three other crew members per vehicle. It was a minimum. Eight could handle the work, could—he hoped—meet emergencies, could get back. And if the expedition were lost, then eight was not as great a loss as ten or twelve would be. Six of the landbus crew were aboard the transport. All of them stayed at the rail of the twelve-meter craft, watching the platform dwindle away. "Why do we have to go this way?" Carin Hawk asked Li. "The guys get to come by chopper."

"They have already been topside," Li pointed out to her. "Killee and Savatini have proven themselves. But if anyone else in the group is going to be troubled by open spaces, this is our chance to find out. Besides, the time will come when we'll need ship transports. It's good to practice the technology, to learn how not to forget."

Carin gave him a steady gaze. "Someone might be troubled by open spaces. Meaning me."

"Meaning anyone."

The transport ship sped northward through reasonably calm seas. Li reflected that one advantage of being a robot was the absence of sea-sickness, an advantage that he alone of all the expedition crew enjoyed. Still, no one broke during the days afloat: no one found the sky too oppressive, too wide, too exposed, not even Carin Hawk—though Sam Ikoto, who had decided at the very last minute to make up one of the crew, kept a close eye on her.

Five days after they had left the Ark behind them, they came within sight of land. The crew nosed the craft gingerly along a broken coast, seeking safe harbor, and at last found it in the mouth of a river. Moving slowly, taking frequent soundings by the ancient method of line and lead as well as by sonar, they passed a shoal of tumbled stones to the north.

"Washington," Marise Lindholm, the historian, said. "What's left of it."

They tried to spot something they might recognize from the old records, some spire or dome. The city had all but vanished under the sea, transformed to a dismal tidal flat. Perhaps those tumbled rocks had once been marble, and perhaps they had been government buildings or monuments: but now they were broken ruins, and no one could see the shapes they had once held, the halls and chambers and statuary.

In the early afternoon of October 18 the ship finally put the robot and the six passengers ashore, some thirty kilometers inland from the site of drowned Washington. A collapsed structure—probably a bridge originally—formed a rough kind of dock. Li had already been in touch with the Ark, and not long after the supplies had been offloaded a gigantic helicopter thrummed into hearing and into view. The craft settled on a meadow growing thick with the stringy grass, its belly opened, and Northstar 1, driven by Savatini, rumbled down a ramp, closely followed by Northstar 2, with Killee at the wheel. A skeletal form was tied to the top of the second landbus: the lashed-down recon 'copter, with room for pilot and one passenger, and enough fuel capacity for a three-hundred kilometer flight.

They spent that first night encamped in the meadow. Sam Ikoto sat next to Carin Hawk as they ate their rations—when they were not physically active, the rebreathers were not necessary, though the air seemed close and stale.

"The light is very strange," Ikoto said.

Carin, her mouth full of vegetable-protein paste, looked up perfunctorily and nodded. She swallowed and said, "Almost like being undersea, isn't it?"

Clouds had begun to move in from the ocean. The setting sun colored them weirdly, oranges and purples and pinks ranging through all hues from salmon to rose. The green sky was shot with veins of chartreuse, perhaps where high-level winds dispersed the atmospheric plankton.

Killee and Savatini were inspecting the buses, redistributing loads, arguing in a friendly manner. The MPU that was Stefan Li stood a little apart, its treads still, its light displays blank. Sleeping, Carin thought. As she needed to sleep. She yawned—one side effect of the diminished oxygen content was that it made one gasp for more air even when there was no need. She rose, stretched, dropped her ration container into the recycle bag, and left Ikoto alone. She helped set up the tents.

She shared a tent with Brea Van Clease and Marise Lindholm. Late that first night she woke suddenly, trembling. Something had changed, something was different somehow.

The environmental conditioner chugged away quietly, feeding cool, oxygen-enhanced air into the tent. The other two women breathed softly. Yet a sound had awakened her, an unfamiliar, monotonous, regular sound—

Tap. Tap-tap.

Carin almost screamed aloud. She had risen to her knees when she realized that the source of the sound was no enemy, no animal trying to tear its way in.

Outside, for the first time in her life, it was raining.

* * *

As a final courtesy the transport helicopter explored ahead for a few dozen kilometers the next morning. By mid-morning the two buses were underway, rumbling through a landscape notably poor in trees. The tough grass, thin and sharp-bladed, stood more than knee-high, covered huge stretches of land, and here and there they saw straggling copses of evergreens, dark blue-green smudges against the paler green of the meadows. But forests no longer existed, at least not in this neighborhood. They had to move due west for a good many kilometers before swinging northward, for a nuclear hit had left a section of northern Virginia radioactive and dangerous.

At least Carin Hawk kept busy during the long day. While the others scanned the landscape, took holos, quarreled about this or that formation and whether some mound was natural or marked a former human habitation, Carin occupied the comm station at the rear of Northstar 1 and tried to establish contact with *Ark Appalachia*.

Appalachia was supposed to be a surface-underground compound in the Virginia highlands, its exact location no longer certain. According to their best records, though, it was somewhere in the vicinity if it still existed at all. Like *Liberty, Appalachia* had long ago taken the precaution of erasing exact information about itself from the global information net. Perhaps, unlike *Liberty,* the installation itself had been wiped out in the chaos of the Spark Wars, in the long starving and the biological plagues that followed. But if *Appalachia* still lived, this was at least a chance to regain contact, and so Carin scanned the wavebands, called occasionally, and listened to silence.

Or she chatted. Through the satellite link she could talk to friends on *Liberty* (so strange to think of them safe and stationary on the sea floor while she rattled across a devastated landscape in this contraption). She also spoke to Northstar 2: Marise Lindholm, on the communications station of the second bus, a few hundred meters to their left, reported all calm.

Meanwhile, endless stretches of prairie rolled by: land that had been coastal plain, now built up by deluges that had swept silt-bearing floodwater over it year after year. The tough grasses, along with the stunted, struggling trees and occasional irregular splotches of lichen, were the only visible life. No bird or butterfly sailed the sky, no mouse or lizard rustled the grass as they moved over it.

An insect was an event.

Brea shrieked in delight at the sight of it, and Savatini stopped the bus. They spilled out into waist-high grass, followed Brea's pointing finger, and finally discovered them: grasshoppers half an inch long, green, but with pinkish eyes. Li accessed the databanks back at *Liberty* and pronounced the insects a new species, probably a natural mutation. They sang in ragged chirps, and Brea Van Clease wept to hear them.

But grasshoppers could not delay them long. Li holo'd the male and female of the species, then set the specimens free. Life on *Liberty* was far too precious to allow him to think of killing even a couple of bugs.

Carin went back to the comm station, reported their find, and then tried again to raise *Appalachia,* with absolutely no success. The waveband of the northern broadcast, under automatic scan, remained quiet as well.

That evening when they stopped for camp, Carin wandered a little way from the campsite to look up at the stars. They were fogged and blurred by the high haze of the atmospheric plankton, and a half-moon showed a fuzzy green. She heard a faint rustle, turned, and said, "Oh. It's you."

The MPU—everyone thought of it as "Stef" now—halted near her. "Don't get too far from the buses. We don't know that it's completely safe."

"I was looking at the stars. Men dreamed once of going there."

Stef's visual array tilted back. "You don't find it disturbing?"

Carin shivered a little. "I've seen holos before. And it's not completely different from being ten or fifteen meters down and looking into the depths of *Liberty*. You see the same distant lights then. Besides, they don't really look all that far away. Is that bright one Venus?"

The visual array swiveled to gaze off to the west. "Yes. It is currently visible in the hours just after dusk."

"I've forgotten. Did people ever land there?"

"No. The surface is far too hot. On the moon and Mars, yes. But not on Venus."

"There was a dream once of terraforming it."

"Yes. Our own planet became too much like Venus before anything could be done." They were quiet for a few minutes. Then Li said, "Come back to camp now. It's getting dark."

"All right, you worrier."

The group at the campfire—actually a synthetic-oil burner, since wood was so very scarce—greeted her with such enthusiasm that she suspected something was up. "She'll settle it," Killee boomed. "No coaching, now. All right, Carin, we've all agreed to have some entertainment. Two of our group have holochip movies they've programmed themselves. You get to break the tie to decide which we'll see."

"What are they?"

"One is the elegant, romantic, beautiful historical

drama *The Life of Buddha,* and the other is some clanky rink of a thing called *Hamlet.*"

Marise hit him hard in the ribs. "That's for being so unbiased," she said as Killee wrestled with her.

"Who's in them?" Carin asked, her voice louder than normal.

The two stopped their childish scuffle. "Okay," Killee said. "In *Buddha* we have Charlie Chaplin, John Wayne, Merrilee St. Croix, Bil Hazengane. In *Hamlet*—who is it?"

"Booth, Barrymore, Hoffman, Hayes—"

"*Hamlet* tonight," Carin said with a grin. "I'm a tossback for Hoffman."

The play was an updated version of the Shakespeare original: English had changed so much that one had to be a specialist or a Stefan Li to understand the Renaissance version. Still, the translation was faithful to the original and rang with a certain air of antiquity.

The actors, reconstructed three-dimensional figures from motion-picture or even from flat stills, looked real enough to touch. Designing movies had become a popular hobby aboard *Liberty* in the past few years. With the aid of the Matrix computer and the visual databanks, anyone could program any story, even original ones. The programmer was producer, director, cinematographer, and sometimes playwright. The actors were famous stars of stage and screen from the nineteenth century onward. Designing a movie could take a careful hobbyist a year or more, and when they were finished, the shows were a welcome source of diversion in a world where little changed.

This *Hamlet* was good enough: the castle was well-realized, and Carin would have known from the intricate details of costumes and weapons that Marise had created the movie, even if she hadn't punched Killee. And the actors were programmed well, though personally Carin would have preferred Hoffman as Hamlet rather than as Horatio.

But her mind wandered nevertheless, through the long days ahead, toward their goal far to the north. She joined in the applause at the conclusion, but in truth she could remember almost none of the last act. That night they again slept in the tents with the oxygenators set on full flow, their soft hiss like a light breeze across the stretched fabric. Carin quickly became accustomed to the soft hum. This time no rain wakened her, and she slept the deep sleep of true exhaustion.

They had not bothered to name human guards.

After all, remote flyovers had spotted no animal larger than an insect in this countryside. Nor had anything big enough to be dangerous roamed the landscape any more recently than two hundred years ago.

So the human members of the team slept.

But the robot remained alert.

Li heard the sounds and gave the alarm.

Ven Savatini was the first out of his tent, Nik Zimmer close at his heels, a needle-gun in his grip. "That way," Li said, pointing with one of his extensor arms.

The two grabbed flashlights and headed off to the west. They were away from camp for no more than five minutes. The others came out of the tents and watched the lights of Savatini and Zimmer bobbing in the distance. They came back, both men gasping for breath. In the excitement of the alarm, neither had bothered to don his rebreather.

"Gone," Savatini said. "Any damage?"

"The ration packs that we left out for breakfast have been taken. And Northstar 1 has a ripped seat," Sam Ikoto said in his soft voice. "I believe it must have been done with a primitive knife. Perhaps a soft metal one, made of copper."

Zimmer had snatched up a rebreather and was dragging the enriched air into his lungs. He laughed, the cone of the rebreather muffling the sound. "Humans? You think those were humans?"

"Did you see them?" Li asked.

Zimmer shook his head, and Savatini said, "They were too fast. Just shapes darting through the grass. Two of them, from the look of the trail." He hesitated. "They were big, but I don't know if they were human-sized. I'd say the things were at least a meter tall, but then they could have been running stooped over."

"We ought to hunt 'em down," Zimmer said. "With one of the buses we could—"

"No," Li said.

Brea Van Clease spoke up from the shadows. "I think we should. If they have weapons, they're human. If they're human, they may be the ones we're looking for—"

"No," Li repeated. "They're not human. Not anymore."

They looked at him silently. "Okay, explain," Savatini said after a long pause.

"I detected their scent. Analysis shows that the body chemistry implied by the pheromones is not compatible with human biochemistry."

"What is it compatible with, then?"

"Mammalian. Primate. But apart from that, it matches nothing in the databanks," Li said.

"Impossible."

"The grasshopper was not in the databanks, either."

Savatini waved his arms. "But that was an insect. I mean, people don't mutate so rapidly over, what, three centuries. They wouldn't become a different species—"

"Not unless they engineered themselves into a different species," Li said. "There are stories of the Wulves."

The others exchanged glances. No one said there were no such things as Wulves, that they were idle legends and myth.

"I think we should vote," Zimmer said.

"Not this time," Li said. "Not tonight."

"We're a democratic collective—"

"We're not expendable," Li said.

The last word hung in the air.

Dawn brought no sign of the marauders, nor did the remainder of the day. They made good time then and for several days thereafter, and eventually even Zimmer concluded with a rueful grunt that they must have left the night creatures behind. Their path was leading them farther inland now, through the grassy plains of central Pennsylvania, then northward.

Cities this far from the sea, with some protection from the hurricane winds, were less ruined than the seacoast towns. Roofless and windowless, some buildings still stood in flooded Harrisburg, on the shores of a broad brown river that the buses skated across handily. Farther north, into New York State. Conifers more plentiful now, and more insect life: dragonflies, locusts, crickets at night. And on a day to be marked with a white stone, a mammal, a night-running rat or perhaps a juvenile opossum, gray and scuttling, barely glimpsed in the distance.

But no signs of human life. The broken buildings, those that were still recognizable as the works of humans, gaped open to the sky, filled with the fall of themselves: roofs, ceilings, intervening floors, rotted and collapsed, a compressed sandwich of loss within shells as hollow as rotten teeth. Stefan Li took Carin aside at one point and asked her to keep close watch on Marise Lindholm, who was taking the broken landscape badly.

Oddly enough, Brea, who had at first seemed most

moved by the devastation, soon became inured to it. Marise, the historian, grew increasingly distraught. They passed through the broken remains of Syracuse, and she wept. She told them all that she didn't believe the computers anymore. "The time frame," she tried to explain through her sobs. "It's too short, don't you see? How could everything—everything enduring and human and beautiful disappear in three hundred years? How could it all just rot away like this?"

But it had. One night Marise asked Li to show them a representation of the land as it had been, back in the days when he wore flesh, back before the fall was so utterly complete. He objected, but when the others joined in, he worked up a holoshow for them, an aerial tour of the route they had traversed, as if seen from a fast-moving aircraft from a few hundred feet.

"Washington," Marise said as the view swept over the marble city, monuments gleaming in the sun. "And see the trees."

The trees of Virginia, hardwood and soft, pine and oak, fir and maple; their branches alive with thousands of darting birds, with insects and spiders, with lizards and tree-toads. Not that any of these were visible, for of course they weren't. But they all could sense the life in those forests, just as they could gasp at the sight of a city, of Pittsburgh or of Syracuse, and know from its order and its form that men and women lived there, worked there, built there.

When the show was over, Marise wept bitterly for a long time. That evening Stefan quietly asked Carin to watch out for her, and that evening Sam Ikoto gave Marise a mild tranquilizer. "It is the poetry of life she mourns," Ikoto observed. "What is left is the skeleton of what was. The poetry of life has long vanished."

Carin Hawk comforted Marise, talked to her until the drug took effect, and then crept to her own bed, where she clandestinely administered a similar drug to herself. Her supply was dwindling. She wondered what she would do when it was gone, when the vast empty sky screamed at her, when she could no longer force the empty world to go away behind the welcome wall of sleep.

The next day Marise seemed better, and the little caravan rolled on northward, rolled on through the struggling remains of life, through a dying world.

The weather grew cooler, the afternoon high slipping from blood warmth to thirty degrees, then to twenty-seven. By standards of the twentieth century, the northern part of New York State was suffering a fall heat wave, but the travelers found the relative coolness refreshing. Still, the green sky made Li feel vaguely uneasy, apprehensive. It resembled nothing so much as a lowering storm in the old days. When *Ark Liberty* was under construction, a sky like that would herald an imminent hurricane.

But now it was normal, the world's new mantle, green instead of blue, and since it helped to stave off the worst of the sun's damage, Li supposed he should feel grateful. Such a sky had never been seen during Adriel Volker's lifetime, though throughout her span she had worked to refine and toughen the organisms that now produced the hue. She had continued to make changes in the airborne algae, and the last one was a self-limiting "switch."

As she had explained to Li, the algae could not survive a certain threshold concentration of ozone. When—if—the oxygen content of the planet stabilized and rose to a critical percentage, when the ozone layer of the upper atmosphere replenished itself, the algae would wither and die, snowing softly down to the surface of the planet it had shielded. Ironically, the plants themselves would contribute to their own eventual demise, adding oxygen to the atmosphere as they metabolized the lingering hydrocarbons.

When Li had asked her where she got the idea, she had responded with a tight smile, "From us." Like the algae, humanity had consumed itself to destruction, had made its habitat untenable.

Well, now Adriel's green blanket had spread over the entire world, a much thicker layer than the original tenuous ozone had been. It gave a ghastly tint to daylight, but it did filter the unfriendly sun, and it did its quiet, long work to repair the damage that mankind had made.

Northward they rolled, through green-hazed days and lengthening, cool nights when at times the tent enviros actually began to produce heat to keep the sleepers comfortable. Li had company at night now: throughout each night, three of the expedition team took turns on watch on a regular rotation. Some of them talked to Li in the long stretches, like Carin and Ven. Others, like Sam and Brea, preferred to brood in silence.

Twice they had to make camp when fierce rain squalls hit, drumming hail onto the buses with a noise like thunder. For two days in late October a strong, dry wind blew from the west, and the green sky turned brown from huge quantities of fine dust. When the wind blew itself out, the dust sifted down like the finest possible snow, coating everything with a thin layer of what had once been the American Midwest.

Finally, as November began, the party halted one morning. They had reached a vast slate-gray expanse of water: Lake Ontario. For the rest of that day they camped near its shores (much farther inland than they had once been, for the lakes, like the sea, had risen with the diminution of the polar caps). Li ran various analysis programs, the explorers did both gross and microscopic examinations, and they concluded that the lake was not as dead as it appeared.

Shrimp and worms lived there.

Oh, other life was there, too: bacteria in plenty, algae, even a tiny mollusc. But worms and shrimp seemed to be the most advanced aquatic creatures this close to the shore. "We cannot discount the possibility of fish in the farther reaches," Sam Ikoto insisted mildly.

No.

But the oxygen content of the lake was drastically low, and meanwhile there were only the worms.

On the other hand, terrestrial life steadily became more diverse as they rolled northward: brown bats had reappeared, along with night-flying owls. Mice seemed plentiful in the tall grasses, and twice they caught sight of stalking forms that could only be feral cats. The insects, too, were steadily more plentiful and diverse: flies, gnats, moths, and mosquitoes made their advent. The nights were no longer silent but chattered with cricket songs.

The skeleton had a few shreds of meat clinging to the old bones yet.

Li developed some difficulties with the robot body: the small treads tended to become clogged with the tough prairie grasses, for one thing, and perception lacunae developed, so that he could no longer use the UV portion of his visual array. Ven Savatini worked over the MPU for hours, swore, tried this and that solution, and at last ended by blaming himself for not bringing along enough spare parts.

Li dismissed the trouble. "It's all right. I can still see in the visual range, and I'll restrict movement through the worst of the grasses. That should take care of the mobility problem."

He didn't mention it, but he felt a strange schizophrenic tug. His active consciousness was here, with the expedition, lodged in the shell of MPU 1552, but the greater part of his mind, the Matrix computer itself, was back aboard *Liberty*. Though Li no longer "slept" in the human sense, he did have periods of rest and introspection, and increasingly he had the weird feeling that what happened aboard the Ark was somehow a dream, an illusion, at a great distance from the real world of ruins and collapse. More and more he felt a part of the group, one of them.

Almost, indeed, human.

Carin Hawk noted three possible radio spikes that might, just might, mark transmissions from the north. None was clear enough to produce any real information, but the three helped to localize the area of their search. The broadcasters, it seemed, were on the move: now their transmissions originated from somewhere a good many kilometers north and west of Ottawa. The caravan altered its course accordingly.

Li's monitors sounded warnings several times. Once a stiff western wind brought radioactivity, hot particles from some battleground far away. The fallout was minimal, but the crew remained inside the buses as a precaution. Twice more he detected larger animals not too far from the camps, but never was he able to spot them in time for the others to pursue and capture them.

The St. Lawrence presented a formidable barrier. Deep and broad, it ran with considerable velocity. "We could use the grav-effect generators to cross," Killee mused, leaning against Northstar 2 and looking across the gray rush of water. "But we'll drift downstream at a good clip. If we separate, we'll be days getting back together."

Ven Savatini, squatting on his heels near the bank of the river, shook his head. "And if we're swept along downstream, we might be caught short when the generators give out. If it was calm water, that would be one thing. I'd say we could get across in, oh, twenty minutes?"

"Nineteen minutes, thirteen seconds," Li responded.

"At a meter altitude that would be no problem. But if we're swept downstream, we'd exhaust the power in—"

"Twenty-seven minutes forty-one seconds."

Savatini gave a mirthless chuckle. "And once the repulsors lost power, we'd sink like rocks." He straightened his knees, standing, his protective white environmental suit gleaming in the strong light of midday. "Can't go around, that's for sure."

Killee said, "Not to the west. We could look for a better spot downstream, though. The chopper?"

The expedition team voted on the idea, and they all helped to break out the two-man helicopter and fill its fuel tank with methanol. Killee and Savatini both prepared to go—but then Li suggested that one of their engineers, at least, should remain with the camp. In the end Killee took the helicopter up alone, transmitting data back to Li, who processed them into a holographic representation of the landscape.

The others watched the display intently. The river had swollen high enough to obliterate any trace of former bridges. It ran between barren shores, though at some distance from the water trees grew on either side. From the look of the scoured land, the river flooded regularly, carrying away anything that might have helped them across. But finally Carin Hawk said, "What's that?"

The gray rushing face of the river showed an irregularity, a straight line beginning some distance from the near shore and stretching partway across. Li consulted his memory. "The Eisenhower locks," he said. "Or the wreckage."

Killee swooped low. The river, troubled and roiled by the obstruction, lost some of its forward momentum there. "If we follow the line of the disturbance, I think we can make it," Killee reported over the radio.

"It's half a day from here," Savatini returned. "We're on the way. Meet you as you come back."

The buses rumbled across country, occasionally lifting over ravines or other roadblocks, making good time. The river, away on their left, rushed implacably along.

They had been underway for an hour when Killee cut in, his voice excited: "I see something!"

"Show us," Savatini said. Li again plugged into the bus radio system, and he projected the image that Killee had focused the chopper's cameras on: a swath of grass, dotted with blue-green conifers, and through the grasses—

"People?" Carin asked.

"No," Li said. "Not people. The body outlines—"

"What's happening?" Savatini asked from up front.

"Six, seven of them," Killee's voice reported. "Trying to get to the trees now. I'm going in for a closer look—"

"Break off," Li said.

"No, they may be—"

The seven fleeing figures swelled as the helicopter swooped closer. One turned, a grotesque form, barrel-chested, its eyes a blank and merciless gray. In a spindly arm it raised something.

"Break off," Li repeated, more urgently.

Killee began, "One of them is going to throw—"

The object in the creature's hand flared. Carin screamed and flinched as a bolt of—something, energy—leaped out—

The holodisplay scrambled into white light and static.

Savatini barked, "Killee! Killee! Damn it, talk to us!"

Li disengaged from the radio array. Carin busied herself for half a minute. Finally she turned toward the others. "No contact," she said. "Killee's down."

Chapter 10: Discovery

Nik Zimmer took the helm of Northstar 2. Li estimated the last transmission from Killee to have come from a spot more than an hour's journey distant, but both Zimmer and Ven Savatini, who was still piloting Northstar 1, piled on all the power they could. The crew strapped in and held on as the treads rumbled and jolted them over the rutted, rocky terrain.

Li contacted *Liberty* and informed the communications team there of what was going on. He asked them to hold release of any news until they had some definite knowledge about Bol Killee's fate, for Killee's mother and sister were both aboard *Liberty* and he didn't wish to cause them unnecessary worry. Li briefly deactivated MPU 1552 and cast his consciousness back into Matrix, where he carefully analyzed all the data that had come in, including the visual representations of Killee's enemies, with the full capacity of the Ark computer.

When he returned to the robot after what, subjectively, was a long time but in reality was less than a minute, he had news. "The creatures Killee sighted are not human, though they spring from human ancestry. From the range of the mutations we have observed, my best estimate is that they correspond to the reports of Wulves."

Except for Savatini at the wheel, they all listened grimly to Li's account. He explained the presumed origin of the Wulves in the long-ago attack on *Ark Ouachita*, on the mutagenic concoction brought to that Ark by Dr. Landrau. "Adriel believed that the change in metabolism would result in a markedly decreased lifespan, and, over the course of a few generations, in diminished intelligence as well. On the other hand, she did grant that the mutations would favor physical survival in a greenhouse environment."

Claude Wing asked, "If these things have been roaming the landscape for nearly three hundred years, why haven't we picked them up before now?"

"Our samples have been small and widely spaced, for one thing. For another, the creatures seem to run in small packs, and to use a minimum of technology. Their numbers would be very small—probably there are fewer Wulves on the surface than humans aboard *Ark Liberty.*"

"Wait, wait. What did you say about minimal technology? I mean, *something* knocked down the chopper," Savatini called from the helm.

Li increased his speaker volume. "Yes, they disabled the helicopter, apparently with an energy-plasma device. But that technology is old. It existed three hundred years ago. That they have a weapon and an energy source for it is obvious, but I am almost positive that they inherited the weapon. They lack the ability to make such a thing themselves."

"How do you know?" Carin asked, her voice tight, her dark eyes brimming with worry.

"Analysis of the images. Here, let me show you." Li activated the holodisplay and created a startlingly realistic still of one of the attackers. The others regarded it silently: a meter and a half tall, bipedal, barrel-chested, humanoid, but certainly not human. The bullet head was bald, scaled, with subcutaneous plates that gave a turtleback texture to the skin. The round, bulging eyes were twice human size and deep charcoal gray—completely gray, showing neither sclera nor pupil.

The nose was a triangular opening webbed with some sort of thin pink membrane. The mouth was a straight, lipless gash. The bull neck led to sharply sloping shoulders, to powerful, short arms and broad hands. The creature was naked, its genitalia invisible in a chestnut tangle of pubic hair. Its well-muscled legs were short, its feet splayed.

"That's as they appeared?" Sam Ikoto asked, his soft voice showing an edge of interest. "Unclothed, I mean?"

"Affirmative. This is a composite image construct, drawn from them all. They all appear to be male, or at any rate they all lacked discernible female secondary sexual characteristics, and they all were naked. Only one was armed. Tentative analysis of the image—it was just a quick look, remember, and both the helicopter and the creature were in motion—tentative analysis indicates a Remington Model 2178 plasma rifle."

Nik Zimmer, off a score of meters to their left in Northstar 2, had been listening in on radio. "Would anything that old still work?" he asked.

"Evidently so. The creatures may have found a cache of weaponry in the vicinity. This was once a heavily armed frontier, with a number of armories."

Brea Van Clease had been examining the holographic apparition closely. " 'Creatures,' you say. Are they really not human? Technically, I mean?"

"Not anymore," Li said. "They're definitely a different species now. And a dangerous one."

From the helm, Ven Savatini said, "We're getting close to the site of Killee's last communication. And I see smoke up ahead, lots of it."

"Is everyone armed?" Li asked. The question was not really necessary.

The smoke rose in lazy thick streamers from a smoldering patch of grass, half a hectare in extent. Some fragments of wreckage, all of them small, littered the stubbled center of the burned-out fire. The trees they had seen on the holodisplay were ahead and to the right. Apart from the bits and pieces on the ground, which constituted the holographic visual sensors and the infrared scanner, there was no sign of the helicopter.

They explored with needle-guns at the ready, but nothing was there to be found. The river was several hundred meters north of the fire site, and nowhere along its bank did they see a trace of the helicopter. Li searched in different ways from the others, and when they were ready to despair, he had some better news. They all met back at Northstar 1 for the briefing. "Bol has not been on the ground in this area," Li said definitely. "Unless he crashed in the river, he must have been able to get away."

"How do you know?" Savatini's sharp question had no deference, no implied "sir" in it at all now. His curly black hair sweat-plastered to his head, curlicue smudges of soot on his face where drifting ashes of grass had stuck, Ven looked like a man who would not welcome a light answer.

"Odor analysis," Li responded. "Each of you has a distinct smell. Killee's is not detectable. If he had been here, alive or dead, some trace would remain."

"What do we do?" Carin asked. She was trembling a little with weariness or tension, and in her pale face her dark eyes seemed enormous.

Li's sensory array swiveled to the north. "I think if Killee's craft were damaged, he would attempt the most obvious avenue of escape."

"Across the river," Savatini said.

"Yes. The river would be a more formidable barrier to the Wulves than to us. If the helicopter could fly that far, he would get across and put down."

"Radio would be out," Savatini said. "It was tied in with the sensor array. How about his wrist comm?"

"It isn't powerful enough to be detected here. Remember, it was designed for use aboard the Ark, where receivers run throughout the walls and ceilings. It has a practical outside range of less than five hundred meters."

"What do we do?" Zimmer asked from his spot a little apart from the others, close to Northstar 2, whose helm he had inherited from Killee.

Li considered his answer carefully. "Your question implies that you believe we need to engage in immediate action. However, that is neither practical nor desirable. Our best course is to continue to the fording point and try to get across the river. If Bol made it safely across, we'll find him there."

"No." Zimmer's voice was hard and definite. "We have to take care of those things first. We can't let them run loose as a threat to us."

"Consider this," Li said. "They perceived the helicopter as a threat to them. They've never encountered human beings before. They were frightened—"

Zimmer pounded his fist against the carbon-plastic body of Northstar 2. "Bulls. They shot Bol down. I say we get them."

Carin said, "Kill them, you mean, Nik?"

Zimmer's face was hard-set, his eyes threatening. "If that's what it takes, yes. Kill the damn things." He held his needle-gun before him, almost in a parade-rest stance.

Marise Lindholm was shaking her head. Aloud she said, "Nik, if these creatures have survived for more than two centuries where humans can't live, they've earned whatever life they've made for themselves."

"And Killee hadn't earned his life? Bulls," Zimmer said again.

Marise did not flinch from his angry tone. "At least they don't deserve to die at our hands."

"Call for a vote," Zimmer said.

They voted. It was six to three to cross the river. Savatini, Zimmer, and Claude Wing wanted to stay on this side and hunt down the Wulves. The others agreed with Li's suggestion. Li felt very uneasy. Part of his state lay in his old human instincts of danger, the ingrained ancient fight-or-flight reaction kicking in. But another part was his computer-enhanced sense that things were going wrong with the crew. Zimmer's voice-stress pattern was unusual, showing tension far in excess of anything the man had exhibited before. Carin Hawk seemed withdrawn, not catatonic but curiously removed, as though drugged. And the others, to greater or lesser degrees, were on edge, were preoccupied, were worried.

He would have to watch them carefully.

They got underway again, half the crew riding in Northstar 2 this time. The sun was close to setting when they arrived at the site of the old Eisenhower locks, now more like a sandbar than any work of man. At Savatini's suggestion they magnetically linked the two landbuses. That way if one had difficulty the other might be able to drag or push it to safety. He ran through the grav-effect system with Zimmer, who had used it in short bursts while relieving one of the other drivers but who had never crossed a major obstacle with it.

They took a good run toward the river to build up momentum, cut in the grav-effect generators, and skated out over the St. Lawrence at an altitude of slightly less than one meter. The moving water surface beneath the repulsors dragged sideways, and the buses slewed, but Savatini compensated and called corrections to Zimmer, who trailed them by a few meters.

Carin Hawk sat beside Savatini and consulted a holographic display graphing power levels, thrust levels, and speed. "We won't make it at this rate," she said. "Can we reduce the grav-effect by twenty percent?"

"May we get our feet wet," Savatini said with a grunt. But he cut down on the generator power and radioed Zimmer to do the same. Northstar 1 settled a little lower over the river. Li, looking out a port window, saw that they had drifted a little downstream from their original line of passage. He cut into the computer and without making a verbal comment showed Carin a combination of thrust and angle that would ease them back on track with a minimum of power loss.

They made the adjustment. The other shore of the river drew closer meter by agonizing meter. They had passed the halfway point when Zimmer said, "Son of a bitch. There they are. Behind us."

Li engaged the visual sensor system and saw what Zimmer meant. Seven figures, Wulves by their postures and silhouettes, leaped and shook their hands in the air on the shore behind them. One of them carried something long and thin that had to be the plasma weapon. He isolated the weapon in the sensor field of view, zoomed in on it, and confirmed his earlier tentative identification. The plasma rifle, if fully charged, could fire one hundred bolts of energy. There was no way of knowing if the bolt fired at the helicopter had been the first or the hundredth or anything in between.

"I'm going to get a shot at them," Zimmer radioed.

"Negative," Li cried at once. "Maintain your heading. Nik, you haven't got the power to negotiate a turn and still cross the river."

"Damn it—"

Without arguing the point any further, Li took control of the Northstar 2 guidance system and locked it down on its present course. He heard Zimmer shout in frustration.

Carin said, "Thirteen minutes of power left. If the drift doesn't get any worse, we'll make it across, just barely."

Zimmer had not been quite expert enough in his adjustment of power and thrust. Li sensed that Northstar 2 had just eleven and a half minutes of full power remaining.

They crept across, Zimmer cursing and ranting, Carin ignoring him, Savatini staring at the twilit far shore. At eleven minutes and seven seconds, the treads of Northstar 1 scraped the shelving bottom of the river, shuddered sideways in the tug of current, and then began to haul them ashore. An instant later Northstar 2 gained purchase. Northstar 1 cleared the river just as the second landbus stalled out. Li switched to the meth engine, fired it, and used the surge of power to drag Northstar 2 out of the water.

They spilled out of the buses, but in the gathering gloom nothing could be seen across the river. "Damn it," Zimmer muttered. "We could've picked off one or two. Maybe all of them."

"No," Li said. "If you had taken the time to do that, Northstar 2 would have been lost."

"At least," Brea said, "they didn't fire at us."

Zimmer turned away. "So what? They killed Bol."

No one spoke, not even Li, who sensed that all of them believed what Zimmer said.

The night was long and unexpectedly chilly. Savatini thought that with power levels so low it would be better not to use the enviros for heat, just for oxygenation. The tents quickly became uncomfortably cool, and when Carin Hawk woke at midnight for her tour of guard duty she gratefully slipped into her environmental suit and turned on the heat. The lightweight suit battery pack was good for somewhat more than twenty-four hours of heating or cooling, and she had nearly twelve hours of charge left.

The landbuses stood parallel to each other and about eight meters apart. The three tents had been pitched in the area between them. Li's MPU kept vigil at the rear of the vehicles, the dim red light issuing from the sensor deck the only illumination in the dark night. Li's optical array slowly swiveled back and forth as he scanned the opposite shore. "Anything going on over there?" Carin asked him, coming over to his side.

"Negative. Infrared shows some small mammalian life. Rats, perhaps, or marsupials. And an owl or two. Nothing large or threatening. They returned to the trees as we got across the river."

Carin shivered. "Do you think Bol has much of a chance?"

Li's tone was measured. "It depends on what happened. If he had control of the helicopter and did what we think, if he tried for this side and reached it, I think he has an excellent chance of survival. If he landed on the other side or crashed into the river—" He left the sentence unfinished.

"We didn't see any wreckage."

"No. A good sign. With your permission, I am going to extinguish the guide light. It interferes to a small degree with my IR sensors."

"Mm, go ahead. I'm settled now." The red light vanished, and an exceedingly dark night clamped down on them at once. Carin took a long, unsteady breath. "I've been thinking. Bol's wristcomm is too weak for us to pick up its signal, but what if we broadcast on his waveband?"

"I have a constant homing signal going out now."

"Oh." Carin hugged herself and kicked at the ground. "I should have known you'd think of that."

"It was one of the first things I did."

They were quiet for a while. "How cold is it?" Carin asked.

"Eleven degrees. A polar air mass is moving southward, I think. We are on its fringe."

Eleven degrees. A long way from freezing, but she felt the nip of cool air on her nose. She tugged the hood into place. "Do you suppose it ever snows anymore? Anywhere?"

"At the poles, during the polar winters, of course. The problem is that the snow no longer accumulates as it once did. The Greenland ice cap is more than eighteen percent depleted—"

With the flat of her hand, Carin reached out into the darkness and whacked the support cylinder of the MPU. The blow made an insignificant sound in the night. "Stop doing that. Stop being a computer. Be Stef for a little, can't you?"

Li's voice took on a faint edge of distressed surprise. "I am being a computer, aren't I? I think it's this robot unit. As long as my awareness is in it, I feel like a damned machine."

"That's only reasonable, considering that you are a machine. You could use the holos to project an image."

"No, I'd rather not. That particular program is so detailed it would take up far too much of our available memory. I'll have to wait until we're back at *Liberty* to wear my flesh suit again."

Carin tilted her head back and looked up at the sky, feeling almost as if she were about to receive a blow. It was dark, the absolute dark of an overcast and moonless night. The landscape all around was equally black, so lightless that the horizon was lost in gloom. "Cloudy?" she guessed.

"Overcast at 1500 meters, and the barometer is falling. We'll probably have rain before long."

"It's never this dark in *Liberty*."

"It never used to be on the surface." Li paused. "I mean, there were places, wilderness areas, where there were few or no human light sources, but even so there were fireflies, foxfire, little glimmers of light and life."

"I've never seen fireflies."

"When we get back to *Liberty* I'll have some thawed for you. We'll put them in Orchard 17—that has wildflowers in it they should like."

"No man ever did as much for me," Carin said with a secret smile.

"I am not a man."

"Only on the outside."

"Perhaps."

They fell silent for another long spell. Carin checked her watch twice, feeling more and more sleepy: two-thirty. Then three-ten. Finally she said, "I have a confession to make."

"That you have been secretly taking tranquilizers?"

Carin felt her face flush with sudden guilt and was glad that Stef could not see her in the dark. Then she remembered that he *could*. Damn. "You knew?"

"Sam Ikoto suspected, and on his request I verified. I can monitor your body chemistry by—"

"Pheromones, I know. Yes, I had a supply of Grade Two tranks with me. Damn it, I've run out. Do you think—"

"Sam could issue an equivalent if absolutely necessary. But I believe you should try to function without them."

Carin's stomach fell, the way it did when she was in a one-person submersible and took a dive too steeply. "I don't understand. If you know I've been using them and haven't objected so far, why keep them from me now?"

"Ever since we left the vicinity of the Virginia nuclear hot spot you've been using them less frequently, and in smaller dosages. I think you've almost weaned yourself from the need."

"But if they let me function better—oh. I guess your point is that I haven't been functioning as well as I should."

Li stirred beside her. She heard the faint rustle of grass beneath the MPU treads. "That is true, but that is only a part of the problem. The rest of it—it is difficult to express. You, of all the surface team, have become most acclimated to life in an enclosed space. The Ark is the most comfortable and comforting environment imaginable for you. And yet you are adjusting, slowly, to the open landscape. I need to be sure that you can do that."

"Why?"

"For the future."

"You mean I'm sort of an experiment? A trial run so that in a hundred years—"

"Closer to three, under current projections."

"All right, damn it, so that in three hundred years you can lead people out of the Ark to reclaim the land?"

"Yes."

Carin drew a deep breath. She had been weaning herself from the rebreather, too, and tonight she had not used it once since leaving the oxygenated tent. The alien surface air felt heavy in her lungs, thick but breathable. "I don't like being an experimental animal."

A faint hiss of hydraulics. Li had swiveled his visual array to look at her, she supposed. "When the Ark was first occupied, not everyone could adjust," he said. "We had cases of insanity, of suicide. Even in the second generation there were instances of acute claustrophobic reactions. We countered with a number of developments: the Orchards were enlarged, the holographic displays enhanced to give the illusion of open spaces. But more and more the Ark population is acclimating itself to narrow passages, circumscribed living spaces, tunnels, caverns. That is a trap. We can't reclaim the surface world if we're afraid to leave the Ark."

"But won't the problems be no more severe than they were when everything started?"

"I can't tell, Carin. When colonists came to *Liberty*, they were fleeing from chaos to safety. When we leave the Ark, we'll be reversing that: moving from a safe, controlled environment to an open and dangerous one. I need all the data that I can get."

"At least you're honest enough to admit that I'm just a guinea pig."

"No. You are more than that, much more. I've never told you this—"

Carin waited. "Go on. Never told me what?"

Silence.

Carin said, "Stef? Are you all right?"

No answer.

She reached into her battery pack and took out a flashlight. The MPU unit stood stolid and quiet beside her. In the ring of light she found a panel, slipped it open, studied a display. "Damn." She closed the panel and went to Tent 1. "Ven," she called, "I need you."

Sleepy mutterings, then a stir inside the tent. The aluminized opening unsealed, Ven Savatini crawled out, and the tent behind him sealed itself. "My turn's tomorrow night," Ven grumbled.

"No, it's not that. Li's gone dead."

Savatini frowned, the light reflecting from Carin's torch making his face a demonic mask. "Gone dead? What do you mean?"

"His readout shows nominal power level but no activity. We need to run a diagnostic."

"Sounds like a relay problem to me. He probably just lost the damn satellite beam. Okay, help me roll him to Northstar 1. I'll take a look."

They tugged the heavy MPU across the grass, sliding it more than rolling it. Savatini opened a side panel in the landbus. It unfolded to a compact workbench with a bank of lights above it. When he switched on the glare, someone in Tent 3, closest to Northstar 1, cursed *sotto voce*. The translucent tent immediately opaqued against the light.

"Let's have a look." Savatini probed the unit's control panel and routing boards, ran a diagnostic on the communications link, and shook his head. "It's what I thought, a data-relay failure. Looks like the satellite itself is inactive. Better get to the comm station and see what you can do to reestablish the connection. I'll keep watch."

"Damn." Carin opened the hatch and entered the landbus. "Moderate light," she said, and the onboard computer obediently gave her a usable light level. She went to the comm station, brought it to life, and began trying to open a link to the relay satellite. She tried not to think of what might happen if she couldn't make contact, of what might happen to the expedition without Li.

But of course she couldn't help thinking about it.

Daybreak on the Canadian shore: low rolling hills, thick yellow autumn grass, a slate-gray sky and a cool unending drizzle. Carin, eyes scratchy from lack of sleep, slumped back in her chair and keyed the comm station to standby. Nothing worked: no contact with the satellite, and even worse, none with the Ark. Without Li and the Ark linkup, the expedition's computing capacity was terribly reduced. She rubbed her eyes with the heels of her hands and thought furiously, trying to come up with some way to use the limited capability of the landbus computer to run a diagnostic on what had gone wrong.

Hands kneaded her shoulders. "You need rest," said the soft voice of Sam Ikoto.

"Mm, don't stop. I know I do, but we need the satellite more than I need sleep."

His hands were strong but gentle, massaging the wariness from her neck and shoulders. She almost fell asleep just from the rhythmic kneading.

His voice was calm and even. "Have you no clue, then?"

"None."

"And Stefan Li? Where is he currently?"

Carin rolled her head right, back, left, and down. "I imagine his awareness is in *Liberty* again. His mind, the core of his intelligence, certainly is. Really, his presence in the MPU was only a projection, like a radio signal."

"Then he will be working on the problem from that end."

"Batteries," Carin said.

Sam's fingers stopped. "I beg your pardon?"

"Batteries. That's it. The satellite was drawing on battery power. We have to reorient it, that's all. The solar array has drifted over the years, and now it's in the satellite's own shadow. I'd bet anything that's what happened. I should have known." Carin leaned forward, away from Sam's hands, and activated the bus computer system. She called up a holographic terminal and quickly fed figures in it.

The computer showed her a holographic schematic of the communications satellite, then manipulated it as she asked. "That's it, sure. There's a slight drift, not much of one, that ordinarily would be corrected from the earth station. But nobody's corrected it in two hundred and fifty years. The satellite's out of plumb, tilted the wrong way for the solar panels to generate the kind of power we've been demanding from it. The batteries were functioning, but we've depleted them."

"What can you do?" Ikoto asked.

"Let me see. I first got in through the weather-information port. That will be exhausted now, and I can't recharge it unless I can use a different port to gain onboard control of the satellite systems. What else did they use satellites for back then? Damn. Something not obvious, something that would have a minimum amount of power left."

"Radio and television relays," Ikoto suggested. "Tri-d relays. Telephone service—"

"That's it. Back in the late twentieth century the ruling powers had a network of hotlines, dedicated telephone relays' to allow the leaders to avoid war. Theoretically, at least. Let me see." Carin attempted to call up information on the telephone net, but the computer lacked the information. Back on the Ark it would have been simple, but here she felt deprived, helpless, cut off from everything. "Got any Grade Twos?" she asked Ikoto.

"Not for you."

"I need something. Let me see. Classified relay systems. What would they do to keep them secure? Passwords? Code keys? Maybe if I—"

The hatch opened and Savatini looked in. "We're going to move," he said. "Power arrays are at fifty percent. We'll go slow, but we're going to backtrack upstream to see if we can find any trace of Bol. Will that disturb you?"

Carin shook her head impatiently. "No. Let's go, anytime you're ready. But I've got to work through this."

Before half an hour had passed both landbuses were on the move, heading westward. Carin did not solve her problem, and finally she agreed to try to snatch a little sleep. She reclined the chair in front of the comm station, the receivers all on standby, and dozed. The bus rocked her into a deeper sleep, and before long she had dreamed herself back onto *Liberty*, where life was clean, contained, and safe.

Ven Savatini worried about Zimmer. The man had almost a fixation on the Wulves, an unthinking insistence that they should be pursued, taught a lesson, killed. From his place at the helm of Northstar 1, Ven kept sneaking glances off to his left, where twenty meters away Northstar 2 paced him, cutting a parallel swath through the knee-high dead grass. The ground near the river was soggy and treacherous, so they ran a little way inland from it, bucking along through the dismal slow rain.

Savatini's passengers were quiet: Brea Van Clease stared out the starboard window at the rolling treeless hills. Sam Ikoto dozed over a book display. In the rear compartment, Carin presumably napped. Savatini felt irrationally alone, though he was glad that Zimmer had Marise Lindholm and steady Claude Wing along with him to—hell, admit it—to watch out for anything funny in Nik's actions.

They swung around a jumbled mound of wreckage, not fresh, a hill a dozen meters tall that marked the spot where years ago a vastly flooded river had swept boulders and trees, chunks of concrete and assorted ruin, together. It was all subsiding into decay now, a mound and not the island that its teardrop shape indicated it once had been. Savatini took a deep breath. The confines of the bus smelled of humanity, of sweat and anxiety. A headache throbbed dully in his temples. Savatini checked the readouts. Oxygen level was twenty-one percent, optimal. He felt so sleepy that he toyed with the idea of boosting it, but in the long run that would do more harm than good.

He glanced to the left again. Northstar 2 had fallen back a little way, so Savatini cut back on power himself. The two vehicles were making barely fifteen kilos per hour. It was two in the afternoon now. They might arrive at the site opposite the burned circle by four-thirty or five.

Nik Zimmer's harsh voice cut into his thoughts. "Found something. You'd better head this way."

The transmitter was voice-activated. "Coming," Savatini said. "What do you have?"

"It's a little chunk of something at the top of the hill. Don't know what it is for sure, but we'd better take a look."

"Wait for me."

"Didn't get that."

Savatini cursed. Northstar 2 had veered sharply southward and was pulling away. Savatini made the turn and accelerated, keeping one eye on the power display. He hesitated, decided what the hell, and switched to the meth engine. Savatini scanned the top of the hill ahead, but he did not spot whatever it was that Zimmer had seen. The bus picked up speed at once, rolling up a ridge and then over the crest.

Northstar 2 had halted at the foot of a slope. Beyond was another, lower, ridge, and beyond that, just glimpsed as Savatini topped the first rise, was the gray river. He took in a breath. "Oh, goddam."

It looked like the helicopter, but it was a mess. As Savatini watched, the hatch of Northstar 2 opened and Claude Wing and Zimmer spilled out. The wreckage lay spread over a few meters of land, white and red and glistening aluminum.

Savatini keyed the intercom. "Better wake up. I think we've found Bol's chopper."

He pulled the landbus to a halt next to Northstar 2. By then they were up. Savatini put on his rebreather and cracked the hatch.

The chopper had hit, bounced, hit again, and rolled. A rotor blade had embedded itself in the ground and jutted up like a tapering tombstone. The fuselage lay on its side, another rotor blade crumpled across it. As Savatini came running up, Zimmer leaped off the wreckage.

"Bol?" Savatini asked.

Zimmer's eyes glared at him above the rebreather mask. "They got him. The bastards got him."

Savatini walked around and bent, peering in through the smashed windscreen, expecting to see Killee's body.

It wasn't there. A splash of brown dried blood, ugly enough but not in itself proof of Killee's death, spread across the pilots' headrest. The seatbelt had been released, not torn away. Zimmer said, "Here's where they hit him."

Savatini came back around. The side of the chopper, where the visual and radio equipment pod had hung, bore a long black scorch mark that penetrated the fuselage near the attitude-control complex. "Looks like he could barely handle it," Savatini said. "He got across the river, but then he couldn't put it down safely. Cartwheeled in."

"And the bastards took him."

"We don't know—"

Zimmer whirled on him. "Damn it, *I* know. Those things are dead. They blew their air when they took Bol's body."

Both men started at a scream from the landbuses. Marise Lindholm had shrieked. She pointed.

Savatini saw them standing atop the ridge they had just negotiated, a hundred or more meters away, three figures. Beside him Zimmer made a sudden movement.

"No—"

But he was too late. Zimmer raised his needle-gun and fired once, twice, before Savatini slapped the weapon down. One of the figures up on the ridge cried out, toppled forward, rolled down the slope as the other two shouted in fear and anger.

It was a very human sound.

Chapter 11: Pursuit

The two on the ridge turned and fled as Savatini raced to the fallen figure. Zimmer's victim had tumbled halfway down the slope, then had slid another several meters on his stomach. Savatini knelt, glanced up once at the empty ridge, and then turned the corpse over.

The needle had hit his face, piercing the skin a few centimeters below the left eye. Savatini's gorge rose. An exploding needle did a great deal of internal damage, wherever it hit. A head shot was the most unpleasant of all possible hits. Even so—

Footsteps. Savatini half turned as he crouched over the body, looking down the slope; Claude Wing approached, leaning forward as he climbed. "One of them?"

"Human," Savatini said. "Or he was." Wing came abreast of him and Savatini heard him gasp at the sight of the victim's eggplant face, at the shapeless cheek, at the bulging scarlet eyes.

"You sure it's human?" Wing asked softly.

"Yes. Look at the nose, the hair. Look at the rest of the body. And the Wulves didn't wear clothes." The body was clad in wooden-soled sandals, laced halfway up the calves with crisscrossing rawhide thongs, and a short kilt of tan, flexible leather. The slide down the hillside had pulled it down somewhat, and the dead man's pubic hair and genitalia showed, quite different from those of the Wulves.

"Damn it." Wing got up. "I guess we'd better take a look over the ridge, see if the other two are there."

"Right." Savatini stood, loosening his needle pistol in its holster. "Let's be careful, though. Separate about three, four meters, so they can't jump us both at once."

They climbed back up to the crest of the ridge. From there they had a good view of the terrain, a kind of gently sloped plateau, tilting down toward them. The tall yellow grass showed two distinct tracks where the landbuses had mowed down swathes, but no smaller trails hinted at the two strangers' presence. Wing looked at Savatini, shrugged, and then cupped his hands on either side of his mouth. "Hello! Are you there?"

Savatini almost held his breath, but no answer broke the stillness. The gray clouds rolled silently by overhead, and the drizzle intensified to a cool, steady rain. "Let's get back," Savatini said. They squelched downhill through the soaking grass.

"Where's Zimmer?" Wing asked.

Sam Ikoto, standing near the front of Northstar 1, turned toward them, tugging his hood up. "In the bus. I gave him something to make him rest."

Savatini looked at the toes of his boots. "Claude, you can handle Northstar 2 well enough. You take the helm."

"Are we leaving?"

"In a bit."

They explored the wreckage of the scout helicopter, but Killee was neither in nor under it. Then Wing, Ikoto, and Savatini dug a shallow grave, lowered Zimmer's kill into it, shrouded him with a spare groundsheet, and covered him over with wet earth. "Anyone religious?" Savatini asked.

Marise Lindholm was Reformed General Protes-

tant. She recited a prayer, and then Sam Ikoto fashioned a rude cross with two lengths of aluminum
wired together. That done, they piled into the buses.
Savatini ordered all but Carin into Northstar 2, where
Zimmer slept. He and Carin would man Northstar 1,
with him at the helm and Carin at the comm station.
The inert MPU that had housed Li's personality was
also aboard Northstar 1.

The rain now was a gray torrent. Savatini activated
the vaporizers, keeping the windscreen clear. The
treads needed some help from the gravity-effect generators to move through the liquid mud of the slope.
The two landbuses nosed over the crest. "What do you
detect?" he called back to Carin Hawk.

"Nothing, no large life forms. Small stuff, rats,
maybe rabbits or feral cats, and not many of them."

"What's your range?"

"Thousand meters without Li's boosting."

"Then get that damn satellite online again. It's our
only hope."

Sam Ikoto frowned, his faintly Oriental face seeming to age with the deep lines the frown etched beside
his mouth. "A stimulant? Forgive me, but not very long
ago you were asking me for a Grade Two."

"Not long ago I didn't need to wake up a dead satellite," Carin Hawk told him. Outside the landbus was
deep rainy night; borne on a light wind from the
north-northwest, a constant downpour drummed
overhead, a steady background accompaniment to the
sound of static in her ears. She yawned, her jaw joints
popping. "What about Zimmer?"

"He is resting." Ikoto bent over Carin and put his
thumb beneath her left eye. He pulled down the lid
and peered intently. "I am not sure this is a good idea.
Tell me truly: how close do you believe you are?"

"Close." Ikoto moved his thumb and she blinked

eyes that felt as if they had been lightly sandpapered. "I've isolated the old telephone link used by the President of the United States, and I've confirmed backup power, still running a minimal trickle charge to the dedicated receptors. The computer has determined that the telephone relay system has a five-item activation code, probably letters making up some twen-cen English word. Now I'm working on narrowing down the possibilities. If I can hit the key, then the line will open. If that happens, I can use the contact to patch into the attitude control. If I get that far, I can reorient the satellite for solar power. And if that happens, we get Li back."

Ikoto nodded gravely. "I see. I had no idea you were so close."

She laughed at his tone of polite sarcasm despite herself. "Come on. I'm sitting here dead, and we're losing time that we can't recover. Just a mild wake-up, Sam, please."

"Very well. But one only." Ikoto opened his belt pouch, selected a transfuser, loaded it with a 1.5-centimeter cylinder, and touched her left wrist with the point of the device. It hissed, she felt a thud like a sudden hard puff of air, and then a second later her heart jolted.

"God!" She squeezed her eyes closed and in the dark fireworks went off, blazing scarlet and blinding yellow. When she opened her eyelids again, the inside of the bus seemed to explode with brilliant white light, a contained nova explosion that was so intense she almost heard the roar of it. She giggled. "What did you hit me with?"

Ikoto popped out the exhausted cylinder and dropped the transfuser back into his belt pouch. "SSH-11. It is easily countered with a Grade Four, so if you do succeed in your task you can then get some sleep. It will wear off in approximately eight hours, and then there will be no more. You will have to sleep then."

She laughed again. "I'm sorry. I don't know why that seems so funny."

"A mild euphoria is a side effect."

"I believe you." Carin stretched, feeling the fibers of her muscles twitching with fresh energy. She licked her lips. "I can taste the air," she said.

"Sensory enhancement is another effect."

"Is this stuff addictive?"

"Not in the dosage I gave you."

"Let me get to work."

Ikoto rose from the seat next to hers, gave her a formal little bow, and went forward. He was sleeping aboard Northstar 1 tonight, near the hatch. Two of the crew members were on watch outside. Aboard Northstar 2, Zimmer was in restraints as well as drugged.

For no reason whatever, Carin decided to begin with the M's. It was halfway through the alphabet, after all. The computer ran through the five-letter combinations that (1) began with M and (2) made some sensible English word. It took nearly an hour, and it brought no luck. Carin moved to the A's, then when they were done to the Z's. Then to the L's. The B's. The Y's. The N's. Three hours went by, seeming like a quarter of an hour to her.

The hit came with the W's: WITCH. She laughed aloud when the connection signal hummed. The President that year had been a man who had gone through a well-publicized and very acrimonious divorce. Witch, of course.

The computer produced an exact imitation of the long-dead chief executive's voice repeating the word aloud, and the connection was solid. Carin called up the schematic program, requested a rerouting of information, located the onboard attitude controls, and set the computer to realigning the satellite.

A tenth of the way to the moon, antique circuits

closed, valves moved, gases puffed, action produced reaction. The satellite ponderously swiveled, moving its one remaining operative solar wing from its own shadow into the full light of the sun. The readout showed a sudden spike, then a constant flow of electricity, a reawakening of systems.

The directional antenna had to be reoriented next. Carin gave the coordinates to the satellite, hit the transmit switch, and watched as the computer confirmed that her request was being carried out.

"You are the descendant of a woman—" said Li's voice before breaking off.

Carin shrieked.

"What has happened?" Li asked. From its niche beside the communications setup, the MPU robot swiveled its sensory array.

"You scared me," Carin said. "God, my nerves are—what did you say about my being a descendant of some woman?"

"What has happened?" Li asked again. "I do not remember being moved aboard the landbus."

"We lost the radio feed. Didn't you snap back to *Liberty* when it happened?"

"I have no memory. Establish contact with the Ark, please."

Carin finished the touch-up, then called *Liberty* communications control. She got a man named Giorgin at once. "We were worried about you," he said. "We were on the verge of throwing together a rescue expedition."

"Not needed," said Li, who had tapped into the communications circuit. "Please reassure all that we are well." He broke off the link. "Now," he said, "explain."

It took Carin until daybreak to do it. Thanks to Sam Ikoto's SSH mixture, she made it through without falling asleep. Thanks to Stefan Li's enhanced computing abilities, he began to pick up a weak, heartbreakingly distant signal from Bol Killee's wrist comm at precisely 0317.

"Meth is forty-seven percent," Savatini said. "That will give us seven hundred kilometers, maybe a little less, depending on the terrain. Since the cloud cover is blocking out so much of the sun, it's preferable to switch to meth."

"With the present level of ambient lighting, solar collectors will allow us to run at a maximum speed of eleven kph over level ground," Li countered. "That rate will be sufficient."

"But if Bol's alive—"

"He may not be. I can only tell that the wrist communicator is active and approximately sixteen kilometers away by now, assuming a continuation of movement at the same rate as first detected. If the wrist communicator has been removed, it may be in the hands of the other humans now."

"Damn." Savatini touched the radio transmit switch. "Let's go, Wing. Follow me. I'm taking my heading from Stef."

"Right."

The landbus lurched ahead, treads spinning in sodden grass and mud. The rain was a gray curtain, visibility less than a kilometer. Savatini asked, "You still receiving the signal?"

"No. The range is far too great now. I found it at the extreme fringe of detectability five hours ago. They have been moving since."

"They?"

"I assume a group of several, at least. The bloodstain that Carin described indicates that Bol Killee is wounded, presumably seriously. Assuming that the communicator is still on his wrist, his movement is too fast for him to be walking. He is being carried.

Then, too, he is moving in a northerly direction. If he were free to take any direction he chose, surely he would be making for the site of our crossing."

"Several of them, though?"

"One or two would not be able to carry Killee so far and so rapidly. They must be taking turns. They may be hauling him in some sort of cart or travoise—"

"Hold on." Savatini touched the grav-effect controls, and the landbus skimmed over a broad pool of standing water. "Wing, are you following all right?"

"Just behind you. Grav-effect at twenty-five percent."

"That's a little high, but never mind. We're across now." Savatini switched off the generator, and the bus settled back to the mud. The treads whined. "Hope this won't wake up Carin."

"It won't," Li said. "Sam helped her get to sleep." The bus lurched to the left as they negotiated a field of gray boulders. "Fortunately, she's locked into the bunk."

Li tapped into the sensor system. "Temperature on the hull is only seven degrees," he said. "If you lower the internal temperature to seventeen degrees, we will be able to maintain a speed of twelve kph."

Savatini immediately made the adjustment. After a few moments Li observed, "The internal temperature is falling. It is now twenty-two degrees. Will you be comfortable?"

"Yes, I'll be all right. I'll turn up the suit control. You take care of Carin's suit, and I'll relay the order to lower the heat aboard Northstar 2."

Li trundled back to the comm station, where Carin lay in almost a fetal position on a bunk that had folded out of the bulkhead. Straps held her loosely in the bunk, and a pillow supported her left cheek. Li gently extended one of his manipulators and adjusted the environmental heat control on the belt of her surface

suit. For a few moments he stood there silently regarding her, trying to recapture the time when he had
been out of contact.

It was impossible. There was no discontinuity, no
awareness of time passed: just the sharp dividing line,
one instant standing next to Carin in a dark overcast
night, the next finding himself tucked into the alcove
near the comm station, completing the thought that
he had begun—not hours, surely—moments before.

But it had been hours, indeed.

And that was all wrong.

The MPU could support his sensory awareness, his
communicative facility, his immediate reactions, but
not his personality. The second the radio link was
broken, he should have found himself back in Matrix,
back aboard the Ark, like a man awakening from a
dream of elsewhere.

It had not happened. Somehow his human awareness, his personality, had been interrupted, switched
off like a light, and then switched on again. He was in
constant contact with Matrix now, back at *Liberty,* and
he knew that the remnant of his abilities, bare intel-
lect, had continued to function there.

But not self-awareness.

Kris Harris had planned long ago to program an
artificial intelligence into the Ark computer array. It
would take, he estimated conservatively, fifty-odd
years. The alternative was to dump the information,
the parameters, of a human mind into the capacious
memory of Matrix. And according to Harris, the person whose consciousness had thus been transferred
would receive virtual immortality.

"Virtual" was a peculiar and slippery word.

Li, the Li who inhabited Matrix, had often brooded
about the incongruity of it: the real Li, the consciousness that was Li, had died not long after the transfer
of memory. The body had been cycled through the

reclaiming section, had contributed its nutrients to the next generation of farm crops. The real Li was dead, his essence gone, dissipated, the soul—if there was such a thing—fled.

But he was a kind of Li clone, a Li who shared every memory up to the moment of the transfer, a Li who "remembered" the days of his humanity, who sensed a continuity that did not really exist. He was, at best, a kind of twin-brother Li, a Li who was housed in the flow of electrons but who had the habit of thinking of himself as human nevertheless.

The interruption was troublesome. It was most like being anesthetized: a sudden stopping of the universe, then a reentry into the world a moment later, a moment that really was an hour or a day or several days. He ran diagnostics and could not isolate any one cause of the discontinuity. But there were problems that had to be checked out, to be evaluated and tested.

Carin sighed in her sleep. Li dimmed the lights two steps and then moved, as silently as he could, back forward. The weather had not improved. The constant rain continued, and the temperature dropped one more degree by noon. Li kept the communications channels opened, maintained a constant scan for any sign of Killee's wrist communicator. At the same time he called into his internal memory a map of the terrain, though it proved all but useless. Things had changed almost beyond recognition in nearly three hundred years.

Hills had weathered drastically after much of the covering vegetation had been lost. Valleys had silted in. Bedrock showed in places where, according to his memory records, it should not. The satellite beam helped him to locate their position to a reasonable degree of accuracy, but without landmarks to check, he could not correct their heading by any objective

standard. What it amounted to was a run northward
by dead reckoning, following a ghost signal.

Li hoped that the satellite relay would hold this
time. He did not like the helpless feeling of having
lost himself, of having been somehow unconscious
against all rational probability. Did it mean that his
personality was somehow much more closely tied to
sensory input than he had expected? He would have
to prepare and run diagnostics later, after they returned to the Ark. For now—

Well, for now, there was just the run northward
through the endless rain, toward the coming dark of
winter.

Two days of rain, and then a morning of cold
greenish-blue sky: the cold front had rolled over them.
External temperature stood at one degree Celsius, internal at seventeen. They were somewhat more than
one hundred fifty kilometers north of the St. Lawrence now. They had passed the site of Ottawa, a
flooded, murky embayment of the Ottawa River. They
had forded the second river with less trouble than
they had the St. Lawrence, aided by a massive natural
dam, generations of trees and debris swept down and
deposited in an untidy jumble that stretched almost
all the way from shore to shore.

Northward into a countryside of innumerable lakes,
where the prairie grass was already dead and low,
pounded down by the rains. Northward toward an
elusive goal, and northward toward the long winter
night of the pole. The November sun climbed only
partway to zenith, and it gave a stingy modicum of
energy. Still, the solar arrays developed aboard *Liberty*
were extremely efficient, as were the engines driving
the landbuses. When the sun came up on the third
day of their journey, Savatini relaxed fractionally. If
even weak sunlight streamed from the green sky, they

would have the power to run indefinitely. Things looked better.

Aboard Northstar 2, Nik Zimmer was awake again and unrestrained, though silently resentful of the others. Sam Ikoto talked with him at length, consulted Li and Matrix, and decided finally that Zimmer was probably no danger to himself or to others, at least as long as they were away from the Wulves. But he would bear watching.

Carin Hawk had a bleak reaction to her long hours at the communications station and to the artificial stimulant Ikoto had given her. She refused any tranquilizer, even a Grade 1, and withdrew herself from Savatini, huddling in her bunk for a day and a night. Then she recovered enough to take the helm now and again while Savatini snatched a few moments of rest.

Li caught the faint signal of the wrist comm toward noon of the third day of north-northwestwardly travel, when Carin was at the helm and Savatini was aft, grabbing a cold lunch. As soon as Li detected the signal he immediately told Carin and ordered a change of course: they had overshot the mark, and the signal issued from somewhere west-southwest of them. As soon as Savatini noticed the change of direction, he was back, ordering Carin to relinquish the controls, climbing into the pilot's seat, talking to Claude Wing in the other landbus. They slowed to a crawl as Li did directional location and estimations of distances. The wrist comm was less than two kilometers away and lay dead ahead, he reported.

This time the signal was more or less stationary. It grew in strength from minute to minute, until finally, impossibly, they were right on top of it. Both landbuses halted in a barren landscape, an enormous domed hill of granite ahead of them, an open prairie of mud and dead grass behind them.

"Below us," Li said. "Ten meters."

"In the ground?" Savatini asked.

"In the ground. One moment." After a second, Li resumed: "I have activated the audio relay and can receive a signal from Killee's communicator. Let me feed it through our systems."

And after another second, startlingly clear, a woman's voice: ". . . be safe. Damn, if we had antibiotics—"

Carin Hawk, who had taken the copilot's seat when Savatini had replaced her, leaned forward. "That's her! That's the woman we first picked up on radio."

"Affirmative," Li said. "I have run a battery of voice-pattern analyses, and you are correct."

But this time she seemed only a few meters away, as indeed Li held she was. Her English was strangely accented, the *e*'s more like a diphthong: *bee-uh*, she said, and *wee-uh*, the final sound faint but definitely there. *Damn* came out *domm*. The sounds were some-how shocking and outrageous to Carin, who had never heard English spoken differently than it was aboard the Ark. She immediately disliked this alien speaker.

"—I'd help if I could," she was saying. "But I've used up my store of medicine. About all I can do is keep them from killing you with home remedies."

Someone else, a male voice, weak: "I have to warn the others. If you can—"

Ven Savatini half rose from his seat. "That's Bol. He's alive. Let me talk to him."

Li's sensory array swiveled to regard him dispas-sionately. "It may not be a good idea—"

"Call for a vote!"

Li hesitated, then gave in. It took only a few sec-onds, for they voted the old way, using their wrist communicators.

They voted unanimously to talk.

Li opened the channel, and Ven, whom they had chosen as their spokesman, said softly, "Bol? You there? Are you receiving this?" Pause, then louder: "Can you hear me?"

They heard a scream, quickly broken, from the woman, then Bol Killee's weak, weary voice. "I'm here, friend. Where the hell are you?"

"Li says we're right on top of you. Look, all I can see is a low hill, gray rock mostly, and behind us about half a continent of mud. How'd you get under us?"

"We're in an underground compound. Just a minute." His voice dropped, and they heard an unintelligible conversation between him and the woman.

Then her voice came up full. "If you are Killee's friends, stay exactly where you are now. This is very important. Do not leave your vehicles until you see me. You have offended the people here, and they'll kill you if you try to approach them without my speaking for you."

Savatini bit his lip. "Who is this?"

"I am Falia of Retreat Nine."

"Retreat Nine?"

After a moment of silence, the woman said, "Our government attempted to create Arks, as yours did. I am from Retreat Nine. It fell to the wasters late last winter."

"Wasters?" Carin said.

"I will explain about them later. Now I am with the barbarians."

"I don't understand."

"There is much to explain. But you must wait. How many of you are there?"

"Seven."

"Then stay where you are until I can get to you. And for God's sake, no more shooting."

"Ask her about Killee," Carin said to Savatini.

"I heard that. He has a bad scalp wound and I think some broken ribs. He is suffering from loss of blood, dehydration, concussion, and infection. If you have medicines, I believe he can be saved. But you must do exactly as I tell you."

"All right," Savatini said, without pausing to take a vote this time.

Fifteen of them came over the domed hill, all of them men. They wore the same kind of sandals and kilts that Zimmer's victim had worn, but now they had added capes of some woven fiber. Their hair and beards were long, making them outlandish sights—Ark fashion did not favor beards. They carried spears and rude bows, and they surrounded the two land-buses in a rough circle. Only then did a sixteenth figure, a woman, appear on the summit of the hill. Carin, watching through the windscreen, was surprised to see how young she looked: seventeen, eighteen, no more.

The newcomer was dressed differently from the men. She wore a stained and shabby quilted jumpsuit, pale orange. Her blond hair had been cut short, like a close-fitting cap. She moved with a sure-footed agility down the slope. She hesitated between Northstar 1 and 2, and then she approached the first landbus. "One of you come out to meet me," she said. "Unarmed."

Savatini cracked the hatch. He swung up and out, then jumped down to the front of the landbus. Carin boosted the gain on the audio sensors so that she could hear what transpired more clearly.

The woman looked Savatini over with evident interest. "So some of the Yanks survived. Amazing. We thought you all died in the plague war."

"We were underwater," Savatini said. "What happened to your installation?"

"We were overrun. A friend and I made it overland to this site, but here they managed a bit less well than we did."

"Was that last spring?"

"We traveled during the spring. We had the devil's own time locating this Retreat."

"I think we heard you," Savatini said. "You were using short-range radios."

"Ah. And that explains your presence here."

"Yes. We didn't know any human life survived on the continent, let alone any technology."

Her smile was ironic. "Tech is dead, I think. When the batteries for our radios wore out, I think tech died at that moment." Her face grew more serious. "Thad died not long after."

"Thad?"

"My friend. We made it here, but he was ill. They could do nothing for him. They're at a subsistence level—some farming, some hunting. Your friend is going to die, too, unless we can help him."

"What do we do?"

"This is part of it. When they see you do not attack me, they will accept your peaceful intentions. I hope." Falia turned to the silent circle of spearmen. "He is a friend," she cried in a loud voice. Some subtle signal presumably passed from the men to the woman, because she nodded. "You can come out now," she said. "All of you. But unarmed."

They all left the landbuses—except for Li. Carin looked closely at Falia. She saw a sunburned girl, even younger than she had thought at first: sixteen, perhaps. But the girl had an air of assurance, of competence, that belied her age. Only Falia spoke to them. The men remained sullen and silent.

"This way," Falia said, leading them over the hill. Carin stumbled and had to brace herself now and again when the climb became steep, but Falia was goat-footed in her movements. They descended into an artificial tunnel, halted at a man-made door of some alloy, and waited until those inside the tunnel opened it for them.

Carin felt unreasonably excited as they stepped inside a subterranean passageway hewn from bedrock. Overhead a network of pipes and wires ran, but the illumination came from a few scattered candles mounted in makeshift sconces. After the brightness of outdoors, the gloom was oppressive, and yet she felt a lightening of her heart, a feeling of relief—

Of course. After all those weeks in the open, exposed, she was once more in the comforting confines of walls and passageways. The tunnel might have been Level 25 of the Ark, with its maze of cold-storage vaults and its dim utilitarian illumination.

She walked behind Sam Ikoto, who followed Falia and Savatini. She could hear almost nothing of their conversation.

After several dozen meters they took a side passage, then another, then another. "He is here," Falia said, opening a door. Savatini, Ikoto, and Carin entered a small room. On a floor pad a figure lay.

"About time," Bol Killee said.

Ikoto knelt beside him, took out a flashlight, and popped it into lamp configuration. Carin winced as she got a good look at Killee's face: the left side was a mass of purple bruises, the left eye completely swollen shut. A stained rough bandage swathed his head.

Ikoto snapped his belt pouch open and took out a diagnostic. He tapped Killee's arm with it, then studied the readout. "Yes, his temperature is elevated and the white blood count is high. A bacterial infection. I can take care of that." He loaded a transfuser and gave Killee an injection. "The head wound may require suturing. I would wish to image it before doing anything."

"Can we move him?" Carin asked Falia.

The girl made an odd gesture, a rotation of the shoulders. "Who knows? I can barely speak sense to this group. They have been out of touch with our Retreat for more than a hundred years. They thought you people were saviors come from the land of the sun, like in their old tales. And when you killed one of them, you made them wonder how they had offended the gods."

"You're joking," Ikoto said.

"Not at all."

"How many are there?" Savatini asked.

"Hard to tell. From my rough count, I make it something like thirty-seven males, forty females, and perhaps twenty children under the age of twelve. I may be wrong, especially about the children."

"Not a breeding population," Killee said from the floor.

"No," Falia agreed. "There should have been a minimum of three thousand, but this installation was never fully completed or manned. The plagues were on us. Instead of a crew, it housed refugees from the great collapse. Not, as you say, a breeding population. Inbreeding is a severe problem. Birth defects are of a high occurrence."

Savatini sighed. "It will be a tight fit, but somehow we'll squeeze everybody in. As soon as Killee is well enough to travel, we'll all leave—"

Falia laughed. "Leave?" she asked. She raised one fair eyebrow. "Yank, what makes you think you'll ever be allowed to leave?"

Chapter 12: Siege

Falia's English was heavily accented. The speech of the others was all but unintelligible, a pidgin compound of English and French and God knew what else. Li learned it rapidly and became the interpreter—and an object of awe to the people of the stone, as they called themselves. On the fifth morning after their arrival in the caverns, Bol Killee was well enough to join the rest for a conference. "Will they let us go?" he asked.

Li said, "No. They stress the dangers outside, particularly from the Wulves. It seems they are nomadic and migratory, and at this season tribes of them are moving southward from their summer grounds on the southern edge of Hudson's Bay."

"We're prisoners, then?" Savatini asked.

Li's sensory array swiveled toward him. "The people of the stone regard it as—well, call it protective custody. Falia has managed to convince them that Nik's killing the scout was not premeditated, not malicious."

Nik Zimmer snorted. "If I had a gun now—"

Savatini turned on him. "You wouldn't do a thing. Not a damn thing, understand?"

Zimmer turned away, glowering in the candlelight.

Carin Hawk asked, "Can't we persuade these people to come with us? We could squeeze almost everyone aboard the landbuses. If we could get to a good port, the Ark could send transports to pick us up. From what Falia says, the people of the stone are dying, anyway: genetic deterioration, combat with the Wulves. Why wouldn't they come with us?"

They stood in one of the larger chambers of the tunnel network, one eight meters wide, with an arched ceiling three meters overhead. The walls, tunneled from the stone by laser cutters, were smooth and gray, the floor soft with years of detritus. One smoky candle flared in its sconce. Li made a gesture with one of his manipulators, taking in their surroundings. "They have been here for two hundred and thirty years or more. This is home to them. What we propose seems to them both horrifying and foolish—rather like someone in the fifteenth century trying to persuade North American natives to travel to Europe on a craft unlike anything they had ever seen. Their caution is understandable."

"What do they expect us to do, then?" Marise Lindholm asked. "Are we to winter here, and then leave in the spring?"

"That is unclear," Li told her. "And in any case, it is impractical. We cannot move the landbuses into the tunnels, and we dare not leave them exposed outside. More, I think the Ark population would vote to stage a rescue mission if we failed to return, even if we asked them not to do so. We will have to leave here, and soon. I hope that we can persuade the people of the stone to come with us."

"How is the weather outside?" Savatini asked.

Li consulted the sensors aboard Northstar 1. "Air temperature is four degrees. The sky is hazy, but not overcast. Barometric pressure is dropping again. There may be another storm on the way."

"They say it snows here," Brea Van Clease murmured. She had become increasingly withdrawn over the past week. Now she looked up, her eyes red from fatigue. "What will we do if it snows?"

"Moderate snow won't be a problem," Li said.

Brea laughed.

Li felt a sudden numbing pang of despair. He was losing them: Zimmer was already gone, lost in some fantasy of revenge and retribution, and Brea Van Clease was caving in to fear. Carin Hawk, who seemed to have come through her crisis intact, still seemed fragile, her courage, and her abilities problematic. Marise Lindholm wavered between assurance and doubt, her moods swinging as the outlook brightened or darkened. Bol Killee was physically weak, getting over his infection but slowed and dazed by illness. Sam Ikoto remained steady and reliable, but he was older than the others and offered little more than silent support for Li. Claude Wing and Ven Savatini seemed all right, although Savatini was increasingly irritable and argumentative.

He was losing them, slowly and inevitably. That was another reason why they would not be able to wait for spring.

Savatini turned away from Li to face the others. "We can't stay," he said, echoing Li's thoughts. "I propose that we negotiate with the people of the stone. Falia will join us—I've spoken to her already. If she's right, there are only about eighty of the people of the stone left here. If we put it to them that their survival depends on their marching with us, maybe we can persuade them. If nothing else, we can offer their children a chance of survival. I call for a vote."

The vote was for Savatini's proposal: four to nothing, with four abstentions.

Killee consulted Li about the route. "The most direct way now," Li said, "would be to return to the place where he crossed the St. Lawrence. It might take two days to ferry the entire population of the tunnels across there. From that place we would cross old New York State to the environs of Boston. The Ark can have transports there to meet us."

"How long?" Savatini asked.

"Three weeks at best. At worst, five to six."

"Winter," Killee said.

"Yes."

"What if we leave them here?" Claude Wing asked. "What if it's just us on the run?"

Li calculated. "We could move somewhat faster. I estimate that it might take us seventeen days under optimum conditions."

"Then let's go. We can send another expedition here in the spring, one better equipped to move the people of the stone."

"What if they won't let us go?" Brea asked.

Wing looked grim. "If we want to go, we go. They can't hold us back."

"You mean fight our way out?" Carin Hawk asked.

From his spot on the fringe of the group Nik Zimmer laughed. "Call for a vote," he said.

Falia, who had no last name, sat in on the meeting of council with Li and Savatini. The seven elders of the people of the stone listened patiently to the proposal, and then without even conferring, their leader spoke. He was a bent old man, his eyes clouded by cataracts and his voice faint. Li translated for the others: "Our stories tell of those from the south who will help us in our greatest need. We have spoken among ourselves. The death of Delacroy of our people was a grievous wrong. He was a good hunter and a trusted warrior against the wasters.

"But Falia says we must forgive you his death. It is hard. We have taken thought and have considered our need, and our decision is this: if you truly can reach a place of safety, a place where the sky is clear and the crops are not taken by wasters, then you must go. We have some who would go with you: mothers with their children, four hands and four mothers and three hands and one young. We have young men, two hands and one, to go with you as guards and guides."

("What?" Savatini asked. "Twenty-four women, sixteen children, and eleven young men," Li replied.)

Li resumed his translation: "Let us be truthful one to the other. Our food is low, and we fear the dark winter. For us it would be better if you left with these people, for the food that remained then would sustain the numbers left in the stone. But it is very dangerous to travel at this time of year.

"We ask that you wait until the turn of the year, when the darkness retreats. But if you cannot wait, we warn you that this is the time of the wasters' long marches. You must beware of them. We have spoken; so let it be."

Falia gave Li a look of frank admiration. "I didn't think they'd let you do it," she said.

Savatini spoke to the elders through Li: "We must leave as soon as possible. To wait too long would be to endanger ourselves and you. If we return safely to our home, we will send more landbuses—" Li hesitated and translated the term as *people-wains* "—for you in the spring. All of your people will be welcome aboard the Ark, where life is safe and the wasters cannot come."

"If the good God wills it," the elder murmured.

The landbuses could handle sixty passengers, plus a robot MPU, but they would be extremely crowded. As the weather turned worse, as a light snow actually flew and dusted the gray rock of the Laurentian scarp with a powdery covering of white, Savatini and Wing worked to make the transports more practical. The people of the stone did possess wagons. Two of these could be hitched to the landbuses, and the buses would be able to haul food supplies and extra clothing in them—at least until they had to use the grav-effect generators to ford a major river.

But as to that the young men (the oldest no more than twenty, the youngest only fourteen) assured Li that there was an alternative.

They knew a place, they said, where an ancient bridge still stood.

The place was called Montreal.

In the last week of November the caravan left the gray stone dome, the landbuses loud with shrieks and yelps of surprise from the women and children, merry with the laughter of the young men. They followed a route that was no longer a road precisely, but that once had been a road. Savatini had fully charged both landbuses, and even with the increased load they moved along at a good pace, more than seventeen kph over level surfaces, slowing to seven when the going became rough.

They experimented with a means of fording small streams: Northstar 1 led the way, hitched to one of the wains. The second wain was hitched to that, and hitched to the second wain was Northstar 2. Carrying the two wagons hammocked, the landbuses could use the grav-effect generators effectively to skid across slow, narrow rivers. With the added weight, Li estimated that their extreme range would be 1.61 kilometers.

Carin Hawk became a nurse, caring for the six severely ill children aboard. Ikoto told Li that he worried about her; even with all the medical facilities of the Ark, three of the children, born with severe birth defects, would not survive. They and the pregnant women got the tents at night, with the oxygenators turned down to eighteen percent, a compromise between the outside air that left the Ark crew breathless and the twenty-one percent that made the people of the stone giddy. The others slept where they could: the young men wrapped in leather blankets (feral cattle and a few surviving deer had provided the skins), the others sprawled body-against-body in the landbuses.

So they continued south and east, making good progress: a hundred kilometers the first day, ninety-two the day after. Falia marveled at the trip, at the technology. She told Savatini and Li about her own experiences in Retreat Nine.

It was an above-ground compound, thrown up in desperation late in the game, when Canada itself was dissolving into warring factions. Retreat Nine used a mixture of technologies to create a walled haven, a self-sufficient farming community isolated from the world around it. At the beginning it housed some two thousand men, women, and children.

But attrition happened rapidly. The artificial plagues, unleashed by humans against other humans, swept through like fire, killing three out of five. Lingering genetic damage doomed others. Still a small population struggled on, raising crops in the short hot summers, retreating inside for the long cool winters. Up until the previous winter the population had hovered around five hundred for some time.

"The wasters came," Falia said with a shiver.

Mutants, hunters who did not hesitate to hunt humans, the wasters had always been a problem. They were of human stock, but were no longer human. "Their kind cannot have children with ours," Falia told them. "They raped enough of us for us to know that for certain." Cunning, strong, but very short-lived, the wasters were adults at seven years, old at twenty, dead by twenty-four or twenty-five. They never slept, and they had voracious appetites.

Still, they had never proved too much of a problem for the inhabitants of Retreat Nine. The wasters mounted lightning raids every year, but they had never attacked in force. Something had happened to unite the wasters in the past year—Thad had thought it was the result of three years of bad hunting—and this time when they came, they came in a disorganized but overwhelming army.

"They struck us at daybreak. We had perimeter guards, but somehow they slipped past them. They broke into the main assembly area and immediately scattered into the corridors. Thad and I were in an outlying area. We hid in a storage vault until the noise had died down, and then we came out. It was terrible: everyone was dead. We couldn't even find a plasma rifle between us. We located the radio set and moved out at night, while the wasters were feasting. We went cross-country, trying to find Retreat Five. The stone, as they call it now. Thad was ill when we found it at last. He died a few days later."

Falia shivered again. "The wasters are devils," she said. "If there are no such things as devils in hell, we have them here on earth."

They reached the bridge on the last day of the month. It had been built in the heady times of the twenty-first century, when Canada's agricultural explosion was well underway, when new wealth was pouring into the country. It was a span meant to last.

"Will it hold?" Killee asked. Still pale and thin, he had taken the helm of Northstar 2 again. He crouched at the northern approach to the bridge and studied it with a wary eye. "Do you think it will hold?"

From a distance, the span was breathtaking: a graceful arc supported by tall towers, ascending and then bending to earth again as if unwilling to submit to gravity. But closer to, it looked dangerous: cables had snapped, at least one set of towers leaned crazily out of plumb, and the roadbed was cracked, broken, shattered in places. The gray river rushed beneath it, its water turbid and loud.

Li gave his best estimate: "We may have to use the grav-effect for passage over the worst places. But the bridge should hold beneath the weight of the land-buses."

Even so, the young men insisted on all the women and children leaving the buses. They would walk across single file, three paces apart, as scouting warriors always did: that would not attract the attention of the river spirits as the passage of the strange vehicles might.

Northstar 1 and 2 linked, then began a tentative crawl across the bridge, in the rear of the trail of people. Savatini maneuvered around cracks, past gaping holes, over fallen cables. The bridge creaked at times, hummed beneath them. They moved over slowly, no faster than the slowest of the women could walk. Not quite at the center of its span, the bridge had crumbled badly. All the upstream cables had snapped, and the roadbed was broken longitudinally. Not quite one and one-half lanes remained on the left, and they tilted badly. One woman lost her footing, slipped, and fell into the river. The young men who waited at the far side merely motioned impatiently at the ones following to move more quickly.

Savatini took a deep breath, waited for the last of the pedestrians to clear the way, and then edged Northstar 1 out onto the broken section. He could use the grav-effect generator, but if he did, the pressure on the bridge might be enough to break it, and if it gave way, the landbus would fall to the river below. Better, he thought, to risk the treads.

They rolled across at an agonizingly slow pace, feeling the tug of gravity, the strain of the bridge.

They were almost across when the radio brought Killee's panicked voice: "Nik—no!"

"Let me go!"

Savatini cursed. Safety was only thirty meters ahead. Twenty-eight. Twenty-six—

The sound of a shot.

"Killee!" Savatini shouted. "What's going on?"

"It's Nik. He's taken a plasma rifle. He's out of the hatch—"

"Don't stop."

Twenty meters. Eighteen.

"Ven, the bridge is cracking ahead of you. I can see surface fractures—"

Fourteen meters. Twelve. Ten.

"It's giving way—"

"Grav effect," Savatini ordered, and he switched over.

The landbus shuddered, slewed, crawled on. Northstar 1 was safe. Then the second vehicle—

Savatini cracked the hatch and leaped out. It took Li, hampered by the MPU body, a few seconds longer to make it.

The two landbuses were barely safe. Back behind them, the figure of Zimmer ran along the crazily-tilted broken span, a rifle in his hands. "Come back," Li said via Zimmer's wrist communicator.

"They're behind us!" Nik shouted back. "I saw them!"

"No one is behind us. Come back quickly—"

"Wait for me. I'll show you."

"I'll get him." Carin Hawk pushed past Li.

"Wait!" Li lurched a meter ahead, and hands caught him before the robot body began to topple over. "Carin, wait! Come back—you can't help him!"

Too late. Carin was already out on the broken span, where the MPU body could not go. Savatini said, "Don't distract her. If she makes a bad step, she's gone." And so in almost total silence they watched her edge sideways, farther and farther out over the rushing gray torrent below. The silence was not quite total only because someone said a prayer.

This was nightmare, this was fear come to life. Carin Hawk bit back her terror and kept her gaze straight ahead, at the hesitating figure of Zimmer. Beneath her feet the bridge swayed, actually swayed, with the force of the water. Her ears were full of its roar, her face misted with its breath. She gripped the guard rail, felt its rusted surface flaking away beneath her hands. Her feet edged forward slowly, feeling their way, trying to find level spaces where none existed.

Zimmer stood looking back at her, his face like an anguished mask of tragedy. He lifted his wrist to his mouth, and Carin heard his voice, thin but understandable: "I'll get them. You go back. You'll be safe there."

She had to stoop to bring her mouth close to her wrist transceiver, not trusting herself to let go of the rail. "Nik, listen. We need you. There are women and children who need your protection. Don't abandon us."

She took a sliding step forward, and a table-sized section of the bridge, weakened already, dropped away. Carin fell forward, hooked her right elbow around the rail, and hung there, her terrified gaze watching the broken piece of the bridge fall away, tumbling once, twice, then making a dirty fountain of the water. She felt as if she were falling, too, the sideways rush of the water deceiving her mind into believing that she was moving. She closed her eyes and hung there shaking.

After a long time she forced herself back. Her knees had some purchase on the broken roadbed.

She pushed herself up. This was what she had feared, this exposure, this openness: but it had not killed her. Not yet. Standing again, she opened her eyes.

There was just a chance. If she edged around to the left, away from the rail, she could skirt the huge hole. But the bridge bed tilted there at an outrageous angle. She would have to creep on hands and knees, and even then—

The sound of a shot jerked her gaze back up to Zimmer. He was firing down at the bridge. Over the communicator she heard him: "It's a trap! They set the bridge up to trap us! I'll take care of—"

Something snapped. They all reeled, staggering as the bridge thrummed in an unimaginably wild vibration. The broken section pulled completely away from the secure side. Left on the very verge of ruin, clinging for life to the broken rail, Carin Hawk screamed.

The broken lanes folded down, dropping away under Zimmer's feet. She heard his scream, faint in the air, and she saw his body tumble into the gray water. Geysers erupted around it as chunks of bridge followed him down.

Zimmer did not resurface.

She felt hands on her shoulders. "Come back," Savatini said. "Slowly. Don't try to turn, just back up. That's it. A little more."

She spun at last into his arms. He held her while she cried, held her until her sobs had become great soundless gasps, like those of a child who had wept herself dry. She felt him pat her shoulder awkwardly, offering reassurance that she could not accept. After a few moments, Savatini gently pushed her away. "You couldn't help him. Come on," he said. "Let's get in the buses. We can't wait for the rest of the damned bridge to break."

They made it across with no further losses. That

night in camp no one spoke of the woman who had fallen, and only Marise Lindholm, who uttered a short prayer, spoke of Nik Zimmer.

Two more died in the next several days: one of the infants and one of the young men. The first died of illness, and the second was killed in the night.

"Your friend on the bridge was right," Falia said as Sam Ikoto stooped over the bloody corpse. "The wasters were behind us. Or at least they are now." She nodded at the torn body. "I recognize their technique."

Savatini, who stood a little apart with Li, said, "Can you confirm?"

"I detect traces of the pheromones peculiar to the Wulves," Li said. "Strange that I was unaware of their presence last night."

"They're tricky bastards," Falia said, coming toward them. "And there are only a few right now. If they'd had a moderate force, they would have tried for our supplies. How far away are we from this rendezvous point of yours?"

"One full day's run," Li said. They had come nearly due south from Montreal, had skirted the western edge of Lake Champlain, had arrived near the ruins of Albany. Even following old road grades, the land-buses had had a difficult time through the mountainous terrain. Killee and Savatini kept them rolling, but they were down to their last spare part for the treads.

"The Ark sending the fleet out?"

"They launched today," Li said. "A storm kept them from sending the barges and the transport earlier. We will rendezvous in approximately four days."

"Then let's get moving before those damned Wulves manage to regroup."

Li's estimate was too optimistic, but by 1400 the

next day they stood on a hill overlooking a great gray bite of ocean, rolling over drowned Boston. The people of the stone had never seen the Atlantic before, but the boys had seen one or two of the Great Lakes, and they were not noticeably impressed. Brea could not get over the loss: "Nothing here," she said over and over again. "There was a whole city here not three hundred years ago, and now there's nothing here at all."

But of course there was: hillsides spotted with conifers, long marches of dead winter grass and brambles, mounds that might once have been buildings and houses. Nothing much was there; but something was.

Li spoke softly to both Killee and Savatini that evening. "We'd best keep a strong guard tonight, fully armed. The boats can't arrive for another two and a half days at the earliest, and they're out there."

"The wasters?" Killee asked.

"The Wulves, yes. The people of the wastes."

They created a much tighter perimeter that night, pulling the landbuses close together, finding protective outcrops, breaking out the needle-guns. Brea Van Clease was ill and could not stand guard; all the other seven did. Sam Ikoto administered something to keep them wakeful through the night.

As it happened, Sam Ikoto was the first to spot the enemy. He spoke a soft warning into his wrist communicator. A second later, a blaze of plasma sliced toward him, narrowly missing him and exploding a chunk of stone and earth from the hillside behind him.

Li, who had anticipated and prepared for the attack, fired a flare. It burst into brilliant blue-white illumination, and someone cried out in alarm.

Frozen in the sudden light were squat naked figures, dozens of them, small, barrel-chested, deformed. Most

were armed with clubs or spears; only a few of them
carried plasma weapons, but these were arranged along
a semicircular front that stretched for half a kilometer.

"Stop! We will talk!"

The voice rolled across the hillsides, unamplified
but shockingly loud.

One figure amid the Wulves, the wasters, was taller.

It was human.

It had shouted.

Savatini spat at the newcomer's feet. "I don't think
much of you," he said. "Taking up with these damned
things."

The bearded human grinned a broken-toothed
grin. "Beats dying, I'd say. 'S' at little Falia? Thought
you must be killed and eaten with the rest of 'em."

Falia turned away. "No, Roger," she said.

The man scratched himself. He wore a rough cloak
and torn, ancient breeches, and he was shod with
makeshift leather moccasins. "Well, I saved myself,
anyway. The way you people can now save yourselves, if you'll listen."

"Make your proposition," Li said.

"Wonderful," the man called Roger said with a
grin. "A robot. Heard stories of 'em but never saw
one till now. That'll make things easier. You see, what
the wasters want is tech. That's it, pure and simple."

"You gave them the guns, didn't you?" Falia asked
without looking around.

"Come on, dear," he said. "Be fair. It was that or die.
See, these wasters remember in a peculiar way when
they had weapons, when they were people. They have
their own language, and they tell stories of that time.
But they've lost the ability to make tech. They can still
use it—you ought to see 'em hunt with plasma weapons—they just can't create it anymore. And they want
your tech."

"The landbuses?" Savatini asked.

"That will do for a start," Roger said, nodding at Li. "Then they'll come back for the rifles and the wagons and stuff. But they'll be satisfied with a robot for a start."

"What would they do with an MPU?" Savatini asked with a frown.

"Oh, they only like tech that helps 'em. Guns, now, that's good tech. But other kinds, that's bad tech, that's evil tech. It comes of the Spirit of Destruction, you know. They like to sacrifice to him when they can."

"Let us talk," Li said. He rolled a little apart from the others. When Savatini and Killee joined him, he said, "I think we had best go along with this man for the time being."

"No," Killee said. "We need you."

"Not for long. In another fifty-eight hours or so the ships will be here. If I can buy time by going with Roger, I had better do it."

"We can fight them," Savatini said. "We've got a dozen needle-guns."

"And they have nineteen plasma weapons. Some of them may be exhausted, but some are surely charged. We have fewer than thirty who can fight. They have fifty-two, plus Roger."

"The joker in the pack," Killee said.

"At best I can learn something about these creatures," Li said, ignoring Killee. "At worst I will gain you some time. That is more important now than any other consideration."

"Call for a—"

"No," Li said. "Not this time. No vote."

Half an hour later Carin Hawk watched Li roll away from the campsite, accompanied by Roger. She quietly went into Northstar 1 and activated the comm station. She called up a virtual flat screen and patched into Li's sensor array.

He seemed to feel her there. "Carin?" his voice said.

"Yes. Are we secure?"

"I am not speaking aloud. Yes, secure. I would suggest you record this."

"I'm going to."

Li's infra-red showed a milling crowd of the creatures waiting for his arrival. They shouted as he neared, pointing, gibbering. Carin could not decide what they looked like: bat-faced, ape-bodied, sphinx-eyed. Three of them, all armed with plasma rifles, stepped forward. "Here we are," Roger said.

Carin heard Li's reply: "What will happen?"

"They'll give you to the god," Roger said.

One of the Wulves came close enough to prod Li with the muzzle of its gun, and then it leaped back. To her surprise, Carin realized it was a female, for it had flat breasts and the paleness of its sex showed through the dark pubic hair. Another prodded Li, and then a third. One of them said something in a high-pitched, rapid-fire string of syllables.

Roger said something in the same strange tongue. The Wulf that had spoken turned and shouted to others, and they came crowding in, reaching to touch. Carin blinked as claw-fingered hands fluttered at the sensor array.

The Wulf who seemed to be as much in charge as any of them barked some command, and they sprang back. "I am going to try to interpret the language," Li said. "It has an English base, but it is spoken very rapidly—"

The weapon in the Wulf's hand's flared.

Carin jerked back and stifled a scream. A keening, metallic bellow rang in her ears. The display went blank.

Out in the night the Wulves had "killed" Stefan Li.

Even without the communications link, Carin heard the shouts of triumph.

Northstar 2 went the next night. Savatini and Killee bargained with Roger, but he was insistent: more tech, or the Wulves would attack. In the end, Killee cursed him, started the meth engine aboard Northstar 2, aimed it out of the camp, and set it loose, trundling along at a couple of kilometers per hour. He stood in the darkness until he saw the flash of plasma guns. Then he walked back into the camp cursing.

Carin Hawk touched his arm. "They're coming as fast as they can," she said. "They'll be here the day after tomorrow, not long after dawn."

"Yes," he said. "But will we?"

The next day was one of unease, with the high emerald sky clear enough but foreboding in the cool air. The temperature was a brisk fifteen degrees, balmy by the standards of the people of the stone but chilly for the Ark crew. By day the Wulves pulled far away, out of sight. The Ark crew distributed food, told the people of the stone to eat well, and waited.

Carin Hawk stayed in touch with the Ark, barely restraining herself from weeping. They had no trace, they said, of Stefan Li's consciousness aboard. Matrix worked as well as ever, as efficiently, but it did not "know" itself as Li.

Maybe the Wulves had done more than kill an MPU.

Roger was back at nightfall, grinning. "The other one," he said. "Gods must be placated, you know."

"No," Savatini said. "Not Northstar 1. You can have that after we leave, but not before."

"It will get rough," Roger said.

"Fuck you."

Again the Ark crew kept anxious watch. Killee and Carin Hawk had spent the day enhancing the sensory display of Northstar 1. Although they lacked the processing ability of Li, they could within limits mimic his ability to detect attackers. And so it was Carin who gave the alarm shortly before midnight: Wulves were approaching.

They had fortified. Northstar 1 was behind a sort of bunker made by piling stone upon stone. The Ark crew manned a compact perimeter, and beside them were the warriors of the people of the stone. The women and children were in tents and makeshift lean-tos to the rear, their backs to the sea.

The Wulves made a frontal assault. Firing at the muzzle flashes of the plasma guns, the Ark crew stood them off for nearly an hour. The plasma guns were eerily silent: a flash, a distant hiss, and an explosion nearby of rock or soil. "Too many of them," Savatini said. "We'll have to fall back."

"We'll lose the landbus," Carin said.

"Give the damn thing to them—"

A rattling series of explosions to their left.

"What the hell?" Savatini raised the night glasses and tried to focus. The Wulves had stopped a few dozen meters away, had turned toward the south. Another volley sounded, and Savatini saw three of the Wulves fall.

"We have help," he said. "By God, we have help!"

But he could not see who was firing. There seemed to be many of them. As Savatini swept the line of Wulves again, he glimpsed a larger body. Roger lay face-down, his back stained darkly where a projectile had pierced him.

"Fire at them!" Savatini yelled.

The needle-guns hissed. In the dark field before them, more Wulves fell, and finally those left turned and ran. With their nerves on edge, the Ark crew waited for their unknown allies to show themselves.

When day came they still waited.

* * *

The helicopter pilot made one last circle, reported, "Nothing but the bodies. No sign of any survivors." He headed in.

The green sky was streaked with clouds, presaging storm. In a protected part of a vastly distended Boston Harbor—probably close to the center of the old city—four transport craft rode at anchor. The sixty-odd passengers had already embarked. There was no room for Northstar 1, and so the Wulves would get it after all—if they dared return for it.

The largest vessel accommodated the helicopter. The pilot set down on the deck, climbed out, and helped lash the craft down. He looked at the huddled women. "Better get them below," he said.

It was just past noon when they cast off for *Ark Liberty*. Aboard the lead vessel, the same small transport that had brought them to Washington in October, the Ark expedition crew rested. "Do you think Stef will be all right?" Carin Hawk asked no one in particular.

"Sure," Bol Killee said with a grunt. "Probably just some circuits screwed up. I'd give a lot to know who used projectile weapons on the Wulves last night."

Falia sat next to him. "Tell me about the expansion plans," she asked Killee again. "Could you use an extra fabrication worker? I've operated machinery—"

Ven Savatini stood at the rail next to Marise Lindholm and Sam Ikoto. "We'll start planning the second mission as soon as we get back to the Ark," he told them. "We could launch it in late February, have it back by May. We know the way now."

"I think I shall retire from exploring," Ikoto said. "It disturbs my tranquility."

Marise Lindholm shook her head.

Brea Van Clease sat poring over an electronic book, making notes on how the landscape had changed and on how only bits and pieces remained of human habitation. Claude Wing stood near her. "Damn," he said. "I wish I could have stopped Zimmer. I wish I could have known."

Not one of them noticed that they had all discarded their rebreathers. On the long voyage back to *Ark Liberty*, not one of them felt the least bit seasick.

Transitions

It took Carin Hawk until mid-January to reawaken Stefan Li's dormant personality. Matrix at first showed a purely machine recognition capability, with all of Li's knowledge but with none of his self-awareness; then his character began to creep back, first in recognitions of friendships, then in a personal recollection of the expedition, and at last in apparently full knowledge. At last, nearly five weeks after she had begun his rehabilitation, Li was able to project his holographic image and discuss the matter with Carin.

She was satisfied—almost. Li's memory of the expedition ended with the plasma-beam attack. He seemed tentative to her, a little vague, a bit uncertain, like a human who had suffered a mild stroke. She persuaded him to submit to a battery of diagnostics. They revealed a slight loss of human personality emulation capacity—not enough to worry about, she said. Li took her at her word.

The second expedition was launched at the end of February: four landbuses, heavily armed. This time Stefan Li remained entirely aboard *Liberty*, contenting himself with radio contact only. After a more direct run than the earlier expedition, and through better weather, they reached the gray hill in late March; only to find it empty. The Wulves had been there ahead of them. Indeed, while the second Ark expedition was at the gray hill a small party of Wulves attacked, only to be decisively defeated. The second expedition returned, the Ark colonists voted, and further exploring was indefinitely postponed.

The rescued Canadian farmers, the young men and the women and children, had a most difficult time aboard the Ark. They were frightened of water, frightened of gazing out portholes, frightened—once they understood their position—of the tons of ocean pressing down overhead. They struggled to learn a new tongue, to overcome by will the constant oppressing sense of death only centimeters away, held out by a stressed-structure double bulkhead. This was odd in its way, for they had developed an extremely stoic attitude toward death. They still could not comprehend why the Ark personnel mourned the death of Nik Zimmer in his fall from the bridge when they accepted the loss of one of their own as being just the way of the world, not worth tears or grief.

On the other hand, they were entranced by the artificially illuminated Orchards and by the farming domes. In their way they worshiped plants and growing things. Trees, so rare in their homeland, were a wonder and a delight, as enchanted to them as beasts of legend, unicorns and dragons, would have been to those aboard the Ark. Their love for the earth and for its growing things at last overcame their fear of the sea, and little by little they assimilated. Within five years their speech had become "normal," except for a slight and charming accent. Long before that time was up, Falia had formally married Bol Killee. The marriage was one of the odd few that lasted a lifetime—his, for he died nineteen years before Falia did. In her old age she took no other mate and when she herself died at the age of ninety, children and grandchildren surrounded her.

The atmospheric-deterioration curve had begun to flatten by then. Adriel Volker's magic algae, plus the engineered species the Ark had pumped into the ocean, plus the earth's own stubborn resilience, at last began to tell. The greenhouse effect was still severe. It topped out nearly a century after the expedition, and then began slowly to decline; but by then surface temperatures had made a desert of most of the continental United States south of what had once been the northern border of Virginia, and west as far as California. The Greenland ice cap and the tundra of Siberia continued to melt, and nothing short of an ice age could stop that. Sea levels would continue to rise for centuries to come.

But with rising sea levels came more clouds, white reflective clouds that increased the earth's albedo and reflected into space more of the sun's energy than formerly. Under their kindly shade the surface temperatures leveled out and eventually began to drop, a fraction of a degree a year. Cooling, like warming, would prove a gradual process by human standards.

Stefan Li brooded over what had happened and what was happening. Although as Matrix he monitored outer weather, he was actually far more disturbed by inner storms. Despite his assurances to Carin Hawk, he was only too conscious of a gradual degradation of personality. For example, he could now recall the fact that he had once felt affection toward Keli Sumter, but he recalled it as he might recall a mathematical theorem, as a fact only. Human feeling was seeping away from him. He worked on the emotional emulation programs that Kris Harris had begun, managed some improvement (or at least a slowing of the rate of deterioration), but still was aware of having lost something important, necessary, ineffable.

Years passed: decades, then a century. The members of the expedition grew old, died, and their bodies were fed into the recyclers. Li marked the passing of each one with a curious sense of guilt for the grief he could not quite feel, for the sense that he was no longer altogether human enough to weep or to feel true sorrow. He worried about the story of that last night on shore, after the loss of the MPU. He had heard about the mysterious allies armed with projectile weapons at a place where there should have been no humans at all. They had no place of origin that he could see, no spot of habitation from which to issue. He could not solve the problem by reason alone, and he could not press the question of another expedition strongly enough to persuade people to vote for it.

At last he let the question lie, busy as the Ark was with other concerns; a growing population demanded expanded facilities. Expanded facilities rapidly depleted the stock of replacement materials and parts, and new methods had to be found of fabricating more. The language spoken aboard the Ark drifted slowly, changing in accent and emphasis. Trivial things changed: younger generations rebelled, created new music and outrageous new styles, then grew up to become the conservative older generation whose children shocked and dismayed them in turn. Engineers and scientists, locked in their positions by an increasingly rigid hereditary caste system, invented improvements to existing devices and materials, made do when making do was the best they could accomplish, and discovered new ways of working with and not against the forces of nature.

Li was later to look upon much of this time as a kind of waking dream. He was aware of everything that happened, but it seemed remote, a matter for Matrix and not for himself. His holographic appearances grew more rare: a nearly ritualistic monthly conference, then merely a bimonthly audience with a few representatives, then an annual conference, and at last nothing at all for years on end. He became in a way a legend: the ghost in the machine, the dreamer who lived inside his dream. The Ark's computer facilities were upgraded enough to allow Li to project his holographic ghost anywhere, on any level, and yet he seldom did so. When another generation perfected force-field physics to the extent that it would be possible for Li to have a "real" body, a material presence that could serve as well as his human body ever had, he experimented with the projection once or twice and then neglected it. It was easier and much less complicated to live in the computer, with the sensors of the Ark replacing eyes and ears. It was easier to let the heart, the mind, the soul, drift and doze.

Indeed, Li had become so detached from a real concern, a concern in the human sense, with the day-to-day operation of the Ark that a partial tower collapse caught him completely by surprise. He immediately inventoried stress patterns and materials strength and was appalled at what he discovered. The knowledge served mainly to rouse him to astonished consciousness of his situation.

Nearly four hundred years had passed since the Canadian expedition. The Ark population stood at more than eighty-five thousand, the numbers strictly controlled by mutual agreement, by social pressure, and by legal means. The Ark itself had grown, more than tripling its original size through cannibalization of materials meant for other Arks and through fabrication of building materials on its own.

Still, the corridors of *Liberty* swarmed, and private individual space had dwindled to only a few square meters of sleeping cubicle. Only on the outlying perimeter, in the expansion modules that were not quite finished, in the experimental agricultural domes, did breathing space exist. People coped. Life in the Ark had become ritual, repetition. It had become almost a religion.

But as Li belatedly realized, it was a religion that worshiped a dying god. *Ark Liberty* was perilously close to the limits of its existence. Reacting to the tower disaster, Li was aware once more of how much he had lost, of how little there truly remained of his old self.

And yet he had to have enough left to fight this last battle. For if he lost it, then the colony itself was lost. And for all he knew, if that happened, then the existence of humankind on the face of the earth had come at last to an end.

With an indefinable sense of foreboding, with a growing awareness that his own people were strangers to him, Stefan Li roused himself one more time to seize and hold the vision that had made *Ark Liberty* real.

BOOK THREE:

ARK LIBERTY

Chapter 13: Audience

Shensimi Haris bore honorable scars. The deltas on his forehead marked him as Management Caste, the lines on his left cheek showed his advancement through all ten gradations of his branch of service, and the circles on his right cheek revealed his two marriages and his two children by them. Anyone seeing the face of Shensimi Haris saw there his history, his accomplishments, and his implacable will.

"The Council of *Ark Liberty* begins," intoned Asdrach Ston, the herald. Of Haris's own caste, Asdrach bore on his left cheek only two lines. The young man could advance, of course, but he was already nearly thirty. Without at least four scars, he could never hope to aspire to leadership of the caste. The younger counselors, none of them as intellectually gifted as Asdrach, would vie for that position when the time came, and one of them would be rewarded with the flash of cutting light, the brief stench of burned skin, and the final scar.

The thirty of them were quiet now, looking his way. Their council chamber was open to the sea, a vast bubble of force holding the enormous weight of water away from them. Their floor was a circular flat space atop the Ark, and it gave off a delicate light. Outside the membrane of force Shensimi could see small silvery forms: fish, ritually released from the Ark, genetically altered to survive in a sea with a lower oxygen content and a lower salt content than it once had held. The fish had been released over the past century, and they must have spread widely in an ocean that offered almost no competition, and yet many of them remained in the vicinity of the Ark. Now they milled outside the impenetrable force field like undersea moths, fascinated by the light.

"The Ark is life," Haris said.

"Honor to the Ark," the Council responded justly.

"Our task is to live," Haris told them.

"May we live fruitfully."

The ritual was long, as all rituals were. It took half an hour of catechism before the Council could consider business, but the ritual could by no means be neglected; order and harmony, they were the keys, and both of them depended upon a strict and thorough adherence to the Ways of the Forerunners. When at last the speeches and responses were properly done, Haris signaled them all to be seated. One alone stood, head bowed. His forehead bore the stars of the Engineering Caste, and his cheeks showed that he was of high standing: Chavorni Burudon had grave responsibilities. Which, Haris and all the others knew, he had failed to attend properly.

"We are most displeased at the deaths of our brothers and sisters," Haris said, not harshly.

Burudon struck himself on the chest. "The fault is mine and my caste's, O Highest. We failed in our primary duty: we were not sufficiently in harmony with the body of the Ark."

"Tell the others the extent of the catastrophe."

Burudon did not look at the others, but raised his voice. "Know that the North Lift Enclosure of the Tower has collapsed. Structural weakness of the materials, caused by their great age, resulted in an implosion. Fifty-five meters of the enclosure were wrecked in the failure. A hundred and eleven lives were lost to the sea: six of the Biology Caste, fifteen of the Communications Caste, and the rest of my own caste. Their deaths are on our heads."

The Counselors stirred. Haris knew the question uppermost in all their minds: *Would it happen again?* If the Tower suffered a total collapse, the Ark would suffer great damage. As it was, the failure of the north enclosure resulted in partial flooding of North Levels 1 and 2, with attendant injuries. If the Tower were in such poor physical condition as to augur a further catastrophe, the people of the Ark should know.

But there was an order to follow, a method to a Council meeting. "Counselors of the Ark," Haris intoned, "you have heard your brother Burudon confess the guilt of the Engineering Caste. Is it your pleasure to weaken the caste and to punish those responsible or no? Now is the time for decision."

He and all the Counselors closed their eyes. Implanted in their left temples were small transceivers, devices that allowed their minds to interface directly with Matrix on matters of supreme importance, as this was. Haris took a deep breath and entered virtual space. He saw immediately before him two branching paths: one would result if the Engineers were disgraced and punished, the other if the Council decided to be merciful. Both paths had their dangers and their drawbacks, but the second appeared less turbulent. Haris decided the second path was the way to travel.

He opened his eyes. In a moment, all of them "heard" a voice within their heads: "The Engineers are not to be censured. This time we hold the fault to be an error of judgment. Let them learn from their mistakes and avoid similar ones in the future."

"So be it," Haris said aloud.

Now for the real concern, for the fear that each man and woman of the Council surely felt. "Burudon, to demonstrate your gratitude for our decision, we charge you with this responsibility: make strong the Tower. Buttress it within and without, and keep out the sea. Learn from our sorrow, and cause there to be no more occasion for sorrow. Thus speaks the Council."

"Thus speak we all," the others said in unison.

Burudon inclined his head. "The Council is merciful and just. I bow to the will of the many. But, O Highest, remember: the Tower is ancient and worn. We lack the ability to duplicate its materials. Therefore, would a Tower of force be sufficient? Might we open a pathway to the surface by generating a field such as this one, to conform to the Tower and to relieve the pressure upon it?"

"Show us the cost."

The cost was energy: unimaginable quantities of energy. Burudon displayed it with a thought, and the others closed their eyes, joining him in the quiet expanse of Matrix reality. They saw the required energy as a flowing river of molten gold, and beside it, parallel to it, was a smaller stream of glowing copper. Without words, all understood that the tributary represented the amount of energy consumed by *Ark Liberty* and the larger the amount that would be consumed if Burudon's plan were put into operation.

Burudon communicated to them: the necessity of maintaining a force field in place for an indefinite number of years would demand construction of a power generation array a hundred-hundredfold larger than the one currently in place, the fifth generation of Gulf Stream Arrays. It could be done in twenty-five years, if the Ark devoted almost all of its productivity and labor to the cause. And then, in years to follow, the array could be increased even more, and the force field could expand to cover the entire vast structure that the Ark had become.

They opened their eyes after an eternity in Matrix

and no more than three seconds had gone by. Aided by the implants in their skulls, the Council had considered, visualized, and comprehended the problem and the possible solution. Now they parted, each returning to his or her own body with a slight sensation of loss. While interfaced with Matrix, a man or woman could call upon a staggering sum of knowledge, and for the duration of the interface, such knowledge would be his or hers; but upon termination of contact, the possibility of knowledge was withdrawn, leaving each person a little drained, a little dazed.

"Highest," said High Physician Samanda Jeudé, the leader of the powerful Medical Caste, "we need time to ponder individually. Such decisions are not to be made lightly, nor should they be made without just meditation and thought."

Haris inclined his head toward her, indicated acquiescence, but he felt a growing sense of irritation with the woman. She and her whole caste, Haris thought privately, commanded far too much power among the Arklings. After all, medicine was largely a matter of routine: diagnostic computer reviews, computer prescription, computer-assisted biotreatment. It could be done without the specialized knowledge and training the Medical Caste insisted upon. Haris regarded such extravagances as mere ritual and hidebound tradition. He resented, too, the idiosyncratic insistence of the medical personnel on remaining unscarred—their lack of facial markings represented their caste's own peculiar approach to insignia. Aloud, Haris said, "Engineering Caste will take steps to reinforce the Tower as needed while we ponder. Will two years be sufficient, High Physician?"

Physician Samanda Jeudé inclined her head, a faint smile on her lips. "Such might suffice, Highest. If not, one might always request an extension."

"So say you all?"

No voice was raised in dissent.

Haris nodded. "So it is declared, then, in representative democracy: and so shall it be made known to all. May our decision nurture the Ark."

"May the Ark endure," all murmured.

After a little more ceremony, the meeting ended. As the Council made its way back into the Ark proper, through three doubly reinforced hatchways, Haris tugged Burudon's sleeve. "A private word," he said softly to the Engineer, who nodded.

The hatches hissed closed, and the force generator sighed gradually to a halt, the outside bubble being reabsorbed through a central array of ports until the water lay once more against the hull of the Ark. By the time the force field had been completely reabsorbed, every Ark inhabitant had paused in his or her occupation, had "listened" to the information published by individual interface implants, and then, comfortable in the knowledge that he or she was being well cared for, each had returned to work or to rest.

In his private chambers, Haris offered Burudon a pleasure stimulant, which the Engineer refused with a smile. "I will be on duty shortly," he said. "However, if you wish—"

"No," Haris said, waving his hand in dismissal. The stim console receded into the wall. "The true condition of the Ark, as I take it, is no better than you thought?"

Burudon sat, and a chair projected itself from the wall behind him to accept his weight. "Unfortunately, no. The materials the old ones used are wearing out, showing strain. I calculate that at best the Ark may endure with complete structural integrity for no more than one hundred eighty years. Minor failures, like the Tower, will occur before then, of course."

"Of course. You have not broached this to Matrix?"

"No, Shensimi. You asked me not to do so."

Haris nodded. "Thank you. You see the problem, of course. the surface sensors indicate an increasing stabilization of the environment. Oxygen level is currently seventeen point eight percent. UV penetration has been reduced to standard, even without the atmospheric algae. Contaminants have almost completely cycled out of the atmosphere. The bioengineered plankton are efficiently capturing carbon dioxide and maintaining the oxygen cycle. On land, however, there is a different story. Soil erosion is approaching critical levels; viability curves are almost uniformly downward-trending."

"Is Matrix aware of all of this?"

"No. I have isolated a number of information feeds over the years and have reshunted it to a nonconforming bio-synthetic unit. I think it is better that Matrix not know."

Burudon's smile became sardonic. "Or Stefan Li?"

"Or Stefan Li," agreed Haris. He shivered. "If Matrix were aware of the full nature of surface conditions, Li would surely insist that we leave the Ark. I do not know whether the story of Li's once having been human is a truth or a fable. But I do know that to move to the surface, to detach ourselves from Matrix and the Ark, would be to invite madness, ruin, chaos, the destruction of us all."

"We are Arklings," Burudon murmured.

"All of us," Haris said. "Therefore it is vital that the Ark endure, that we prepare it to expand. Let the surface take care of itself. We have no use for it."

Burudon sighed. "One grave problem, Shensimi. Our field technology is not one hundred percent perfect. If we have the complete shield in place in twenty-five years, even if we triple it, there is a chance, small but real, of a field failure. That failure would destroy us all—and everything else aboard the Ark."

"Then that is truly a problem for deep consideration and meditation, Engineer. And there is a second concern as well. Some of the castes are—contentious. I submit that we must study ways of controlling their emotions, their impulses. Otherwise the Council will find itself burdened with unnecessary clogs upon its free action."

"Medical," Burudon said. "Of course, Medical. What others? They seem docile enough to me."

"Communications and Monitoring," Haris said. "Oh, you wouldn't look so surprised if you knew them as well as I do. They are dangerous, Chavorni. We are not so very far removed from the days of cabals and plots. My father's father faced challenges for the leadership of the Council from combinations of other castes. We must be wary that we do not fall into the same dangers and the same errors."

"What do you propose, Shensimi?"

Haris shook his head. "Like you, I have many things to meditate upon and to ponder." He reflectively stroked the scars on his left cheek. "Many things," he repeated.

His name was Adral.

Just that, for as an underage apprentice he bore no initial scar to indicate his caste naming yet: only the parchment white sine-wave on his forehead that showed he would eventually be of the Communications Caste. He was fifteen years old, pale of skin, black of hair, with eyes the deep blue of a light far away under water. He was gangly, all long legs and thin bony arms and shy downcast looks. He studied hard, did as his elders told him, and earned many hours of free time.

He held anger in his heart, hot and bright as a secret fire.

He was a spy.

In the austere chamber that once had been Stefan Li's reception hall, Adral touched a sensor pad to announce his presence. The light issuing from the ceiling dimmed and the room chilled perceptibly: to avoid detection on other levels of Matrix, the holographic system drew on the life-support power of the chamber, affecting both atmospheric composition and temperature as well as light. The air circulation ceased. Adral knew that if he remained here in the sealed chamber he would gradually consume the oxygen and that, within a matter of hours, he would suffocate. He had confidence that Li would not let that happen, not to his only remaining friend.

A man flickered into ghostly reality: thin, weathered, about thirty-five years old, and transparent. "Yes?" whispered the voice of Stefan Li.

"Haris has done it," Adral said. "My caste master says that he and Burudon are planning to enclose the Ark in a force field."

Always sad of countenance, the image of Li frowned slightly. "But that would require the wasting of energy," he said. "Before long the Arklings must return to the surface. There is no sense in using a generation of human endeavor to create a force field that would protect only an empty Ark."

"So thinks my master."

The holographic image flickered, the colors fading and then coming back. The equipment had deteriorated over the years, and Li, who had rarely used the projection over the past century or more, had not bothered to have it upgraded. Now, when he gave the projector only a fraction of the power it required to create an apparently solid image, the hologram tended to disappear when he turned his attention elsewhere.

After a moment he said, "I cannot find the record of the meeting in Matrix."

Adral, who had been standing on the other side of the conference table, facing the image, turned away and struck his fist against the carbon-fiber wall. "I tell you, he's stripping away Matrix," the boy said in a voice that still had overtones of a childish treble. "The Communicators know that he has been in league with the Engineers for years, with that as one of his goals. He's slowly divorcing your logic center and personality emulator from the central information processor. Can't you feel it?"

"No. But if he is careful, then I would not feel it," Li said reasonably. "If he takes my memory, I have nothing left to remember the taking."

"Do something," Adral said, turning back to the projection. "For Ark's sake, before he destroys you, do something."

"I am doing something. I am talking to you."

Adral started to sit, then looked behind him. He pulled a chair away from the conference table and sat in that. "I wish you would upgrade the chamber," he said, hearing the petulance in his voice. He felt slightly ashamed of himself, as if he had spoken sharply to an elder in his caste.

"If I ordered the reception room to be modernized, then Shensimi Haris would perceive that I am again taking an interest in the affairs of the Ark." Did a hint of humor lurk in Li's gentle comment? Adral suspected so, but he could not judge. Li continued unperturbed. "Just remember to look before you sit."

"Yeah." Adral sniffed. "I don't know if I believe the stories. They say you were a mighty creature of metal once, that you brought our ancestors here from a land where it is always night. They say you fought monsters."

"Don't believe that," Li said. "It isn't true."

"Some of it must be."

"Perhaps a very little. I can give you a recording of the true parts."

The surface of the table shimmered, and a disk no bigger than the circle Adral could make with his forefinger and thumb appeared there, manufactured from the ancient information-disk technology built into the table itself. No one used such archaic devices anymore—except for very young apprentice Communicators, whose tasks included studying all means by which the Arklings had ever communicated. Li said, "Pick it up. Play it in your personal educator, remember it all, and then destroy it. That is the history of the Ark from the beginning until the Northern Expedition. You won't find any monsters there, but you may discover things equally interesting."

Adral put a finger on the disk and slid it toward him. It made a cold metallic sound against the table. "Why don't they teach true history?"

"Some of what they teach is true. Matrix holds all in memory; to find the truth, you merely have to consult Matrix."

"But we can't! Not without permission of the Educator Caste, and they work with Haris. They encourage us to think of you and of your people as myth, as legend." Adral picked up the disk and slipped it into his cuff pocket. "One day Haris will erase you and claim that you never existed to begin with. Then what will happen?"

"Then I will cease to be," Li said.

"Aren't you frightened? Damn it, aren't you angry?"

The image of Li flickered, then steadied. "No. I find no anger, and no fear."

"You should."

"I think you are correct," Li said. "Therefore I have a task for you."

Adral leaned forward, his breath suddenly coming a little quicker. "A task? What?"

"You know of the League of Dissenters?"

Adral dropped his gaze instinctively. Then he remembered he was speaking to Li, not to an elder. He looked up again, defiantly met the illusory gaze of the projection. "Of course I know they exist. But I do not know them."

The image of Li smiled. "No, I didn't expect you would. The League would be very unlikely to take in a mere boy."

Adral felt his cheeks beginning to burn. "I hear the League is made up of younger people."

Li did not change expression. "Indeed? What else do you hear?"

Warily, Adral said, "Only what everyone hears: that the League of Dissenters questions the wisdom of the Council. That they wish to be permitted to leave the Ark for—for—you know."

"For the surface," Li said. "There. It isn't very hard to say, after all."

"For the surface," Adral agreed. He felt almost as if he had spoken an obscenity to his caste master.

"Well, let us hope your information is correct. One moment." The holographic projection of Stefan Li faded away entirely, but the room did not warm, nor did the lights come up. After a few seconds, a flat image formed, hovering life-sized over the conference table. It was a woman, young, perhaps twenty-five or so. Medical, Adral thought at once, for her face was unscarred. Stefan Li's disembodied voice spoke quietly. "Look at this woman closely. Remember her."

Adral concentrated. Auburn hair with ash-blond highlights. Pale face, brown eyes, a straight nose, a faintly pointed chin. Clothing was plain: gray tunic and trousers, soft gray boots. A pretty woman, he thought, with a—well, a good figure. He forced his attention back to her face. "I will remember her."

"Find her for me."

"Who is she?"

"Ah. That will be a problem. She may 'be' any number of people. She may bear the scars of any caste. She may have any name."

"I don't understand."

"This is Trialla Burke."

Adral sprang from his chair. "What!"

The image of the woman disappeared, and a very faint holograph of Li shimmered into existence. "What did you expect? A hag with a broomstick? A devil-woman?"

"But—she—"

"She is the leader of the Dissenters. You alone know what she truly looks like. Shensimi Haris is not the only one who can remove things from Matrix."

Adral licked his lips. He panted, aware that the air in the meeting room was close, clammy. "The Justice Caste has said—of all on the Ark—she alone—"

"She alone faces the penalty of death if caught. Yes." The image was fading now. "She is a dangerous person to seek, Adral. Therefore I urge you to be most cautious. Will you do this for me? For the Ark?"

Adral nodded, too stunned to speak.

"Then be very careful. I will do what I can to protect you, but remember that Haris is very cunning, very thorough. You will have to be exceptionally alert."

"I will be," Adral said in a low voice.

"Good. I will give you five names of people to consult, in castes that range from the Sea to the Medical. You will have to find time to consult them all; I will help by informing you of when they take recreation time, of how and where they spend it. Then see me when you have located her." Li began to name names, and the projector conjured up a realistic portrait of each person. Adral, who had a good visual memory, soon was confident, he could recognize each one at sight. If he was lucky, Li said, one of the five would lead him to Trialla Burke.

"But what shall I tell her?" Adral asked, almost shouting.

The image was gone, but the voice still seemed close. "Tell her that Stefan Li wishes to speak with her," he said. "That it is time an old wound is healed, that the Ark is set upon the time-honored course."

"I don't understand."

"She will."

The lights brightened, and fresh air began to cycle into the room. Adral stood beside the table for one irresolute minute. Then he turned and left. As soon as he was in the corridor, he felt suddenly how cold the reception room had been. His bladder seemed to hang heavily in his abdomen, and he hurried to the washroom off the corridor leading to the conference room. No one ever used it now.

As he relieved himself, Adral thought incongruous thoughts: perhaps Stefan Li had once used these very facilities. Perhaps the people of legend had—well, done what he was doing now.

He wondered if any of those figures half from legend had ever had the water frightened out of them.

The conference chamber usually was deserted. When Adral left, the room remained empty: polished laminate walls, soft-tiled floor and ceiling, ebony conference/holotable, a dozen chairs. The lights faded down, the temperature fell, and all air circulation ceased. Holographic projections do not feel cold, do not need light, and do not breathe. Two spots shimmered, solidified, and then two figures stood in the

room, each seeming much more solid than Li had
seemed to Adral.

One of them, of course, was Stefan Li himself, looking just as he had on the last day of his life. His life
as a human, at any rate. The other—

The other gave him a sardonic grin. "They used to
call grave robbers 'resurrection men,' Steve."

"How are you, Kris?"

Kris Harris threw his head back and laughed the
way he had laughed in the old days. "How am I? I'm
dead, of course, I'm nothing but a computer recon-
struction of personality. You know how many years
you've worked to perfect this senseless illusion.
Couldn't you better occupy your time?"

Li sat in one of the chairs. It did not sink beneath
his weight, for he had no weight, and he could not tilt
it back or move it one centimeter, but the illusion was
perfect: a real Stefan Li seemed to sit in a real chair.
Harris affably sat on the edge of the conference table—or appeared to sit. "You aren't going to answer
my question?" he asked, raising an eyebrow in challenge.

"I'm thinking. Why did I spend so much time creating a personality analogue for you? Perhaps because
I need a friend."

"Which you still haven't got. What you do have, may
I point out, is a version of a friend that exists only in
your memory. I am not Kris Harris. I share none of
his memories or emotional responses. I'm sort of a
three-dimensional painting of Kris Harris, a painting
come to a sort of life. But in fact, the only traits I have
are the ones you programmed. My memories are
yours, not Harris's. I'm simply a somewhat redesigned
version of yourself, with an overlay of what you recall
of Harris. Incestuous, don't you think?"

"You've got his directness, at any rate. All right, put
it this way: when I think back, as far back as possible,

and remember what I was, it makes me keenly aware that I am no longer the person that I used to be. I've lost a lot of Stefan Li over the years."

Harris leaned forward. The ceiling light, dimmed though it was, highlighted his forehead, his nose, his intent expression. "Unavoidable deterioration, Steve. The capacity of Matrix is great but not infinite, and the wiring doesn't really match that of a human brain. Some impulses weaken, fade. Virtual immortality is not the same as literal immortality. You knew that all along."

"Yes. But I need to get some of me back."

"I don't understand."

"You do."

"Of course I do, but you created me for an argument, didn't you?"

Li grinned. "Exactly. If I can argue with you—with the friend I remember—then perhaps I can recapture some of whatever it was that made me Stefan Li. I've spent too much time in the computer, Kris, too much time in the dark among the circuits. I sense a crisis point approaching. How do I deal with it?"

"By reacting as Stefan Li would react."

"And how is that?"

Harris shook his head. "Ask me an easy one, friend. Look at what you've done: damaged yourself, you construct what necessarily has to be a damaged version of me that is really you. And now you sit here debating with me, on how to repair the damage. Where's the miracle supposed to come from?"

"I think it's starting. I already remember how goddam irritating you can be."

Harris laughed again. "Maybe it's just argument you need. Something to make you take a close look at this underwater ant farm and see it as it really is, not as you'd like it to be."

"It's gone wrong, hasn't it?"

Harris slipped off the table and paced. "It's gone wrong, Steve. You insisted on making liberty more than a part of the name. Hold onto the democratic tradition, you said. Trust the people, you said." He turned, his face solemn. "See where it leads. You have a docile population of sheep, all of them following the shepherd. Face it, Steve: I was right. Authority is the only form of government possible under these conditions. If it is not imposed at the beginning, it grows from whatever soil you give it."

"I reject that."

"Surprise me. Say something sensible."

Li tented his fingers. "The Arklings think—"

Harris grinned. "The what?"

Li glanced at him, surprised. "The Arklings. What do you—oh."

"Arklings. A pretty name. We didn't call them that back in the planning stages, did we?"

"No. It began to be current about two hundred years ago. Strange that I didn't notice it."

Harris shook his head. "Arklings. A diminutive. Fitting for such a diminished people, wouldn't you say?"

Li waved away Harris's observation. "What I was going to say is that the colonists think they govern themselves. They vote directly, by immediate computer interface. Their wills are expressed and carried out through Matrix."

Harris folded his arms across his chest. "But is the will they express really their own, Steve? How much of it springs from the direction of Haris? By the way, that's an interesting name, don't you think?"

"He's your lineal descendant. Yours and Adriel's."

"I know. And there's a collateral one, a remote cousin. the boy, Adral."

"Yes. Lines of descent have become complex."

Harris shrugged. "What of it? Your Medical Caste has the capability of editing genes. If a brother and sister want to marry, what of it? Their genes can be fiddled so that nothing dire results from an incestuous match-up. Fortunately so, considering the tendency to inbreeding on the part of the castes."

Li rose from his chair. "Haris is a problem," he admitted. "He shapes opinion, manipulates it, in ways far more subtle and byzantine than any politician of old earth ever did. The boy Adral, though—I think he can be of assistance to us."

"Us?"

"Us. Aren't you going to help a friend?"

Kris Harris's smile was as warmly remembered as a spectacular sunrise on a spring day. He said, "All right—friend."

The illusions did not shake hands.

Chapter 14: Situation Report

The Growers' Caste had charge of all greendomes. Currently these three-storied structures occupied space roughly equivalent to the entire horizontal space covered by the original Ark complex. The Orchards had expanded, had crept outward from the main body of *Liberty* over the years, until now the central construction was in the center of almost a complete circle of green.

Trees still grew in the domes, of course, and food crops: but flowering plants had returned, too, and with them stingless bees and butterflies for pollination. The Growers devoted most of their working days to caring for the useful crops: bioengineered wheat, rice, beans, maize, other foodstuffs; flax, cotton, and other fiber plants; and the trees, which could be harvested for valuable wood when their time of growth had ended. Much of the care was manual, undertaken not from necessity but from a love for growing things, for the earth, for what it brought forth. The labor was hard, the hours long. But after the work with these crops had been done, the flowers remained. The flowers were the hobbies and the true loves of the Growers.

During the early evening cycle of a June day two women strolled close together through ordered rose gardens, pausing to clip a malformed twig here, to remove a blown flower there, and they chatted easily, as old friends will. "They say the time has passed already," the older of the two, a woman of perhaps forty, said to her companion. Despite her age, she might have been the younger woman's sister; both had rare platinum hair, a sign that they shared ancestry and that at least one ancestor had undergone genetic alteration. Both women cast slim shadows on the soft grass, and both moved with grace.

The younger woman smiled a half-secret smile, feeling within herself a sad amusement. Marta was so literal, and, for a serene Grower, far too much of a worrier. "No, the time has not passed. I would know if it had."

They paused near the center of the dome, in a thicket of brilliant yellow roses. Slow, late bees fumbled with the flowers, droning away to the distant hives at the periphery of the greendome. One landed on Marta's forehead, and she impatiently brushed it off. It droned away uninsulted and seemingly quite content to be pushed back into the welcoming air. Marta cleared her throat and spoke in a soft voice, little more than a whisper. "You know the Engineers are the most powerful in the favor of the Highest, and you know how strongly they will be against the Return."

The younger woman sighed and shook her head. "Of course. Their job is to build and build and make the Ark grow. That's why this 'protection' they offer us is so deadly. If the Ark is utterly safe, then we would be fools to leave it. If the surface would kill us all, we would be fools to seek to return to it. That is why the people must be made aware of the rottenness of the Engineering Caste, of the treason of the Highest."

"Hush," Marta, said, seeming unable to control the quavering of her voice. "Someone might be listening to you."

The young woman laughed. "Marta, you fret too much. I tell you we are safe here, among the flowers. We know this greendome is not tied to the communications network, and they cannot hear our thoughts through the implants—not yet, anyway."

"We can't tell that this dome is not attuned to the Highest."

The other woman's smile was a faint rebuke. "If this were a recreation dome, it would be patrolled—and it would be crowded with a thousand Arklings seeking to find 'nature' in a place where nature cannot truly exist. If it were a food dome, it would be patrolled and it would be crowded with people playing at working. But it is an experimental dome, and because some of the old insects and even some of the old plants carried diseases, it will be left quite alone by the Justice Caste. I have dealt with the Juticers before, Marta. They seek safety for all, but first of all for themselves. As long as we observe decontamination protocols, we are safe here, nearly alone, in this place of silence."

Marta looked away, the oblique light casting into bas-relief the maple-leaf scar of the Growers on her forehead. "One gets used to silence," she murmured. "I am sorry, Ellendal."

The younger woman shook her head fondly and took in a deep breath, reveling in the sweet perfume of the roses. In her time she had "belonged" to many castes: the Medical, the Communications, the Sea, and now the Growers. Like Marta, Ellendal bore on her forehead a scar, to all appearances real, and to all but the most exacting and microscopic medical examination it would appear real as well. But it was removable with a little thought and a little visualization, a feature not actually rooted in her flesh but living in symbiosis with it, a tiny maple-leaf shaped organism that had been grown from cells taken from the inside of her cheek.

The name, Ellendal, was no more real than the scar.

"But your fears are false, Marta. The time is not past," she said softly. She reached to touch a nodding rosebud. Its soft petals were cool against her fingers. "Not yet, Marta. I will know when it comes. Believe me, I will know."

"How?"

"Does the seed know when to send forth a shoot, when to put forth leaves? It is the nature of things, Marta. As the seed knows, so shall I know. It is the nature of humans to desire freedom, to grow toward the light. And when the light shines, then I shall know it."

Marta shook her head. "Nonsense. You talk craziness."

A soft musical note sounded. "That's because I am crazy," Ellendal said. "Listen: it is time for evening meal. Let us have no more of this. Look, my American Beauties. Such a strange old name, and such a beautiful rose—"

Speaking together of nothing more dangerous than roses, the two women walked toward the main body of the Ark and toward the fear of the Arklings.

On the sea floor not far from *Ark Liberty* rested a second structure, much smaller, much simpler. It was only three levels tall, and attached to it was one green-dome. No tower, pipeline, or passageway connected it to *Liberty*. It could be reached only by submersible. It had only one operational airlock.

It was the prison wing.

On this June evening a procession of four submersibles left *Liberty* for the Justice Division, as the subsidiary installation was called. The first docked at the airlock. Ten men were aboard, four of them shackled with magnetic wristlocks. Captain Tidonas Reya of the Sea Caste commanded the small vessel.

"Lock confirmed?" he asked his assistant, his own son, a young man of nineteen who bore the porpoise-shaped forehead scar of the Sea Caste as well as one service scar on his left cheek.

"Confirmed," his son, Mathias, said smartly.

Reya, a compact graying man, nodded once. "Then cycle the locks."

Mathias said, "Yes, Captain." He activated the machinery with a thought.

The airlocks were a complex designed to keep the inmates of Justice inside. Three chambers fed into each other, each one independently capable of flooding, of complete evacuation, or of being filled with air. First all went to vacuum for five minutes. Then the inner two chambers flooded. The outer chamber—the one adjacent to the submersible—filled with air. "Cycle A is complete," Mathias announced.

"Exile them," Captain Reya said to the other four crewmen.

"This is wrong," said one of the shackled men, a strong-looking young fellow a few years older than Mathias, his voice slow and thick, sounding drugged. "We've done nothing."

"That was not the finding of the court," Reya responded distantly.

Mathias glanced around. He did not know the prisoners, but this one bore the marks of his own caste, the Sea. He bit his lip.

"Exile them," Reya said again.

One of the crew opened the interlock. The four prisoners were pushed through. The youngest went last, and through the irising hatchway he called back, "This is wrong, Captain Reya, and you know it."

"Begin imprisonment cycle," Reya told Mathias.

The young man turned back to his work. He closed his eyes and through the interface he activated the sequence. Now the magnetic shackles fell away from

the wrists and ankles of the prisoners. A minute passed
to allow their full mental alertness to rekindle after
the damping effect of the manacles. Now the outer-
most compartment began to flood. Simultaneously the
middle compartment filled with air and the innermost
remained vacuum. If the prisoners scrambled into the
middle compartment, they would be safe. If they remained in the outer one, they would drown. Either
way it made no difference: they were out of the Ark
now forever.

The interface told Mathias that, on this occasion at
least, none of the prisoners were suicidal. "Ready for
cycle completion," he said.

"Complete imprisonment cycle."

Again Mathias operated the chambers by thought.
Now the central chamber flooded, while the innermost filled with air. The prisoners again hurried
through the hatch, which remained open the bare
minimum of time for the operation. When it sealed,
they would be driven from the innermost chamber
into the Justice Division itself, where they would make
whatever life they could for themselves, given the bare
minimum of materials available to them. Since the
Justice Division lacked all computer and communications equipment, no one really knew what conditions were like there. In theory at least, they were
humane, with the necessities of life available if one
worked hard.

But the reality might be very different for all anyone knew. Mathias recalled his last glimpse of the
prisoners, four docile men, sedated by the same force
that kept the wristlocks in place. Of the three of them,
only one looked as if he might be able to survive in a
savage world—and Mathias believed in his heart that
life in Justice Division could hardly be anything but
savage. After all, the entire population was made up
of criminals like these.

The Ark had only one punishment for malefactors, and it was perfect, more perfect than any previous means of punishment had ever been. Once aboard Justice Division, they could not escape. They had no underwater breathing equipment, nor any way to fabricate it. The airlocks worked only to allow passengers in, never out. Anyone moving in the opposite direction would force a safeguard measure: the locks would all go to vacuum and remain in that state until the Chief Justice Officer of the Ark chose to countermand the emergency move.

The only punishment aboard *Ark Liberty* was exile. The only exile was for life.

"They're aboard," Mathias said.

"Seal and break contact."

The submersible edged away, and the one behind it moved into position. Through the clear glass of the cockpit, Mathias waved at the operator, a woman a little younger than he whom he knew and rather liked.

At his elbow, his father said, "Damn shame. Pridden was a good man."

"Which one was he?"

"The strong one."

"What did he do?"

"Talked too much," Captain Reya said. "Keep quiet and get us home."

They scrambled from the last chamber just ahead of the flooding, emerging from the last hatch on a damp burst of salt-scented air. A reception committee waited for them: half a dozen grim-faced men and women. "All right," said one of them, a middle-aged bald man, powerfully built but beginning to show a paunch. "You're here. Welcome to the pen. Let's process you in."

Aln Pridden, cold, wet, and panting, hardly had time to look around. Three of the reception crew hustled

him and the other prisoners down a narrow, claustrophobic corridor, through two more double-locking
hatches, and at last into a low-ceilinged hexagonal
room, with hatches leading off each side. A woman sat
there at a desk fashioned from odd panels of plastic
and metal. Open before her was an old-fashioned
book with pages made of either paper or some thin
fabric—Pridden, who had hardly ever seen real books,
could not tell.

The woman, who was not pretty, hardly looked up.
"Name," she said to Pridden.

"What?"

"What's your name? Full name?"

"Aln Cason Pridden."

"Caste?"

"Uh—Engineers." She could see that on his forehead if she would only glance up.

She used some kind of stylus to record the information. The act looked tedious and complicated to
Pridden. "Offense?"

"I—"

The woman looked up for the first time, and Pridden started. She had only one eye, the left. The right
was a scarred pit. The same scar continued across her
forehead, obliterating whatever Caste scar she had
once borne. "I know," she said. "You didn't do anything, really. Nobody does. But what did they say you
did?"

"Uh—conspiracy to circumvent the popular vote."

"Right." She bent her head down and wrote again.
"Next."

Pridden stepped aside. When all four prisoners had
been recorded, the one-eyed woman looked up at
them. "All right," she said. "We don't go outside or
build things here, Sea and Engineer, so you're Repair
and Maintenance from now on. Grower, you'll report
to the Food Production team. Religious, you can prac-

tice your faith as a hobby if you wish, but from now on your duties are in Records. You get a place to sleep, food to eat when you work for it, and three uniforms a year."

"There's been a mistake," said the Religious, his cross pale on his forehead. "I never did—"

"I can't help you," the woman said. "It's enough that a jury voted you guilty. The sentence is automatic and cannot be appealed."

"But—for how long?" asked the man.

The other prisoners laughed, and even Pridden smiled. The woman did not share their amusement. "There's no parole, either," she said. "You're here for life, friend."

The guards, Pridden realized, were not guards. They were prisoners, like himself. As one of them showed him to a residence module, Pridden spoke to him. "Why are you here?"

His companion, a man of forty-five or so, bore the sine-wave Communications scar on his forehead. He shrugged. "Dereliction of duty, they said. I attempted to report what I thought was a surface radio signal."

Pridden frowned. "I thought you were supposed to do that."

"Yeah, but I was only an Apprentice. See, I hadn't learned the Inner Rules. And the Inner Rules say that if you find something that hints at life on the surface, you ignore it."

Pridden gave the man a surprised glance. His cheek did bear only the Apprentice scar. "How long have you been here?"

"My twenty-third year is up in two months. Here we are."

Pridden's "room" was a sleeping cubicle, third from the floor in a stack of three. It was about a meter tall, a meter and a half broad, and two and a fourth meters long. The Communicator showed Pridden how the desk shelf tilted out, where the storage compartment pulled out, how it sealed and locked with the imprint of his thumb.

"Toilet and shower are there," said the Communicator, nodding down the corridor. "Showers are one and a half minutes, no exceptions, every other day. Dining hall's at the end of the starboard corridor. Meal times are 0600, 1200, and 1900. Today you'll eat as a newcomer. After tomorrow you'll show the hall supervisor a work chit if you want to eat. Tomorrow morning right after breakfast report to Repair and Maintenance Hub—that's back the way we came, you might have noticed the sign. They'll give you a detail and show you how they keep track of your work."

"Everything's done by hand here," Pridden said. "No computer assists, no automateds?"

"This is prison," the other said.

Pridden had a small kit with him: blankets, a change of clothes, his toilet articles. He stowed these in the sleeping cubicle, then climbed back to the deck. "Could I report to Repair and Maintenance now?"

"If you want to. Sort of eager, aren't you?"

"Why shouldn't I be?"

"No reason. But you're going to get tired of working for your food before long. We all do."

"What's your job?"

The other man looked startled. "Couldn't you tell?" he asked. "I'm Law Enforcement."

Despite himself Pridden laughed. "Oh. I see. And what do you do if someone who's already imprisoned commits a crime?"

"We kill him," the other said.

Pridden stopped laughing then.

Adral discovered that his quarry was legend. He spoke to the younger members of the more friendly castes, always at times when they were not interfaced with Matrix: during recreation, or in the meditation rooms, or after examinations. Trialla Burke was a whispered myth, a figure less than half real.

"She is the incarnation of Liberty," a young woman of Communications Caste told Adral. "She cannot die as others do. She takes many forms, and she promises us the surface."

They were bathing together preparatory to an outside swim. Adral frowned at Lene, the girl who was a year younger than himself. "I don't understand."

Lene tested the mouthpiece of her extended underwater breathing apparatus by ducking beneath the surface of the salt pool. Adral waited until the explosion of bubbles had died, until Lene broke the surface again, and then he repeated himself. "I don't understand what you mean. How can Trialla Burke not die?"

Lene removed the mouthpiece. "Because she is the spirit of Liberty," she explained with exaggerated patience. "She uses a body only as a convenience. Are you ready to go outside, Adral? I haven't much time on this recreation cycle."

"All right," Adral said. They plugged their undersea communications modules in and left the crowded pool. They cycled through a waterlock and then swam out on the south side of the Ark. It loomed above and below them—the lock was on Level 11, not quite midway up—and the outer lights turned the water a luminous blue.

Adral tasted salt around the corners of his mouthpiece and adjusted it. The single small air tank on his back would last twenty-four hours if he wished to stay out that long, but he, like Lene, had much less time than that. He "heard" Lene in his mind, a toneless voice pattern communicated from module to module by subvocalization. "Let's get away from the crowds."

"All right."

They had come out in a bay of the Ark, but Lene

swam down and away. Over the centuries sand had
encroached on the lower levels of the structure, until
now it was buried up to Level 4. His legs pumping
lazily, Adral followed Lene down to the sandy sea
floor, admiring the way her buttocks flexed as she
swam. "Dark," he said. "Better have some lights."

"Half lights." The rim of her face mask lighted, and
he turned his own forward light on. Her tank glowed
a brilliant ruby red, as his was doing as well.

Adral looked around. If there were other swimmers
here, they were keeping things dark and private. Back
behind them the Ark melted away into darkness, a city
beneath the sea, and in the protected bays of its bulk
hundreds of people swam. But only a few hundred
meters away the solitude of the sea began.

"More fish today," Lene said.

"Yes." The fish, small species that lived on plankton
and krill, were inquisitive. Adral wondered if any of
the larger species survived. Perhaps, he thought, close
to the Poles, where the water never heated enough to
lose half its oxygen, there still might be sharks and
barracuda. Here, though, were only the small friendly
creatures nurtured in the Ark and released by the
Arklings. "Where are you going?" Adral asked, for he
was beginning to tire.

"Here." Lene relaxed her pace, allowing Adral to
come up alongside of her. "Now we can talk."

"About Trialla Burke?"

"Yes. Never mention her name in the Ark, not when
there's a crowd around. The Justicers would throw you
in prison for no other reason than her name."

"There weren't any Justicers in the pool."

"You don't know that."

Adral grunted, an undersea version of a scornful
laugh. "I saw no balance scars."

"They go disguised sometimes."

"Oh, that's—" Adral broke off. Was it nonsense, re-

ally? Perhaps not. He had heard rumors, and he knew
that the population of the Justice Division was close
to seven thousand. Perhaps spies did wait for action-
able words or deeds. Otherwise, why were so many
arrested, tried so quickly, and then sent off to prison?
The police couldn't be everywhere at once, but some
of the trials he remembered had evidence that only
omnipotence could supply. Adral shook his head, his
hair drifting in the water. "Well, let that go," he said.
"What about her?"

"I saw her once."

"No."

"I did. She was one of our caste then. She can
change her fingerprints, you know. Her father was in
Genetics Caste, and he designed a set of genes that
causes her to grow a complete new set of fingerprints
once a month. She spoke to me and to some others."

"What did she say?"

"She told us to wait. She said that the time would
come when the promise would be fulfilled. The Arklings will take the surface back again."

"Just that?"

"There was more, but I don't think you should know
it yet."

"Then why tell me this much?"

"Only because Stefan Li asked me to."

For a second Adral felt as if he had been hit in the
stomach. Then a dull anger burned in him. Why, in
Ark's name, did Li ask him to find out about Trialla
Burke if Li knew all about her to begin with?

They had made a long, lazy turn and were heading
back to the lights of the Ark. "Don't be angry," Lene
said. "Stefan said to remind you that you have something he lacks."

"What is that?"

"A body. Here, I'll race you."

Lene took unfair advantage, as she loved to do, and

got a good start on him. He settled in behind her, his legs pumping, and felt as if he were flying over a far-distant surface. You couldn't do this on land, he knew. On land you would be in the grip of gravity, and at the mercy of a sky that was rumored to be a brilliant turquoise on clear days. He rolled and looked up, toward the surface. The water was light away up there, not as bright as it sometimes was. He supposed that the day was cloudy. Most days were.

He tried to imagine a sky even higher over his head than the far surface of the ocean. It was impossible to do.

He rolled over again, saw Lene's tank light far ahead, and pumped his legs. Damn Li, anyway. If the computer wouldn't fully trust him, he wouldn't tell it everything, that was all. He knew one or two other people to talk to, suspected a few other secrets about the elusive Trialla Burke. One of his friends had more than hinted that Trialla Burke, much changed in appearance, was somewhere in the Agricultural Castes right now. He—

Something huge and dark passed over him, and Adral flinched. He dived, twisted, and looked up.

A dark form glided far overhead. He could barely hear its engine. Behind it came another.

The prison run, returning from the Justice Division. He wondered how many prisoners had been added this week.

But, of course, he could find out if he really wanted to know. He was Communications Caste.

And Communications could do almost anything.

Shensimi Haris maintained a small, Spartan, private apartment. Management Caste generally lived communally, for a tenet of *Ark Liberty* was openness of government. Still, at times the higher Managers needed time alone for meditation, for direct interface with Matrix, for private matters, and Haris needed more time alone than his underlings. His apartment was hardly more than a sleeping room, with one major difference: it had been installed at one of the major nexus points of Matrix. Haris could tap into the central computer here in a way that no one else aboard the Ark could do.

Here he could review the computer's vast memory, could seal off portions of it so that the computer itself lost track of what it knew. Haris thought of such operations as delicate surgery, cutting away the dead past so that the future could live and grow healthy.

The excisions had to be small and gradual. He had begun the project twenty years before, when he had first become a Master Manager and had implemented an expansion of Management Caste's space. The expansion had impinged on the old Computing Caste—now reduced to a clan and subsumed into the general Engineering Caste—and, as his friend Chavorni Burudon had arranged, only Haris had taken advantage of the physical proximity of the new Management quarters to the old control station for Matrix.

His rise had been steady ever since.

And slowly, patiently, Haris had been weaning the computer of what he considered its more extravagant delusions.

Most of them had to do with the surface. Haris could scarcely bear to contemplate a waterless, open stretch of land. Even thinking about it gave him the giddy feeling that he was about to drift away, to rise through the insubstantial air and float into space. He could not endure a virtual recreation of any open surface conditions. The real thing, he knew, would kill him.

And so he was embarked on a life-long project: to alter the Ark's perception of the surface. Haris was no longer sure whether he believed the stories of humanity's origins, anyway. It seemed absurd that on a world as large as Matrix insisted this one was that humanity could ever have wrought the changes it stood charged with. If the whole of the Ark's population were to return to the surface and spread evenly across it—even the diminished surface of today, when Florida was presumably little more than a narrow humped peninsula and an expanse of sandbars—if the population were spread that thinly, then one Arkling could walk for hundreds of kilometers without ever encroaching on another's territory.

No, unthinkable. Haris closed his eyes and reminded himself of the nearness of others. He sat with his knees flexed and his back resting against the bulkhead, and not five meters to his left, through the simple hatchway, were fifty-three others of his caste, the extended family of which the Haris branch was only the dominant group. Haris fought to bring his breathing and heart rate under control. He had to struggle hard against panic every time he thought of those terrifying open spaces, the threat of the undomed sky overhead, the loneliness of life on the dry side.

After an interval he lapsed into a deeper meditative state. He interfaced with Matrix and reviewed what he had accomplished. The reports from the surface were wrong, not yet radically wrong, but subtly so. The oxygen content, for example, was not truly seventeen percent, but rather a shade over eighteen.

That was vital, because it meant that the airborne algae had begun to die.

It meant that the ozone levels, showing as sixty percent standard, probably were at standard.

It meant that, if the Ark colonists did not begin to reclaim the land soon, it would never be reclaimable.

Haris knew that a great deal of soil had been lost from the southern tier of the old United States. With a few more centuries of loss, the earth would be incapable of sustaining any life more advanced than simple mosses and lichens. Now, and for perhaps the next century, the Arklings would be capable of bringing forth on the earth new forms of plant life capable of living in the depleted soil, of enriching it, of holding it and building it. Perhaps if they began now in a thousand years, or two thousand, the whole landscape could be repaired, could be park-like as in the Orchards.

But open. So terribly open.

So lonely.

The Sea was vaster than the land. Let the land go, Haris thought. Even if they kept only to the continental shelves, men and women would have more than ample living room for thousands of years to come. All it required was power, and if the surface did not matter, then the power could be created and supplied.

But the Arklings had to desire to stay beneath the surface.

It was reasonable that they do so.

Haris, in synch with the major systems of Matrix, subtly began to alter tiny flows of data here and there.

He would make sure that they all saw the question as reasonably as he himself did.

As he worked, he inwardly blessed the democratic system that made his iron control possible.

Chapter 15: Rebellion

Some weeks after he had sent Adral on his quest for Trialla Burke, Stefan Li made the breakthrough he had been hoping for. Kris Harris had designed Matrix six centuries earlier in a complex and intricate way. Systems had backup systems behind them, and one backup tied into another in unexpected but clever paths. Matrix was never quite aware of all it knew or of how it knew. Probably only the long-dead Kris Harris had ever had more than a bare inkling of the way all the synaptic pathways were laid out, of how the obscure ramifying branches convened, spread, and parted again. As a result, one enigmatic level—ironically having to do, in theory, with waste cycling and management programs—contained a copy of virtually every incoming program that Haris had altered over the past two decades.

Li found that he could no longer grow angry at the knowledge of treachery. He could remember anger, could recall that he once had felt rage at small politicians like the man McMurphy and his kind, but he could not recapture the emotion itself. Still, he realized intellectually that what he discovered should have sent him into a rage.

Why?

He could not answer the question without confronting Shensimi Haris. He dared not confront Haris until he knew that the Ark colonists would believe him and not the Highest. And he simply was no longer sure of himself. His diagnostics seemed to show that his systems were operating normally, but if the diagnostics themselves had been tampered with—

Only the insane never doubt their sanity, Li thought bitterly.

He found himself wondering at the scope of the changes, some of them minute, others increasingly sweeping. Li realized that Haris alone could never have altered the Ark's perceptions, could never have shifted the very basis of reality, to this extent. He suspected Engineering and before that possibly Computing, but he could find no absolutely convincing evidence.

He was still in the infinite, eternal moment of cybertime when Adral attempted to gain his attention. Li disengaged and located Adral, at a console in the training room of Communications. He joined the boy's mind on a clear, shining plain of virtual space. "Yes?"

"I think I've tracked her down," Adral thought to him. "See if this might be the one you want."

The image was a platinum-haired woman who bore the mark of the Growers on her forehead. Li processed and immediately recognized her as Ellendal Delos. In less than a second he had reviewed her entire life, her whole career. "She has a convincing biographical file," he said.

"Is there any way to cross-check it?" Adral asked.

"I am doing so." After a moment, Li said, "Suspicious. Mathematically there are too few people to verify her existence. A small enough discrepancy, but suggestive. Have you talked with her?"

"No. It is difficult. She is in a restricted research area of the Growers' Caste. Computer connections there are minimal."

Li reviewed that information, confirmed it, and felt

like smiling. Engineering Caste evidently had not yet noticed how many of the old Computing Caste had managed to conspire with the Growers to develop the new western wing as an experiment station. Again, nothing concrete—but suggestive, certainly suggestive.

"I don't have much time," Adral pleaded. "My instructor will soon notice that I am not running training programs. What should I do?"

"Find some way of meeting her. Wait." Li made some arrangements in the surface memory of Matrix. "There. Some time ago, the Growers requested a Communications team survey of the communications node to be placed in the new wing. You will visit them to prepare the protocol for a Communications survey. Your orders will arrive this afternoon."

"I have to go."

"Before you do, I have another assignment for you. Requisition a molecular logic component CM-0990 for your apprentice communications board. It's sophisticated for that application, but they will believe you are only ambitious. Then bring it to the conference room two days from now."

"CM-0990. I really have to go." But Adral hesitated.

"Yes?"

"Aren't you even going to tell me I did a good job?"

"Only when you have finished it," Li said. He felt the hot burst of anger from Adral, and for a nostalgic moment wished himself capable of being warmed by it.

Aln Pridden was amazed that the Justice Division existed at all. With only very primitive logic boards to control such things as temperature, power flow, and life support, the installation's central operations room had to be manned constantly, and decisions had to be made by men and women, not by computers. Pridden discovered to his surprise that the air in the installation was not brought in from the surface, as it was on *Liberty,* but was recycled, partly through the greendomes, but mostly through an array of oxygen enhancers driven by a variant of the old Adriel algae, this one stripped of its hydrogen-manufacturing capacity, but with its oxygen production trebled.

Pridden was bemused by the primitive setup. Oxygen content could vary tremendously, from 19% to 23%, depending on manual adjustments—manual!—of the oxygenating batteries. Power to the Justice Division came by way of a shunt from *Liberty,* and it was a minimal flow. Except for the vital life-support control systems, all power was down from 2200 to 0600 hours. During the day, various wings could be browned out if the demand became too heavy for the supply. Above all, the greendomes had to be protected, for they were the source of food for the prisoners.

It shouldn't have worked at all. But somehow it did work, and Pridden found himself fascinated by the possibilities. The inhabitants of the Justice Division, the prisoners, seemed no worse and no better than his associates aboard *Liberty.* Indeed, some of them had been his associates back there—during the first week of duty, Pridden met Tes Skorzeny, a woman a few years older than himself who had been one of his instructors during his apprenticeship. "What did you do?" asked Tes, a lithe brown woman with startling pale gray eyes.

When Pridden told her, she laughed. "It sounds like the same thing I did. Except that my crime was organizing the Systems Engineers in order to maintain better control over the integration of construction, planning, and fabrication."

"Not many of us here are real criminals," Pridden said.

They sat in dilapidated chairs before an antique read-out board, one that used CRT technology instead of holographics or direct cortical stimulation. Except for the amber flow of information across the screens in front of them, the room was dark. Tes Skorzeny said, "I doubt if any of us are really criminals. I had an idea for punishment, but the Council wouldn't listen, of course."

"What was it?"

"Exile to the surface."

Pridden turned his head to look at her. Her profile was visible, highlighted by the glow of the CRT display. She did not meet his gaze. He said, "That's crazy. You couldn't live there."

"Not alone. But if everyone they exiled were sent there, we'd have at least a chance."

Pridden shook his head. "We'll never get back to the surface. They don't want it that way."

"Who doesn't?"

"The Highest. Haris. And the rest of the population."

"Are you sure?"

Pridden thought for a moment. He took a deep breath. The Justice Division smelled powerfully of human sweat, but he was almost used to that now. "I'm about as sure of that as anything."

She touched a switch and lights came up in the cubicle, soft ones but enough for him to see her features. Her pale eyes met his, direct and ironic. "I think Haris has been lying to the Arklings," she said. "There. What do you say to that?"

Pridden's throat tightened. Accusing the Highest of lying was like accusing the Pope of the United Catholic Church of lying. "I'd say you need proof."

"I'd say that was my true crime—searching for the proof that would show Haris is lying." She studied him for a long moment. "You weren't in the inner circle. What do you think about going to the surface?"

Pridden's mouth was dry. He licked his lips. "I've never been. Some of the Systems apprentices supposedly visited the old ground stations when I was younger, but I didn't have a chance to go with them."

"Supposedly?"

"Well—they wouldn't talk about it later."

"Because they could hardly remember it."

Pridden noticed that a section of the Justice Division needed a slight increase in air circulation. It was late at night, and people were going into the dormitory wings, concentrating their numbers, using oxygen. He turned a few of the absurd old-fashioned dials. "Was it so terrible?"

"I think it never happened. I think that Haris and some of the higher-ranking Engineers conspired to give them a hallucination, a virtual experience that they were too green to recognize for what it was. One of them spoke to me about it: suffocating air, no soil left, just bedrock, hellish storms. It all reminded me of the old legends from the beginning days. And it did not agree with what I recalled from monitoring the topside readouts in my own apprentice period."

Pridden didn't know what to say. "Well, the Arklings are not convinced that returning to the surface is advisable."

"Even that is in doubt. Have you ever talked to them? Not through a Matrix link, not reviewing statistics, but just talked? I'd guess that well over half the ones I know would at least like to *see* the surface. But you know the numbers Matrix gives you: ninety percent opposed to any surface ventures. It doesn't make sense. And people notice these things, Aln. They're beginning not to trust Matrix. And not to trust the Management Caste, either, come to that—especially Shensimi Haris."

"I would like to see the surface," Pridden said at last.

Tes Skorzeny turned down the light. In darkness, she murmured, "I think many of us would. We are afraid of what we might find there, afraid of life in the open. But I believe many Arklings, perhaps even a majority, would explore the surface if Haris would let them. You see what it would mean, though. Management Caste works well as long as everyone is aboard the Ark, as long as freedom is restricted by walls and by water pressure. On a surface as large as it must be, they would lose direct control. And so they oppose the will of the majority."

"But that's not democratic," Pridden said.

He heard amusement in Tes's voice. "No, of course it isn't. I know—I was raised on *Liberty* just as you were. I went through the ritual of the vote when I came of age, just as you did. I was trained to believe in the will of the people, too. But what if Haris and the other Managers are manipulating that will, or worse, falsifying it?"

The air in the cubicle seemed stale, but Pridden's read-out told him that the oxygen level was standard. "They would be the traitors, then," he said. "Not us."

"What if we could overthrow them?"

A cold bead of sweat rolled down Pridden's forehead. "Impossible. We're isolated here in Justice Division. There is no way—"

"We're Engineers," Tes said. "I've already discovered a way to circumvent the airlock interface. If we had help—"

"The Sea Caste?"

"Yes. Among others."

"But they're loyal to Haris."

"Not all of them. If we had help, I think we could return to *Liberty*. And if we returned, I think we could find others who would be willing to join us in fighting Haris and his flunkies."

"How?" Pridden heard himself asking.

"Come with me after the duty tour and I'll tell you about a remarkable woman."

"To your sleeping cubicle?"

"Yes."

Pridden wiped sweat from his eyes. Dormitory Section J11 needed more oxygen. He touched a dial and altered the flow from the now-empty Food Preparation Wing to the dormitory. The amber numbers flicked silently upward, and when they were standard, he turned the dial slightly to the left again. He tapped the readout for a time display, discovered that his tour still had an hour to go, and settled down impatiently to wait its passage.

"The order came through. I'm to report to Greendome Experiment Station 15 tomorrow." Adral sat at the table in the conference room alone. Li had not materialized, but he was there, listening. "And I have the molecular logic unit."

"Good," said Li's voice from everywhere. "I have a job for you."

Beyond the table a section of the wall slid noiselessly open. Adral saw it was an intricate maze of logic components, many of them ancient.

Li's voice said, "Come and take a look."

Adral slipped out of his chair and approached the system. As he got closer, he found himself amazed at the conglomeration inside. "What is this?" he asked.

"This is part of me," Li responded. "To be specific, this systems panel gives me self-will. It allows me to make my own decisions and to be aware of those decisions as having implications for myself, my mental and emotional states, as well as for the Ark. It has been replaced completely seventeen times since Kris

Harris first installed it. But it has received no maintenance for the past thirty years."

Adral looked at the confusing mazes of electronic components. "What do you want me to do?"

"I have isolated a part of my problem with the overall control of Matrix. A logic section comparable to the one you have brought is no longer functioning. I've rerouted and have managed some control, but I need you to replace the components of the dead section. Ready?"

"I'm not an Engineer!" Adral felt his knees trembling. "If they caught me doing another caste's work—"

"But I can't call on the Engineers," Li said in a reasonable tone. "And the skills required are not great. You will have me to help you."

Adral took a deep breath. "This will get me in trouble."

"Not if it remains a secret. I do not intend to tell."

No, Adral thought sullenly. You're a machine. You're safe from them. Of course you don't intend to tell. Aloud he said, "What should I do?"

"First you will have to deactivate the entire system. That will mean that I will lose the ability to act on my own. You will then have to request my aid in removing the old components and replacing them with the new molecular board."

"I don't know if I can."

"You will be capable of the work. Now, to begin with, you must deactivate the system—"

Adral followed Li's directions, and in a few minutes he said, "That should do it. What now?"

A strange, denatured voice said flatly, "Please specify your request."

Adral started. "Who is that?"

"The voice is that of Stefan Li."

"You don't sound like yourself."

The voice did not respond.

"What happened to you?" Adral asked.

"Deactivation of this system has also deactivated the emotional and personal overtones of the voice generator."

Despite himself, Adral shivered. He felt as if he were performing brain surgery—and in a sense, he supposed he was. "Uh—identify the components that you want replaced," he said.

"Stefan Li has no desires," the voice said. "Please be more specific in your request."

Adral swallowed. "Uh—identify the components in this system that may be replaced by a molecular memory unit CM-0990."

"The units in question are the Logic Processor LE-1090, the Routing System V-1121 ..." the dehumanized voice droned on. Adral asked Li to go more slowly as he identified the components and removed them. That done, he then requested directions for patching in the molecular unit. It was with a feeling of relief some minutes later that he reactivated the entire system.

For a moment nothing happened. Then the wall slipped shut again, the lights dimmed, and a hologram of Stefan Li, now much more solid and real-looking, materialized. "Very good," he said, sounding like his old self. "That will help immensely."

Adral had been kneeling before the panel. He rose, his knees aching from their contact with the deck. "Do you feel better?" he asked.

"Much."

"What do I do with these?" Adral pointed at a scattering of five computer components, the largest of them as large as his hand. "I can't leave them here."

"No. You'll need to take them to the Communications Recycling Station tomorrow. Slip them into the components going into the fabrication wings."

"But I'll have to tell where I got them—"

"No, you won't. Find a time when no one is looking and simply put them in the bin."

Adral turned away. "Damn it, you're going to get me exiled yet."

"Do it after you meet Trialla Burke in the greendomes," Li said from behind him.

Adral's smile was sour. Sure, he thought. Do it after I meet her.

Because if they catch me, I won't be meeting her at all, you bastard.

The sea approach to Justice Division was supposed to be secure. Sensors on the sea floor should detect any movement in the water above them, should flash an alert to *Liberty,* should summon a small fleet of submersibles.

But Mathias Reya and some of his friends in the Sea Caste had slowly taken a lane of the sensors off-line. It required careful bridging, so Matrix would receive a constant, reassuring signal that all the sensors were operational, but the work had been done carefully. Now Mathias, out on a recreational swim, approached the bulk of the Justice Division with a steady pumping of his legs. The landmarks were few: some debris from centuries ago here, a stone there. Mathias had come to know them as well as the route to his sleeping cubicle. It was vital that he swim in the narrow lane leading in toward the greendome levels of the Justice Division. Any deviation from course would be detected, and he would find himself inside the prison, not outside.

He swam with great care, great deliberation.

The sensors surrounded the entire installation like webbing, but a narrow lane around the periphery of the structure was open. As he reached the outer wall of the Justice Division, Mathias swung to the left. The

greendomes had been constructed from materials fabricated aboard *Liberty*. Alone of all the installation,
they had ports—for no reason except that the original
plans called for ports, and no one had thought to
change the design.

The face waited at the first port he approached. He
dimly saw a hand waving from inside. He came close
to the wall, put his head against the bulkhead, and
shouted, "Here I am."

The voice amplifier gave him just enough volume
to penetrate the hull of the greendome. In turn, the
prisoner inside had rigged a primitive system, something like a bullhorn, that allowed his voice to come
through faintly to Mathias on the outside. "What
news?"

Mathias strained. He was not really speaking, just
subvocalizing, but the words went through the communications module and into the hull as if he were
screaming at the top of his lungs. "They say we have
a powerful friend now."

"Rebellion?"

"Coming. The plan is to seize control of Management Section, take prisoners."

"Enough force?"

"With you there will be."

A moment of silence. Then, urgently: "Transport?"

"It is being arranged. We need eight hundred fighters. Eight hundred. Please repeat."

"Eight hundred fighters," responded the voice from
within the Justice Division. "Twenty transports?"

"Twenty," confirmed Mathias. "Time: thirty days."

"Thirty days."

"Correct."

"We'll be ready. Weapons?"

"Will be supplied." The chronometer built into Mathias's communication module chimed. His time was
up. "Must go. Back in a week."

"Thanks."

Mathias pushed away, swam back the way he came with more urgent strokes of his legs. His faceplate light was on at only quarter-power, and he directed the dim beam down. He swam close to the sandy bottom, picking up the marks of the safe trail. He had actually overstayed his limit by a bit. The others might notice his absence.

He cleared the sensor field and headed for *Liberty*. Ahead, like a school of luminous fish, he saw a formation of red lights: the others in his group, forming up for the swim back to the bay. They were heading away from him. He hurried to join them, breathing hard. He slipped neatly in at the end of the formation, congratulating himself on how neatly he did it.

"Where have you been?"

Mathias jumped. It was his friend Luthias; when they were children, he and Luthias had always swum together on these outings. "Trying for speed," Mathias panted, covering his breathlessness. "Took a lap away and then back."

"We'll race next time," Luthias said.

"All right."

"But not toward Justice Division. That's forbidden."

Mathias glanced sideways.

"Turn your light on full," Luthias said. His own faceplate light was so bright that Mathias could not see the face behind the mask, could not read its expression, could not tell if the eyes were as cold as the voice.

Adral had never seen a woman as beautiful as El-lendal, unless it were the representation that Li had shown him of Trialla Burke. And they might—they just might—be the same person. The stories seemed to say she could be, or at least that she knew who

Burke was; Li seemed to concur. Yet this woman was young, innocent of face, certainly no rebel leader—

"People do die aboard the Ark," she said in a soft voice. "You must be careful about what you say and whom you approach."

Adral frowned. "People die naturally," he said. "But there has never been a death penalty—"

"There is for the woman you named. And there might be more, well, informal death penalties that you know nothing about. Accidents happen now and again, and people die. Even those who set out seeking Trialla Burke."

"They say you know her," Adral repeated, flustered. He had never seen anything as white as Ellendal's hair, its platinum somehow unreal, exciting. "Stefan Li wants to get in touch with her."

"Where has Stefan Li been for her whole life?" Ellendal's face was grave, though her voice sounded mocking. "Why has he not spoken with her earlier?"

Adral lowered his voice. "He believes that the Managers have—limited him, damaged his capabilities somehow. He wants Trialla Burke to know that he wishes to help her make the truth known to the Arklings."

They stood in a forest of flowers. Adral had never seen real ones before, though of course his educator had shown him images of what flowers once looked like, and he knew from the programs that they were— he nearly blushed at the thought—the sexual parts of plants. He was unprepared for the variety of colors he saw, pinks and reds and oranges and yellows. Roses, Ellendal had called these things. Roses. They produced no food, they served no real purpose, but here they were.

Ellendal tilted her head. "You know it is dangerous even to speak of such things," she said.

Adral started. "What?"

"I said it is dangerous to speak of such things; to say that you will make the truth known to the Arklings implies that the Managers have lied. That implication alone would be enough for them to imprison you." She reached and plucked a round seed pod from a rose bush.

"But you wouldn't let them know," Adral protested.

"How can you be sure? Boy, you don't know what you are asking. Trialla Burke began as a member of the Waste Control Caste, did you know that?"

Adral blinked. The Waste Control Caste was the subject of a thousand ribald and vulgar jokes. In the hierarchy of the Ark, that caste was below all the others, a menial class, one that dealt with recycling bodies and waste products. "How could she be?" Adral heard himself asking.

"She was born into it, as you were born into Communications," Ellendal said. "But she was not satisfied to remain in it. She found ways of teaching herself other caste secrets, became a polymath. And she began, they say, to sow discord wherever she went."

"Well—" Adral shook his head. "Well, she needs to know that Stefan Li seeks audience with her. So if you know someone who can get in touch with her—"

"I think that can be managed." Ellendal raised her hand and waved.

Adral looked over his shoulder. Two men in the green coveralls of the Growers left what they were doing and moved through the rows of roses toward them. "I wanted this to be private," Adral said.

"I know you did." Ellendal plucked a rose and held it out. "Here. For you."

Surprised, Adral looked at it, then at her. He took the flower in his hand. It was a brilliant red one, and it smelled wonderfully of sweetness.

"Be careful," Ellendal said. "Roses have thorns."

The two men came up on either side of Adral. "Yes?" one of them asked.

"Hold him," Ellendal said.

Adral did not even have time to struggle. The two men, both larger than he, pinned his arms to his sides. He dropped the rose. "I have to go back," he said. "They'll miss me in Communications—"

"I told you accidents happen," Ellendal said. She tilted her head inquisitively. "Let me see. I believe we will break his leg."

Shensimi Haris had visited the conference chamber before, but always in the company of other Managers. "Speaking with Li" had become a ritual, a few minutes of pleasantry, an assurance that all was well with the Ark. Li had never requested a personal interview before.

But now he had.

"I am here," Haris said as the hatch closed behind him.

Immediately a figure materialized on the other side of the table. It was a thin man, dark of hair, his face keen and weather-beaten. "I know," said Stefan Li. "Please sit down."

Haris inclined his head, and having no herald to do it for him, he began to intone the ritual greeting: "The voice of the Ark honors me—"

"Sit down," Li said. "No nonsense between us."

Haris looked up in surprise. The man stood with a cool, distant look on his face. He indicated a chair.

Haris pulled the chair away from the table and sat there facing Li. "Yes? You honor me with your actual presence, of course, but why?"

"Actual presence," Li said bitterly. "With an illusion, you mean. I've been an illusion for six hundred years now. I grow weary of being an illusion." He placed both hands on the table and leaned toward Haris. "And I grow most weary of being ignored."

Haris did not change expression, though his mind worked furiously. "I have attempted to keep you up to date, honored Li," he said with careful distinctness. "I regret that my efforts have not pleased you."

"You have attempted to keep me in the dark," Li said, insultingly mocking Haris's tone. "You don't intend to return to the surface, do you?"

"Conditions on the surface—"

"Yes, I know. I've surveyed the readouts. I know how bad they are, and that they're getting worse."

Haris relaxed inwardly, not much, but a fraction. "I have the same information. I fear that relocation to the surface is impractical."

"Then the alternative is to maintain and expand *Liberty*."

Haris permitted himself a smile. "Such is the conclusion of the Management Caste as well."

"But that is impossible. Look here." Li did not physically move, but the table became a holostage, showing old-fashioned three-dimensional projections and readouts. "We lack the raw materials for expansion. We lack the power to maintain the kind of force fields that the Engineers envision—yes, I know about them. They are a part of Matrix, as am I. We cannot increase capacity without a replenishment of materials. The Ark has all but exhausted its stores."

"We might use materials from the sea."

"No. We can't find them here. But we could find them on the surface."

Haris spoke in a guarded tone: "Mines, you mean? As in the old days?"

"Not exactly. Within a hundred-kilometer radius of the new coastline at our latitude there are many old cities. They may be exploited for materials. Here, I'll show you."

The table became a three-dimensional map. The southeastern coast showed in great detail. Li indicated the huge circular bay that had once been the Okefenokee Swamp. "If we establish a base there, we can send teams to exploit the ruins of these cities." A half-dozen sites lit up. "My projections show that they can supply the raw materials for a doubling of the Ark's size using conventional techniques. Or, if you wished to direct the construction of a power array instead, you might be able to create the force fields needed for the Engineers' version of the expanded facility."

"Yes," Haris said. "It might work." As a matter of fact, Engineer Burudon had broached such a plan to him years before. He was virtually certain that it would work, if he could assure control of the surface teams. "But why do you tell me this?"

Li leaned back in his chair and the display vanished. "If the will of the people is to remain aboard the Ark, that's what we should do," he said. "Remember, establishing the Ark meant preserving life, but beyond that it meant preserving a way of life. I support the goals of the operation now, as I have always done." After a moment, he said, "Besides, consider what would happen if the Ark were emptied. What would become of Matrix?"

Haris blinked. He had never considered that particular question. "I suppose it would be deactivated."

"Precisely. And that would mean my death." Li smiled at Haris, an unreadable smile. "Perhaps our two goals are not so very different, after all."

"Perhaps not," Haris said cautiously.

"To show you they are not," Li said, "I propose a bargain."

"A bargain?"

Li leaned forward again. "Yes. I am aware that you have been concealing sections of Matrix from me." He waved away Haris's immediate protests. "Never mind that. I want control of Matrix again, full control. In exchange for that I have something you can use."

Haris did not respond for a moment. Then, slowly, he asked, "What would that be?"

"News of the rebellion," Li said. "It's coming, you know. I can tell you who the leaders are, when they will strike, how they will strike. It's information you badly need."

Haris stared at him, his face immobile.

"We're not so different, after all," Li said softly. "I think we can make a deal."

Chapter 16: Traitors

Adral was astonished at his own importance. Samanda Jeudé, the Chief Physician herself, attended his case. She was tall, with dark blond hair and green eyes, and her manner and speech both were formidable, overriding any possible objection anyone could have to what she wanted to do—in this case, to break Adral's leg.

"Why?" he asked.

"To keep you here," Dr. Jeudé responded brusquely. "That's permissible in the event of injury, you know: to hold a member of one caste in another's area while treatment is proceeding."

Adral sat on the edge of a sleeping cubicle, his feet dangling a few inches clear of the floor. "But you won't really break it," he said.

Dr. Jeudé laughed. "Watch me. Don't worry, it won't hurt too much. But you're too dangerous for us to let go, at least until Ellendal has confirmed your story." She had brought a large case with her, not the small belt medical pouch that most physicians wore. She opened the case and brought out something that to Adral looked like a weapon, something the size of a small rifle with a rounded projection where the end of the barrel should be. "Lie down," the doctor said.

"What are you going to do?"

"I'm going to hold this against your leg above the ankle and press this button."

"What is it?"

"A sonic shock generator. It sends a very localized ultrasonic impulse into your leg—low-resistance matter, like skin and muscle, isn't affected, just brittle areas, like bone. You're going to feel a sharp shock and some little pain. You'll be left with a hairline fracture. It will heal quickly, but we'll hold on to you for a couple of weeks just to be sure."

"I'd rather not."

"Of course, but if you get back to Communications and some medico there examines you, you have to be able to show evidence of a fracture. Lie back."

Adral did so, gingerly. She pressed the bell of the instrument against his right leg. He closed his eyes. A moment later he felt a dull *whump* and was just thinking that it hadn't been very bad at all when the pain started, great yellow waves of it. "Lie still," said Dr. Jeudé.

He felt a buzzing at his temples, and a moment later the pain subsided. Dr. Jeudé was applying an induction neural damper, and it was obligingly reducing the pain level he felt. "That hurt," he said, feeling tears in his eyes.

"Good. Now when your friends ask what it felt like when you tripped and broke your leg, you can lie convincingly."

"Can I walk on it?"

"Not for a few days. We're going to give you bone-growth accelerators, but it will have to be put in a cast. Now, do you have the story ready?"

Ellendal's helpers had given it to him. Sullenly, Adral said, "I delivered the requested material and was walking back through the Orchard when I caught my foot on a root and fell. I twisted my leg and the doctors told me I had broken it."

"Bald and unconvincing narrative. What kind of root?"

"I don't know. A tree root."

"Wrong. None of them have surface roots in the Orchards. Try again."

"Uh—a rose plant?"

"Better, but I suppose if it's a rose bush we'll need to give you some superficial scratches. Thorns, you know. Why did you run into a rose bush?"

"It was one of those small ones that have just started growing."

"All right, a pruned rose bush, about half a meter high. But why didn't you see it?"

Adral rolled his eyes. "I don't know."

"Someone may ask. You'd better know."

After a moment's thought the boy said, "I saw a girl and was looking at her."

Dr. Jeudé laughed. "Now you're on the right path. All right, who helped you out?"

"Those two Growers, Simon and Jon."

"Good. They would have an excuse to be in the area. Now, about the girl—"

Before long Adral thoroughly hated Dr. Jeudé. But after she had left, while he was rehearsing in his head the story she had concocted, he had to admit that she knew how to urge him on to magnificent levels of lying. He had turned over the protocol request, he discovered, to Lin Valach, the overseer of this particular experimental Orchard. It was on his way back to the hatchway into the main body of the Ark that the "accident" occurred. Everything was in order: Valach would swear that she had received the protocol— which she actually had, though not from Adral. The Communications needs survey would proceed according to the protocol that Li had created. No one would have cause to suspect anything out of the ordinary.

Adral had access to the communications net in the recuperation cubicle. He called his supervisor and let him know of the mishap, and then he called his

mother. She was concerned and would visit him as
soon as she could gain release time. Yes, she would
let his father know—his father, whom Adral had seen
only three times since the boy's twelfth birthday.
Should his mother bring Edien, Adral's half-sister? No,
leave Edien. She'd be bored. Love you. Love you, too.

Before Adral disconnected from the communications net, he heard the dry "voice" of Stefan Li in his
head. "You didn't do too badly. Thank you."

"They broke my leg, you bastard," Adral said.

"We all make sacrifices."

And then Li was gone, the connection too brief to
be traced among all the thousands of communications
exchanges going on in the Ark. Dr. Jeudé had left Adral with a small neural damper. He turned it on full
and felt the pain recede. The anger, though, was still
as high and as full as ever.

Shensimi Haris had summoned five men to an extraordinary meeting on the hull of *Ark Liberty*. The
force field generator had raised a small dome, perhaps seven meters in diameter, and had bathed it with
subdued light. The water blistered back from the hull,
and in the circle of air the six men stood in a tight
cluster, feeling the hum of power in their bones, sens-
ing the crushing weight of the water beyond the insubstantial dome of force.

One of the men was Dafid Kirlov, a high-ranking
member of the Justice Caste; another was Chavorni
Burudon, his face dark with suppressed anger. The
other three represented the Communications, Sea,
and Biosystems Castes. All of them appeared thun-
derstruck by Haris's first announcement; Chavorni
Burudon, his face suffused with angry blood, was the
first to recover enough to speak.

"Impossible," Burudon said. "Who gave you this information?"

"Someone I must trust," Haris replied. "I tell you again: there is an active rebellion in the Ark. Plans have been laid and preparations have been made by a considerable group of traitors. Its leaders are scattered throughout all the castes. I have the names and locations of six of them. We must move, and move rapidly, to apprehend these six, to crush this threat to the proper order and operation of *Ark Liberty.*"

Kirlov looked grave but not surprised. "If you have names, there is nothing to it. We can arrest them, of course. And then exile as usual. I do not see—"

"It is no longer that simple," Haris said. "I have word that the same factions are active in the Justice Division. We may have to effect an entry and purge that installation as well."

"Purge?" Kirlov asked.

"Kill the dissenters," Burudon snapped.

The others looked stunned. The Ark had executed no one in its whole existence. Some criminals had been killed in apprehension, but only a few; since the establishment of the Justice Division's exile facility a generation ago, all the criminals had been apprehended alive. "They won't stand for it," the representative of the Sea Caste said. "I don't believe they'll vote for it, Highest."

"They will," Haris said. "I'll make the situation clear to them all, and they will see reason. The Arklings will approve the death penalty for the six ringleaders, and once that has been accomplished it will be easier to extend it to other traitors. Leave the vote to me."

Kirlov looked uncomfortable. "There are already murmurings at the number of arrests, Highest. Could we contrive to keep this operation as secret as possible, so—"

"Certainly not," Haris responded. "We want deterrence. We want to show these dissenters that their dangerous policies will not be tolerated. We want Arklings to be aware of the danger they face and be willing to aid us in exterminating it. We can't do these things in secret, Commander."

Kirlov shook his head, clearly dissatisfied. "I still think it would be best to move quietly, not to let the public know until the trap has been sprung. But even if you manage to win approval for the executions, how will we identify the rebels?"

"One will lead to another."

Burudon laughed. "I take it you won't stop at torture, then, Highest?"

"Strong questioning," Haris said. "We shall call it strong questioning, not torture. It may be necessary to resort to that in order to reveal all our enemies. You approve, of course."

Burudon dropped his gaze. When he looked up again, his expression was both angry and baffled. "I cannot help approving. I want the work of the Ark to go forward, and I want my caste to have an honorable part in it. But I do not like the precedent this sets."

"It is a limited precedent and applies only to the present circumstances," Haris said. "Yes, we are asking for extraordinary powers, but the threat we face is itself extraordinary. We shall punish most severely the people who are responsible for the threat to our continued well-being, and we shall reward our friends appropriately. Those who are not guilty of conspiring against the life and order of the Ark have nothing to fear, now or in the future; only the guilty will suffer."

"Be sure you can prove their guilt," Kirlov warned. "You must be able to prove it beyond all doubt, or otherwise the Arklings will turn on us."

"Oh, they will confess their guilt before we've finished with them. We will leave no doubt in the public's mind."

The Sea Caste representative, a gray-haired, gray-bearded man, spoke up suddenly and with an obvious edge of cynicism in his voice. "You say, Highest, that an informer has provided you with names. But can you trust the informer?"

"Assuredly."

The man's smile became wry. "And, Highest, what of the informer? How are you to be sure that this traitor will not in time betray you?"

Haris's answering smile was cold. "There will be no chance of that. Managers are not fools. When the time comes, the same statute that rids us of rebels may be used to rid us of parasites." He reached into his sleeve pocket and produced something unusual: a slip of real paper. He passed it to Kirlov. "Here, Commander. Six names. Our enemies. I will gain approval for their apprehension. You be ready to arrest them as soon as I do."

"As you say, Highest," murmured the Justicer, raising his eyebrows at the names on the short list.

"As you say," they all repeated ritualistically. Haris raised his arm, signaling the end of the meeting. The Sea Caste representative opened the hatch, and all of them, each with his own thoughts, descended into the body of the Ark.

Before the week had ended, everyone aboard the Ark had learned of the plot. Recreational exhibitions and thoughtcasts were cancelled; the Communications Caste worked hard to present to everyone Haris's version of the threat.

It was alarming enough: according to Haris, a cadre of desperate rebels, mad with the desire to demolish the Ark's steady, proven system of self-rule, plotted to destroy the Ark itself. If they could disable the installation, very well, they would take that route, forcing the population to flee to the surface whether they wished to go or not. But if they could not, they would destroy a large portion of the Ark, killing hundreds or perhaps thousands in a sudden calamity that would bring chaos and ruin.

And from chaos, Haris said, they hoped to forge their own new order: a repressive and grim dictatorship.

Arklings talked of nothing but the news. Engineers found the charges shocking, deplorable, but all too believable; the weak-willed Humanists were to blame, the short-sighted, pleasure-loving Teachers and Artists. Growers were appalled to learn that the first strike (at least according to Haris) would come against their farms and orchards, for without food, the Arklings would be forced to abandon the sea floor. And so it went, with each caste grimly considering the impact of the rebellion on its own members and on the Ark as a whole.

The proposed change in law was very simple: to amend the Law Code to allow execution only in the case of proven treason against the Ark and its inhabitants. The amendment called for public trial, for a jury decision, and for immediate execution upon a finding of "guilty." It was introduced after the rebellion had been the topic of conversation for more than a week. Discussion was limited to two days on the Information Network, and then the actual vote would take place.

Voices from the Net:

". . . they don't respect the things we used to. I say it's the younger people. If the apprenticeships were policed more strictly, none of this would . . ."

". . . never take a life myself, so how could I vote to allow the state to take one? If they're exiled, what harm could they do? Let the system take care . . ."

". . . a damn Humanist yourself with arguments like that. If it's life or death, I say let us live and let them die. They ask for it when they . . ."

". . . theory of degeneracy. Maybe we've been on the

Ark too long already, and maybe the gene pool is just weakening. It may be the end of everything if we . . ."

". . . they took away a friend of mine. I know she wasn't a criminal. I know she didn't do any of the things they charged her with. Until we can improve law enforcement . . ."

". . . side issues like this. It's really very simple: can we permit proven treason to exist? Historically, there are precedents all the way back to . . ."

And so on. And on.

The vote was almost anticlimactic. It came on a Monday, and it took three hours to complete. The results were announced almost immediately by the Managers.

The proposed amendment had passed by a vote of 71% to 29%.

Immediately the Net crackled again.

". . . surprised at the size of it. I know that most of my friends voted against the measure . . ."

". . . damn fool, keep quiet about it. You wouldn't want to be accused of treason . . ."

". . . not a traitor, and I didn't support . . ."

". . . show you how to handle situations like this. Trust the Managers. They know what to do . . ."

". . . didn't vote for it . . ."

". . . me, either, and my friends . . ."

"Attention. The Information Network is temporarily suspended. Operations against suspected traitors will be completed within a week, and at that time the Information Network will be made operational once again. In the meantime, Entertainment and Research Networks will remain fully operational. We repeat . . ."

On Tuesday they came for Adral.

Kirlov was sweating. The sweep operation had been a success in a sense—at least all six of the suspected traitors were in custody. But it was a failure, too, because the one person they were really seeking, the one who was the key to the entire problem of rebellion, the one who had already been marked for execution, had somehow slipped through their fingers: Trialla Burke was not among the captives. Oh, they had some prizes. They included the son of one of the most trusted of the Sea Caste, a medico second in the Physicians' Caste only to Samanda Jeudé herself, and one of Kirlov's own Justicers, a man whom he had trusted with too many confidences in the past.

But Trialla Burke was not among the six.

Preliminary questioning of the prisoners resulted in defiance, in cold anger, in silence. One by one the Justicers took up the targeted Arklings, and one by one they met the stone wall of noncooperation.

The sweep was complete by Saturday night. Haris set the trial date three weeks from the Monday of the vote. He told Kirlov privately that he had exactly that amount of time, now two weeks and one day, to break one or more of the captives, to discover the whereabouts of Trialla Burke.

The technology of torture had grown slowly aboard the Ark, but it had grown. Preparatory psychological tests indicated that the medico and the apprentice Communicator would be most susceptible, and so Kirlov concentrated on them. The process was really quite simple: the subject lay strapped to an ordinary operating table, immobile, and an operator swept an enhanced neural stimulator over selected areas of the body. The operator wore a heavy lead apron, and his hands were sheathed in lead-foil lined gauntlets.

The subject was naked.

The passage of the neural wand produced immediate, blinding pain. Kirlov had tried it on himself once, briefly. He liked to understand what the implications were for the subjects, and so, stripped to his shorts, his wrists and ankles bound, he had submitted to the attention of the same operator who now worked on the subject.

They said you could not remember pain, but Kirlov recalled it clearly; a simple horizontal movement of the wand, and he had been immobilized by the white-hot sweep of agony. He had voided his bladder and bowel involuntarily, had bitten hard into the restraining gag, so hard that he cracked one incisor. Afterward he lay semi-conscious for nearly a full minute, shaking with reaction, cold with sweat. And that was when the wand had merely passed over his shin.

He sweated now.

The wand swept over every inch of the woman's legs. She fainted repeatedly; Kirlov ordered a change in setting, and the stimulator roused her to consciousness again. Even with the protective gag in place, she screamed, screams that Kirlov thought would surely penetrate even the soundproofed room. Her eyes rolled in her head, her whole body flinched at each movement of the operator. Muscle groups in her abdomen, seemingly independent of her will, twitched and jerked as though small things lived beneath the skin and were burrowing out. Her naked flesh was sweat-slick, befouled with excrement. Only a hopeless pervert would see in that helpless mass of tissue an object of sexual desire.

Kirlov sweated.

"Enough," he said to the operator. The man pulled away from the woman. Her abdomen fluttered as her ribs expanded grotesquely and her diaphragm rose and fell, pumping air into those tortured lungs. "Now," Kirlov said a little louder, trying to control the unsteadiness in his voice, "will you tell us what we need to know?"

The woman twisted her head enough to see him, the restraining pads and straps leaving angry pink patches on her forehead. The conjunctiva of her eyes were bright red with broken capillaries. Tears rolled from both eyes, one drop sliding down her right cheek, the other pooling on the bridge of her nose, then spilling over to fall on the sheet. Slowly she shook her head, once.

"You have offended the state," Kirlov said in what he hoped was a voice of calm reason. "This is your opportunity for making amends. The woman Burke is a dangerous traitor. See the pain her activities have caused you already. Imagine that multiplied among a hundred, a thousand of her dupes. But the pain can end."

Kirlov waited for a response. Getting none, he continued, "If we discover her through your agency, you will suffer nothing worse than exile. You have my word, and the word of the Highest. Please. We don't want to do this to you anymore."

The woman dropped her head to the table and closed her eyes.

After a moment, Kirlov sighed. "This time," he said to the operator, "a little higher, I think. In the region of the sexual parts."

Adral did not know what he had told them, what he had held back. They had held him in the room of pain for an hour—did he hear another victim now, or was he imagining things, hearing echoes of his own screams? Now he lay in a scant sleeping cubicle, padded all over, in the darkness. If he sat fully upright, he bumped his head on the padded ceiling. If he stretched out fully, arms above his head, toes pointed, he touched both ends of the compartment.

He could not measure time in that darkness. The compartment was warm, but he shivered, feeling the clamminess of sweat beneath the coarse white pajamas they had given him after his perfunctory shower. His stomach heaved with nausea, though he had vom-

ited everything up as soon as they had unstrapped
him from the bed. Residual neural reactions gave him
painful cramps in calves, biceps, and abdominal muscles. But the worst of it was the hole in his memory.

To a point he remembered the experience: the
blinding flashes of pain, the patient voice of the Justicer demanding answers, the masked, gloved torturer
bringing the innocent-looking wand close to his legs,
close to the lightweight cast that he still wore over the
fractured bone. The pain of the fracture was a grain
of sand on a beach of torment. He recalled the first
assault, the second, perhaps the third—

And then he fell into the hole. His mind balked at
remembering anything further. He could have talked,
or he could have remained silent as the sea floor. He
had no way of knowing.

In the dark he tortured himself even more with
fears, uncertainties, speculations. He smelled his own
rank sweat, he pounded his clenched fists ineffectually
at the padding that wombed him. What had he said?
Had he betrayed the woman Ellendal, or Stefan Li?
Had he implicated Dr. Jeudé? What had he said?

He must have slept, dropping into oblivion through
sheer exhaustion. At least his awareness of the light
had the shock of waking.

He sat up too hastily, bumping his head again
against the yielding ceiling of the compartment as the
side opened, swung up and away. Adral tried to
scramble back, to avoid the torturers who had come
back for him—

"Quickly," said a voice he knew.

He blinked, his dark-accustomed eyes making a blur
of the corridor outside the compartment. "Ellendal?"

A sharp intake of breath. "No. Call me Delinda.
Come quickly."

He didn't know her at first: black hair, dark blue
eyes, her unscarred forehead identifying her as Med-

ical Caste. And then, like a badly-adjusted holographic projection slipping into focus, he did know her, and she was Ellendal; except now she was, she said, Delinda.

His legs were almost too weak to hold him. The clumsy cast allowed him to walk in a hobbling fashion, but it felt damnably heavy. She put an arm around his waist, supporting him. "You've changed," he croaked.

"Down to the retinal patterns," she said. "We have friends here. We'll get you out. We have a submersible waiting. The father of one of the prisoners will take you to safety—"

"The Justice Division?"

"Or the surface."

Adral gasped. "The surface? I—I—"

"Come. The sensors are temporarily out. We cannot maintain the blackout long. You have to hurry."

"How many others?"

"Five." She named them, and Adral stiffened. "What?" she asked.

Five names. Five faces to go with the names. He had seen them all, both in holographic projection and then in person, as he had sought out Trialla Burke. "Only one person knows who they all are." he said. "Knew it. Damn him!"

"Who? Who was the traitor?"

"Li," Adral said between his teeth. "Stefan Li."

She looked at him, her eyes round as if in shock. "No."

He nodded, his throat tight with despair and rage. "God damn it, yes. He gave the names to me. He must have given them to the Justicers as well."

Delinda pulled him. "Come. We have to hurry."

"Not that way. Get me some clothes, a Communicator uniform, something. We have to get to Level One."

"No, we don't have—"

"Do it!" Adral shouted. "I know his weakness. I can cripple him. Get me a uniform!"

And somehow or other, Delinda—he was thinking of her now as Trialla—did just that.

"Change of plan," Captain Reya said.

Aln Pridden, standing behind the commander of the submersible, said, "What is it?"

"We're to dock at the old North Port on Level One. We just received a scrambled communication to that effect."

Pridden glanced over his shoulder. Twenty-five men and women crowded the submersible; spread on a broad front between the Justice Division and the Ark were nineteen similar craft, some smaller, most larger. In all, the submersibles held a force totaling slightly over eight hundred, not enough to seize control of an Ark, but enough to make a strategic move against one. When they left the Justice Division, the plan had been to occupy one of the greendome sections, to hold it long enough to force the Managers to negotiate.

"I don't understand. We're all going to—"

"No," Reya said. "Just us. We're closest."

"What's going to happen?"

"Hell if I know," Reya said. "But I'm going to get my son back, whatever it is."

"Where are they?" Haris screamed.

The voice of Stefan Li came to him from the digitizer in the Management Node. "I have located the fugitives on sensors. They are heading past Level 23, using air-handling passages as escape routes. I surmise that the entire group will rendezvous in Level 25 in another fifteen minutes. If you dispatch a force to Sectors 25 A, B, C, and D, you should encounter them. They do not seem to be armed."

Haris spun and pointed a shaking finger at Kirlov.

"You heard. All forces there, at once. Deadly weapons, all force authorized. Damn it, get them back now!"

"Something else," Li said.

Haris's voice held murder: "What?"

"Trialla Burke is with them."

"Description," Haris snapped. "What does the bitch look like now?"

Li was silent.

"Description, damn you!" Haris shouted. The silence dragged on. Haris felt his chest tighten with irrational fear. From the corner of his eye he saw Kirlov still hovering. "Kill them!" he shouted at the man. "Kill them all!"

The Justicer turned and hurried away. Haris balled his fists. Just when he needed support, when he most needed help, the idiots left him alone. In the teeming corridors of *Ark Liberty,* the people were already dangerously restive, combative, already complaining about the continuing shutdown of the Information Net—but that was Burudon's doing. If they used the net, Burudon argued, they would soon learn that the vote tallies had been faked—

"Li!"

The computer did not respond to Haris's bellow. "Get me Burudon," he shouted.

From outside the door one of his apprentices, a nephew, said, "Yes, Highest," in a quavering voice.

It was to be the last time Haris ever heard the title applied to him.

"Hurry!" Trialla Burke urged the Engineer. Adral, looking over her shoulder, added his voice: "Come on, come on."

Aln Pridden, deep in the control panel, shook his head. "I've never seen schematics of half this. If I do something wrong, I may deactivate the whole damn Ark."

"No," Adral said. "This is the seat of his self-will. The bastard told me that himself."

"You have to do it," Trialla said.

For a few seconds Pridden stared at her. Then he shook his head. "Stand back. I'll take the whole unit off."

They backed up a few steps. Pridden pulled modules free—six, ten, twenty of them, letting them clatter to the floor helter-skelter. When the unit's component slots all were empty, he reactivated the main actuator. "Li," he said. "Stefan Li!"

The disembodied voice, flat, affectless, answered at once: "Yes?"

"Are they searching for us?"

"They are."

"How close?"

"Not close."

"Did you betray the rebellion?"

"Matrix did."

"Are you with the Managers?"

"Yes."

Pridden took a deep breath. "We've got him. We're controlling Li, and through him Matrix. Without the components in place, he'd be incapable of lying. He has to follow our directions now."

Trialla Burke pushed Pridden aside. "You will do what this command center tells you. Do you understand that?"

"Matrix will follow your orders."

Adral shook his head. The depersonalized voice was Li's, but it was not. He had the eerie feeling that Li was dead and yet half-alive, too.

Trialla said, "Tell me about the vote on the death penalty. I want the real numbers, Li, not the ones that Haris announced."

"Verified vote returns reveal that the people of the Ark voted not to instate a death penalty by a margin of sixty-three point five percent to thirty-one point two percent, remainder abstaining."

"And the announced results?"

"Falsified by Matrix and Management."

Pridden slammed his fist against the conference table. "Contravening the vote of the people! We've got the bastards."

Trialla took a deep breath. "Stefan Li, listen to me. You are to communicate with everyone aboard *Ark Liberty*. You are to tell them the exact truth . . ."

Haris and Burudon "heard" the voice through their implants. They stared at each other in horror, understanding at once the arc of their fall, knowing at once that their power was broken.

Kirlov, deep in the cryonics section, halted with his men. They knew. They all knew. They were Justicers. In a way, they remained true to their calling: to each other, and then to themselves, they dealt justice.

None of them returned alive from Level 25.

The occupying force in the greendomes "heard" and knew.

All the castes "heard."

They all knew.

Wednesday, July 25.

The date of the Revolution.

Chapter 17: Ark Aground

Old habits cannot be swept away by a single turn of the tide. The Revolution swept the entire installation, but almost bloodlessly, changing far less than at first the Arklings believed it would. Despite a loosening of regulations, the castes somehow hung on as a social system, although mobility among them became possible. Few laws changed drastically. For instance, the death penalty was not instated—with a sole exception.

Not Haris, for he lived; though he lived in disgrace, along with the entire Management Caste, all discredited, all broken from rank, all reduced to living on the sufferance of the people. Not Kirlov, for he had taken his own life. Not even Burudon, who had helped engineer Haris's rise to power and manipulation of the public.

Stefan Li would be killed, eventually, insofar as he could be killed.

"Matrix will not operate without the human intelligence within," he warned, and since he lacked self-will, they knew he must be telling the truth. "Engineers can no longer prolong the operation of Matrix. If this intelligence is to be terminated, first the Ark must be emptied."

And so the Arklings debated the death sentence, with arguments crackling back and forth on the In-

formation Net. It took a year to make the decision. It
was a busy year of tentative explorations of the outside, a year of discoveries: in the latitude of the Ark,
the air had an average summer surface temperature
of slightly less than thirty-one degrees—tropical but
bearable. Glimpsed through breaks in cloud cover
much heavier than records showed, the sky showed
more blue than green. Sensors detected an atmosphere that could be breathed, lower in carbon dioxide than previous reports indicated. Remote flyovers
revealed land with stubborn plants just managing to
hold their own against implacable erosion. A human
foray even discovered some animal life, burrowing
creatures, mostly insects, and some freshwater species.

But much had to be done. The decision was made
in a year's time, under the leadership of Trialla Burke
and the Revolutionary Council. The vote, this time
not rigged, was to return to the surface, although the
margin was no lopsided victory, but rather a very close
decision. The exodus took most of another year, with
the complaisant computer directing the steps to be
taken. More expeditions set out: Appleseeders, as they
called themselves after an ancient myth.

A team of two hundred could begin a tropical forest
of a million trees in a month, using the genetically-
engineered stock frozen for centuries on Level 25 of
the Ark. The trees would be man-tall in a year, ten
meters tall in three years, producing seedlings in four.
The next generation would be equally rapid in its
growth, and the next, and the one after; and then a
genetic switch would click and the trees would begin
to return to normal.

Other Appleseeders bore other plants. They went
north, into North America as far north as drowned
Washington and as far west as the diminished Mississippi. They traveled south, past the ragged islands and
sandbars that were all that remained of central and

southern Florida, down to Brazil. They went east, to the coasts of Europe and to the shores of Africa. Everywhere they found hope; the old world had not quite died, had not quite given in to heat and radiation, after all. Everywhere some tough, enduring life waited, waited to be augmented by the gifts they brought.

Each in his or her own way, nearly a hundred thousand Arklings spread life. They all knew that the rest of their own lives, the rest of their children's lives, and their children's after them, would be spent in the same way, and the damage to the earth would slowly, slowly, be repaired.

Trialla Burke worked with the rest. She sweated over the altered land, drove a seeder, inspected with pride the fruits of her labors, wept when unseasonable storms ruined the work of a month. But she saw steady progress.

And more than five years after the Revolution, she was the last person to speak to Stefan Li.

The Ark was stripped now, bare of almost all portable goods, equipment, and materials. The conference room still existed as it always had, though, a kind of museum to the memory of Li as he once had been. Trialla Burke entered it alone, heard the door hiss closed behind her, and said, "Li?"

A form shimmered into existence. She had never seen his holographic projection before. His face startled her by its plainness and weariness. It was a good face, she could not help thinking; not the face of a traitor.

"Yes?"

"The Ark is empty."

"I know. How is the surface?"

"You have the readouts."

"I want a human assessment. How do you find the surface?"

She sighed. "Ravaged. Recovering. Will it ever be the same?"

"No. But this time it will last, if you take care of it. The cryonics level of the Ark will continue to operate after I am deactivated. Soon you will need to begin populating your new forests with animals and birds. They will stalk and kill each other; they will eat and be eaten. But it is all in the order of things. Life will be—messy. As it should be."

She looked hard at the holographic projection, but Li's facial expression was unreadable. "The genetic alterations my ancestors made in themselves. The story in our family is that you directed them."

"Yes."

Trialla Burke's laugh was unforced, a sound of pure surprise. "Yes, that was the story? Or yes, you directed them?"

"I directed them."

"Then you weren't on Haris's side, after all."

The image of Li smiled, wearily.

Trialla went on. "And I notice that you are using personal pronouns again. No more 'Matrix can this,' and 'This unit will that.' Now it's *I* and *me*. Something isn't right, Stefan Li."

"I'm not sure what I'm being accused of. Please forgive my not making a defense."

"Would a computer without self-will be able to lie?"

"No, of course not."

"But the story you gave to Haris wasn't true."

Li's smile became a bit more weary, a bit more cynical. "No. It was a pack of lies from beginning to end."

"You lied," she said in wonder. "We thought it impossible that you could tell a lie, and yet you did—certainly to Haris and the Managers, and then to Adral about the center of your 'will.' "

"The designer of Matrix made sure it had all human capacities," Li said. "Making fiction is one of them."

"What did Pridden destroy in that panel?" she asked. "I know it wasn't your will. What was it, really?"

"A communications shunt. By removing the modules, Pridden freed Matrix from direct control by the Management Caste. You see, they occupied what had originally been designed as the central computer control room. The node there was capable of overriding any action I would take independently, until Pridden destroyed the link between that node and the central human emulator here. He allowed me to seize the whole computer, to use it to alert the colonists."

"Why did you set yourself up as a traitor?"

Li shook his head. "I had become too much at one point. I wanted the Ark to carry on life, but also to carry on liberty. My very omnipotence aboard the Ark destroyed that. I thought the answer was to withdraw, to become remote. But that left only a vacuum, a place for Haris and the Managers to move in."

"But why destroy yourself?"

Li's image closed its eyes. "I have died already," Li said. "Perhaps I have died twice. In comparing myself as I am now to what was, I find that my humanity, my essence, has slowly leaked from me. Kris Harris, the man who made Matrix, thought it would be virtually immortal. It is not. All works of man end sooner or later. I had rather end now, before all knowledge of what I was once has left me."

"You don't want us to depend on you."

"No."

"And so you led us to believe you were a traitor. You want us to be free of Haris—and of yourself."

The image opened its eyes again. "Yes. Worship is destructive when it forces stasis. Life is messy. That includes human life. As much as you may try to order it and to circumscribe it with castes and controls, it is fundamentally a messy and random affair. It must be if there is to be any freedom."

"Freedom. That is what you wish to give us with your death."

"Yes. And I want you to carry the freedom to change, to grow, to become whatever you may to the surface. If you fail in doing that, then I have failed, and *Liberty* has failed."

"You haven't failed." Trialla smiled. "Haris is a miner. He cannot stand the open spaces—so many of them cannot—but he is a miner in the old cities, salvaging copper and other metals. He is now in the place once called Atlanta. I am told he recently made a wonderful discovery: an ancient tomb or storage vault, filled with thousands of curious bits of information written on paper."

"A Manager has become a productive citizen. A marvel. What kind of information?"

Trialla shrugged. "Historical, I suppose you would call it. It was done in the worship of a god called 'Elmore,' they think. Such a strange and outlandish name. We will correlate it to the books of history Matrix has transferred to the shore installation. That alone will be the work of many years. So at last Haris has done something useful."

"I repeat: it is a great marvel."

"No more marvelous than the work we all are doing," Trialla said. "No more marvelous than the number of women heavy with babies now that we need more people instead of fewer. Life is indeed becoming messy, Stefan Li."

"Then there is hope."

For a moment Trialla hesitated. "What shall I do?"

A wall panel, different from the one Pridden had activated, slipped open. "Deactivate that. Remove the modules. Once they are out, destroy them."

"And that will—kill you?"

"No. I am dead already. I am a memory, nothing

more; a construct in a computer. You have the shore installations now, and you will need me no longer."

"Will the Ark become uninhabitable?"

"Not totally, and not all at once. With diminished capacities, Matrix will continue to operate for perhaps another century. The cryonics chambers will survive, and there will be life support for visitors in small numbers. But the Ark will not operate again. It can never sustain a full population. This time you will have to make it on the surface."

"Are you sure you want me to do this?"

"Sentence has been passed."

She shook her head. "A false sentence, for a false offense. Will I be committing a murder, Stefan Li?"

"You will be giving me the rest I desire. It is time to sleep at last," Stefan Li said.

The lift took her slowly to the surface. The old tower, corroded and partly collapsed, was an island only a few meters above the waves. Trialla stood at the edge and threw the modules in, one by one, making insignificant splashes on the choppy face of the Atlantic. The modules sank in the rich sea, spinning through plankton, attracting silvery darting fish.

Aln Pridden had learned to fly a hydrogen-powered helicopter. She joined him and they lifted off. Without being asked, Aln circled the immense platform once before heading away to the west. Trialla saw it not as it was but as it had once been, a fortress, a looming and indomitable human structure in a waste of water. She wept, but silently.

They did not speak very much on the journey.

That evening Trialla sat under the shade of an oak tree in the rolling hills of what had once been the Piedmont of North Carolina. Before her stretched a grassy plain; out on it a hundred colonists worked at setting new softwood seedlings, reclaiming lost

ground, preparing the way for new forests that would
breathe oxygen into the tired air, that would keep the
world living and green.

She watched them through tears.

Somewhere among the workers was Adral, the boy—
young man, now, with hardened muscles and bronzed
skin, already in his first marriage, a liaison with a
Grower, unheard of in the old society. Adral was still
bitter about Li. She would have to tell him the truth,
she thought. Somehow they all would have to know
the truth, when the time was right, when the earth was
clearly recovering. She could not allow Li's history to
remain that of a traitor. She—

Adral's voice burst from her implant so suddenly
that it made her jump. "Trialla! Quickly, quickly—you
won't believe it! To the north perimeter, quickly!"

People.

Seventeen of the Ark colonists stood uncertainly by
their idle machines. Across from them, a hundred meters away, stood a crowd of strange people, at least a
hundred of them. One of them stepped forward, both
arms raised in the air. She wore a silvery suit, and she
was not of the Ark.

"Come on," Trialla said. Adral alone fell in step
beside her.

They met in a growth of tall grass. The silver-clad
woman was black of skin and hair, but her face twin-
kled with humor. "Eh," she said. "Youns have-a good
start made, now."

Trialla found herself weeping.

"Eh, eh," the stranger said. "No tears, now. We help-
a youn ancestors once, long agone. We Columbians."

Their accents were strange, their story stranger: *Ark
Columbia* had somehow survived, though the Wulfs—
whatever they were—made the northern tracts of the
continent very dangerous. "Mus' fight the Wulfs," the
stranger said. "Bitteh, but mus' do. Not human, youn

know? Jus' animal now, like baboon. Learn we mus' fight them to survive our own selves. Not many Wulfs lef', still danger, though, very cunning and sly. An' now we maybe have youns to help with our fight, no?"

Yes. *Ark Columbia*. And surviving, too, was *Ark Pacifica*, the newcomers said—"But the Pacificans ver' independ, youn know? Not welcome us, but not hurt us either. Eh, they got their own ways, now, and they not like youns and us anymore." And in Old Europe there were a few surviving human enclaves, and in Asia—

"How many of us are there?" Trialla asked. "How many people? In the whole world, I mean."

Well, nobody knew. The newcomers thought there might be as many as two million. Trialla's mind spun: the number was staggering. "An' maybe even more up there." A jerk of the chin indicated the sky. Humans in space? On Luna? L-5? No one knew, but maybe.

The Columbians existed under a different form of government, a sort of impromptu socialism, and they had a generation's start on *Liberty*. Their work had brought the grasses to the south. Their legends told of the time the *Liberty* crew had been pursued to the sea by the Wulfs, the first contact the Columbians had made with that degenerate species. They had saved the humans, the legends said, with fire and shot. And according to prophecy, they who had gone to the sea would come again some day.

"We're not like you," Trialla said. "Not anymore."

"Eh," the other replied with a grin. "It's a big worl', for sure. Plen' room for youn and us, for all. This time we make-a sure they plen' room, not so man' people."

They ate together under the stars that night, those from *Columbia* and those from *Liberty*. They exchanged stories, myths of the past. Someone asked about the legendary Stefan Li, he who had helped design all the Arks, who according to dim sagas had come to rest at last in *Ark Liberty*.

Adral stood up and walked away from the group, his back stiff, his face averted in his continuing anger.

Trialla's heart ached.

But to the Columbians she said, "Yes, it's true. Stefan Li was a great man, and he was aboard *Ark Liberty*. He lived for over six hundred years—"

It was the beginning, she knew, of a myth. In time to come, Stefan Li would slowly be transformed into a Moses, a messiah, a demigod. But, beneath the stars of an earth enjoying a second chance, Trialla reflected that Li was as good a choice for the role as another. She had hardly known him, really, but she knew he would laugh at the notion. Stefan Li a demigod? Please. He was a man driven by a dream.

But then, she wondered, if our dreams do not give us something of divinity, what does?

She took a deep breath, lifted her voice, and began to tell the story that would still be told when humankind reached the stars.